"DO YOU HAVE ANY IDEA HOW BADLY I WANT YOU RIGHT NOW?"

Relief spread through her. "I rather hoped you did." Laura managed a shy smile. "Because I want you, too."

Brent captured her lips, teasing and tasting. Then suddenly he tore his mouth from hers. "We have to stop."

"Why?" she frowned up at him.

"Because I didn't invite you here for a one-night stand."

"And I didn't come here for one." She fought down equal measures of uncertainty and frustration. She longed to tell him she'd waited half her life for him, and she didn't see any reason to wait anymore. "Brent," she sighed. "We practically grew up together. Would it be so wrong if we skipped the 'getting to know each other' stage?"

A laugh escaped him. "I never know what to expect from you." He stood and pulled her up beside him. "Even on short notice, I think I can manage something a bit more romantic than the sofa."

His words brought a blush of heat into her cheeks.

"Never be embarrassed by the things that give you pleasure," he whispered in her ear.

DRIVE ME WILD

JULIE ORTOLON

A DELL BOOK

Published by
Dell Publishing
a division of
Random House, Inc.
1540 Broadway
New York, New York 10036

Cover art by Anton Markous

ISBN 0-440-23618-5

Printed in the United States of America

Published simultaneously in Canada

March 2000

10   9   8   7   6   5   4   3   2   1

OPM

FOR KEN

whose encouragement,

patience, and love

gave me the freedom to go after a dream

A special thanks to Austin anchorman Larry Brill, as well as former news pros Anne Wentworth and Linda Zimmerhanzel, for answering my hundreds of questions about what goes on behind the scenes. Now let's hope I got it all right.

To Heda Christ, a huge thanks for driving me all over Houston in search of the perfect neighborhoods, houses, and restaurants—and for showing me how to load film into my own camera!

And of course, thanks to fellow author Cynthia Sterling for, well . . . *everything*.

CHAPTER
1

"**H**ey, Michaels!" a gravelly voice shouted over the clamor of the newsroom. "Telephone!"

Brent Michaels turned from the bank of TV monitors to see Connie Rosenstein, his news producer, waving a receiver over her head. The cord stretched across her cluttered desk to his immaculate one. "You want to take it?" she called.

He glanced at one of the digital clocks mounted on every wall of the Houston newsroom. He had fourteen minutes, twenty-six seconds to air. Plenty of time. "Who is it?"

"Claims to be an old high school friend from . . . Beason's Ferry?" Connie shrugged as if that meant it could be any one of a hundred people.

Brent's chest gave an odd lurch at the mention of his hometown. "Did he give a name?"

"No name. But it's definitely not a he." Connie's wink belied her tough-as-nails New York demeanor.

Brent stared at her, unable to think of a single person he'd classify as an old friend from high school. A whirling click jarred him back to his senses as the tape finished downloading the satellite feed for his lead story. Handing the tape to a runner, he crossed to his desk. This close to airtime, the chaos was migrating down the hall to the control booths and set, leaving the newsroom quiet.

Connie exhaled a cloud of smoke as she handed him the phone and gave her watch a warning tap.

"I'll be right there," he assured her with a smile to hide his tension. Once she'd joined the exodus, he glanced at the receiver in his hand. He hadn't been back to Beason's Ferry since the day he'd left for college, had almost forgotten that sinking sensation in the center of his chest that came from being an outcast. How could something so simple as a phone in the palm of his hand bring it all back?

Taking a deep breath, he steeled himself and brought the receiver to his ear. "Brent Michaels here."

"Brent! Thank goodness I caught you." The soft voice conjured an unexpected memory of honeysuckle. "I'm so sorry to bother you right before the news, but I couldn't take a chance on waiting."

Something in that voice made his pulse pick up speed. "Who is this?"

"Oh, goodness." The honest laughter triggered his memory, and he pictured white-blond hair pulled back in a ponytail and wide blue eyes behind Coke-bottle glasses. "It's Laura. Laura Morgan."

"Laura *Beth*?" The air left his lungs in a rush of relief.

"Bre-ent. . . ." She dragged the name out in a teasing scold. "I used to count on you, at least, to call me Laura—even if the rest of Beason's Ferry still insists on Laura Beth."

"Little Laura Beth Morgan." He propped his hip on the desk as he remembered the awkward, skinny kid. As the daughter of the town's doctor and most prominent citizen, she should have had the easy life. Oddly, though,

Laura had been nearly as much a misfit as he, which was probably why he hadn't thought of her the moment Connie mentioned an old friend from high school. While they had gone to school together, he'd never considered her a part of the high school crowd. Of course, he'd never exactly been part of the crowd either. "Good Lord, Squirt, how long has it been?"

"Fourteen years, seven months, and ten days. But who's counting?"

He laughed. "Only a math brain like you would remember something like that."

"It has nothing to do with brains," she insisted crisply. "A girl never forgets her first kiss. Not that that brotherly peck you gave me the day you left was all that memorable, mind you," she added quickly, making him smile.

That, at least, hadn't changed. Laura had always been able to make him smile. "Well, I didn't want to shock you, just give you something to remember me by."

"I would have remembered you either way," she said quietly, with the slightest touch of hurt.

Confused by a barrage of emotions her voice had stirred, he strove to keep his tone light. "So what has you tracking me down after all these years?"

"I'm running interference, if you must know the truth."

"Oh?" He could feel the old wariness tightening his chest.

"You remember the annual Bluebonnet Homes Tour?" she asked.

"Beason's Ferry's biggest festival?" He scowled. "How could I forget?"

"Well, I'm on the fund-raising committee this year."

"And?" he prompted.

She gave a heavy sigh. "You remember Janet Kleberg?"

"Big head but no brains. The cheerleader who made passes at me behind the school gym but wouldn't be caught dead talking to me in the hall? Yeah, I remember her."

"That's not fair," she chided. "Janet would have given her eyeteeth to go out with you, as would most of the girls in this town. You're the one who snubbed them."

"I was just saving them the effort," he said. "So what's ol' Janet Kleberg up to these days?"

"Actually, it's Janet Henshaw now. She married Jimmy right after graduation."

"My condolences to both of them."

"They're divorced."

"My congratulations, then."

"Anyway," she continued in an exasperated tone, "Janet is the chair of the fund-raising committee, and she's come up with a rather, uhm . . . imaginative idea."

"Spill it, Squirt."

He heard her take a big breath before she spoke in a rush, as she always did when she was nervous. "They want to have a *Dating Game* reenactment, like the old TV show, the one that used to run when we were kids?"

"I'm familiar with the show." Brent checked the clock. He had eight minutes and twelve seconds until airtime. He'd need exactly one minute, twenty-eight seconds to reach the set and take his seat.

"Yes, well." She cleared her throat. "They want to get a celebrity for the bachelor, so we can sell more tickets."

"And?" He could feel the trap closing around him.

"And, well, you are the nearest thing to a celebrity to ever come out of Beason's Ferry."

"Let me get this straight." He rubbed at the tension in his chest. "Back when I lived in that snobby little town, I couldn't have asked out a 'decent' girl without the town fathers hauling me into some back alley for a little talking to. And now, just because I'm on the evening news, they want to pay money to watch me ask one of their daughters out on a date?"

"That's not exactly how I would have phrased it, but I see you get the general idea." She fell silent, as if waiting for his answer. "So," she asked at last, "will you do it?"

"Absolutely not."

"It's for a worthy cause."

"Restoring old houses is not a worthy cause, Laura. A children's hospital, or aid to indigent elderly, now there's a worthy cause."

"Brent, you know how important tourism is to this town. The Homes Tour has put us on the map."

"Sorry, it's just not something I can get worked up about." Out of the corner of his eye, he saw Keshia Jackson, his coanchor, leave makeup and head for the set. "Look, Laura, it's been great hearing from you. I mean that, really. Maybe we could get together sometime, but—"

"Brent, wait." Panic edged into her voice. "I know this town doesn't mean anything to you, but it's my home, and I care about it very much. Not just the town, but the people who live here. This festival is important to us."

"I realize that. But what's important to Beason's

Ferry and what's important to me are not the same thing. You of all people should understand that."

"No, I never did. You always cared deeply about things, as deeply as I did. Until it came to this town, and then you'd turn your back without a second thought. How am I supposed to understand that, Brent? It makes no sense."

"It makes sense to me." Pinching the bridge of his nose, he realized nothing had changed. He and Laura were still the same mismatched misfits they'd always been. She was still trying to save the world, and he was still taking it head-on with shoulders squared and fists clenched.

"I'm sorry," she offered softly.

"No," he sighed. "I'm the one who's sorry. For a lot of things."

"I had no right to ask," she continued. "I shouldn't have even called. I should have known you wouldn't consider such a thing—"

"Would you stop," he said. God, he hated it when she sold herself short. Besides, even if he would never admit it out loud, the thought of returning to Beason's Ferry as the conquering hero had been a nagging temptation since he'd moved back to Texas two years ago. In brief moments of fancy, he imagined everything from a homecoming parade complete with a big brass band to the wary frowns of the town fathers wondering what "he" was doing back in town.

"You're not considering it, are you?" she asked hopefully.

He didn't answer.

"Because if you are, I just want to point out that it'd

only be for one weekend. The first weekend in April. If you don't have plans."

He didn't, unfortunately. He closed his eyes as resignation settled over him.

"You can spare one weekend . . . can't you?" she asked in a soft, sweet voice that made him think of homemade peach cobbler served in the shade of an old oak tree amid the scent of fresh-cut grass and honeysuckle vines. "Would you do it for me?"

If anyone but Laura had made such a request, he'd have hung up the phone. But deep down he realized he wanted to go back, if for no other reason than to see her again.

"All right." He let out a pent-up breath. "I'll do it. On one condition."

"Absolutely. Anything."

"I want you to be one of the bachelorettes."

"I can't do that! It'd be cheating."

He grinned. "That's my price, kid. I refuse to be stuck for one whole evening with some bouncy nitwit like Janet."

"How did you know she plans to be a contestant?"

"Lucky guess." He rolled his eyes and noted the time. Three minutes, eighteen seconds. "Is it a deal?"

"I'm not getting up on a stage in front of the whole town and making a fool of myself."

"Oh, but you'll ask me to do it, is that it?" he asked, knowing he had her there. "What do you say, Laura? I'll do it if you will."

"Oh, all right." She blew out a breath. "But I have a condition of my own. You have to promise not to pick me out of hand. At least consider the other contestants."

"No problem," he agreed absently. Standing, he

straightened his silk tie. "Right now, however, I really do have to go."

"Okay, okay." A hint of mischief entered her voice. "I'll have Janet call you with the details. Bye, Brent."

"No, wait—" The phone went dead. He glared at it for a moment, then laughed. Laura Beth Morgan. Who'd have thought he'd hear from her after all these years? He wondered what she looked like without a mouth full of braces.

⌐⌐

Laura sagged with relief as she hung up the phone. She couldn't believe she'd actually called Brent Zartlich, or rather Brent Michaels as he was now known. What choice had she had, though? The fund-raising committee had met that afternoon. If she hadn't rushed home, frantically looked up the number for the station in Houston, and placed that call, Janet would have been the one to contact him.

Laura cringed at the thought of Janet blithely putting her foot in her mouth—and Brent turning her down cold. Now all she had to worry about was how the people of Beason's Ferry would treat Brent when he arrived. Surely his homecoming wouldn't be that bad. In the years since he'd left, people's attitudes toward him had done a complete about-face. Whereas they'd once called him a sullen loner with more pride than sense, people now delighted in saying they "always knew that boy would go places."

The question was, how would he react to their new attitude? His moods could be as unpredictable as the weather in Texas.

The grandfather clock down the hall chimed the hour

of five. Right on schedule, her father, Dr. Walter Morgan, entered the wood-paneled den. Though he now used a polished black cane, he still carried himself with dignity. His stoic features showed no more emotion than usual, though she noticed the grooves about his mouth looked deeper this evening. So many people thought of him as aloof since her mother's death, but few of them knew the full story.

Her heart ached as he lowered himself into his leather easy chair. "Can I get you anything before I start supper?" she asked. "A glass of iced tea?"

Her father made a sound that she took for a yes as he aimed the remote control at the console TV. His easy dismissal never failed to hurt her. She longed to do something to make his life easier, happier. He wanted nothing more than a clean house, his meals served on time, and to otherwise be left alone, mired in twenty years of widower's grief.

Standing, she smoothed her skirt and started for the door. She stopped at the sound of Brent's voice as his image filled the screen. The sight of him made her breath catch, as it did every night. Though his dark hair was now expertly trimmed and his body had filled out, he still had the most riveting blue eyes she'd ever seen, and a devastating smile.

How clearly she remembered that smile from those long-ago Saturdays, when Brent would come to mow her father's yard. The first time he came, she couldn't have been more than ten. Brent had been a much older thirteen. She'd recognized him instantly as the boy from the outskirts of town, the one people always whispered about. As he pushed the massive mower over the large expanse of lawn, he reminded her of her father, daring the world to offer one word of sympathy or help.

Perhaps that was when she'd started lying awake at night dreaming of grown-up things: like children of her own to laugh with and love, and a husband to notice how hard she worked to transform their house into a home.

And in those dreams her husband always looked like Brent.

She sighed now, watching him read the news into the TV camera. He had indeed come a long way from the guarded boy the girls of Beason's Ferry had been forbidden to date but had been labeled drop-dead, grade-A gorgeous. His projection of confidence had earned him the admiration he deserved, and his success made her heart swell with pride.

When the station cut to a commercial, she came back to the present. She needed to call Janet and let her know what she'd done. Even though Brent had agreed to do the show, the former Beason's Ferry cheerleader was not going to be pleased, for Laura had stolen Janet's excuse to call Brent herself.

Heading for the kitchen at the back of the sprawling old house, she almost wished he had said no. Then she could cling to the possibilities spun of girlhood dreams. Another part of her, the daring part she tried to ignore, tingled with the anticipation of seeing him again. No matter how staunchly she lectured her heart, she couldn't stop it from racing away with the thought that maybe, just maybe, this was her chance to make those dreams come true.

CHAPTER
2

"He's here! He's here! He's here!" a high-pitched voice sang out over the sounds of the crowd on the courthouse square.

Laura glanced over her shoulder to see Janet barreling straight toward her, or rather straight toward Tracy Thomas, who stood in front of her in the food concession line. Janet's long dark hair and generous figure made a striking picture in the midday sun.

"Omygod!" Tracy, an equally pretty blonde, squealed. "Brent Michaels is really here?"

Laura's heart leapt as her eyes darted about the square. Beneath the stately magnolia trees, throngs of people meandered through the arts and crafts booths. From the south side of the square, country-western music blared from the bandstand, while the scent of barbecue filled the air.

"You actually saw him?" Tracy asked Janet. "Where?"

"Over at the bed and breakfast. And you'll never believe what he drove up in." Janet waited a heartbeat before she blurted, "A Porsche!"

"Ohmygod!" Tracy cried. "You are so lucky, and I am

so jealous! If only I weren't pregnant." She gave her distended stomach a disgruntled look.

"Your husband still wouldn't let you enter the show, even for charity," Janet pointed out.

"You're right," Tracy pouted. "Besides, Brent would likely pick you anyway, and then I really would hate your guts."

Like most of the town, Tracy assumed Brent would pick Janet from the bachelorette lineup. And why wouldn't he? Janet had a figure to make men drool. Even the weight she'd gained from having three children was in all the right places.

Laura, however, strongly suspected Brent had already made up his mind—to pick her. Not because he had some deep-seated urge to take her out, but because she'd never given him cause to suspect her infatuation. If he'd known of her attraction, he'd have avoided her as he did all the other girls in town who had set their sights on him.

The thought of a grown-up Brent choosing her for a date sent a fresh attack of flutters through her stomach. Biting her lip, she wondered what Janet's reaction would be. For that matter, what would Greg's reaction be! No, better not to think about Greg.

"Oh, Laura Beth." Janet turned as if just noticing her. "Miss Miller asked me to help set up the stage over at the opera house. But you're so much better at that sort of thing. Would you mind terribly taking care of it?"

"Not at all." Laura forced herself to smile as she mentally added stage decorating to her growing list of responsibilities.

"Thanks!" Janet squeezed her shoulders and kissed the air beside her cheek. "You're such a peach! I just don't know what the committee would do without you."

Laura fought the urge to roll her eyes as the two women hurried away, no doubt to spread the news of Brent's arrival. For the thousandth time, she kicked herself for making that call four months ago. But how could she have known the women of Beason's Ferry would treat Brent's return like the Second Coming? And the more ridiculous the women acted, the darker the scowls grew on the faces of the men.

If only she'd let Janet make that call, then Brent would have said no, and this whole fiasco would be over. At least, she thought he'd have said no. He'd always despised the popular crowd back in high school.

On the other hand, maybe his returning was for the best. Once this weekend was over, the little fantasy that flickered deep inside her heart would finally and effectively be snuffed out. Sure, Brent had been her friend when they were kids; he'd even given her her first kiss—a chaste little peck that had nearly made her swoon—but Brent Michael Zartlich was not, definitely *not*, going to come roaring back into town someday to sweep her off her feet and declare his all-consuming love for her.

Things like that did not happen to women like her. They happened to famous women, stunning, exotic, romantic women. While Laura might have a hopelessly romantic heart, she was neither stunning nor exotic, and it was high time she accepted that fact.

"Laura Beth," a tight voice said from behind her, "I'd like a word with you."

Greg. Her shoulders slumped for a fraction of a second before she turned to face her sometimes boyfriend. "Hello, Greg. Are you enjoying the art show?"

"Well, yes, I . . ." he started to answer, then squared his shoulders unexpectedly. "I'd enjoy it a lot more if you weren't about to make a laughingstock out of yourself in front of the whole town."

"Greg . . ." She stared at him, amazed by his boldness. "What are you talking about? We already discussed this, remember? I agreed to be one of the contestants to help raise money for the Homes Tour."

"I know what you said, but, well . . ." His hazel eyes blinked with agitation behind gold-rimmed glasses. "I just don't like the idea of you competing with other women to go out with some—some pretty boy."

She hid a smile at that accusation, since Greg, with his fair coloring and baby-smooth cheeks, was far closer to being "pretty" than Brent would ever be. In fact, when Greg Smith had moved to Beason's Ferry as the town's new pharmacist five years ago, she'd found him very handsome in a shy sort of way. In some ways, she still did.

Greg straightened in a rare show of determination. "Laura Beth, I insist you withdraw from this—this spectacle."

Her amusement faded at his direct order. "I can't," she said. Reaching the front of the line for the concession stand, she turned her attention to Jim Bob Johnson, who ran the booth for the Optimist Club.

"Hey there, LB." Jim Bob gave a big wink as he rolled his toothpick to the opposite side of his mouth. "How are you today?"

"Just fine, JB, and yourself?" she asked.

"Fine and dandy." He straightened the red ball cap on his head. "So what can I get for you today? A sausage wrap? Chop' beef on a bun?"

The aroma of meat smoking on the pit behind him made her mouth water. "Make that one wrap, two chop' beefs, a roasted ear of corn, two Cokes, and a large lemon-ade.''

"Whew-ee! You sure must be hungry." Jim Bob grinned.

From the corner of her eye, she saw Greg reach for his wallet. "I've got it," she insisted, with money already in hand.

Greg's face fell. "That's the third time this week you've refused to let me buy your lunch. If I didn't know better, I'd think you were trying to avoid me."

Rather than address that sensitive issue, she glanced down at her slender figure clad in beige slacks and a cream silk blouse. "You think all that's for me?"

Two red blotches appeared on Greg's cheeks, and she felt instantly guilty. He was such a nice man, the last thing she wanted to do was hurt his feelings. Sooner or later, though, she had to tell him her feelings for him had cooled. The moment the food came, Greg gathered it up, leaving the drinks for her to carry.

"So you'll withdraw your name?" he asked as she led the way toward the art booths with him close on her heels.

"Greg, I can't." She wove in and out of the crowd, smiling at friends and neighbors. "It's entirely too late to withdraw, even if I wanted to."

"Dag-nabbit, Laura Beth, you can't do this. We're practically engaged!"

"Since when?" She stopped in her tracks, and he nearly plowed into her.

"Oh, I know we agreed to think about it for a while, but everyone knows we'll tie the knot eventually."

Guilt nettled at her conscience. Six months ago, when Greg had proposed, she'd tried to say no. She really had. Only the word *no* seemed to have slipped from her vocabulary. In the end, she'd agreed to think it over and let him know. She'd assumed six months of silence was answer enough. Apparently she was wrong.

Shaking her head, she continued on to a booth that sold hand-painted T-shirts, where she delivered the sausage wrap. Fetching lunch was not something the festival volunteers usually did, but so many of the artisans manned the booths by themselves that Laura couldn't help herself. "Here's the wrap and the change you needed."

"Gee, thanks!" The Houston woman looked surprised that Laura had actually returned with her money. "You are so sweet."

Blushing at the compliment, Laura hurried on to the next booth, where a couple from the Hill Country sold wooden cutouts of cows and chickens and pigs. While she gave them their sandwiches and soft drinks, she thought over Greg's proposal. If she had any sense at all, she'd marry the man. He was considerate and responsible and attractive. What more could a woman ask for? He was everything she'd dreamed of having all those lonely nights while she was growing up. Except he wasn't Brent.

Brent, however, was a dream. Greg was real.

Unfortunately, every time she pictured herself as Mrs. Greg Smith, she felt as if she were suffocating. How could she explain that to him without squashing his male ego? Turning back to him, she took the roasted ear of corn, which was still in its warm husk. "Greg, when this weekend is over, I really think we need to talk."

"I'd like that, Laura Beth." His face softened with a smile. "You know I always enjoy talking to you."

She stared at him, seriously tempted to bean him

with the ear of corn. Couldn't he sense that she wanted to break up?

"After all," he said, stepping closer to touch her arm, "we haven't had much time together lately, what with you working on the Homes Tour, and me so busy with . . . well . . . you know."

She shook her head when he couldn't come up with an excuse for his own lack of time. Truth was, he never *did* anything. He worked. He watched TV. He played golf. That was it: Greg Smith's life in a nutshell. Not that there was anything much to do in Beason's Ferry, which was why so many of her classmates had gone off to Austin and Houston and never come back.

Continuing down the grassy aisle, she wondered what her life would have been like if she'd attended a big university rather than commuting to Blinn College in the neighboring town of Brenham. A sense of melancholy stole over her, as it always did when she imagined life outside her own small world. So many times, even after meeting Greg, she'd wanted to ask: Is this it? Is there nothing more to life than this? Brushing off the depressing thought, Laura neared a booth at the end of the row that was filled with bright, colorful paintings.

"My savior!" the artist exclaimed at her approach. Melody Piper was a regular artist at the Homes Tour, and Laura considered her a friend. The woman's vibrant orange hair was as vivid as her artwork, and clashed brilliantly with her pink tie-dyed T-shirt, purple leggings, and army boots. Silver dragon charms and crystals hung about her neck and dangled from her ears. "I thought I'd expire from hunger before you returned."

Smiling at Melody's exuberance, Laura handed over

the ear of corn. "As usual, the options were limited for vegetarians."

"Anything. I'm famished," Melody said as Greg came to an abrupt halt. His eyes riveted on the woman's shocking attire. Lowering her voice, Melody asked, "Have you had a chance to think about my offer?"

Laura glanced toward Greg. The last thing she wanted to talk about in front of him was the possibility of her becoming Melody's housemate in Houston. She hadn't even had time to think the idea over. Not seriously, anyway. Giving Melody a warning look, she asked, "How's the show going?"

"Fabulous!" Melody said, picking up on her message. More crystals and dragons flashed as she waved a hand toward a blank spot in her booth. "I sold the big monstrosity, which means now I have to rearrange my entire display to fill in the hole." She turned to Laura with a speculative gleam in her eye. "I don't suppose you'd care to help me."

"I'd love to, really, but I can't." Laura gestured toward the nineteenth-century opera house that overlooked the square like a grand old diva. "I have to go help the drama students set up for our *Dating Game* show."

"Oh, that's right." Melody grinned. "I'll bet ya five bucks that news guy picks you."

Greg drew up sharply. "Laura Beth would never throw good money away on some frivolous wager."

A slow smile spread over Melody's face as she turned to the bristling pharmacist. "Wanna bet?"

"Melody," Laura quickly interjected, "I don't believe you've met Greg, my . . . friend."

Curiosity sparkled in Melody's eyes. "So this is

Greg." She extended her hand in a limp-wristed fashion. "I've heard so much about you."

The blotches in Greg's cheeks went crimson. He hesitated, then took the beringed hand, looking uncertain about whether he should kiss it or shake it. "Good to meet you," he mumbled.

"So, Sir Gregory," Melody cozied up to him, "how'd you like to save a damsel in distress?"

"Yes, of course." Laura leapt on the idea while Greg looked patently horrified. "That would be perfect. Greg can help you rearrange your booth while I go help the students."

"But—" He turned to Laura with pleading eyes.

"Good luck with the rest of the show," she called out to Melody with a parting wave.

"You, too," Melody called back. "And if Brent Michaels picks you, you owe me five bucks."

As Laura crossed the street, she breathed a sigh of relief. Now that she had slipped free of Greg, she turned her attention to a much bigger problem: getting through the next few hours without making a fool of herself.

～⌒⌒

Stepping out of the Boudreau Bed and Breakfast, Brent took in the scene before him. Visitors from across the state crowded the streets as they funneled into the historic town. Many of the cars slowed to a crawl as the passengers caught their first glimpse of the fully restored homes.

Across the street stood the Homes Tour's crown jewel: a turn-of-the-century mansion elaborately painted in burgundy, green, and gold. Amid the towering live oaks and blooming azaleas, the town daughters strolled in Southern Belle costumes that had been handed down from mother to daughter to sister to friend since the Homes Tour began more than fifty years ago. Pedestrians lined up, fanning themselves with walking tour pamphlets as they waited for their turn to get inside.

A wry smile tugged his lips. For most of his growing-up years, he'd felt just like those tourists: standing outside, longing for his turn to be welcomed across the threshold. Only the threshold he'd wanted to cross was an invisible ring around the whole damned town. As an illegitimate kid being raised by an alcoholic grandmother and two hell-raising uncles on the outskirts of town, he hadn't been accepted into Beason's Ferry society. Why should he be, when his own mother hadn't even wanted him enough to bother sticking around?

"Oh, look! It's him!" One of the "Southern Belles" pointed in his direction.

With parasols twirling, she and her two companions waved. "Hello, Mr. Michaels." Coming to the waist-high fence that enclosed the front lawn, one of them called across the street, "I'm Susie Kirckendall. I bet you don't remember, but my mom, Carol Sawyer, went to school with you."

Yeah, he remembered. Carol had been one of the bolder ones who'd enjoyed flirting with the boy who'd been declared off-limits for respectable girls; although he figured she'd have run home screaming if he'd ever acted on her invitation. Pushing aside the unpleasant memory, he waved back to the three teenagers and watched them fall into fits of giggles.

How ironic, he thought as he moved on down the street, that now, when it no longer mattered, the cream of

Beason's Ferry welcomed him with open arms. They'd even hung a banner across the main street into town that read "Welcome Home Brent Michaels" in big red letters.

All right, so it didn't say Brent Zartlich, but he refused to let that bother him.

It shouldn't bother him.

He was the one who'd dropped his last name in favor of an altered form of his middle name. Still, the subtle connotation was there, that they welcomed him only because they no longer considered him one of those white trash Zartlichs.

Changing his name, however, didn't sever his relations. He debated going out to the house at some point during the weekend to say hello to "the family." Not that his two remaining uncles constituted much of one. Whatever he decided, he was just glad he didn't have to worry about running into them in town. On a Saturday afternoon they'd either be sleeping off hangovers or working on new ones. His grandmother had died of lung cancer years ago. Brent had been working as a news intern in New Mexico at the time.

A twinge of guilt pricked him for not coming home for the funeral, but money had still been tight back then.

He shook off the regret as he reached the corner. The familiar scent of barbecue cooking on the courthouse lawn stirred old hungers that had nothing to do with food. The lively strains of fiddle music underscored the hum of pedestrian traffic. He realized they'd set up a bandstand on the south lawn. People filled the tables ringing the dance floor, like an outdoor honky-tonk. Apparently the Homes Tours had gained popularity in the past fourteen years.

Taking in the whole square, he realized other things

had changed as well. Fischer's Hardware was now an antique shop, as was the old feed store. The five-and-dime had a colorful display of handicrafts in the front window, and the pharmacy had added an espresso bar. An espresso bar in Beason's Ferry!

"So there you are," a crisp, no-nonsense voice said from behind him. He turned to find Miss Miller, his old high school English teacher. His body instantly stiffened, as if he'd just been caught cutting class. She gave him a reproachful glare. "And here I just walked all the way over to the B and B to fetch you."

"My apologies, Miss Miller." He tried out one of the ratings-winning smiles that had landed him an income in the six figures. "I would never dream of inconveniencing you. Although it is a lovely day for a walk."

She snorted as if to say she'd have none of his fancy talk; he was in trouble, and that's all there was to it. Fourteen years, and the woman hadn't changed a bit. She still wore her hair in a neat cap of hair-sprayed curls about her angular face, although the color seemed to be more gray than blond now. Bifocals obscured a pair of piercing blue eyes he swore could see through walls and read boys' minds. In deference to the warm weather, she wore a cotton shirtwaist dress that accentuated her overly thin figure.

Through the top half of her glasses, she took in his khaki slacks, polo shirt, Italian leather belt, and loafers. He knew he looked every inch the successful business executive relaxing at the country club. He'd worked to perfect the look and had practiced it until he wore it with ease. He'd forgotten, however, that fashion in small towns tended to run fifty years behind the times. In

Beason's Ferry, aging farmers wore khaki, and then only to work in their fields.

"I suppose this will have to do." Miss Miller pursed her thin lips in disapproval. "You haven't time to change. We'll need to get you backstage at the opera house before the show begins."

He glanced at his Rolex. "I've got a good seventeen minutes. Plenty of time."

With a snort, she turned and led the way down the crowded sidewalk.

He fell in step beside her. "I see quite a few things have changed around here."

She followed the direction of his gaze to the newly painted storefronts. "Yes, I'd say a great many things have changed, in appearance anyway, since Laura Beth formed her Beautification Committee."

"Oh?" He raised a brow. Laura forming a committee didn't surprise him. Her getting the credit did. Back in school, she'd belonged to a dozen different clubs. Only while she did all the grunt work, girls like Janet and Tracy stole all the glory.

"Speaking of Laura," he said offhandedly, "she is one of the bachelorettes I'll have to choose from, isn't she?"

Miss Miller gave him a quelling stare as they reached the corner. "You know perfectly well I can't reveal the names of the entrants."

"You're right," he conceded as they started across the street. He never could flirt, talk, or wheedle his way past Miss Miller on anything. Her unwillingness to bend was what he'd always admired about her. If she hadn't pushed him to study harder and aim higher, he'd probably be driving a gravel truck like his uncles.

He wondered what she'd say if he told her the pen

and pencil set she'd given him at graduation had sat on his desk in every newsroom where he'd worked. The memory of the day she'd given it to him still tugged at something deep inside him.

Reaching the stage door, he hesitated. How did a man thank a woman for changing his life? "Miss Miller?"

She turned with a puzzled frown.

"I, uh . . ." He didn't know how to say it now any more than he had back then. ". . . just wanted to thank you for keeping the dogs at bay these past few months."

For a moment, he thought she'd seen past his hasty recovery and might actually smile. Instead, she gave a nod. "An apt phrase. If I hadn't taken over, those girls would have pestered you day and night."

"So," he gave her a teasing wink, "who besides Janet and Laura will be on that stage?"

Her eyes narrowed. "Don't you practice your wiles on me, young man. These lips are sealed tight."

Cocking his head, he gave her his sexiest grin. "I don't suppose I could just pick you for my dream date and save us all a lot of trouble?"

She stared at him a moment, looking inside him in that uncanny way she had. "Why, Brent Zartlich, I do believe you're nervous."

He snorted and hoped that covered up what she had seen too clearly.

"You just remember one thing when they get you on that stage," she said. "A sense of humor goes a long way in life."

This from a woman whose face would crack if she ever gave in to a full-fledged grin, he thought.

"Now don't you do that." She wagged her finger at him. "Don't you turn all sulky and sullen."

"I've never sulked a day in my life," he insisted.

She shook her head. "Like I said, some things never change." She started to move past him through the door but stopped. "I will tell you one thing, Brent Zartlich. A few speech lessons and fancy clothes don't change who you are. If the people of this town were too blind to see what a bright, sensitive boy you were back then, then you shouldn't fret over their opinion now. You just go in there, give the audience their money's worth, and be done with it. You got that?"

He stifled a grin. "You don't have to make it sound like I'm about to do a striptease."

Her narrowed gaze bored into his. "By the time this nonsense is over, you may feel as if you've done exactly that."

CHAPTER
3

A sense of humor goes a long way in life. Brent repeated the words in his head as he stood waiting backstage. From an opening in the backdrop, he had a partial view of the set. Huge psychedelic flowers in orange, yellow, and lime green contrasted sharply with the rococo trim and frescoes of the opera house's decor.

Two bar stools sat on the half of the set he could see, one for him and the other for Mayor Davis, who was already greeting the audience. Brent assumed similar bar stools awaited the three bachelorettes on the other side of the partition that divided the stage.

Laura would be sitting on one of those stools. He wondered again what she looked like now, what she'd been doing with her life, if she was nervous about getting onstage. Surprisingly, knowing she'd be going through the next few minutes with him settled his own case of stage jitters, something he hadn't experienced in years.

Mayor Davis's voice rose in volume. "So, y'all help me greet our celebrity bachelor, Brent Michaels."

This was it. Brent took a deep breath, pasted a smile on his face, and walked onto the set with a casual wave to the crowd. If he knew one thing, it was how to play his self-made role: Brent Michaels, the charming, confident all-American male.

Mayor Davis greeted him with a handshake and a hearty thump on his back. Microphone in hand, the mayor turned back to the audience. "Of course, most of y'all recognize this handsome face from the evening news, but those of us here in Beason's Ferry knew this boy long before he was anything special."

Brent's smile never wavered, even as he wondered if the insult was Freudian or intentional.

"Now, Brent," the balding mayor said as he turned to him with mock sternness. "As you know, we've gone to great lengths to keep the identities of the three young ladies confidential. But why don't you assure the folks here that you've had no contact with any possible contestants since you agreed to be with us here today."

"None whatsoever," Brent said. "Except for Miss Miller. Unfortunately, she turned me down for a date, so I guess I'll have to pick someone else."

A chuckle rippled through the audience.

"And we do have three lovely candidates for you to choose from," the mayor said. "So, Brent, before we introduce 'em, why don't you tell everyone what it is you look for in a woman?"

"Well, I'll tell you, Mayor Davis," Brent said, playing along with the sexy tone of the game show. "I'd have to say my taste in women runs about the same as my taste in cars: I like them sleek and sophisticated."

"Fast, eh?" The mayor wiggled his brows.

A laugh from the crowd saved Brent from having to respond. Not that he would have bothered to explain what he really longed for in a female companion. Over the years, he'd developed a vague image of a self-assured woman with refined manners and taste, a woman who embodied all the things he only pretended to be.

"Well, Brent, I doubt any of these young ladies are fast, mind you. But what do you say we introduce 'em one at a time, so you can hear their voices?" The mayor referred to his cue cards as the first of three spotlights popped on to light the other half of the stage. "Our first lovely contestant has always loved watching sports—when she isn't watching you report the news, of course."

"Of course," Brent said agreeably.

"She says," the mayor tilted his head to read the cue card through his bifocals, "if you pick her, she'll do whatever it takes to *cheeeer* you up."

From that not-so-subtle hint, Brent knew contestant number one was Janet Kleberg, former cheerleader for the Beason's Ferry Bulldogs.

"Hello, Brent!" Janet shouted through the loudspeakers. She sounded so chipper, he pictured her holding her pompoms.

"Now, contestant number two," the mayor glanced at the next card in his hand, "claims to be a homebody but says she wouldn't mind going out with you because your smile reminds her of Donny Osmond, on whom she's always had a crush."

Brent bit back a laugh as the audience let out a collective *oooh*. Contestant number two had to be Laura. She knew he'd cringed in disgust whenever the girls had compared him to the squeaky-clean Donny Osmond. So she was trying to keep him from picking her, was she?

An awkward silence fell.

"Uh, contestant number two," the mayor called. "Honey, do you think you could manage to say hi to Brent, here?"

"Hello, Brent," someone said through the speakers. Did that soft, low voice belong to Little Laura Beth? He didn't remember her sounding quite that grown-up on the phone.

"Now, contestant number three," the mayor continued, "is a horseback riding enthusiast who competes annually for the barrel-racing championship at the county livestock show and rodeo."

"Howdy, Brent" came a booming voice Brent didn't recognize. So they'd managed to get at least one contestant he hadn't grown up with.

"Okay," the mayor said as he motioned Brent to a bar stool. "You ladies take your seats, and let's get started."

On the other side of the partition, Laura fought off a fresh wave of nerves as she took the middle stool. She never should have agreed to this. She felt like a drab mouse caught in the headlights. Of course, seated between Janet, in her figure-hugging floral sundress, and Stacey, in her brightly colored western shirt and denim skirt, maybe no one would notice her.

Over the sound system, she heard Mayor Davis explaining how they'd asked Brent to come up with questions that wouldn't give the identity of the contestants away. "So, Brent, you got those questions ready?"

"I sure do," Brent answered in his clear, deep voice. She could hardly believe that after all these years of thinking about him, he was seated mere feet away with nothing but a thin partition blocking him from her view. The thought of stepping around that partition in a few minutes and seeing him face to face made her pulse flutter. "Bachelorettes, now that you've heard what I look for in a woman, I'd like to start by asking each of you what you look for in a man. Contestant number one?"

Janet gave a little squeal of delight at being the first one asked. "Well, Brent, I like men who are into sports, especially *running*." She emphasized the last word since Brent had been the star sprinter on the track team, a sport that required little interaction with team members. He'd once confided to Laura that he liked sprinting better than the longer races because it absorbed the runner's mind completely, blocking out everything but straining muscles, breathing deep, and getting to the finish line.

Janet leaned forward as she added, "I think a sweaty man in running shorts is just about the sexiest thing there is."

Laura blushed as an image from the past came to mind, of Brent wearing thin nylon shorts and no shirt as he'd practiced on the track every day after school.

"Oookaaay," Brent said, and she braced herself, fearing she'd be next. "Contestant number . . . three."

She slumped in relief as Stacey, a teller from the First Texas Bank, sat up a bit straighter.

"I like a man who enjoys the great outdoors," Stacey answered. "One who's open and honest but isn't afraid to get a little *wild*."

Laura laughed, since Stacey's voice had dropped to a suggestive whisper at the end. The other women on the fund-raising committee had encouraged them to get into the spirit of the game, to be fun and provocative. Janet and Stacey definitely were that.

"Contestant number two," Brent said, and she jumped, realizing he was talking to her. "What do you look for in a man?"

She tried to think of something provocative to say,

but her mind went blank. "I, uhm, like a man who's . . . there?"

Someone in the audience boomed with laughter, making Laura cringe.

" 'There'?" Brent repeated. "You mean as in constantly near you—or there as in somewhere else?"

"Yeah," a heckler called out. "That's what my wife likes me to be: somewhere else."

"No," Laura explained, "as in around, reliable. Someone who doesn't grumble about doing a few household chores."

"Dream on, honey!" A woman called out this time.

The mayor cleared his throat. "Perhaps we should move on to the next question."

"Certainly." With the ease of a man accustomed to public speaking, Brent segued smoothly into his next question. "As we all know, the fastest way to a man's heart is through his stomach. So, contestant number three, if we were dating, what tantalizing entrée would you fix to show me how much you care?"

"Let's see." Stacey thought for a moment, then smiled. "I'd pack a picnic lunch and spread a blanket in the shade. Then we could hand-feed each other pieces of my home-fried chicken . . . and lick the juice off each other's fingers."

Brent laughed, sounding more amused than embarrassed, which helped Laura relax. Maybe he'd pick Stacey, which would solve everything. She'd still get to see him but wouldn't have to suffer Greg's hurt, Janet's anger, or any teasing from the people in town. "Contestant number one," Brent said, "what main course would you serve?"

Janet flipped her hair behind one shoulder. "I'd fix

you a nice *juicy* steak and serve it by candlelight . . . in the nude."

Half the audience gasped while the other half roared with laughter.

"Well, that would certainly get a man's attention." Brent chuckled. "Which brings us to contestant two." His voice warmed, letting her know he'd guessed which one was her. "What tempting delicacy will you offer me to show you really care?"

Anything you want, she nearly said, then scowled at herself. "If I really wanted to show I cared, I sure wouldn't clog your arteries with a lot of cholesterol. I'd serve you baked fish and steamed vegetables."

The audience gave a good-natured groan that brightened her mood considerably. As long as he didn't pick her, she'd be saved from mortification.

"Last question," Brent announced. "Contestant number one, as a man with a definite sweet tooth, I'd like to know what dessert you'll offer to top off our steak dinner?"

"Cheesecake," Janet responded seductively. "With my special cherry topping. It's so tart and creamy, it'll just melt right in your mouth."

Laura closed her eyes and prayed the floor would open beneath her. Even for Janet, that answer was way over the top.

"Contestant number three?" Brent asked.

Not to be outdone, Stacey lowered her voice to a husky purr. "I'd feed you a nice rich slice of chocolate cake, so I could lick the icing off your lips."

"Well, that certainly sounds . . . interesting." Brent's suggestive tone made the audience laugh. "All right, number two, you're on. What sweet thing are you going to tempt me with?"

"Wholesome oatmeal cookies." Laura smiled broadly when the audience moaned. Even if Brent recognized her voice, no man in his right mind would pick a woman who sounded this boring.

"All right, contestant two, I'll bite. Why oatmeal cookies?"

"Because even if they're loaded down with all that butter and sugar, at least the oatmeal has some nutritional value."

"Wholesome and nutritious, eh?" The deep sound of his chuckle warmed her inside.

From backstage, a bell clanged. "Time's up," Mayor Davis announced, as the *Dating Game* theme began to play. "And now it's time for us to learn which contestant our bachelor will pick for the romantic dream date we've arranged at the Riverwood Golf Course and Country Club." The music died as a hush fell over the room. "Which will it be, Brent—Tart and Creamy, Wholesome and Nutritious, or Chocolate-Covered Lips?"

"Well, Mayor, I'll tell you, when it comes to sweets, a man just couldn't ask for more than warm cookies straight from the oven. I have to go with contestant number two."

Laura's mouth dropped open as the audience applauded. No. He couldn't have picked her. He just couldn't have!

Stacey at least was honest enough to look disappointed, and a good enough sport to give Laura a hug. Janet, on the other hand, tried to act as if she didn't care one way or the other. All Laura could think was: *There's been a mistake. He promised not to pick me out of hand.*

On the other side of the partition, Brent managed to

keep his smile intact as Mayor Davis draped an arm about his shoulder. Now that the show was over, he looked forward to being alone with Laura. At least with her, he could relax and be himself.

"You made a fine choice there, son. A mighty fine choice. Now what do you say we introduce you to the ladies you didn't pick?"

"Sounds good to me," Brent said.

"Contestant number three, come on out here and meet Brent Michaels."

A tall, lanky woman with straight brown hair and western garb stepped around the partition. "Stacey here is a right fine little barrel racer when she isn't working as a teller at the bank."

Brent gave the woman a dutiful kiss on the cheek as the mayor thanked her for being such a good sport.

"Now," the mayor said, "while you may not have recognized the voice, I'm sure the face will bring back some fond memories. Contestant number one was head cheerleader for the Beason's Ferry Bulldogs. Janet, come on out here and welcome Brent home."

Janet appeared, looking every bit as built as she had in high school, if not a bit more so with the extra curves she'd acquired. Tossing back her hair, she crossed to Brent, her gait lacking its usual bounce. Her normally bright eyes narrowed to dagger-thin slits as Brent kissed her cheek.

"So are you ready to meet your dream date?" the mayor asked as Janet left the stage.

Brent nodded and took his first real breath since the show had begun.

"This next little gal is someone you're sure to remember. She was three years behind you in school, but as I remember, you used to mow her daddy's lawn. Your dream date is everyone's favorite little darling: Miss Laura Beth Morgan. Come on out here, Laura Beth, and let this fella get a look at you."

A woman appeared around the screen, slender and graceful in beige slacks and a cream blouse. Brent glanced past her, looking for Laura. Then his eyes shot back and widened. "Laura?"

A smile softened her face, a face that was both familiar and new. Gone were the glasses and the ponytail. In their place, blond hair waved softly to her shoulders, framing the delicate features of a woman. Not a stunning woman, but one who possessed a poise he'd never suspected.

Her conservative attire lent her an air of elegance as she came to him. When he enfolded her in his arms for the obligatory hug, his senses filled with the homey scent of honeysuckle and baby powder. The innocent fragrance sent an unexpected rush of arousal shooting through his system.

When she stepped back, she smiled up at him. He held their joined hands out to the side and stared in disbelief. "Good Lord, Squirt. You grew up."

Her response was the same unpretentious laughter he remembered from their youth. Only now it had a throaty quality that could sink into a man's blood and drown him in desire. But this was Laura. Little Laura. The kid who inspired brotherly affection.

Rising on her toes, she kissed his cheek. "Welcome home, Brent."

CHAPTER
4

"You were supposed to at least consider the other contestants." Laura cast Brent a sideways glance as they left the opera house and crossed the street. She hoped if he noticed the heightened color in her cheeks, she attributed it to the afternoon heat rather than his nearness.

"I did consider them," he insisted. She shook her head, laughing. "What?" he asked, the picture of innocence. "You think I only picked you because I recognized your voice?"

"Uh-huh." Reaching the grassy square, she stopped beneath a magnolia tree to escape the sun. The crowd had thinned, and a blessed breeze ruffled her shirt. "It certainly wasn't because of the provocative answers I gave."

"Actually, it was because of the provocative answers you *didn't* give." He looked thoroughly disgusted, and so wonderfully male, she felt light-headed standing next to him. "Do women really think all they have to do to get a man is offer him their body?"

"Some women, I suppose." She frowned, hoping he couldn't see the pulse beating in her throat.

"Well, they're wrong. Mostly. I mean—Never mind." He shook his head, seeming more amused than irritated. She marveled at his light mood, realizing he'd shed some of the brooding darkness she'd found so heart-wrenching when he was a teenager. Not that she found this mature Brent any less intriguing.

Hoping to disguise her attraction with the familiar teasing they'd often exchanged, she leaned forward and drew circles on his chest with her fingertip. "Are you saying you picked me because I played hard to get?"

He looked startled by her touch and pulled back with a nervous laugh. "Sorry," he said. "I'm just not used to you looking so—" His gaze made a hasty trip down the length of her, then darted away. "What time should I pick you up?"

"Seven, I suppose." She frowned, wondering what her looks had to do with him pulling away. "The country club is expecting us at seven-thirty. After dinner, there'll be live music and dancing in the ballroom."

"Lawrence Welk, no doubt." He glanced at his watch as if impatient to get away from her. "I can hardly wait."

"Look, Brent." She crossed her arms. "I realize today was uncomfortable—for both of us."

"Actually, it wasn't that bad."

"It wasn't?" She frowned.

He shook his head, chuckling. "You should have seen Mayor Davis tugging at his tie every time Janet answered a question. I've never seen a grown man turn that red."

"Well, he couldn't have been more embarrassed than I was." She laughed, releasing the tension. "Can you believe the things she and Stacey said! I wanted to die when they offered to lick your lips and serve you in the nude."

He laughed as well, a sensuous sound that stirred something deep inside her. "That was pretty, um . . . intriguing."

Her laughter stilled as she watched him, noting little

details about his eyes that the TV screen didn't show, like the tiny lines to either side, the dark spiky lashes, and the flecks of silver within the navy-blue depths.

"What?" he asked self-consciously.

"Nothing." She looked away. "I just . . . wanted to thank you for being such a good sport."

"You're welcome." For a moment, he studied her in turn. Then a grin came slowly over his face. "Though I expect to be well paid."

"You what?" She blinked at him as erotic images of the two of them together played across her mind.

"I meant with dinner." He grinned in reproach at the conclusion she'd drawn—a conclusion he'd probably wanted her to draw, the wretch. How could a man be so exasperating and so endearing at the same time?

"That was the deal, wasn't it?" he asked. "One night on the town with a beautiful woman, compliments of Beason's Ferry?"

"Well, I don't know about the beautiful woman part," she tried not to blush and failed. "But you will be well fed."

"I can hardly wait." He disconcerted her by wiggling his brows.

"Would you stop?" She laughed and thumped him on the arm with her fist.

"*Ugh!* I'm wounded." He staggered back with a hand clasped to the arm she'd hit.

"Just pick me up at seven." She sighed.

"Whatever you say, Squirt."

The single word stiffened her spine. "Yeah, well, see you then, Zartlich."

As she turned to leave, she chided herself for getting so flustered. In spite of the sexual undertones of their exchange, she knew Brent had only been teasing. Obviously, he still thought of her as nothing more than a little sister.

~~~~~

At five minutes to seven, Laura stared at the pile of clothes strewn across the white eyelet comforter of her canopy bed. The situation was hopeless. Utterly hopeless. She had absolutely nothing to wear.

Why didn't I buy a new dress?

Because everyone in town would have known about it and laughed behind her back. *Poor Laura Beth thinks Brent Michaels will pick her.* Only—he had picked her.

And now I have nothing to wear.

For the third time, she snatched up the simple black dress with the scooped neckline and three-quarter sleeves. She held it in front of her as she stood before the free-standing mirror. It looked like what it was: her funeral dress. Maybe she could snazz it up with some jewelry—and look like she was trying too hard.

Tossing the black dress onto the white wicker chair, she reached for a pink cotton shirtwaist with a lace collar. She studied her reflection, then slumped in despair. The dress looked more appropriate for an afternoon tea party than a dinner date.

She needed something sophisticated—not sweet. Something subtle—but not *too* subtle. Something sexy! Every woman had at least one sexy dress in her closet, didn't she? In desperation, she turned back to the bed, hoping some slinky number in bright red would magically materialize.

"Mmm, mmm, girl, ain't you dressed yet?"

Laura glanced up in "Clarice. Thank goodness you could come on such short notice."

The elderly maid came over to straighten the clothes on the bed. "What you cleanin' your closet for at a time like this?"

"Never mind that." She waved the woman away. "I'll pick all this up later. Right now I'd rather you see about dinner. Daddy's been grousing for the past hour."

Snatching up a navy-blue suit, Laura turned back to the mirror. She'd always thought the suit a bit conservative, even for her, but men frequently complimented her when she wore it.

"If I know Dr. Morgan," Clarice said, "he ain't grousing 'cause his stomach's empty. He's grousing 'cause his baby's going out with a man. A real man."

"Clarice." Laura blushed. "I've been on dates before."

The woman gave a rude snort, which Laura ignored. Clarice liked to think she was too valuable a maid to be fired. And she was—though certainly not for her house-cleaning abilities. She'd been coming in twice a week to clean for as long as Laura could remember. Laura had come to consider the older woman a friend. A surrogate mother. She could never fire her, even if Clarice had grown too old to do much more than dust. Clarice had grandchildren to support and a bad back. Besides, Laura didn't really mind taking over the heavier housework without reducing the woman's pay.

The rumble of a motor sounded beyond the open window. Startled, Laura dashed over to peer outside to find a yellow Porsche pulling into the drive.

"Oh, no," she breathed as she clutched the sheer curtains to her breast. "He's early."

"More like you's late."

Laura glanced at the thin gold watch on her wrist. "You're right. Clarice." She sent a desperate look to the maid. "Would you do me a favor, please, and run downstairs to get the door before my father does?"

"If you say, though I sure hopes you gonna wear something other than *that* fer your date." The woman cast a meaningful eye at the ivory-satin-and-lace garter belt that held up Laura's stockings.

Laura blushed. Her preference for sexy underwear was only a small rebellion and one she preferred to keep from her father. If he had any idea what she wore under her proper outerwear, he'd think she'd inherited her mother's wild streak. "The door, Clarice. Please?"

"I'm going, I'm going," the woman grumbled. "But if I was you, I'd wear the blue suit."

"You don't think it looks too churchy?" Laura asked, frowning at the outfit.

"With that short skirt?" Clarice cackled, a twinkle in her eyes. "Fine pair of legs like yours is just begging to be showed off. 'Sides, never hurts to advertise the merchandise, if you know what I mean."

"Clarice!" Laura started to scold, but the woman had already headed down the hall. She glanced at the navy-blue suit. Was that why men liked the the outfit? Because it showed off her legs?

The thought of displaying her legs to Brent made her heart hammer so hard, she almost rejected wearing the suit. Almost.

Stopping in the circular drive, Brent cut the engine on the German sports car. The silence seemed startling after the rumbling purr, as if nothing so crass as noise would dare disturb the sweeping lawns of the Morgan house. For a moment, he stared up at the century-and-a-half-year-old structure, with its red brick and white columns.

A smile tugged at his lips. Who'd have imagined that Brent Zartlich would ever be welcome at this imposing front door? To take Dr. Morgan's daughter out on a date, no less.

Climbing out of the Porsche, he tossed the corsage box into the air and caught it neatly. The garish mum, which had arrived at his room that afternoon, made him think of all the things he'd avoided to save his pride: homecoming dates, prom night. Tonight would make up for all of it. And he couldn't think of anyone better to share his triumph with than Laura.

Bounding up the steps, he rang the bell, which sat above a historical marker and between two plaques proclaiming the occupants Sons and Daughters of The Republic. A series of chiming notes drifted through the solid cypress door.

No sound followed. Glancing down, he dusted a speck of lint off his pearl-gray Yves Saint Laurent suit. The chirping of birds and the scurrying of squirrels drew his attention to the lawn. He frowned in disapproval. Whoever had taken over his old job as lawn boy wasn't keeping the boxwood properly trimmed or the mulch turned under the azaleas.

The door cracked open, and a wizened face peeked around the panel, a face as gnarled and dark as the old oak trees that shaded the lawn. " 'Bout time you got here."

"Clarice!" He laughed in surprise. "What in the world are you doing still working here?"

"I'd like to know that myself." Her grin showed a mouthful of teeth too white to be real. "You'd think these folks could learn to take care of themselves after all these years."

Brent stepped into the foyer and had the oddest sensation of stepping through an invisible wall. He'd never been through the front door of this house. He soaked in the feel of the entryway, with its gleaming antiques, its wood-plank floors, and the stairway that curved gracefully upward to the second floor.

"Mmm, mmm, mmm." Clarice shook her head at him. "They sure must be feeding you right in that city of yours."

"Good enough." He glanced surreptitiously at the carved rococo mirror over the Chippendale entry table. He would never have thought to mix those two styles, but somehow the blend created an air of inherited wealth. He'd have to keep it in mind for his own house in Houston.

"Who's there?" a deep voice demanded from beyond the formal parlor. Brent peered into the softly lit room, where evening sunlight filtered through lace curtains to glow against a Queen Anne coffee table laden with porcelain knickknacks.

"It's Mr. Brent to pick up Miss Laura Beth for their date," Clarice shouted back, then lowered her voice. "As if he didn't have the sense to figure that out for himself."

The smile that started to form on Brent's face stiffened when Dr. Walter Morgan appeared in the doorway at the far side of the parlor.

"So it is." The doctor's angular face registered no

readable emotion as he assessed Brent's attire. "Well, you certainly have come a long way since the days when you used to mow my lawn."

Keeping his own expression bland, Brent adopted his news announcer's voice. "Good evening, Dr. Morgan. I hope you're well."

"Passing fair." The man came forward with the aid of a cane to stand before Brent. His tall frame refused to bend despite the arthritis evident in his hands. Thin white hair had been scraped straight back, emphasizing sharp cheekbones and cool gray eyes. "If it weren't for seeing you on the news, I'd never have recognized you . . . coming through my front door."

Brent ignored the reminder that he would never have been extended the privilege of using the front door instead of the back if he weren't a news anchor. "Word in town has it you sold your medical practice to join the ranks of the retired. I hope you're enjoying retirement."

Dr. Morgan glanced toward the maid. "Clarice, inform my daughter her . . . 'date' has arrived."

"Yes, sir." Clarice climbed her way up the stairs, and neither man spoke until her footsteps faded.

"I understand you put on quite a show today in town," the doctor said.

"Just giving the audience their money's worth," Brent answered evenly.

"From what I hear, Janet made the usual fool of herself. Stacey, however, is normally a sensible girl. If the bank hadn't insisted she participate out of some misguided sense of civic duty, I'm sure she'd have avoided the whole nonsense."

"No doubt." Brent resisted the urge to glance at his

watch. "But then, it was all for your daughter's favorite cause."

"Which is the only reason Laura Beth participated." A hard gleam came into Dr. Morgan's eyes. "But then, everyone knows she's always had a soft spot for charity cases. No doubt she wanted to spare the fund-raising committee the embarrassment of an empty chair on that stage when no one else could be persuaded to participate."

Brent kept his expression completely blank, while inside every muscle in his gut tightened. No matter how far he'd come, no matter what he accomplished, to some people he would always be the bastard kid raised on the edge of town.

"I do hope," the doctor said, "as you take Laura Beth out this evening, you'll remember this is a small community. I would hate to see my daughter's name linked to any unsavory gossip as a result of her charity work."

"I'll try to bear that in mind," Brent said with a forced smile. "But then, we poor folk do have trouble remembering how to behave when we're out among polite society."

"Hey, Brent!" Laura's voice rang out from the second-floor landing as clear and cheerful as the chimes on the doorbell. "Sorry to keep you waiting."

Relief washed over him. Everything would be fine now. He would get away from town and spend a nice relaxing evening with a friend. And that's all he and Laura were, friends.

Or so he thought until she rounded the first newel post and the air left his lungs. There at eye level were a pair of incredibly long, shapely legs. He tried not to gape as she skipped down the stairs in a blend of youth and grace. In contrast to the exposed legs, the rest of her looked prim and proper. The lapelless navy jacket floated nearly to the hem of the short navy skirt. A cameo pin fastened the white silk blouse at the throat. She'd swept her hair into a perfect French twist.

"My goodness," she said, taking in his suit. "Don't we look nice."

Brent felt an absurd flush of pride. Over the years, he'd learned to view his appearance with detached objectivity, as nothing more than an asset to his trade. Yet in that moment, with Laura smiling up at him, he felt as if she'd complimented *him*.

Then her eyes lit on the corsage, and laughter slipped past the hand she pressed to her lips. "Oh, dear." She made a valiant effort to regain a straight face. "Janet's corsage."

He glanced down at the enormous white mum and devoutly wished he'd tossed it in the trash. He should have known Janet had arranged for it in the expectation that she would be his date. The thing was as big as a high school spirit corsage, minus only the ribbons, cowbells, and glitter. "If you'd rather not wear it, you certainly won't hurt my feelings."

"Don't be ridiculous." She smiled up at him while her father looked on with a scowl. "I never received a single mum when I was in school. I'm not about to pass up the chance to wear one now. Besides, pea green is such a delightful color on Janet, don't you think?"

He grunted as he went to pin the corsage to her jacket—and discovered her blouse wasn't as prim as he'd thought. He could see the lacy pattern of her bra through the fine silk. He jerked as the pin jabbed his finger.

"Oh, and Dad?" Laura said over her shoulder. "Clarice will have dinner ready any minute. I'd appreciate it very much if you'd let her go home as soon as she's finished cooking."

"I don't see why you couldn't have cooked dinner and left it on the table," her father complained. "That woman burns everything."

"I'm sure she can handle heating up leftovers and tossing a salad," Laura said as she checked the corsage.

Dr. Morgan gave a snort that conveyed his doubts about Clarice's abilities in the kitchen. Then his gaze dropped to his daughter's feet, and his brows snapped together. "You'll ruin your ankles in those high heels."

"Dad." Laura's eyes narrowed with warning. "I'll likely be in late, so don't wait up."

"I'll expect you to wake me when you do get in," he said gruffly.

"Good night, Dad." She kissed his cheek.

Brent offered his arm, more than relieved to make their escape. To his irritation, the good doctor stood at the doorway and watched as he helped Laura into his car. Out of pure frustration, anger, or maybe just for the sheer hell of it, when he climbed into the driver's seat, he threw the car into gear and laid ten feet of rubber down the circular drive.

CHAPTER
5

"What did he say?" Laura kept her eyes straight ahead, not sure she wanted to hear the answer.

"Who?"

"My father." She shot Brent a look for his obtuseness. "What did he say to you?"

"Nothing," Brent insisted as he turned onto the main road out of town.

She propped her elbow on the window ledge. "I knew I should have been waiting downstairs when you arrived." Brent didn't say a word. She glanced over and saw the tension in his face. "I'm sorry. Really, I—" She broke off at the sound of his chuckle. "What's so funny?"

"You." He turned toward her, and his eyes filled with fondness. "You haven't changed a bit."

"I have, too," she insisted, then frowned. "In what way haven't I changed?"

"You're still flying to the aid of the underdog. Only, Laura?" He grinned. "I'm not the underdog anymore."

"Oh, well, no, of course not." She wondered if she'd offended him. He seemed so self-assured, but currents flowed beneath the confident facade, little glimpses of insecurity that reminded her of the boy he'd once been.

"I'd much rather talk about you, though," he said.

"What the heck has Little Laura Beth been up to all these years?"

"Nothing." Her mouth twisted in a derisive smirk. "Absolutely nothing."

"Oh?" From the corner of her eye, she saw his brow lift. "Am I to take it you aren't entirely happy living in Dullsville?"

"It's not the town. It's me. I just feel so . . . restless! Like my whole life is passing me by."

"Then why have you stayed?"

"You know why." At his confused look, she jogged his memory. "Dad had a heart attack right after my mother died. He needed me to take care of him."

"Laura . . ." His laugh sounded more surprised than amused. "Your mother died when you were, what, seven? Surely your father's over it by now."

Some things people don't ever get over. She wished she could say the words aloud, but the truth about her mother's death, and all the sordid details leading up to it, were things neither she nor her father shared with anyone. As a result, people had the misconception that she'd led some idyllic life with storybook parents. But under the surface, she suspected her home life wasn't much happier than what Brent had endured.

Was that why she'd always felt drawn to him?

She'd often wanted to talk to him about her parents, but habit and loyalty made her tamp down the impulse even now. "It wasn't just my father's heart attack that made me stay. There were . . . other considerations."

"Like what?" He gave her an incredulous look, obviously ready to dispute anything she said.

"Like the fact that my father's office manager quit without notice the summer after I graduated high school.

He needed someone to help out until he could replace her."

"Let me guess." Brent held up his hand. "He never found someone to put up with him long enough to fill the position, right?"

"Wrong," she said. "I discovered I liked managing a doctor's office. And I happen to be very good at it. Or at least I was." She heard the disgruntled note that crept into her voice and frowned. Whining was selfish, and she had too much to be grateful for in life to waste time crying over the things she didn't have.

"Was?" Brent scowled. "Aren't you working anymore?"

She shrugged. "Dad sold his practice."

"So? Just because he retired doesn't mean you had to quit working."

She glanced out the window to watch the stately oaks that lined the backcountry road. One after another, they slipped by . . . as uneventful as her days. She'd tried to tell herself over the past months that charity work was enough. She didn't need money. So why did she feel this compelling need to do something with her life? Why couldn't she be content as Dr. Morgan's coddled daughter?

"He made you quit," Brent guessed. "Didn't he?"

"He didn't *make* me do anything. We both felt the incoming doctor deserved the right to hire his own staff rather than be saddled with Dad's old one."

"Yeah, right."

She crossed her arms and refused to admit she agreed with him. There'd been no reason for her to quit when her father retired, but giving in to his wishes had been easier than living with his quiet condemnation. That, and she hadn't realized how useless she'd feel without a job.

"I'm sorry." Brent sighed. "I didn't mean to get you down. I should know better than to discuss your father."

"I'm not down," she insisted. At his dubious look, she decided he was right. Her father was a topic that had always thrown up barriers between them. What they needed to do was lighten the mood. "Although you're right about one thing." She crossed her legs and leaned toward him, in an effort to look playfully seductive. "My father is the last thing we should be discussing—on our first hot date."

"Hot date?" For one second, he looked as if he'd swallowed his tongue.

Surprised by his discomfort, she carried the teasing further in her best Southern Belle accent. "What else would you call it, when a girl's out with a boy who makes her heart go all aflutter?"

An odd frown passed over his features as his gaze fell to the region of her heart. Then his eyes slipped lower, and the crease between his brows deepened. She glanced down to find her skirt had ridden up to show the top of her stockings.

Mortified, she tugged at the hem and sat up straighter. Although, she assured herself, she had no reason to be embarrassed about the stockings. No reason at all. Lots of women wore stockings instead of hose. Especially when the temperature soared into the nineties and beyond.

Chancing a sideways glance, she watched Brent fiddle with the air-conditioning vents. She relaxed a little, relieved to know the sudden heat in her cheeks came from lack of air conditioning. "Speaking of hot," she said, "it sure is warm tonight. For April, I mean."

His hand went back to the steering wheel as he stared straight ahead. "Yeah. Hot."

She puzzled over his sudden withdrawal. *He* had no reason to be embarrassed. Unless her wearing stockings bothered him. But that was ludicrous. Surely he didn't think her choice of underwear had anything to do with him.

They turned off the two-lane county road onto a four-lane divided drive bordered by lush green grass and blooming redbud trees. Pillars of red granite and geysers of water shot into the air, marking the entrance to the Riverwood Golf Course and Country Club.

Brent had thought he'd be able to relax once they reached the club. After all, he'd always been comfortable with Laura, they were away from Beason's Ferry, and the country club was exactly the type of atmosphere he'd grown accustomed to in recent years. Maître d's, wine stewards, starched linens, and fine cuisine should have distracted him from thoughts of Laura's legs.

Or so he'd thought.

He couldn't quit thinking about the long, slender legs he'd watched skip gracefully down the stairs. It was the stockings that did it. Those damned stockings.

He shifted in his chair and glanced about, looking for the waiter. The soup and salad courses had already been served and removed. Their main course should have been out by now.

"So tell me about Denver," Laura said, leaning forward to cradle her chin on her laced fingers. "Was it any better than Albuquerque?"

"What?" He turned back to her, frowning as he noticed how the soft lighting enhanced her skin. The faint strains of Mozart played in the background. Through the wall of glass beside them, the evening sun lent a golden glow to her hair.

"Denver?" she prompted. Without the thick glasses of her youth, her eyes sparkled like blue diamonds.

"Yes, of course. Denver." He frowned as he tried to remember where they were in their conversation. He'd been filling her in on his years as a reporter between college and when he landed the plum job as anchor in Houston. "Believe it or not, Denver was worse . . ."

He told the story by rote, the way he'd told it a hundred times—embellishing the facts, glossing over the boring parts, and zeroing in on the offbeat wackiness that made the world of broadcast news what it was: exhilarating, challenging, his life's blood.

"You sound like you miss working in the field." Her head tipped, and a gentle smile curved her lips. All that rapt attention made him uncomfortable.

He had no idea why. And he didn't want to know. The reason was all jumbled up with his unexpected attraction to her, and the totally unwelcome thought that her attraction to him was not merely teasing. And why *that* made him nervous, he really did not want to know.

Some emotions, he'd learned, were like the monster that had lived in his closet when he was a kid. A wise man, like a smart kid, instinctively knew which closet doors to leave firmly shut at all times.

The waiter arrived with their steaks and a bottle of

merlot. Brent concentrated on tasting the wine, then tried to focus on his meal. "I suppose I do miss reporting."

"Then why'd you give it up?" she asked, taking up her knife and fork.

"Are you kidding?" He laughed. "They offered me a prime-time anchor position in a major market. Nobody turns down a career rung like that."

"Yes, but if you enjoyed reporting more than anchoring—"

"Laura." He shook his head. "Do you have any idea how much more money an anchor makes than a reporter?"

She studied him a moment. "What if they paid the same?"

"I'd go back to reporting in a heartbeat. Not," he added quickly, "that I don't like anchoring. It has its challenges—the pace is grueling, the hours suck, and I still get to fight with my producer over lead stories and time allotment."

"What more could a man ask for?" she summed up with a smile.

She had the most incredible smile, sweet yet sexy, pure yet bold. For a heartbeat, he lost his concentration. Then lifting his wineglass, he saluted her understanding. "Exactly."

"So," she straightened, "tell me about Houston."

After taking a healthy sip of merlot, he launched into a few stories about KSET, thinking sooner or later he'd land on a topic that would get his mind off Laura's legs and those flesh-colored, silk stockings. At least she wasn't wearing black stockings. Or white. White would definitely be worse. White stockings conjured images of rumpled sheets, lacy lingerie, and a long strand of pearls against satin-smooth skin.

He shifted his weight to accommodate his growing arousal. This was ridiculous. Here he sat in a formal restaurant, surrounded by people—all of whom watched him with avid curiosity—while he mentally stripped Laura Beth Morgan down to her garter belt and stockings.

"Is something wrong?" Laura leaned forward and placed her hand on his.

His whole body stiffened. Staring at her slender fingers, with their neatly trimmed nails against his hard, tanned fist, sent panic shooting through him. He eased his hand away from hers and cut off a bite of steak. "No, of course not."

Laura sat back, frowning as she studied him. He was lying, and she knew it. Something was definitely wrong. Even while he'd told his entertaining tales of broadcast journalism, she'd sensed an undercurrent of tension. She wondered again what her father had said to him. Or was it simply being back in Beason's Ferry that was wearing on his nerves?

Returning to his hometown might have been harder on him than even she had imagined. The performance at the opera house would have embarrassed anyone. She'd certainly been embarrassed by it. And now, since arriving at the restaurant, people from town kept staring at him like he was some oddity. Several people had even come over to ask him for his autograph. She'd laughed the first time it happened, thinking how silly it was. These people had known Brent all his life, and now they were asking for his autograph?

The fifth time had not been so funny, and now, to her

disbelief, she saw Karl Adderson heading toward their table with a cocktail napkin and pen.

"Why, Brent, is that you?" Karl asked as if he'd just been walking by and happened to notice Brent. "You probably don't remember me—"

"Of course I do, Mr. Adderson." Brent rose to shake hands and accept a slap on the back.

Irritated by the interruption, Laura glanced away, toward the wall of glass beside their table. Beyond it she could see the tee box for the first green. Imported African deer grazed along the fairway that cut through the woods.

Superimposed on the tranquil scene was Brent's reflection as he spoke to the owner of Adderson's Grocery. Brent had worked for the man three summers in a row. Mr. Adderson kept Brent's hand clasped in his own while he relayed stories about Brent, as if he were speaking to a total stranger about an old friend. All the while, Brent's smile remained strained but in place. What had happened to the quiet, brooding boy she'd known so long ago? The one who kept everyone at a distance with his dark scowls?

Did the Brent she'd known years ago still exist beneath the polished new facade? Or had he simply exchanged one shield for another? The thought upset her, but for reasons she feared were more selfish than empathetic, for she very much suspected this new shield was designed to keep her out as well.

Mr. Adderson finally left, and Brent resumed his seat. "I wonder how many more of those 'I knew you when' conversations we'll have to put up with tonight?"

"It makes you uncomfortable, doesn't it?" she observed.

"What?"

"People's adoration."

"Oh, that." He tried to laugh it off. When she didn't buy it, he sighed in defeat. "Yeah, if you want to know the truth, it makes me very uncomfortable."

"Why?"

"I don't know," he admitted. "It just feels weird." He looked as if he would leave it at that but surprised her by taking on an urgent tone. "Have you ever felt like . . . like nobody really sees you? Like their eyes are focused about an inch in front of you, not *on* you?"

She stared at him, amazed that he'd so accurately described how she felt at times, as if people saw only what she was on the surface, Dr. Morgan's dutiful daughter, the conscientious citizen, the hard little worker. None of them seemed able to look into her eyes and see that she had sorrows locked deep in her heart and ambitions beyond Beason's Ferry. She was a woman, with needs and flaws and unfulfilled dreams. But she also feared that someday someone would see all the way inside her—and reject the person she really was. "Yes," she said quietly, "I know exactly how it feels."

Before he could respond, the waiter arrived with their desserts. Brent waited until they were alone, then spoke in a voice that held a hint of self-mockery. "When I came back here, I guess I wanted to show all the people who ever looked down on me what a big shot I'd become."

"If you mean you wanted to impress the people in your hometown, you have."

"Only with what I am now, not with how far I had to come to get here. It should be enough, though, don't you think?" His eyes met hers. "I should be happy they only see Brent Michaels, News Anchor, not the kid who used to mow their lawns and deliver their groceries and hustle pool at Snake's Pool Palace.''

"So why isn't it enough?"

"Who knows?" He shrugged. "And once this weekend is over, I'll be back in Houston, so what does it matter?"

She frowned at his feigned acceptance of something that obviously bothered him, but chose to shift the topic slightly. "Did you really hustle pool at Snake's?"

He chuckled at her intrigued expression. "How do you think I made money after I quit mowing lawns?"

Her eyes widened. "But you were only sixteen when you quit mowing lawns. I thought you had to be twenty-one to get into Snake's."

"Oh, God, Laura." He shook his head, laughing. "You really are an innocent, aren't you? Even after all these years." He smiled, as if his words were a compliment, but she felt downright insulted.

Why does everybody in the world live interesting lives but me? She brooded over the question as she ate her dessert. When it was gone, the waiter came to whisk away their plates.

"Will there be anything else, sir?" the waiter asked.

"Nothing for me," Brent answered. "Laura?"

She shook her head.

"Well, then." Brent rose to pull out her chair. "Are you ready for the ballroom?"

She nodded, still lost in thought. Since the meal had been donated by the country club, they didn't have to wait for a bill, although Brent left a generous tip on the table.

"You're awfully quiet," he said as they made their way across the dining room.

"Hmm?" She started slightly. "Oh, sorry."

"You aren't mad about something, are you?"

"Mad?" She frowned. "No, of course not."

He looked less than convinced as he led her to the foyer between the restaurant and the ballroom. A crowd stood at the doorway, waiting to get in. From inside, she heard the band swing into an old Glenn Miller tune.

"I knew it," Brent muttered close to her ear. "Lawrence Welk."

Looking at the crowd inside the ballroom, her heart sank. The last thing she wanted was to go into a room full of people who were craning their heads and gathering cocktail napkins for Brent's autograph. The line moved ahead, leaving her and Brent standing alone in the doorway.

"Well," he took a deep breath, "you ready?"

"No." The word popped out of her mouth of its own accord. "Let's not go in there."

"You want to go home?" He frowned at her.

"I don't know. I just . . ."

"What?" He sounded leery—and perhaps a little hurt. Did he think she wanted to get away from him? Looking in his eyes, she realized he thought exactly that. Somehow this evening, she'd crossed over the line from being his ally to being one of "them"—the people who wanted a piece of Brent Michaels but had never taken the time to know Brent Zartlich.

With a stab of guilt, she realized maybe she was no different from the rest of the town. She hadn't taken the time to truly get to know him beyond a surface friendship, a passing camaraderie between two misfits. Perhaps the fear of exposing her own flaws had held her back.

More than anything, though, she wanted to know Brent—
the real Brent.

"Take me to Snake's Pool Palace," she said.

"Excuse me?" He stared in disbelief.

"You heard me." A slow smile stole across her lips. "I
want you to take me to Snake's."

CHAPTER
6

"Wait. Stop." Brent came to a halt the minute they stepped out the front doors of the country club into the motor court. "I can't take you to Snake's."

"Why not?" Laura grinned up at him, overflowing with jaunty enthusiasm.

"Because . . ." He stared at her face, thinking that for an intelligent woman, she could be really dense at times. "Do you have any idea what that place is like?"

"No. Which is why I want to go." Her expression said she'd never done anything like this and almost couldn't believe she was doing it now.

"Okay, look, if you want to shoot some pool or do some country-western dancing, why don't we drive over to the VFW Hall?"

"I don't want to go to the VFW Hall," she said slowly. "I want to go to Snake's Pool Palace."

"Laura, your father will murder me if I take you to a place like that."

His words made her back go straight as a poker. "Which is another reason I want to go. I'm sick and tired of living my life according to other people's rules. Can't I just once have some fun, like every other normal person in the world?"

She had a point. Not a point he liked—but a valid one.

"Mr. Michaels?" the valet asked. "Will you be needing your car, sir?"

Brent looked at Laura. If she wanted to see the darker side of life, she was safer doing it with him than on her own.

With a curt nod, he sent the valet after his car. "All right, Laura, if you're bound and determined to flirt with disaster, here's how it's going to be. You will not utter one gasp of horror or one word of condemnation all evening. You will stay in my sight at all times. And you will never, *ever* tell anyone where we went tonight, or so help me, I'll come back here and tan your hide. You got that?"

"Does that mean we're going?" Her whole face lit up.

"Do I have a choice?"

With a low, rumbling purr, the yellow Porsche rolled up beside them, and the valet hopped out. "Boy, does this baby sing. You want the top down, Mr. Michaels?"

"Oh, yes, please," Laura answered brightly, as if they were headed for a picnic in the country.

Brent jerked off his jacket and tie and threw them in the backseat as soon as the valet had finished lowering the top. Shoving a tip into the kid's hand, he climbed into the driver's seat and slammed the door.

Laura, of course, waited politely for the valet to dash around the hood and open her door. She climbed in with that innate grace of hers, legs folded neatly together with her ankles crossed and her knees touching.

He gave her a long look, waiting for her to change her mind. She raised a brow as if to say, *Well? Are we going or not?*

In answer, he threw the car in gear and headed down the drive. "This is the stupidest idea I ever heard."

"It'll be fun," she said.

"What are you doing?" He scowled as she peeled off her navy jacket. She folded it neatly with the mum on top and placed it in the back. The wind plastered her shirt to her body, revealing the lacy pattern of her bra through the thin silk. Christ, how could any woman look so prim and so sexy at the same time?

"Somehow," she answered, "I don't think a church suit and corsage would be appropriate attire for a pool hall."

Brent jerked his eyes back to the road. This was nuts. He had to talk her out of this before the rednecks who hung out at Snake's got an eyeful of Laura. They'd be on her as fast as wolves on a newly born lamb.

From the corner of his eye, he saw the wind tug a strand of hair free from her French twist. She reached up to repin it, and relief washed through him. Laura Beth Morgan was going to take one look at Snake's and demand he take her home.

Only, to his horror, he realized she hadn't repinned her hair. She'd been taking it down!

Laura tried to hide her disappointment as she twisted in her seat to study the dark building separated from the road by a gravel parking lot. It wasn't exactly what she'd expected. On the few occasions when she'd driven this backcountry road by day, she'd tried to imagine how the abandoned-looking building would transform itself at night. Garish neon lights would glow in the windows while the throbbing bass of blaring music filled the night air. Couples would lock themselves in passionate embraces against souped-up hot rods and battered pickup trucks. Maybe two drunken cowboys would even stumble out the front door to engage in a bar fight. She'd never seen a bar fight. Of course, the only bars she'd ever been to were the kind attached to respectable restaurants.

"Well?" Brent demanded in the disapproving older-brother tone he'd somehow acquired. "Seen enough?"

She gave him her best smirk. "We haven't even gone in yet."

"Then by all means, let's go in." Brent got out of the car. She waited for him to open her door, but he turned away and headed across the parking lot instead.

"Hey, wait up." She scrambled out of the car, slinging the thin strap of her purse over her shoulder. She knew perfectly well he wanted her to chicken out, but she meant to show him she was made of sterner stuff than that.

The car alarm chirped behind her as she headed after him. She slipped on the gravel and caught herself against an old Oldsmobile. Her father was right, she really would twist her ankle in these shoes.

To her surprise, the car rocked against her. She glanced through the grimy window and caught a glimpse of movement in the backseat.

"You coming, Squirt?" Brent called.

She sprang away from the car, trying not to blush or laugh as she hurried after him.

"What's so funny?" he asked when she reached him.

"Nothing." A giggle escaped.

"Laura . . ." he said in a threatening tone.

"There were . . ." She lowered her voice. "People. In the backseat of that car. You know. Doing it."

"Which car?"

"That one. Back there. Jeez, don't look!" She tried to grab his arm, but it was too late.

Rather than whisper, as she had, he raised his voice. "You mean the one with the bumper sticker that says 'If this car is a-rockin', don't you dare come a-knockin'?"

"Bre-ent!" She covered her face with her hand. He laughed, which was an improvement over the glowering he'd done since they'd left the country club. "Can we just go inside?"

His laughter stopped, and she lowered her hand. The glower had returned. "Laura, look . . ." he hesitated. "I don't know what you're trying to prove here, but we don't have to do this."

She longed to say she wasn't trying to prove anything. But that was a lie. She needed to prove, at least to herself, that just because her life was boring didn't mean *she* was.

"Brent," she said, "I'm twenty-eight years old. An age when most single people are thinking about settling down. Only how am I supposed to do that, if I have nothing to settle down *from*?"

He studied her closely, his face unreadable in the darkness.

"I mean . . ." She fidgeted. "Shouldn't everyone have at least one night in their lives they regret?"

He heaved a sigh. "Just remember you said that, not me."

"Absolutely." Her mood instantly lightened.

"And drop the Girl Scout grin." He headed up the wooden steps to the plain brown door. "Jeez, I keep wanting to ask what kind of cookies you're selling this year."

"Oatmeal." Her grin grew wider.

"Just get in here." He jerked the door open and held it for her.

The smell of smoke and stale beer filled her nostrils as she stepped over the threshold. A hush fell over the stark interior. Directly across from them, two old farmers sat at the bar—not the ornate carved-wood and mirror-backed bar she'd imagined, but a plain wooden bar with plain wooden stools. An assortment of liquor bottles cluttered the shelves behind it.

The two old-timers, in their dirty plaid shirts and baseball caps, glanced over their shoulders to glare at the newcomers. Laura stepped closer to Brent. "It's a little quiet in here, don't you think?"

"It's early," he said, closing the door behind them.

Laura glanced off to the left, where two younger men bent over one of the three pool tables. Plastic imitations of stained-glass lamps bearing beer logos hung over each table, casting beams of smoke-filled light onto the playing surface.

"Would you care to have a seat?" Brent asked with exaggerated politeness. "Or would you prefer to go straight for a game of high-stakes pool?"

"No, no, sitting would be nice."

To her relief, he led her off to the right, where a hodgepodge of tables surrounded a minuscule dance floor. A jukebox sat before a stage that looked as if it hadn't been used in years. Brent picked a table close to the dark-tinted windows along the front wall, away from the few occupied booths along the back. As they settled onto the cracked plastic seats, Laura was glad to see two women at the other tables, even though the women looked as hard and worn as the men.

"I thought I'd order whiskey," Brent said. "What do you want?"

She stared toward the bar, wishing she could toss back her hair and say something provocative like "I'll have the same, on the rocks with a splash." But a splash of what? She'd never had whiskey before and didn't even know what her options were.

"Well, if it ain't Brent Zartlich," a raspy male voice wheezed. " 'Scuse me. Brent *Michaels*."

"Evening, Snake." Brent nodded to the man.

Laura looked up and found herself staring into the eyes of a tattooed snake. It coiled up the entire length of a flabby arm that was nearly as big around as her leg.

"Hey, boys!" the man named Snake called toward the pool tables. "Looky here what the cat done drug in."

Laura looked beyond the tattoo long enough to get an impression of an enormous man wearing a sleeveless black T-shirt. Black hair framed a face that could have been attractive if it were a bit less flabby and a lot less piratical. On second thought, that wicked pirate gleam in his eyes lent him a certain charm.

"Well, well." One of the pool players swaggered toward them. He too wore a sleeveless T-shirt, but his arms were sculpted of hard muscle and bore no tattoos. He had the face of a fallen angel with brown eyes and a mischievous grin. Rather than a halo, he wore a battered straw cowboy hat over his sandy-blond hair. "I don't know, Snake, looks more like something a skunk would play with to me."

"Jimmy Joe." Brent greeted the newcomer in a cool tone without offering his hand.

"And who might this be?" Jimmy Joe's gaze lit on Laura as if he'd just found his father's secret stash of *Playboy*. She blushed, embarrassed yet oddly delighted at the idea of being cast in such a role.

When Brent made no move to introduce her, she held out her hand. "How do you do? I'm Laura M—"

"Martin," Brent interrupted and shot her a warning glare, although she thought his precaution unnecessary. They were far enough outside Beason's Ferry, Jimmy Joe probably wouldn't recognize her name. "This is Laura Martin."

"Girlfriend?" Jimmy Joe asked, taking her hand.

"Friend," Brent corrected in a stilted voice.

"Weeell, in that case—" Jimmy Joe raised Laura's hand to his lips—"I'm right pleased to meet you, Laura Martin. I'm Jimmy Joe Dean," he said, sliding uninvited into the chair beside her. "Sort of like James Dean, but with a Texas twist."

"Yeah," Brent muttered. "The original Rebel Without a Brain."

"And this here's Roy." Jimmy Joe gestured to a bulky man who stood silently staring down at Laura from beneath the bill of his ball cap. The total blankness of Roy's expression gave her pause.

"Have a seat, Roy." Jimmy Joe gestured to the one remaining chair, and his friend did as he was told. "Roy here, he don't talk much," Jimmy Joe whispered, then winked to put her at ease.

She offered Roy a smile, which wasn't returned. On closer inspection, she decided he looked more slow-witted than dangerous.

"How come we ain't seen you around here before?" Jimmy Joe asked her.

"She's from out of state," Brent answered.

Jimmy Joe slapped a hand to his chest. "Now don't you go breaking my heart by telling me you're a Yankee."

"Does she sound like a Yankee?" Brent demanded.

"Hard to say, since I ain't heard her speak much." Jimmy Joe gifted her with one of his fallen angel smiles. "You can speak, now cain't you, darling?"

"Of course she can speak," Brent said, and Laura had to bite her tongue to keep from laughing.

"You know, it's right handy how you do that," Jimmy Joe said to her. "Talk, I mean, without moving your lips. You must be one of them there ventrilo-kist." He turned his smile on Brent. "And this here must be your dummy."

"You boys gonna order something?" Snake asked. "Or sit here yammering all night?"

Brent glanced at Snake. "I'll have whiskey on the rocks, and Laura would like a whiskey and seven—Johnnie Walker Red, if you have it." He'd obviously guessed she didn't have a clue what she wanted.

"What about you, JJ?" Snake asked. "You and Roy want another round of long necks?"

"You bet," Jimmy Joe said.

Laura heard Brent's sigh of exasperation and gave him a sympathetic smile. As Snake ambled off toward the bar, the front door opened and a teenage girl wearing baggy jeans and a skintight T-shirt entered. The shirt stretched over her full breasts and left her flat stomach exposed. Every man's eyes went instantly to the girl. Brent, she noticed, was the first to turn away with a look of mild disgust.

"Speaking of what the cat drug in . . ." Jimmy Joe muttered, but he was grinning from ear to ear.

The girl's eyes scanned the room and lit up when she found Jimmy Joe. She sauntered toward him with her blue jeans riding low on her hips. She had a startling, almost innocent look to her heart-shaped face. Dark brown hair hung straight to her narrow waist. But her eyes, Laura noticed, looked glassy, dilated, and far too old for someone so young.

"Hey there, Jimmy Joe," she breathed as she slipped into his lap. Curling one arm about his neck, she fastened her mouth to his and proceeded to give him a tonsillectomy with her tongue.

Laura glanced away, focusing on the scarred tabletop, the neon beer signs on the wall, the darkness beyond the window. In the window she saw a reflection of the couple kissing, like wavy images from a dream. Her breath turned shallow as she watched them, and deep inside her belly her muscles tightened around an empty ache.

She'd never kissed a man like that, had never been kissed with that deep twining of lips, and bodies, and tongues. Oh, but she'd dreamed about it. Even when she'd kissed Greg, especially on the few occasions when they'd made love, she'd dreamed of kisses that defied politeness and shunned propriety.

Unnerved by her own thoughts, she turned away, and her gaze collided with Brent's. She held her breath as he watched her. No expression showed on his face, but his eyes reached inside her, laying bare her darkest secrets. Could he see all the times she'd lain awake at night with perspiration dampening her thighs as she dreamed of kissing him?

As if in answer, she saw his throat move as he swallowed, and his breath turn shallow and slow. The couple beside them ended their kiss with the wet sound of mouths separating.

Laura jerked her gaze back to the window as every nerve inside her trembled.

"Ja miss me?" the girl asked with a husky murmur.

"Now why would I be missing you, Darlene?" Jimmy Joe asked. "You've been right here all evening."

"Yeah, but I went outside for some air, and I was gone an awfully long time."

"Were you now?" Jimmy Joe asked without much interest. "And here I didn't even notice."

Laura's heart ached for the girl, as if she were the one who'd just been dismissed.

"I don't suppose you saw Bobby while you were out takin' some air, now did you?" Jimmy Joe asked. "He promised to drop by tonight and lose me some money on the pool table."

"Well, I'm sure if I'd seen him, I'd have noticed," Darlene shot back huffily.

Jimmy Joe looked at Brent. "What'd'ya say, Zartlich? You up for shooting some pool, or are you just here to soak up the atmosphere?"

"To tell you the truth," Brent said while staring at Laura, "I'm not quite sure why I'm here."

"In that case," Jimmy Joe set Darlene aside and stood, "why don't we go rack up some balls while you decide?"

CHAPTER
7

Bending over a cue stick, Brent sighted the three ball to the corner pocket, but in his mind he saw the expression on Laura's face while Jimmy Joe had been giving his little teeny-bopper girlfriend mouth-to-mouth. When Laura had turned to him with those dilated pupils and the sheen of perspiration on her flushed neck, something inside his brain had shorted out. In that moment, he'd wanted her, right then, right there, and to hell with whoever watched.

With a savage *crack*, he sank the three ball. Without glancing up from the table—since he'd lose what little control he had left if he looked at Laura—he moved around to line up his next shot. How could he be having these thoughts about her? Laura was sweet, decent, and proper to a fault; she had an understanding heart and generous nature that had allowed her to befriend a boy the rest of the town had shunned. Loyalty alone should be keeping his thoughts in line. Yet try as he might, he couldn't stop the images from popping into his head: images of Laura stretched out on the pool table before him while he did a dozen scandalous things to her body.

Focusing on the eleven ball, he reminded himself of all the reasons he absolutely could not give in to a single impulse pumping through his overheated body. Women like Laura didn't make love to men unless they thought the relationship might lead to marriage. He, on the other hand, had no intention of getting married. Ever. It was not a decision he had made lightly. Nor was it one he would ever reverse. To seduce a woman like Laura would be no better than lying. He knew that. So why the hell wasn't his body listening to his brain?

He smacked the cue ball with such force, it flew off the table.

"Whoa, there." Jimmy Joe laughed as he caught the ball midflight. "This is pool we're shooting. Not skeet."

"Your shot." Settling against the far wall, Brent took up his drink and studied Laura over the rim of the glass. She sat perched on a bar stool next to Darlene, her blond hair neatly framing her face. The brooch still held her blouse closed primly at the throat. She'd crossed her long, silky legs and clasped her hands together over her knee.

With a snort, he shook his head. She looked as out of place as a hothouse lily growing in a garbage heap. He couldn't believe Laura was even talking to that girl. Well, actually, he could. He wouldn't be surprised if she was hoping to take Darlene home, clean her up, and introduce her to some nice boy in the church youth group.

He wanted to shake her, to tell her she couldn't save the whole world no matter how hard she tried. But he wouldn't shake her, because if he put his hands on her, he'd pull her up against his aching groin, cover her mouth with his, and kiss her till they both went weak and breathless.

Damn! He drained his glass of melted ice and whiskey.

Just then someone burst through the front door, allowing in some much-needed night air. "Hey, JJ!" the newcomer called. Brent looked up to see Jimmy Joe's lifelong sidekick, Bobby. "Wait'll you get a load of what's out in the parking lot."

"Do you mind?" Jimmy Joe growled. "I'm lining up a shot."

"Yeah, but you gotta see—" Bobby broke off when he caught sight of Brent. "Holy shit." His boyish face split with a grin. At thirty-three years old, Bobby still looked like the runt of the litter with his curly brown hair and pug nose. "Hey'ya, Brent. Long time no see."

"Bobby." Brent nodded in return as he jangled the ice cubes in his glass.

"Jesus," Jimmy Joe cursed. "You think y'all could talk a little louder?"

"Yeah, sure, no problem," Bobby said in a raised voice. He looked back at Brent and grinned. "I guess I ain't gotta ask who she belongs to." He nodded toward the parking lot, indicating the Porsche.

"Guess not." Brent smiled, feeling an admittedly juvenile but very satisfying thrill of ownership.

"Shit!" Jimmy Joe said as he missed his shot. Straightening, he glared at Bobby. "You mind telling me what was so all-fired important for you to bust my concentration?"

"Nothing." Bobby sent Brent a wink. "Just some old junker I seen in the parking lot."

"Then do you mind shutting up while we play some pool?"

"No, you go right ahead, Jimmy Joe."

"Hey, Bobby." Darlene straightened on her bar stool in a way that called attention to her breasts.

"Yeah, eh . . ." Bobby looked at everything in the room but Darlene. "Hi."

"Jimmy Joe was just asking me if I'd seen you earlier." She leaned back with her arms along the bar as she swung her crossed legs. "While I was out, you know . . . getting some air."

"Oh?" Bobby shifted nervously, leaving little doubt as to who had been in the backseat of the car when Laura and Brent had arrived. "What'd you tell him?"

"What'd'ya think I told him?"

Bobby's eyes darted from Jimmy Joe to Brent to the pool table. "Hey, I get to play the winner."

Shaking his head, Brent turned his concentration back to the game. As long as his winning streak held, he wouldn't have to sit next to Laura. If he didn't sit by her, or talk to her, or look at her too often, he might convince his hormones to cool off.

⁓

Laura realized Brent had been right; the place had been empty when they arrived because it was early. As the evening progressed, the tables around the dance floor began to fill. Smoke thickened the air as a lazy, mournful tune whined from the jukebox. Most of the patrons were men of various ages who'd apparently come to drink beer and gripe about their wives. Still, an occasional couple wandered in. Some of them even ventured onto the dance floor.

She watched longingly as a couple swayed back and forth to a Garth Brooks tune. She'd hoped to dance with Brent tonight and probably would have if they'd stayed at the country club. Then she could have danced and talked with him all evening.

Instead they'd come here.

And Brent had played pool.

She shouldn't have felt resentful—since coming to Snake's had been her idea, but Brent had ignored her all evening. No, he'd more than ignored her; he'd avoided her. She wanted to ask if he was angry but couldn't get his attention long enough to do even that.

"Hey, honey," Snake called to her, "you want another whiskey?"

Laura glanced at the lonely ice cubes in her glass. With nothing to do but sit on a bar stool and chat with Darlene, who talked of nothing but getting drunk and boffing boys, or visit with Roy, who didn't talk at all, Laura feared she may have had a few too many whiskey and sevens already.

"No, thanks," she said. "I think I'll take a little trip to the ladies' room."

As she climbed down from her bar stool, the floor shifted beneath her feet, and she decided she'd definitely had a bit too much to drink. With careful tread, she made her way to the rest room, where she removed the cameo at her throat and unfastened a few buttons of her blouse. Feeling stuffy and warm, she pressed a damp paper towel to her throat and studied her reflection in the mirror. No wonder Brent was ignoring her. Next to Darlene, she was practically invisible.

Digging through her purse, she came up with some blush and a darker shade of lipstick. She combed her hair but decided that created the opposite effect from what she wanted. So she bent forward to brush it upside down. Flinging her head back as she straightened up made the room spin, and she grabbed the sink, laughing as she steadied herself. A glance in the mirror told her she'd gotten rid of the paleness, even if she was a little dizzy. For good measure, she rolled up her sleeves, undid one more button to show a hint of cleavage, and headed back to the bar.

One way or another, she would get Brent's attention.

"Hey there, pretty lady."

"Oh!" She jumped when Jimmy Joe stepped in front of her. "You scared me."

"Well, that's the last thing I'd want to do to a pretty thing like you." Leaning one arm against the wall of the narrow passage, he let his gaze sweep over her. "Yes indeed, the last thing I'd want to do to you."

His sheer arrogance made her smile. "If you're looking for Darlene, she's over at the bar."

"Now why would I be looking for some little girl when I've got me a fine-looking woman standing right here?" He leaned forward to curl a hand about her waist. The earthy smell of dirt and sweat filled her nostrils. "What'd'ya say we rub bellies on the dance floor? Why, my belt buckle is just begging to be shined."

If anyone else had asked her to dance in so crude a fashion, she'd have given them a cool stare and walked away. But Jimmy Joe had a way of smiling right into a woman's eyes that made the proposal seem more like a compliment. For one split second, she considered dancing with him, then laughed. "No, I better not."

"Now why would you go and break my heart like that?"

"Because, Mr. Dean, for all your charm, I get the distinct impression that Brent doesn't like you very much."

"Actually," Jimmy Joe flashed a grin, "Brent hates my ever-loving guts. Which is exactly why you should dance with me."

"That," she said, "makes absolutely no sense."

"Sure it does, considering that he's practically making it with my sweet Darlene on that pool table over there."

Laura looked past Jimmy Joe to the pool table, and everything inside her went cold.

~

Brent braced one hand on the pool table and planted the other firmly in the middle of Darlene's back as she jerked him forward. All the while he prayed that if the twit lost her balance, she'd have the sense to unclamp her teeth from his lower lip. He had to admit, she was quicker than she looked. And stronger, he added, as she wrapped her legs about his waist.

"Mmm," she purred, and slowly released his lip. Her head fell back as she sat upright on the edge of the pool table. "That was really wow."

"Look, sweetheart—" He tried to untangle her arms from around his neck. "I'm flattered, really, but—"

"What's the matter?" She pouted as she locked her ankles at the small of his back and ground her crotch against his. "Don't you like to do it?"

"I love to do it, just not with little girls who are barely out of diapers."

"I'm old enough," she insisted as her nimble fingers attacked the buttons of his shirt. "Old enough to know all kinds of things. Care to find out?"

"Actually, no." He grabbed her wrists and held them

firmly away from his chest. She reeked of stale smoke and beer. "In case you haven't noticed, I already have a date. So why don't you run along and practice your tricks on someone who'll appreciate them? Like Jimmy Joe."

"Cain't." Her eyes danced with mischief. "Jimmy Joe gets real ornery if I bother him while he's busy. And right now, he looks real busy . . . dancing with your girl-friend."

Brent jerked his head toward the dance floor and froze. Laura was locked in the arms of Jimmy Joe, the most disreputable lowlife ever to darken Snake's door. Their bodies rubbed together from shoulder to knee as they swayed to the immortal sounds of Patsy Cline. Laura wiggled, at first, he thought, to get some respectable dis-tance. Then the couple turned so Laura faced him. For a fraction of a second, she went still. He thought she'd seen his warning look, but he must have been mistaken. The next thing he knew, she molded herself against Jimmy Joe as if she'd taken lessons from Darlene.

Jimmy Joe's hand wandered downward to cup her bottom. Brent knew the instant the man felt the garter belt beneath Laura's skirt. Jimmy Joe's hand went still, his head lifted, and a big smile blossomed on his face.

Fury exploded inside Brent's head, blinding him in a red haze as he charged toward the dance floor.

Laura screamed as Brent slammed into Jimmy Joe, knocking him into the jukebox. The music ended with a ragged screech and Jimmy Joe slid to the floor, shaking his head to clear the stars.

She stared in shock at Brent, who stood over Jimmy Joe with clenched fists. "Brent! What are you doing?"

"Get up," Brent growled at the downed man.

"No," Laura cried, rushing to Jimmy Joe's side. "Stay still till we know if you're hurt."

"Settle down, sugar," Jimmy Joe said to her, though his eyes never left Brent. "Us boys are just gonna have ourselves a little de-scussion about squatter's rights. Ain't that right, ol' buddy?"

"Not in my place you ain't!" Snake hollered from behind the bar. Laura felt a surge of relief that someone the size of Snake was there to stop this nonsense. Then to her disbelief, the bar owner gestured toward the door. "You boys wanna bash each other's brains out, you take it outside."

Laura gaped as Brent kicked Jimmy Joe's boots. "You gonna lay there all night, lover boy? Or you gonna get up and let me kick your ass?"

"Just gathering my strength." Jimmy Joe rolled slowly to a crouch as if barely able to rise. Then he lunged without warning, swinging for Brent's face.

Brent ducked and caught his rival with a solid blow to the gut. Jimmy Joe staggered forward, catching Brent in the side with an elbow. Grunting with pain, Brent landed a double-fisted blow in the center of Jimmy Joe's back, sending the man face-first into the dance floor.

"Stop!" Laura screamed when Jimmy Joe scrambled to his feet. Snake came toward them with a baseball bat, and everyone in the bar leapt to their feet. Half of the men looked ready to join the fight, and the women looked eager to cheer them on. Laura stepped between the two combatants. "I will not stand by and watch you two behave in this adolescent manner."

Brent stared at her as if she'd lost her mind. "If you didn't want me to beat him to a pulp, why the hell'd you start this?"

"Why did *I* start it?" She gaped at him.

"Shit, Brent." Jimmy Joe laughed. "Don't these city women know nothing?"

"You!" She pointed a finger in Jimmy Joe's face. "Stay out of this."

"Sure thing, sugar. But if you don't wanna see a fight, you got to stick with the guy what brung ya."

"What's that, some redneck credo?" she snapped. "Besides, I didn't see you throwing a fit when your date locked lips with Brent."

"Hell, Darlene ain't my date. And even if she was, I cain't very well get riled every time she gets horny. Why, everybody in the county knows she'll spread her legs for anyone."

For one moment Laura just stared at him, not quite believing he'd said that. How could she have thought this ignorant jerk was cute? She turned to Brent and stepped out of the way. "Hit him."

Brent pulled back his fist.

"I said—" Snake stepped between the two men—"take it outside."

"I got a better idea," Bobby piped up. When all eyes turned to him, he grinned. "Why don't we settle this down at Hangman's Hollow?"

Brent glanced at Jimmy Joe, and a light came into his eyes. "Fine by me. If you're game."

"Are you serious?" Jimmy Joe looked as if he'd just been granted his fondest dream. When Brent nodded, JJ rubbed his hands together. "Well, shit, boys, let's go."

Laura stood in confusion as everyone in the bar started filing out the door.

"Get your purse," Brent said as he too started to leave.

"Wait a second." She grabbed his arm. "Why are we going to Hangman's Hollow? What are you two planning to do?"

"Why, settle our grievance in a manly and time-honored tradition, of course."

"Which is?"

"Street race."

CHAPTER
8

"Okay, Laura, this is where you get out," Brent said as he pulled to a stop in the middle of the road.

"What?" Laura turned to stare at him.

"We're here." He gestured to the darkness around them, and she realized they'd arrived at Hangman's Hollow. To either side of the road, the convoy that had followed them from the bar pulled up their trucks—the noise of their engines and the smell of exhaust broke the stillness of the night, while their headlights illuminated the charred remains of the Hanging Tree.

"Laura," Brent said, touching her arm, "did you hear me? I want you to wait here until the race is over."

She stared at his face, garishly lit by the headlights, and a sick feeling settled in her stomach. If she let him out of her sight for one second, he'd crash and die. Where that notion came from, she had no idea, but she believed it to the marrow of her bones. "I'm staying."

"Don't be ridiculous." He laughed. "This is not some Sunday drive we're going on. Things could get dangerous."

"Exactly," she said, swallowing down her fear. If she stayed with Brent, he'd be more careful. And if he wasn't, she'd be there to help him. "I'm staying."

"Hey!" Jimmy Joe shouted as he pulled up beside them in a vintage red Mustang Mach I. Beside him, Darlene jumped up and down, making the Mustang rock like a racehorse waiting to shoot from the starting gate. "You ready to get your butt kicked?"

"Anytime you and that worn-out piece of junk are ready to try," Brent hollered back.

As the two men discussed the course, Laura stared into the darkness straight ahead. She couldn't believe she was doing this. They'd all probably die—yet no force on earth could have pulled her from Brent's side. After exchanging a few more taunts with Jimmy Joe, Brent turned back to her. "You sure about this?"

"Positive." Her fingers tightened on the armrest.

"All right," he sighed. "Just make sure your seat belt's tight."

She watched as he tightened his own seat belt, then braced himself with one hand on the steering wheel and the other on the gearshift. She'd never seen him look so intent, so dangerous. So utterly arousing.

Bobby, who'd ridden with Jimmy Joe, stepped into the center of the road and raised both his arms. Behind him lay a narrow bridge known as Whispering Bridge, for the ghosts of the hanged dead that supposedly dwelled beneath it. Concrete pilings stood like sentinels to either side, preventing more than one car from crossing the bridge at a time. Whoever took the early lead would hold it until he reached the other side. But what would happen if both cars reached the bridge at the same time? The shouts from the sidelines grew to a roar. *Oh, my God.* Laura gripped the armrest. *We're all going to die.*

Bobby dropped his hands. Laura's head snapped back as the Porsche leapt forward, taking the lead. They shot over the bridge and were swallowed by darkness. The road rose and fell, twisted and turned, slinging her from side to side. She glanced behind them, into the headlights of the Mustang.

"How far are we going?" she shouted over the noise.

"Around the Simmons farm, then back to the Hanging Tree. Whoever crosses back over the bridge first wins." He glanced in the rearview mirror as Jimmy Joe's headlights illuminated his eyes. "Just try to pass me, you son of a bitch." He jerked the wheel to cut the other car off.

Laura screamed as she fell against Brent.

"You all right?" he called, letting go of the gearshift long enough to steady her.

She stared up at him and saw the gleam in his eyes as he focused once again on the road. "You're enjoying this," she shouted over the wind that whipped her hair into her face.

"Hell yeah, I'm enjoying it! You have any idea how often I dreamed of beating that bragging jackass in a street race? Not that I ever had a chance in that beat-up Nova I used to drive."

He jerked the wheel again to cut off the Mustang. Then the road straightened out, and Jimmy Joe swung onto the gravel shoulder. Dust and rocks flew up from the tires as the Mustang pulled even. To Laura's stunned horror, Darlene leaned out the window, flailing her arms and laughing as she shouted obscene taunts at Brent.

Laura glanced up ahead, where the road narrowed into another series of turns. "Oh, my God, he's going to cut you off."

"Like hell he is." Brent pressed the accelerator closer to the floor, pushing the Porsche to the fine line between speed and loss of control. Seeing the determined set of his jaw, something inside Laura stirred to life: a competitive spirit she never knew she had. As stupid and childish as a street race might be, Brent wanted desperately to win, and right then she wanted it for him just as badly. Just once she wanted the misfit kid to trounce the reigning champ.

But wanting alone couldn't make it happen. Jimmy Joe jerked his car sideways, and Brent braked rather than let his car be sideswiped. In a cloud of gravel and dirt, the Mustang took the lead. Brent moved from side to side until he found an opening and charged ahead on the curve that would take them around the Simmons farm and back toward the Whispering Bridge. On a straight downhill grade, the Mustang barreled back into the lead. As they jockeyed back and forth, Laura realized the Porsche handled better in the turns, but the heavier car had the advantage on the straightways.

They were neck and neck and nearing the finish line when Brent glanced into his rearview mirror and cursed.

"What?" Laura twisted around. Flashing lights appeared behind them as she caught the faint whine of a siren. She whirled back and stared straight ahead. She wasn't going to die tonight—she was going to be arrested! Her father would have to bail her out of jail. Everyone in Beason's Ferry would read about it in next week's paper. DOCTOR'S DAUGHTER ARRESTED FOR JOY RIDING, or reckless endangerment, or whatever they called it. Any minute Brent would pull over, and they'd slap the handcuffs on both of them and haul them away.

Only Brent didn't slow down. He pushed the car to go even faster. "Aren't you going to pull over?" she shouted over the noise.

"Are you crazy?" He spared her an incredulous look.

"But there's a sheriff's deputy behind us." She gave him the benefit of the doubt, in case he hadn't noticed.

"Yeah, I know!" They skidded sideways into another turn, spraying Jimmy Joe with gravel. "Let's hope he's not driving one of their new high-speed pursuit cars."

"And if he is?"

Brent didn't answer. His eyes locked onto something up ahead. She followed his gaze to the Whispering Bridge, with its concrete guard posts.

"Oh, my God." From the corner of her eye, she saw the nose of the red Mustang. Both cars struggled for an extra thrust of speed.

"Come on, baby, come on, baby," Brent chanted as they flew toward the finish line. The Mustang struggled to take the lead, but Brent gripped the steering wheel, refusing to yield. Laura realized Jimmy Joe was going to hit the concrete posts rather than concede the race. Brent was going to win, but Jimmy Joe and Darlene were going to die.

"No!" She screamed and covered her eyes as they plunged onto the bridge.

"Yes!" Brent shouted in triumph.

When no crash followed, she looked up. "What happened?"

"I won!" Brent laughed as they reached Hangman's Hollow at the far end of the bridge. A cheer went up from the men still waiting on the hoods of their trucks. She glanced behind them and was nearly blinded by Jimmy Joe's headlights. At least he'd had the sense to brake instead of crash.

They raced on through several more bends and turns, trying to outrun the patrol car.

"Hang on," Brent called, and in the next instant, his headlights clicked off. They careened sideways, off the paved road onto a gravel drive.

Laura twisted in time to see the sheriff's car whiz by in hot pursuit of Jimmy Joe's Mustang. As Brent continued forward at a slow crawl through the darkness, a sense of relief swept through her adrenaline-charged body. Sliding down in the seat, she let her head fall against the headrest. Her eyes closed as laughter bubbled up inside her.

She laughed between gulps of air, laughed until her sides ached. After a while, she felt the car roll to a stop. The engine went quiet. The silence of the night enveloped her. Still chuckling, she wiped the tears from her cheeks and opened her eyes. The sky arched above her, infinite midnight blue strewn with a wealth of glittering stars. A moment ago, she'd been a breath away from death. And yet she'd never felt so alive.

Hearing Brent laugh, she turned toward him. He too had slid down to rest his head on the back of the seat. Then he glanced at her. Their gazes met. Their laughter stilled.

For endless moments, he simply stared at her eyes, her face, her hair. She held her breath as her heart slowed to a hard throb in her chest, and she longed for him to close the chasm between them.

She wanted him so badly, she feared she was dreaming when he leaned forward so his body loomed above her. He cupped the back of her head in his hand, and his face blocked the sky. She felt his breath and the heat of his body, and she yearned for the touch of his mouth on hers.

The kiss, when it came, whispered against her lips as

he retreated and returned. *Please*, she told him with her eyes. *Please kiss me as I long to be kissed.*

He groaned deep in his throat, and all gentleness vanished. His mouth covered hers, moving, tasting, devouring. His tongue begged entrance, and she opened her mouth willingly, surging up to meet him. Fumbling with his seat belt, then with hers, he freed their bodies to move and entwine. His hands ran over her back, her sides, her breasts. The buttons on her blouse gave way, as did the clasp at the front of her bra.

When his palms cupped her naked breasts, she arched upward. Desperate to feel his skin, she fought with the buttons of his shirt, then buried her fingers in the warm mat of hair that covered his chest. She felt his muscles flex and harden as he pulled her closer.

Her leg bumped the gearshift. His elbow hit the steering wheel. With a muffled curse, he reached his hand down beside her seat. The seat back lowered slowly as he pressed her backward. With her fingers buried in his hair, he kissed her neck, then moved lower. His teeth nipped the rounded swell of her breast. A shiver shot through her as he soothed the flesh with his tongue. Mesmerized by the moonlight, she watched as his mouth closed over one taut nipple. *Yes*, she whimpered, and realized the sound came from deep inside her. She needed him to touch her. Anywhere. Everywhere.

His hand ran downward, beneath her skirt and back up.

"Oh, God," he groaned as he touched the bare skin above her stockings. His breath came in labored pants as he rested his forehead against her breasts. "Do you always wear these?"

"What?" she breathed, unable to think. She

squeezed her thighs to try and ease the ache. Running her fingers through his hair, she longed to feel his mouth once more.

"Stockings," he rasped as he moved upward to hover over her. In the darkness, his eyes caressed her face. "Do you always wear stockings?"

"Yes. I—They're very comfortable and . . . they keep me from getting too hot."

A grin lit his face. "Are they keeping you from getting hot now?"

Her eyes widened as she realized what she'd said. But then he took her mouth in a ravenous kiss. Beneath her skirt, his hand moved over the top of her thigh, making her muscles jump and her skin tingle. She squirmed, not knowing if she wanted more or less until the need inside her became a mindless thing, like a beast clawing to escape. She whimpered in fear of the very sensation she wanted to embrace.

"It's okay," he whispered in her ear as his hand found its way around her damp panties to the core of her ache.

"Oh, Brent, yes . . . please . . ." She wanted to tell him she'd never felt this building urgency. But his finger pressed inside her, and the ability to speak fled.

She gasped as he stroked her with slow, sure thrusts, and her legs fell apart as she welcomed his touch. When his thumb found her sensitive bud, her world shattered; like a hammer striking glass, the pleasure slammed deep into her and splintered outward. She arched in wonder, then hung suspended for an endless moment before spiraling down slowly to earth.

When she opened her eyes, she saw he'd pulled back. With his hand still buried beneath her skirt, touching her intimately, his body had gone utterly still. Shadows hid his face, but she could feel his shocked gaze sweeping over her.

In the next heartbeat, he was gone. He clamored out of the car, not even bothering to close the door. She lay there for a moment with her blouse open, her legs apart. Cool air brushed her skin, sinking straight into her bones.

Mortified, she scrambled to right her clothes. Her hands shook as she buttoned her blouse. She knew so little about sex, but apparently she'd done something wrong. She just couldn't figure out what. If this had been Greg, he never would have stopped so abruptly, at least not until he'd satisfied himself. Not that he was a selfish lover, he was just, well, inept. Or so she'd thought. Maybe she was the inept one. It must be her. Why else had Brent practically leaped from the car to get away from her?

As she righted her seat, she chanced a peek behind her. He stood a few yards away, silhouetted against the night sky, his back rigid and his fists clenched at his side. His shoulders moved as he pulled great gulps of air into his lungs. He raised a hand to wipe his face but stopped abruptly to hold the hand before him as though horrified.

A fresh wave of humiliation washed over her as she realized that was the hand that had been touching her moments ago. He balled the hand into a fist and dropped it back to his side. Without a word or a glance in her direction, he paced away from the car, halted, and turned.

He was coming back. She hurried to tuck her skirt about her legs, then tried to look as nonchalant as possible. Her heart hammered as he climbed into the car and closed the door. From the corner of her eye, she saw that he was facing straight ahead, refusing to even look at her.

"I, eh . . ." He cleared his throat. "I didn't mean for that to happen."

"You didn't?" she asked, then cringed at her inanity. Should she apologize? But for what? She didn't even know what she'd done wrong—other than get more excited than she ever had in her life. She hadn't even known it could be like that: like an explosion igniting inside her and rippling outward in a series of shock waves. She'd thought women who spoke of orgasms were exaggerating.

They weren't exaggerating. If anything, their descriptions fell woefully short. How could she apologize for feeling that, when she desperately wanted to thank him?

He opened his mouth as if to speak, but closed it. After a moment, he sighed and started the car.

They rode home in excruciating silence. When they pulled up in front of her house, she couldn't even look at him. She wanted to jump from the car and run inside, but Brent had reverted to playing the gentleman. He collected her jacket from the backseat, then came around the car to open her door. After walking her up the front steps, he turned to her.

"Laura, I . . ." Another awkward silence fell between them as she waited. Her legs felt strangely weak, and the longer she stood, the more her knees wobbled. If only he'd hand over her jacket, she could run inside and hide.

Instead, she tried for a smile and a casual shrug. "Hey, look, it was no big deal, okay?" With a quick sideways glance, she saw his brow crease as if he were confused, or . . . insulted? She sighed in defeat. "Maybe it would be best if we just pretended tonight never happened."

He gave a mirthless laugh. "How about we pretend the entire day never happened?"

She felt a twinge of hurt to know his homecoming had been that distasteful, and that she was the one who'd talked him into coming back. "I'm sorry," she said. "About . . . everything."

"No, Laura, don't—" He exhaled sharply. "Truth is, it wasn't all bad."

She found the courage to look at him as she tried to decipher which parts he regretted and which he didn't.

A small smile tugged at one corner of his mouth. It was the smile she remembered from their shared youth. His secret friend smile. "If nothing else, I enjoyed seeing you."

She blushed, more from embarrassment than pleasure, for he definitely had *seen* her. "Thank you."

"You're welcome." His smile grew teasing. Only she didn't want to tease, had never wanted to, really. Their banter had always been a shield, and she felt too weary to don it now.

"Then I guess we're still friends?" she asked, her throat aching.

"Of course." He held out her jacket.

Something in the gesture squeezed her heart. As she took the jacket with the wilted mum, her eyes prickled. "Will I see you at the reenactment tomorrow?"

"No, I . . ." He gazed off, in the direction of the highway. "I'll be leaving first thing in the morning."

"Oh. Well. I guess this is good-bye, then."

"Yeah."

She turned toward the door but halted with her hand on the knob. In all her girlhood dreams, her dates with Brent ended the same way: here on the front steps, he'd take her in his arms, kiss her tenderly. Then he'd smile down at her and say: "Sweet dreams, my darling."

She'd flush with pleasure and say: "Always—when I dream of you."

"Until tomorrow, then," he'd say, "I'll see you in your dreams."

Only now, in the adult world of reality, she wouldn't see him tomorrow. She might never see him again. She swallowed hard and forced a smile. "Good night, Brent. Take care of yourself."

"You, too."

She hurried inside, before the tears could fall. For a long moment, she stood with her back pressed to the door, biting her lip as she listened for his footsteps. At last they came, followed by the sound of his car door slamming. And then he drove away.

Earlier, she'd said every woman needed one night in her life to regret. And yet in spite of everything, in spite of the pain in her stomach and the tears that coursed down her cheeks, she knew she would never regret her one night with Brent.

CHAPTER
9

A repetitive ringing sounded in Brent's ear. Blind with sleep, he swatted at the nightstand to turn off his alarm. Instead of his clock, his hand hit a phone. He curled his fingers around the receiver and carried it to his ear. "Hello," he muttered.

"Brent?"

"Hum?"

"Jesus, Michaels, it's friggin' ten A.M. Drag your sorry ass out of bed, you jerk."

"Connie?" He blinked the sleep from his eyes and tried to focus on the digital readout of his clock radio. Only his radio wasn't on his nightstand where it should be. Nothing was where it should be.

With his producer's voice grinding in his ear like a gravel truck, he glanced about the room. The ruffled curtains and quaint country accents brought everything back in excruciating detail.

He was in Beason's Ferry. Last night he'd taken Laura Beth Morgan to Snake's Pool Palace, gotten her drunk on Johnnie Walker Red, then tried to jump her in the front seat of his car.

Groaning, he covered his face. Erotic images taunted his memory of how she'd writhed beneath his slightest touch. Before the images could arouse his body as well, he lowered his hand. But nothing could stop the echo of her parting words: *Maybe we should just pretend this night never happened.*

Not that he blamed her. He'd behaved like some hormone-driven adolescent who forgot the meaning of words like *restraint* and *respect* the minute he became aroused. That he'd behaved that way at all was humiliating enough. That he'd behaved that way with Laura, the closest thing he had to a childhood friend, didn't even bear thinking about.

"Michaels, are you listening to me?" his producer demanded.

"No." He rolled onto his back and dropped his forearm over his eyes. "Jeez, Connie, can't I even go out of town for one lousy weekend without you tracking me down?"

"Not when going out of town gets you plastered all over somebody else's news broadcast."

"What?" His sluggish brain clicked fully awake. *Had someone found out about the street race?*

"Actually, KTEX didn't mention your name, thank God. All their anchor said, in a snide little voice, was 'A local Houstonian donated himself as the prize in a *Dating Game* show for a small-town fund-raiser.' If their cameraman hadn't caught a shot of you standing on the town square with the winning bachelorette, even I wouldn't have known it was you."

"Oh, that." He breathed a sigh of relief. At least he hadn't ruined Laura's good name with the community. Yet.

"What do you mean, 'oh, that'?" Connie's voice rose steadily in volume. "I had three viewers call up and ask if you were leaving KSET. And as if that wasn't bad enough, KTEX's news director called to innocently ask why my hottest anchor was participating in a publicity stunt that *we weren't even covering!*"

"Give me a break, Connie." Sitting up, he swung his legs over the side of the bed, then pulled the covers into his lap. Talking to his producer while sitting in the nude was not his favorite way to start a day. "My donating an evening of my time to an out-of-town fund-raiser is hardly newsworthy in Houston."

"Get off it, Michaels." He heard the click of a lighter followed by Connie's deep drag off a cigarette. "Anything you do that smacks of 'community spirit' and 'goodwill' makes this station look good. On top of that, I hear this Bluebonnet Homes Tour thing draws a big crowd from Houston—and you never even told me about it. Christ, you're the home boy on this team, and you made me look like some ignorant schmuck."

"The term is *Yankee*, Connie. Down here, we say 'ignorant Yankee,' not 'schmuck.' "

"Whatever. You cost me, kid. And you know it."

"Fine. Send a remote down for a couple minutes of footage then."

"You bet your sweet ass I'm sending down a remote. Now, give me a rundown on today's schedule of events."

"Hell, I don't know." He dragged a hand through his hair and tried to think. "If they follow tradition, there'll be a costumed reenactment of the Burning of Beason's Ferry, followed by a barbecue at the city park."

"Perfect." She exhaled into the receiver, and he swore he could smell the smoke coming out his end. "You can do a live feed for the six o'clock report."

"Not likely. I'm out of here as soon as I get dressed."

Although if I stayed, I'd have an excuse to see Laura again. And do what? Apologize? Explain? He shook his head. "I need to get back to Houston. The sooner the better."

"To do what?" Connie scoffed. "Your laundry?"

To get out of this town before I suffocate, he thought.

"All right, all right," Connie groused when he said nothing. "I'll bump the spot up from two minutes to two and a half. But no more than that, so don't start with me!"

"Two and a half minutes for a fluff piece?" Brent scowled into the phone. "What is this, a slow news day?"

"It's a pathetic news day. Besides, footage of kids licking ice cream cones boosts ratings. Throw in a couple disgustingly cute pets, and I'll even use one of your sound bites in our next promo campaign."

"I don't know. . . ." He racked his brain for what he'd say to Laura if he saw her again. They'd ended last night on semifriendly terms. Maybe he should leave it that way.

"Come on, Michaels, you owe me."

"For what?"

She hesitated, obviously scrounging for a reason. "For not bringing this hoedown to my attention in the first place."

"Screening press releases for the weekend reporters is not my job. Try again." Although, he thought, since he and Laura were on friendly terms, there wasn't any reason he shouldn't see her. Besides, what were a few more hours in Beason's Ferry now that he was there?

"All right, jeez." Connie took another raspy drag. "How about this: I'll owe you. One favor, your choice, to be called in at some point in the future."

"Ha!" Brent snorted. "Too bad I'm not taping this."

"Hey, I'm trustworthy."

"Yeah, right," he scoffed as his mind raced. Laura would be at the reenactment. She'd probably organized most of it. A live report would be good publicity for the whole town. He owed Laura that much. "Okay, Rosenstein, just don't conveniently forget we had this conversation the second we hang up."

"Are you saying you'll do it?" Connie choked.

"For two and a half minutes of airtime? What the heck?" he shrugged. Even if it was a throwaway piece any first-year intern could handle, Laura would love it.

"Great." When Connie caught her breath, she rattled off some possible angles and leads for the story.

"Connie," he chuckled, "if you want me to do the story, at least let me write my own lead."

"Yeah, sure, I just thought—"

"Good-bye, Connie." He ended any more discussion by hanging up. The moment he did, his mind went back to Laura.

Should he really act as if last night had never happened? His friendship with her might not have been active over the last years, but he still valued it. Did he want to jeopardize that in order to—to what? Have a romantic entanglement that would lead nowhere? She lived in Beason's Ferry. He lived in Houston. He couldn't exactly see her driving into the city every Saturday to spend the weekend with a man. And he sure as hell wasn't coming back to this stifling little town so he could take her to the City Diner and then kiss her chastely good night at her father's front door.

He thought briefly of a motel on I-10 but banished the thought just as quickly. Laura deserved better than some sleazy affair at a No-tell Motel. She deserved candlelight dinners, soft music, and a chance to relax and get to know her date: which was how yesterday evening had started out.

So why had she insisted they go to a dive like Snake's Pool Palace? Everything about her behavior last night surprised him—especially the erotic scene in his car. He'd barely had a chance to ease into the kiss before she was arching against him and kneading his chest with her hands. He could almost hear that sexy catch in the back of her throat and her breathy sigh when he'd cupped his hand between her legs. She'd been so unbelievably hot and wet when he pressed his finger inside her. And tight. God, she'd been tight.

For one horrifying moment, he'd wondered if she was a virgin. Words like Virginity and Innocence were right up there with Commitment and Marriage on his list of things to avoid.

He liked his women, when he had time for them, to be worldly, sophisticated, and blasé about sex. He didn't have time to worry about things like corrupting or, heaven forbid, breaking some fragile heart.

No, Laura was right. The best thing for them to do was to pretend last night never happened. He should be glad she'd offered him such an easy out. This way, they could keep the memory of their friendship untainted by any prurient complications.

Yes, that was the best course of action.

So why did he suddenly feel so hollow inside?

Maybe it was just the hangover. What he needed was something to eat—something more than the fruit juice and pastries served at a bed and breakfast. He needed a greasy plate of hash browns, eggs, and sausage, served with a gallon of black coffee at the City Diner.

With that in mind, he showered, dressed in slacks and a golf shirt, and left the Boudreau Bed and Breakfast by way of the back stairs. As he turned to cut across the gravel parking lot, he came to an abrupt halt. Bending over his Porsche as if to admire the inside was Sheriff Bernard Baines.

"Shit," he muttered. So much for pretending last night never happened.

The sheriff straightened with a deceptively friendly grin. "Why, hey there, Zartlich."

"Morning, Sheriff." Having little choice, Brent crossed the small lot to shake Sheriff Baines's hand. The man had always reminded Brent of a dark-skinned Pillsbury Doughboy: a very large Pillsbury Doughboy who had played left guard the year the Beason's Ferry Bulldogs went to the state finals. Bubba Baines's fumble recovery and touchdown had won the Bulldogs the title of state champs. It was a claim to fame that had later helped him win the office of county sheriff.

"I heard you were back in town." Pushing back his gray Stetson, the sheriff turned back to the Porsche. "Who-ee, this sure is some car you got here."

Brent never had bought into the poor-dumb-country-boy act. Bernard Baines was as sharp as they came. And Brent had the feeling he'd just walked smack dab into some well-laid trap.

"So what kind of an engine you got under that hood?" Bubba asked, stepping around the front. "A two-eighty-two?"

"No, the nine-eleven comes with a three-fifteen," Brent answered, leaving off any mention of the minor adjustments he'd made that bumped the horsepower up closer to four hundred.

"Three-fifteen." The sheriff whistled. "I bet a car like that can really fly."

"She'll do zero to sixty in six seconds flat, and stop just as fast," Brent answered impatiently. He wondered how long the man intended to toy with him before the jaws of the trap snapped shut.

"You know," the sheriff said as he continued his circuit around the sleek yellow convertible, "it sure is something to have *one* of these beauties come through my jurisdiction like this, but *two* in one weekend downright boggles the mind."

"Two?" Brent blinked.

"Well, sure, hadn't you heard?" Bubba flashed a white-toothed grin. "It's all over town how a nine-eleven Porsche convertible finally whooped JJ's Mustang in a street race last night. Now, the couple dozen folks who witnessed it firsthand all say it was you driving. But I say they'd all had too much rotgut. Why, last night, you were on a date with Miss Laura Beth. And I'm thinking, a smart fella like you has surely got more sense than to take a nice girl like Laura Beth hot-rodding down by Snake's Pool Palace."

"Yes, sir." To Brent's astonishment, he realized the sheriff meant to let him off the hook in order to spare Laura's reputation. It shouldn't have surprised him. Aside from the fact that Laura came from a prominent family, she had always been the kind of squeaky-clean kid authority figures adored; while Brent was the type to get slapped with the whole book for nothing more than jaywalking.

"Speaking of Miss Laura Beth . . ." Sheriff Baines stepped around to Brent's side of the car as he pulled a ticket book from his back pocket. Brent's moment of relief died a quick death. "She helped me and the deputies organize a raffle to buy Little League uniforms for under-privileged kids. She even got the Ladies Auxiliary to do-nate a handmade quilt.''

"Raffle?" Brent frowned at the ticket book. What did Little League uniforms have to do with him getting a speeding ticket? And could the sheriff really write him a ticket this long after the fact, even if he had two dozen witnesses?

"Now I knew you'd want to buy some of these here raffle tickets." Bubba lifted the ticket book. "So I thought I'd save you the trouble of tracking me down.''

"Raffle tickets?" Brent took a closer look at the book and nearly laughed. He couldn't believe he was going to get out of paying for last night's foolishness for nothing more than the price of a few raffle tickets. "Sure, I'll be happy to buy some," he said, reaching for his money clip. "How much are they?''

"Two dollars a piece," the sheriff said. "Or twenty dollars for a dozen. 'Course, knowing how generous you celebrities like to be, I took the liberty of bringing along a whole book.'' Bubba held the ticket book up as if display-ing the top prize in a game show.

"I see." Brent narrowed his eyes at the book. "And the whole book costs . . . ?"

"Two hundred dollars."

"Two hundred dollars!"

"For a hundred and fifty tickets." The sheriff's smile stretched from ear to ear. "Cash or check is fine with me. And of course, it's a tax-deductible donation.''

For one heartbeat, Brent nearly told Sheriff Bubba Baines where to shove his raffle tickets. But pissing off a county sheriff was never a wise move. At least this way no speeding ticket would go on his record, which would save him a lot more than two hundred dollars on his insurance. And Laura's reputation would remain unscathed. Not to mention what would happen if the news wires got ahold of this story. He could just hear the report on the rival station KTEX now: KSET NEWS ANCHOR FINED FOR RECKLESS ENDANGERMENT.

With angry jerks, Brent pulled four fifty-dollar bills out of his money clip. For Laura's sake, he should thank the sheriff for his discretion, he really should, but somehow he couldn't work up much gratitude.

"That'll do it," Sheriff Baines said as Brent handed him the cash. "Me and the boys surely do thank you for your generosity."

"Think nothing of it," Brent grumbled as he accepted the book of raffle tickets.

The sheriff started to leave, then turned back, his expression more serious. "You know, it sure is a shame about that sweet Laura Beth, though."

"What do you mean?" Brent frowned.

"Well, you know how people are around these parts. Once they get a meaty piece of gossip between their teeth, they like to gnaw on it till there's nothing left but bone. Now normally I don't pay it much mind, but it sure does pain me to see folks talking trash about that Morgan girl." Bubba's eyes zeroed in on Brent. "I can only hope, once this nonsense dies down, nothing like it ever happens again."

Brent's anger toward the sheriff spread to include the whole town—and himself. "I assure you, if I have anything to say about it, it won't."

Baines held his gaze a moment longer, then nodded.

"I reckon that's all a man can do." He started to leave, then turned back. "Oh, and rest assured I'll be on the lookout for the driver of that other yellow convertible. He ever comes speeding through my county again, I just might have to haul him in on a DWI. Thing like that can be mighty hard for a man to live down. Even a hotshot celebrity, if you get my meaning."

"Loud and clear, sir."

Sheriff Baines's grin returned. "Reckon I'll be leaving then." He hesitated again. "Oh, just one thing more."

Now what? Brent nearly snapped. "Yes, sir?"

"You might want to check under the hood before you go starting that fancy engine. Looks to me like you're leaking oil."

Brent glanced under the car at the huge oil patch staining the ground by the right front tire. His heart constricted as wild thoughts ran through his head. Had the sheriff vandalized his car? No, Baines wouldn't do that, but Jimmy Joe might. He dropped to the ground to look underneath. A small hole marked the center of a huge dent in his right oil heat exchanger.

"Damn!"

"You find the problem?" the sheriff asked.

"I knocked a hole in one of the exchangers."

"Now I wonder how that could happen with you driving on a nice paved road."

Brent scowled up at the sheriff, who knew perfectly well how it had happened. Brent had hit a rock or a chug hole when he'd veered off the paved road to avoid getting caught.

"Mmm-mmm." Sheriff Baines shook his head. "Like my momma used to say, one way or the other people always pay when they do wrong.'' With that pearl of wisdom, the sheriff ambled away.

Brent dropped his head to the gravel. Staring up at the oily undercarriage, he felt his heart break right in two. *My car. How could I do this to my sweet, beautiful car?*

CHAPTER
10

$\mathcal{B}$etween arguing with the tow-truck driver and the garage mechanic, neither of whom seemed to know how to treat a car with reverence and respect, Brent barely had time to tape a few sound bites on the courthouse square. Snippets from those pretaped interviews would run as promos throughout the day—minus the irritating questions his interviewees kept asking him about Laura Beth and last night's race. Of course, now even his coworkers at the station knew about the race, since they were the ones editing the tapes.

How in the world was he supposed to pretend last night never happened when everybody within three counties had heard about it?

By late afternoon, his concentration was shot. He stood at the top of the hill that overlooked the park and tried to compile some semblance of a story before the camera started rolling. Fifteen minutes away from his cue, and he still hadn't written his intro.

"Hey, Michaels," Jorge, the cameraman—or in this case, camera kid—hollered, "Ms. Rosenstein is asking for a mic check."

Brent glanced up from his notes to fit the IFB into his ear. A similar one fit into the cameraman's ear, but they were tuned to different frequencies so the producer could talk to them together or separately.

"Michaels, you there?" Connie's gravelly voice ground into his ear.

"With bells on," Brent answered, and ran through the sound check by rote.

When Connie turned his earpiece off to talk to Jorge, Brent's gaze wandered toward the city park clubhouse. He could see glimpses of Laura through the window of the kitchen. She'd been there since he'd arrived at the park half an hour ago. His first impulse had been to go right to her and ask how she was holding up under the onslaught of wagging tongues. But he feared that if he made any attempt to approach her in public, a hush would fall over the entire town, and every ear would strain in their direction.

The image brought his temper to a slow simmer. How could normally decent people be so desperate for excitement that Laura's one fall from grace constituted headline news?

God, he hated this town. He hated it as passionately now as he had fourteen years ago. He wished he could do now what he'd done then: get in his car and drive away without looking back. Only his car was being held hostage in a garage by a bunch of morons who claimed it couldn't be fixed for at least a week, maybe two.

"Michaels." Connie's voice once again came through his earpiece. "Give me a run-through of your cues."

As if he had any. Deciding to wing it, Brent raised the microphone so both Connie back at the station and the cameraman before him could hear. "Okay, Jorge, start close on me. I'll say something to the effect of 'During the terrifying days that followed the fall of the Alamo, the

Texas militia fled for the safety of Louisiana with Santa Anna's troops close on their heels. Directly in the path of both armies lay the frontier town of Beason's Ferry.' On that, pull back and swing enough to my left to show the crowd sitting on the slope behind me. When I start talking about the reenactment being an annual event, move in on the cabin that's set up in the clearing at the bottom of the hill."

"You mean that pile of logs they just soaked with kerosene?" Jorge asked with one eye to his viewfinder.

Brent gave him a disgruntled look. Just what he needed: a cameraman with a sense of humor. "Okay, move in on the pile of logs stacked to look like a cabin."

As a prelude to the reenactment, a man and boy, dressed in billowing white shirts and knee pants, were pretending to work in a "field" around the cabin. Closer to the cabin, a woman in an apron and gingham dress hung up laundry while a little girl played at her feet. A doll, which played the exciting role of the woman's baby, slept peacefully on a blanket, oblivious to the drama about to play out.

"Okay, Jorge, when I refer to the 'forerider,' I want you to zoom in on the hill behind the cabin."

"Hold up, George," Connie interrupted. "Michaels, unless that forerider is actually going to appear while you're talking, this is going to get real boring real quick with no people in the shot. George, stay back enough to keep Brent in the picture throughout the feed. As long as we're paying a fortune for that gorgeous mug of his, we might as well use it."

"You got it," the kid answered.

Used to such remarks about his looks, Brent went on without pause to describe how the rider would come galloping over the rise, shouting that the Mexicans were right behind him.

"After warning the settlers," he said, "the rider will charge off to warn the next homestead while the man and boy abandon their tools in the field. The mother will gather her daughters in her arms and flee on foot. They'll travel east toward Louisiana, which, at that time, was the closest gateway from the Mexican state of Tejas into the United States.

"The husband and his son will stay behind to set fire to the cabin, burning everything they own. With nothing left but the clothes on their backs, they will take off on foot to help their neighbors burn down the town and the ferry crossing for which it was named."

"You gotta be kidding," Connie scoffed. "You guys torched your own town?"

"Better that than let it offer shelter or aid to the Mexicans," Brent explained.

"Don't say Mexicans," Connie said. "Say Hispanics. It's politically correct."

"But inaccurate," Brent pointed out. "Santa Anna didn't lead the Hispanic Army. He lead the Mexican Army."

"Then say Mexican *Army*. That sound okay to you, George?"

"Fine with me." Jorge rolled his eyes at Brent. " 'Sides, my ancestors fought with the Texans, along with a lot of other 'Hispanic' guys."

"Oh," Connie said. "Okay, whatever. Brent, that's about forty-five seconds' worth."

"Okay, Jorge," Brent turned in the other direction, "go wide as I describe the Mexican Army, exhausted and starving as they come over that distant rise to find only charred ruins where they had hoped to find a town to plunder. Then come back in on me as I tell how the people in Beason's Ferry paid a high price, but their sacrifice helped Texas win her independence from Mexico to stand as an independent nation for ten years before she joined the United States of America as the twenty-eighth state in the Union. Then, Connie?''

"Right here."

"Take it to B-tape when I say, 'Earlier today, KSET spoke with some of the actors who will perform in tonight's reenactment of the Burning of Beason's Ferry.' ''

"Got it," Connie said. She was silent for a moment as she wrote down her cue. "So, George, you hanging 'round Brent's little burg for the party tonight?''

"You bet," Jorge answered.

"Actually, he's not," Brent corrected, refusing to feel guilty at the kid's disgruntled groan. "Jorge is my ride home, and I plan to leave the moment we're done.''

"Oh, that's right." Connie's snicker ended with a wheezing cough. "I heard you had a little problem with your car. So, Brent, was the sacrifice you made worth winning the title of Texas Drag King?''

"Well, it's better than being named Texas Drag Queen," Brent shot back, unusually irritated by Connie's offbeat sense of humor.

"No, wait," his producer laughed. "I guess that title would have to go to the sweet little blonde you had riding in the car with you. The one who won you as her dream date.''

"I'm warning you, Connie, one more snide word about Laura, and I'll leave you stranded with two and a half minutes of airtime to fill.''

"Sorry," the producer chuckled with a total lack of sincerity. "Stand by for your cue."

Brent exhaled, then rolled his head to relax his neck and shoulders.

"Brent Michaels," someone said beside him. The moment he turned, he knew the blond man with the wire-rim glasses was not a fan seeking his autograph. Belligerence pulled back the man's thin shoulders and set his weak jaw.

"May I help you?" Brent asked tiredly.

"That depends—" the man's smile appeared entirely forced—"on what you're willing to do to help quell this groundswell of gossip Laura Beth's coping with, thanks to you."

Brent sighed. Just what he needed: one more person to give him grief about last night. He hadn't decided which was worse, the accusing stares from the town's respectable citizens, or the winks and grins from the disreputable ones. "I don't suppose you'd care to tell me how my business concerns you?"

The man's eyes widened slightly. "I simply thought, if people saw us talking amicably together, some of these rumors would die down." He glanced at the crowd that covered the hillside waiting for the reenactment to begin. "Although one would think these people would know Laura Beth better than to believe she'd behave unseemly with any man, much less one she hasn't seen in so long, he's practically a stranger to her now."

"Is that so?" Brent had no idea who this guy was, but he'd never seen anyone look so nervous, determined, and angry all at the same time. He could almost admire the guy's grit, if an odd foreboding wasn't crawling up his back.

"Yes," the man said, squaring his shoulders and meeting Brent's eyes. "So if we could manage to look as if we didn't want to tear each other's arms off, I think it would help Laura Beth."

Brent's spine stiffened a fraction more. "Well, I'll tell you, as one of Laura's oldest friends, I'd be happy to do whatever I can to help her. All I want to know is why you're so all-fired concerned about her reputation in the first place."

The man's hazel eyes blinked behind his glasses. "Because I'm Greg Smith."

Brent shifted into an intentionally cocky stance that any redneck down at Snake's would have recognized as an invitation to a fight. "I suppose that name should mean something to me?"

To his credit, the man straightened with indignation rather than backing down. "Perhaps I should rephrase that. I'm Greg Smith, as in the man Laura Beth is going to marry."

Brent felt as if a fist had slammed into his gut. "Laura's *engaged*?"

The man's chin went up a notch, even as his gaze skittered away. "We're, eh, just waiting to set the date before we make the official announcement." Greg Smith cleared his throat. "So I'd appreciate it if you'd at least act as if this were a civil conversation we're having."

Through a red haze of fury, Brent heard the man talk on for another minute or two, even felt the man shake his hand and pound him on the shoulder as if they were the best of friends. Then Greg Smith walked away, calling out for Brent to have a safe trip to Houston and to come back and visit him and Laura Beth sometime.

But in his mind, all Brent heard were the same words

over and over: *Laura was engaged!* The whole time she'd been out gallivanting with him, she'd been engaged to another man.

"Stand by, Michaels," Connie's voice buzzed in his ear. "You're in on three."

The following seconds moved by in a blur. As if completely detached, his own voice sounded like nothing more than background noise to the clamoring in his head. Before he realized he'd even given his report, Jorge lowered the camera and gave him a big thumbs-up.

"Well," Connie said, "that was certainly intense. Not that I'm complaining, but have you ever considered giving up the news biz to become a dramatic actor?"

"Connie?" he said tightly.

"Yes, love?"

"Screw you."

He heard her laugh just before he ripped the IFB out of his ear to toss it and his mic at Jorge.

"Where are you going?" the kid called out as Brent headed toward the clubhouse. He didn't answer as his attention focused solely on his destination.

~

"Hey there," Melody Piper said from directly behind Laura.

"Oh!" Laura jumped, scattering a freshly sliced loaf of bread across the kitchen floor. Her nerves had been strung so tight all day, she startled at every sound. She almost wished that if Brent were going to leave without speaking to her, he'd just do it and get it over with. Another part of her couldn't stop peeking out the window of the clubhouse to store up memories of how he looked working before a camera. Squatting down, she gathered up the slices of bread. "What are you doing still in town? I thought the art show was over hours ago."

Melody raised a brow at the unfriendly welcome. "I came to collect my five bucks."

Standing, Laura cast a quick glance toward the women of the fund-raising committee who were working the concession stand. For once, Janet and Tracy looked too busy serving barbecue through the window to be whispering behind her back and casting dagger-sharp glances her way.

"Yes, of course, your five dollars," she said as she tried to decide what to do with the dropped bread. Finally, she threw it in the trash and headed for a table at the back of the kitchen to fetch her purse.

"You okay?" Melody asked.

"I'm fine, I'm just—" Laura cut herself off before she rattled off the truth, that she was anything but fine. Though no one had said anything to her outright, she knew the whole town was talking about her. Every time she entered a room, all conversation ceased, and she felt like a rabbit caught in a spotlight. If only Brent would leave, she could relax and find the situation a little bit amusing, rather than intensely embarrassing.

"Here you are," she said, handing Melody a five-dollar bill.

"Thanks." Grinning broadly, the artist snatched the money from her hand. "Although I'd waive my winnings for a few juicy details about last night."

Laura cast a horrified glance toward the others as heat exploded in her cheeks.

"That good, eh?" Melody laughed, then seemed to understand the depth of Laura's discomfort. "Never mind. I really stopped by to see if you'd made a decision on what we talked about yesterday."

Laura frowned as she remembered the conversation they'd had about Melody looking for a roommate. With everything that had happened since, they'd never had a chance to talk about it further.

Before she could answer Melody's question, however, the side door of the kitchen banged open, and her heart nearly leapt from her chest. She chided herself for her jumpy nerves, until she turned and found Brent filling the doorway. Silhouetted against the afternoon light, he looked like a conquering warrior come to claim his battle prize. A hush fell over the kitchen as he scanned the room with hooded eyes. When his gaze speared her, she leaned against the table at her back. Her breath turned shallow as he strode toward her.

And all she could think was that he hadn't left without seeking her out. Not that this was how she'd pictured his final farewell. Rather than friendly sorrow, he looked angry enough to devour her on the spot.

"Laura." He ground her name out between the clenched teeth of a false smile. She noticed his chest looked bigger when his muscles were strained with tension.

"Y-yes?" Her attempt at a normal tone failed miserably.

"I'd like to speak with you, if I may."

"Certainly." With trembling hands, she set her purse aside and started to walk past him. His hand clamped onto her elbow as he took the lead. Quickening her pace to keep up with his long-legged stride, she tossed a reassuring smile to the other women. Janet and Tracy gaped while Melody gave her a thumbs-up just before Brent pulled her through the door. He led her toward the back of the clubhouse, where the building shielded them from the crowd.

"Brent . . ." She gave a breathless laugh. "What in the world—"

He released her abruptly and spun to face her. "Why the hell didn't you tell me you were engaged?"

"Excuse me?" She took a step back and came up against the building.

"Don't give me that innocent look." He stepped closer, looming over her. If only she could catch her breath, maybe she could think. Instead, her mind whirled as he turned and paced before her, accusing her of lying to him, or using him, or something to that effect. For an articulate man, he didn't seem to be making much sense.

And then it dawned on her. He was jealous! Brent Michaels was jealous because he thought she was engaged to another man. The wonderful absurdity of it made her feel as light as a helium balloon floating off the ground.

"And what the hell are you grinning about?" he demanded.

"Brent." She struggled to keep a straight face. "I'm not engaged."

He straightened, clearly startled by her light mood. "You're not?"

She shook her head, afraid that if she spoke, she'd start laughing.

"Then who the hell is Greg Smith?"

She sighed, coming back to earth. "Greg is someone I've gone out with off and on for the past few years. At present, we're barely even dating."

"Then why does he think you're engaged?"

"Perhaps because he proposed?" she offered lamely.

"And?"

"I tried to say no, really." She cringed at how weak that sounded. "But I didn't want to hurt his feelings. So unfortunately, I'm afraid he may not have understood."

"Hurt his damned feelings, if that's what it takes. What do I care?"

She studied him a moment. "I don't know, Brent. What do you care?"

"I—" He turned to her with a look of total confusion. "I just care, all right?"

"Why?"

"Because—" He turned away from her, running his hands through his hair.

"Brent?" She hesitated in confusion, then rested her hand on his back and felt his muscles tense beneath her palm.

"Oh, hell," he muttered and spun back to her. She barely had a glimpse of his face before he pulled her into his arms and crushed his mouth down on hers.

Her heart took flight as he deepened the kiss. Passion sparked between them, as hot and fast as it had the night before.

"Laura," he whispered huskily, trailing his mouth along her jaw, her cheek, her neck. "I can't pretend last night never happened." His hands cupped her head as his forehead rested against hers. "I can't forget, because I can't stop thinking about it."

Pulling back, she stared up at him in wonder. "Me either."

Relief washed over his face an instant before he took her mouth in another possessive kiss. If he hadn't had a firm hold on her, she surely would have floated off the ground. She couldn't get enough of his taste on her lips, the feel of his body pressed boldly against hers. "I guess," he managed between kisses, "this means . . . we're not . . . friends anymore."

"Guess not," she chuckled.

"Thank God." He fit her more firmly against him, and she felt how desperately he wanted her.

"Excuse me, Mr. Michaels." An unfamiliar voice jolted Laura out of her euphoria. "Does this mean we're staying after all?"

Her eyes snapped open to meet Brent's equally startled ones, as they both realized they were standing outside in broad daylight with half the town a few yards away.

CHAPTER
11

Brent jerked his head up to find Jorge standing at the corner of the building, his gaze politely averted.

"I'm sorry to, eh, bother you." A smile played at the corner of the kid's mouth as Laura buried her face against Brent's chest. "I just wanted to know if we're staying for the street dance after all."

Brent dropped his arms and moved to shield Laura from view. "Go ahead and load up the van. I'll be with you in a moment."

"The van's loaded."

He gave the cameraman a pointed scowl. "Then go get some barbecue or something. I'll find you when I'm ready."

"All right!" With a whoop, Jorge headed off to enjoy himself.

"You're leaving, aren't you?" Laura asked quietly.

Turning back to her, he saw the resigned look in her eyes. "It's not like I'm leaving *you*, it's just . . ."

"The town," she guessed correctly.

He gave her an apologetic look. "I think we gave them enough to talk about last night, don't you?"

"Yeah." She bit her lip as laughter danced in her eyes. "Good thing we've behaved ourselves since then."

He groaned as he realized the extent of the scene he'd made in the kitchen. "Sorry."

"I'm not." She smiled. "I haven't seen the members of the fund-raising committee so flushed and excited in years."

"I can imagine."

Her face sobered. "So what now?"

"I don't know." He thrust his hands into his trouser pockets. "I'd like to see you, only . . ." He didn't know how to explain without insulting the town she loved so dearly.

She took a breath, as if building up courage. "Brent, since yesterday I've been thinking—about a lot of things. Well, actually, I've been thinking about some of this for years."

"What sort of things?"

She crossed her arms and stared at the ground. "I, uhm, don't suppose you noticed the woman I was talking to when you came into the kitchen?"

"Actually, no."

"Yes, well, she's one of the artists from the show."

He frowned at the abrupt change in topic. "Let me guess. You're going to break the monotony of small-town life by taking up painting?"

"Lord, no!" She laughed. He loved the sound of her laughter, and the ease with which it came to her. "I couldn't paint a straight line if I had to. But Melody lives in Houston. And," Laura glanced up at him, "she's looking for a roommate."

"Oh?" His ears perked up.

"She really only needs someone through the summer," she said in a rush. "Apparently that's a busy show season for artists. Only Melody can't do too many out-of-town shows because she has these two dogs. She claims pet-sitters are expensive, and they don't like to take on Rottweilers; besides she could use the income from renting her spare room, which she's tried to do before, but without much luck—"

"Laura," he chuckled, "you're rambling."

"Yes, well." She fidgeted. "I just don't want you to think I'm trying to chase after you or pressure you into anything. Truth is, I've been thinking about moving to Houston for a long time. You know, to get a job. And a life."

His mind raced as she waited for his reaction. For some reason, his stomach felt tense, even though he couldn't think of a single downside to her plan. Making her father take care of himself would be the best thing for both of them, and her moving to Houston obliterated all obstacles to them dating.

"Well?" she prompted.

He decided to ignore the inexplicable attack of nerves. "I think that's a great idea. When do you move?"

"I don't know." She frowned. "I'll need to find someone to cook for Dad and make sure he takes his medicine. Doctors can be notoriously bad patients, and Clarice refuses to work any more hours. I just hope she doesn't quit the minute I'm gone."

She was backing out of it already. And knowing her father, the man would find a way to keep her chained to that house until she turned old and gray. She'd never leave solely for her own benefit—what she needed was someone else's needs to focus on.

"I have an idea." With a deep breath, he rushed ahead before he changed his mind. "A favor, actually. Apparently my car will be in the shop for a while."

"Your car's in the shop? What happened?"

He stared at her a moment, then laughed. "Wouldn't you know, you're the only person in town who hasn't heard. I knocked a hole in one of the oil heat exchangers last night when I turned into that open field."

"Oh, Brent, I'm so sorry." She laid a hand on his arm.

"Laura." With a playful growl, he shook her chin. "Would you stop apologizing for things that aren't your fault? I'm the one who should apologize for endangering both our lives in that stupid race."

To his surprise, she smiled—an impish little grin that made her look incredibly young and unbelievably sexy. "I guess we're lucky the Guardian Angel of Foolish Boys was on duty last night."

"And that his jurisdiction includes idiot men on occasion." Idly, he ran a thumb over her jaw and felt her shiver. "Anyway, what would you say to driving the Porsche to Houston when it's fixed?"

"Me?" Her eyes went wide. "Drive your sports car?"

"Sure." He pulled her into a light embrace. "You can drive up on Sunday, stay through Monday, to um," he nuzzled her neck, "look through the want ads for a job. And I can," he nibbled her earlobe, "drive you home," he traced his tongue along the shell of her ear, "Tuesday morning . . . or so."

"Won't . . ." He heard her sigh as he kissed the pulse point in her neck. "Won't you be working?"

"Laura," ne chuckled, trailing his lips along her jaw. "I'm an evening anchor. I work two to midnight."

"Oh." She swayed against him as he covered her mouth with his. She tasted of some elusive, salty-sweet flavor he couldn't quite place, but he gladly would have stood there for hours sampling that soft, luscious mouth.

Cursing their lack of privacy, he lifted his head and smiled at the sublime expression on her face.

"Mmm . . ." She blinked. "I guess I could do that." He watched as her eyes focused and her mind began to function once more. "That way I could stay with Melody, to see if rooming with her would work out. Sort of like a trial run."

"Actually, I was thinking—" He stopped himself short of inviting her to stay with him. No sense in moving ahead too quickly on this dating thing. He loosened his arms, to give his body some space to cool off. "Your, eh, idea sounds perfect. A trial run is always a good idea."

"If you're sure you don't mind me driving your car." She looked up at him with those heart-stopping blue eyes.

"Of course not." He took another step back. "I mean, you do know how to drive a stick shift, don't you? No major wrecks, rollovers, or fender benders on your record?"

"Not even a speeding ticket." She gave him a knowing smile.

"Just checking," he said. "But you will be careful, right?"

"Of course. All you have to do is give me a call when the car is ready. Although I'll need a few days' notice to get everything settled with my dad and all."

"Here, let me give you my home address and phone number." He pulled a business card out of his wallet and scribbled his unlisted number on the back. "The garage has the keys. I'll call you with directions when the car's fixed."

As he handed her the card, his fingers clamped down on it. Even as she tugged, he couldn't seem to let go. "You will be careful with my car, right? The gears are very sensitive, and don't hit the brakes too hard or you'll go right through the windshield."

"I'm sure I can handle it."

"Maybe you should drive it around town a few times before you get on the highway, just until you get used to the European steering—"

"Brent."

"Yes?"

"I'll be careful." She plucked the card out of his hand and gave his lips a quick kiss. When she pulled back, excitement shone in her eyes. "So I guess I'll see you in a week or two."

"Yeah, I guess so."

She stood for a moment, long enough for him to think about kissing her again, but something held him back.

"Well then," she said, "if that's it, I'd better get back to helping the others in the clubhouse."

He watched her move away, momentarily distracted by the sway of her hips. With a final smile over her shoulder, she disappeared around the corner of the building— and a wave of terror gripped his chest. He wasn't sure whether it came from the thought of Laura driving his car, or the thought of her moving to Houston.

Taking slow, steady breaths, he reminded himself she was moving to Houston to get a job, not to chase him down or trap him in a relationship. Besides, he had two weeks to get used to the idea or back out completely.

Staring in the direction she'd gone, though, he knew he wouldn't back out. Not yet, anyway. He'd get through this moment of panic the way he got through his first live news report: by concentrating on the present and blocking the future out of his mind.

Not that he and Laura had a future. At least, not a long-term one. Surely she knew that, though, or she wouldn't have assured him so strongly of her motive for moving. He had nothing to worry about. They were both adults. Everything would be just fine.

⁓

Two weeks later, Laura came down the stairs with a garment bag and overnight case. Her father stepped into the foyer as she set down her luggage to rifle through her purse for the keys to Brent's car.

"So," her father said, "you're really going through with this. You actually mean to leave."

She glanced up, surprised to hear his voice after so many days of silence. Greg's stunned reaction to her leaving had been uncomfortable enough, but her father's disapproval hurt far worse. Since he learned of her plans, they'd hardly spoken a word.

Resigned to his disapproval, she returned to searching for the keys. "I have several days' meals labeled in the refrigerator. Instructions for heating are taped to the lids. Your medicine is in your daily pill-minder on the kitchen counter. Although if you'd like," she hesitated, "I could call you in the evening to remind you."

"I can take care of myself, Laura Elizabeth." He straightened with the aid of his cane. "Just don't expect me to lie for you while you're gone."

"Lie for me?" She frowned. "What are you talking about?"

"You don't think anyone actually believes you're going to Houston to look for a job, do you?" His arm shook as he leaned on his cane. "Everyone knows you're running off to spend the weekend in the city with that Zartlich boy."

"I'm twenty-eight years old, Dad," she reminded him with strained patience. "What I do is nobody's business but mine."

"What about me?" He thumped his chest. "I'm the one who'll have to stay behind and listen to all the whispers behind my back. This whole town will say you're no better than your mother."

"Stop it, Dad. Just stop it!" Anger surged up hot and fast. She took a breath to hold it in. "If I'm like my mother, well, fine. For all her faults, I can think of a lot worse people to be compared to than her."

"That's only because you never knew what she was really like. I shielded you from that, thank God."

"Thank God? Thank God!" She gaped at him, not knowing whether to laugh or cry. "I can barely remember my own mother because her name has been taboo in this house since the day you brought her body back from Galveston, and for that you're thankful?"

"You're better off not remembering what she was like."

She stared at him, seeing the hurt behind the bitter words. "I remember she was kind and giving and the most loving mother any girl could hope for. I also remember the way she cried as often as she laughed. I remember how desperately you two loved each other, even as I remember lying awake at night listening to the two of you fight. That's all I know of my mother. All I'll ever know."

"Then maybe it's time you knew why your mother

and I fought so often. Maybe it's time you knew the truth about all those 'shopping trips' she made into Houston."

"Dad . . ." Her shoulders sagged under the weight of regret. "Please. I don't want to go into this, not now when you're upset. Maybe when I get back—"

"As if there's ever a good time to tell a child her mother was a tramp."

"I said stop it! I—" She bit her lip to keep it from shaking. "I know there were . . . other men, all right? I overheard enough shouting matches to know that much."

"They weren't just 'other men,' Laura Beth. They were total strangers she picked up in bars. Is that the kind of woman you want people comparing you to? The kind of woman you want to be like?"

"This isn't like that!"

"And how is it different? Do you deny you're going off to see Brent Zartlich?"

"I'm going to meet Brent, yes—a man I've known most of my life. A man I hope to have a relationship with."

"A relationship." He sneered at the word. "You can dress it up with platitudes, child, but you can't change the truth. Sex outside of marriage is still a sin."

"Maybe you're right. Maybe it is a sin. But I've spent my whole life being good, and what has it gotten me?"

"It's gotten you a decent home, food and clothes, and the respect of this town, that's what it's gotten you."

"It isn't enough. Can't you understand, I need—"

"What? What do you need that you can't get right here in Beason's Ferry?"

"More! All right?" Her body trembled with frustration. "I need more."

"And that, young lady, is exactly why you are just

like your mother.'' He closed his eyes. ''Why do women always chase the very things that will destroy them in the end?''

She started to defend herself, but her throat closed up. ''Dad, I'm sorry,'' she finally said, gathering her bags. ''But I have to go. Please . . .'' Her voice broke. ''Try to understand.''

''Laura Beth,'' he called as she reached for the door. She glanced over her shoulder and saw the worry and pain that lined his face. ''He'll break your heart—you know that, don't you?''

''You're probably right. But I'd rather go after what I want and have a broken heart than stay here and have nothing.''

Her father drew up to his full height, his face contorting as he fought back his own tears. ''Fine then. Go. Give yourself to some white trash bum who'll destroy everything I've ever given you. But I'm warning you, Laura Elizabeth, if you walk out that door, don't ever come back. I'd rather think of you as dead than sit here worrying over you night and day. Do you understand that?''

Her throat closed. ''Good-bye, Daddy,'' she managed to whisper before she crossed the threshold and shut the door behind her.

⁓

Swiping at her cheeks, Laura steered Brent's car onto First Street and headed out of town. Her watery vision made the Porsche's tight steering and touchy brakes that much harder to deal with. Damn Brent's car for needing to be babied. Why did men have to have cars as sensitive as their egos? Damn all men, and damn her father, too.

Well, no, not damn her father. Damn her for letting him get to her. She'd known he'd make a scene before she left. She just hadn't expected him to bring up her mother. That had been a low blow.

Reaching the highway, she eased the car into a nice steady pace. A glance in the rearview mirror confirmed she'd smeared her mascara. She muttered a few more curses as she dabbed at the runny mess. This was supposed to be her big day: her emancipation. And instead of celebrating, she was crying off her makeup.

To heck with that, she decided. Her father could only ruin her day if she let him. Adjusting herself more comfortably in the contour seat, she absorbed the feel of the road through the steering wheel.

She rather liked this image of herself, dashing off to Houston in a Porsche to meet a handsome man. As for the day, she couldn't have picked a better one: the sun blazed in a cloudless sky, and a profusion of wildflowers bloomed along the side of the highway. All she needed now was the right music.

Keeping one eye on the road, she rifled through Brent's eclectic selection of CDs, which ranged from rhythm and blues to good old rock 'n' roll. Passing up the lighter fare, she picked something to set the mood she wanted: ZZ Top.

As she struggled to get the disc out of the case, a car whizzed by in the fast lane as if she were standing still. She jumped at the sound and glanced down at her speedometer. The indicator read seventy miles an hour, exactly the speed limit. One would think that was plenty fast enough for anyone. Yet as she popped the CD in the player, a pickup truck came up behind her so fast, she feared he'd hit her before he whipped into the other lane and flew by.

Dang! She pressed a hand to her pounding heart, then laughed at herself for being so skittish. If this was how fast life moved outside of Beason's Ferry, then she'd just have to get used to it.

Digging through her purse, she found her sunglasses, put them on, and slid lower in the seat. As Billy Gibbons's gravelly voice belted out the opening line to "Gimme All Your Lovin'," she hit the accelerator.

She was tired of being the slowest driver on the road.

CHAPTER
12

$\mathcal{L}$aura's eyes widened with interest when she turned onto the street that led to Brent's house. One block off Westheimer, between the prestigious addresses along Kirby and Shepherd, was a world she'd never believed existed. Even though she'd grown up listening to people talk about Houston's "charming old neighborhoods," she'd never seen them. When she'd come to the city before, she'd driven straight to the Galleria, or some other destination along the main roads, and then gone home. But here on this side street in one of the city's trendiest neighborhoods, she discovered the romantic heart of Old Houston.

Easing the car along the shade-dappled street, she admired the green blankets of lawn, the colorful flower beds, and the stately two-story homes. Behind brick walls, she caught glimpses of garage apartments and the blue reflections of swimming pools.

She spotted the address Brent had given her as she turned the corner at the end of the street. It was a smaller house than the others—more of a cottage, really—nestled between a newly built row of town houses and the imposing wall of a mansion. A rather large cottage, she realized as she cleared the gnarled magnolia tree that shaded the front yard and partially hid the three-gabled roof.

Pulling into the drive, she checked her directions to be sure she had the right house. Somehow she hadn't pictured Brent owning a home that could have graced the pages of *Southern Living*. An apartment in a glass-and-steel high-rise, yes. A country cottage, no.

Yet as she looked up, Brent stepped onto the front porch, and she'd never seen anyone look more at home. In tan slacks and a navy-blue polo shirt, he had the casual look of old money, as if he'd been born on this very street among the quiet wealth and blooming azaleas.

"You found it," he called as she stepped out of the car. His welcoming smile banished any lingering doubts she had about coming to Houston.

"Of course." She took a deep breath to calm the frantic rhythm of her heart. "You give excellent directions."

Reaching the car, he hesitated, as if he wanted to touch her but wasn't sure if he should. He cast a sideways glance at the Porsche. "Any problems with the car?"

"None whatsoever." A mischievous impulse made her add, "Well, except for that speeding ticket I got flying through Katy."

"Speeding ticket?" he said absently, still searching his car for evidence of damage.

"I told the officer to send the ticket to you, since it is your car."

He glanced up, looking confused, then his brow cleared. "Why, you little liar," he laughed. "You didn't get a ticket."

"No." She grinned. *But I should have.*

Cupping her face, he gave her a quick kiss and started

to pull away but came back for a second brush of her lips, followed by a third and a fourth, each progressively longer. By the time he lifted his head, she felt weak in the knees.

"I'm glad you came," he said in a quiet, husky voice.

"Mmm." A warm glow stole through her as she opened her eyes. "Me, too."

"I have to admit, though, I'm a little surprised."

"Surprised?"

He shrugged. "I half-expected your father to pull some stunt at the last minute. You know, some life-threatening emergency to keep you from leaving."

"No." The inner glow dimmed. "Nothing life threatening."

He narrowed his eyes at her. "What did he pull?"

"Nothing," she insisted.

"Laura . . . ?"

"Nothing I want to talk about. All right?"

For a moment, he looked ready to argue but apparently changed his mind. "All right." His mood lightened as he gestured toward the house. "So how do you like it?"

She looked past him to the red brick house with white trim and black shutters. "I love it."

"Really?" Boyish glee lit his face. "Me, too. It still needs a lot of work, though."

"Old houses always do."

"How about I give you the grand tour before we decide what we want to do tonight?"

"Sounds great." Warmth tingled in her belly as he led her up the brick path toward the porch. To her surprise, she felt even more jittery now than she had on their first "date." But then, that had been prearranged. Tonight she was with Brent because he'd invited her of his own accord.

"So, eh, what time is Melody expecting you?" he asked as they climbed the front steps. She glanced at him sideways. *Was he anywhere near as nervous as she was?*

She forced a casual note into her voice. "She said not to hurry."

"Good." His smile, and the subtle meaning behind that single word, sent heat spreading through her even as she preceded him into the cool interior of his home.

"Oh, my," she breathed, captivated by the masculine beauty and understated elegance of the décor.

Recessed lights cast pools of warmth onto the hardwood floors, soft taupe walls, and white molding. In both the sitting room off to the right and the formal dining room to the left, Oriental rugs added splashes of color to offset the dark antiques.

"There are a couple of bedrooms upstairs," he explained as he gestured toward the stairwell. "I use one for an office, the other for a weight room."

Her eyes couldn't help but notice the results of those weights as he led her through the dining room. Her mouth watered at the sight of his tapered back, trim buttocks, and muscular thighs as they moved beneath his clothes.

Beyond the dining room, they entered the kitchen. With her eyes still on Brent, she barely noticed the copper pots hanging over a butcher-block island, the red brick encasing the oven, or the herbs that grew in a window over the sink. She listened more to the richness of his voice than to his actual words.

"And now for my favorite room," he announced.

Passing through a second door, he swept his arm outward. "The den."

Gathering her wits, she stepped into a room that oozed masculinity. Rough-hewn beams, a stone fireplace, and leather furniture lent the room the air of a mountain lodge. Track lights accentuated bold paintings of Santa Fe impressionism. On the coffee table, wrought-iron candlesticks held candles that had never been lit. The room was perfect. Almost too perfect, she thought as she noticed the *Architectural Digests* fanned out on the end table.

The sound of a waterfall drew her to the windows that looked out onto the patio. Redwood furniture sat in a precise grouping about potted flowers. A small water garden splashed in one corner of the yard. It looked like a setting for a photo shoot: beautiful to look at but not quite real. She brushed the odd notion aside. "You must have wonderful parties."

"Actually," he hesitated, "you're the first person I've had over."

She turned to him with a questioning frown.

He thrust his hands into his pockets. "I keep meaning to invite some of the people from work. Maybe after I have the molding in the dining room stripped and repainted."

"Brent," she shook her head, "if you wait until everything is done, you'll never have anyone over. Trust me, I've lived in an old house all my life."

"I know." He shrugged. "But there's still so much to be done, even though it has come a long way."

Cocking her head, she stared at him in amusement.

"What?" He fidgeted, something she'd rarely seen him do.

"You." Smiling, she walked toward him. "Or have

you forgotten what you said when I asked you to help out with the Homes Tour?" When he didn't answer, she deepened her voice to imitate his. " 'Restoring old houses is not a worthy cause.' "

"Did I say that?"

"Yes, you did." She touched his chin with her finger-tip.

"I guess what I meant was, it's not a worthy *charity*. But then I'm not asking anyone to give me money. I'm doing this for me and, well, for the house." He glanced about. "You wouldn't believe how neglected this place was. Even standing among all the other restored houses, no one seemed to realize the potential it had. Either that, or they considered it too small to mess with." His gaze shot back to her, and color crept up his neck. "Never mind. It's hard to explain."

"Brent." She ducked her head to see directly into his eyes. "I understand. Perfectly."

"Thanks." He kissed her forehead.

"So," she asked brightly, "what do you have planned for tonight?"

"Well, let's see." He drew her lightly against him. "We could either go out for dinner and a movie, or . . . we could stay here for dinner and a movie."

"Oh, I get it," she laughed as he nuzzled her neck. "You tricked me into coming here just so you could get a home-cooked meal. Well, forget it, mister." She pressed a hand to his chest and gave him a stern look. "I'm officially on a cooking strike for the next few days."

"Actually, I was going to cook for you. How about something pseudo-Italian?"

She narrowed her gaze. "You are talking about cooking, right? Not picking up the phone and ordering a pizza."

"What a sexist thing to say."

"I'm just checking."

"All right, Miss Smartypants, how does Burgundy beef with parsleyed fettuccine sound?"

Her face lit up. "It sounds fantastic."

"Good, because I already have the meat marinating in the refrigerator. But we'll need to run to the store. I'm fresh out of pearl onions and artichoke hearts."

"Fine with me." She smiled in amazement, deciding she liked this unexpectedly domestic side of Brent. She liked it very much.

Since the day was sunny but cool, Brent put the top down on the Porsche and took the "scenic route" to the grocery store. He wanted to show Laura all the spectacular mansions on the other side of Kirby from where he lived.

"Not that I could ever afford anything like this," he said. "But they are something to look at."

"Would you really want anything so big?" She looked a bit horrified by the idea.

"You bet," he answered. "Who wouldn't?"

She shook her head. "After all these years of living in my father's house, all I want is a place to call my own. It could be a mansion or a shack, I wouldn't care." He watched the wind rumple her hair as she studied the houses. She had an odd blend of contentment and longing that he realized now had always been there. The things she wanted seemed so simple, yet remained just beyond her reach.

Turning back to the road, he took on a teasing note to keep the moment light. "As long as that shack had a white picket fence and a couple of kids in the yard, eh?"

"Maybe." She cast him a sideways smile. "Although there are other things in life besides marriage and kids, you know."

To his surprise, a tiny gleam of wickedness lit behind her smile. His pulse leapt with memories of what had happened the last time they'd been alone in this very car. His gaze darted to the slender legs he'd been trying to ignore. Exposed by her khaki denim skirt, they looked invitingly smooth—and naked of anything but a tan. As if intentionally taunting him, she crossed her legs with a slow, sensual motion that made him smile.

Maybe dating Laura wouldn't end in disaster after all. She seemed perfectly prepared to handle a temporary relationship. Turning back to the road, he allowed himself to enjoy the low hum of tension that had settled in his groin.

When they returned to the house, Laura perched crosslegged on a bar stool in Brent's kitchen as he prepared dinner. The CD player in the den piped a random selection of husky, bluesy tunes throughout the house. Sipping from the glass of wine he'd poured, she watched him with fascination.

"Wherever did you learn to do that?" she asked as he sliced carrots with the uniform precision of a Cordon Bleu chef.

"What, cook?" He shrugged. "The rudiments I learned early on. Not that I had much choice, since my grandmother rarely turned off the TV long enough to remember I was even in the house.''

The rhythm of his chopping skipped a beat. He frowned at the uneven slice of carrot and tossed it into the sink. "After a while, even kids get tired of bologna sandwiches and ketchup soup.''

"Ketchup soup?'' she asked.

"Hey, I was a kid, give me a break.'' He grinned. "Besides, ketchup's free.'' Leaning toward her, he lowered his voice for dramatic effect. "See, I'd sneak in the side door of the Dairy Bar, make like I was headed for the john, and then, when no one was looking, I'd swipe the envelopes of ketchup off the tables.''

"Very clever,'' she said with exaggerated awe, even as something twisted inside her at the image he painted.

"Anyway,'' he said, scraping the carrots into a bowl and moving on to peel the tiny pearl onions, "my culinary skills were ripe for expanding when I landed the job as delivery boy for Adderson's Grocery. I guess it started as simple curiosity, you know, wondering what people planned to do with all that food I put in their pantries. So I . . . peeked through people's cookbooks if I delivered the groceries when no one was home.''

"Brent . . .'' She shook her head. "Why didn't you just ask?''

"I did,'' he insisted. "Once. The woman told me to mind my business and unpack the groceries.''

"Who said that?'' Her spine snapped straight.

He flashed her a grin. "Clarice.''

"Clarice?'' Laura gaped. "But Clarice can't cook, unless you like burnt meat loaf and cornbread hard enough to break a tooth on.''

"I, eh . . .'' he scratched the side of his neck. "I sort

of figured that out later. By then, however, I was already set in my devious ways."

"Clever ways, if you ask me." She shook her head, marveling at how much he'd overcome in life to become the man he was. "You were quite resourceful as a kid. It's something you should be proud of."

"Thanks." Finishing with the onions, he grabbed the bowl of marinated meat and turned to the gas stove. "So," he said with his back turned, "did you ever get around to talking to your friend Greg to explain that your answer was no?"

Her shoulders slumped "I did talk to him, yes."

"And?" Brent's voice sounded casual, but his body looked suddenly tense.

"He seems to have developed selective hearing." She toyed with the stem of her wineglass. "While I told him I was moving to Houston as distinctly as I know how, he seems to think I'm coming here for some sort of vacation to think things over."

"I see. And your dad. Are you going to tell me what he said before you left?"

"I'd rather not." She took a sip of wine and rolled it on her tongue.

"He doesn't approve of you seeing me, does he?"

"Dad doesn't approve of me seeing anyone."

Brent busied himself adjusting the burner flame. "What did he say?"

"Oh, I don't know." She waved her glass through the air in an effort to appear blasé. "Something about the whole town knowing I was coming to Houston for a weekend of sin and debauchery." Even with his back to her, she saw his body stiffen.

"Does that bother you?" he asked quietly.

"What, sin and debauchery?"

"No, the whole town knowing you're here. With me."

"Of course not." She shrugged off the notion, until another thought occurred to her. "Does it bother you?"

"For people to know I'm spending time with a beautiful woman? I don't think so." He laughed as he reached for the olive oil. It sizzled and popped as he drizzled it into the pan. The garlic he added filled the room with a mouthwatering aroma as he lined up the bowls of chopped vegetables and meat. "Now, sit back and enjoy the show."

CHAPTER 13

"*That* was wonderful!" Laura gave a sated sigh as she plopped onto the sofa. Slumping back, she placed a hand over her stomach. "I can't believe I ate so much."

"Glad you liked it." Smiling, Brent took a seat beside her and grabbed the remote control, hitting the play button for the VCR. "You sure you want to watch a movie you've already seen?" he asked as the opening credits for *Up Close and Personal* began to roll. She'd spotted the tape earlier in the extensive collection in his entertainment center.

"Absolutely," she answered. "Like I said, it's been a while. Besides, what could be more appropriate than a movie about broadcast news? Unless you'd rather watch something else."

"No, I like this film." He leaned forward to retrieve the bottle of wine he'd set on the coffee table and topped off both their glasses. "It's even fairly accurate, for the most part."

"Oh?" she prompted, eager to learn more about his line of work. "Is your newsroom as posh as the one in the film?"

"Not exactly," he chuckled. "Behind the slick, fancy sets, newsrooms are usually cluttered and chaotic, kind of like a war zone." Settling back against the sofa, he stretched his arm out behind her. "What I meant by accurate is the way they portray the Robert Redford character, Warren Justice. Newsmen like him, ones who really care about informing the public, are a dying breed. These days it's all ratings and show biz."

"Does that bother you?"

"Yeah, it does, actually. It bothers me a lot." His fingers toyed with the ends of her hair. When she glanced sideways, he seemed more interested in her than in the movie. "I can't imagine ever doing anything else, though. And every once in a while, I get to write a story that matters."

"Like what?"

He told her of the special reports he'd done, from land development scandals to political corruption. As she listened to him talk, she lost track of the movie. He had a passion in his voice when he spoke about uncovering truth and informing the people. Most of the stories he told, though, were from his days in the field, before he'd landed a spot on the anchor desk.

"I still don't understand why you gave up reporting."

"Because the anchor job is one step closer to what I really want to do."

"Which is?"

"News director." He grinned. "Now there's a job that matters. The director I have now, Sam Barnett, is a bit like that." He gestured toward the TV, where Warren Justice was badgering Tally Atwater, a hungry, green reporter, to find the heart of the story, to dig beyond the surface for the human element that would make people care. "Connie, my producer, thinks Sam's an outdated

dinosaur, but I admire the way he cares more about reporting the news than providing entertainment.''

Rather than glance at the screen, her eyes remained
on Brent. ''You really love it, don't you?''

''Yeah. I really do.'' He turned and smiled at her. And
in that moment, she realized she loved him. Truly *loved*
him. Not as a childish crush on the cutest boy in town,
but with the quiet depth of a woman's love for a man.
She loved his confidence and discipline, his integrity and
drive.

As she listened to him talk about his dreams, she
longed for his happiness as much as she longed for him to
return her love. Whether he would ever feel this same
overwhelming pull of the heart toward her, she did not
know. For now, however, it was enough to sit quietly
beside him, to listen to his voice and believe in the possibility of sharing those dreams.

''Listen to me.'' His smile turned self-mocking. ''I
sound like Clark Kent: Truth, Justice, and the American
Way.''

To her surprise, his cheeks darkened with embarrassment. ''No,'' she insisted, and lifted a hand to his cheek,
''you sound wonderful.''

The moment her hand touched him, his gaze locked
with hers. The doubt in his eyes gave her the courage to
not draw away. So many things swelled in her heart, longing to be voiced, but she knew her feelings would frighten
him away. ''Someday,'' she said quietly, ''I know you will
make a fabulous news director.''

A stillness settled between them. He lifted a hand to
touch her face. For one flicker of a moment, she thought
she saw everything she felt reflected in his eyes. But as he

leaned toward her, her eyes drifted closed, and all she could do was feel.

The brush of his lips on hers was like a whispered question, and she answered with a sigh. His hand trembled as his fingertips trailed from her cheek to her neck, and she trembled in turn.

She wanted this—oh, how she wanted it. No matter what the future held, she would have this night forever. She leaned into him, her mouth urgent as she tried to convey her decision without words. His body stiffened for a moment, hesitating before his tongue plunged into her mouth, delighting in what she offered so freely. As she stroked his arms and his chest, his muscles hardened beneath her touch, and her own body strained in response.

His mouth left hers in a desperate quest down her neck, stopping at the barrier of her blouse. She arched her back to beckon him lower, but he didn't respond.

Lifting her lashes, she found him staring at her body, his face lined as if some battle waged within. He moaned as he brought his mouth back to hers, hard, demanding. She opened her blouse with trembling hands. He needed no further encouragement to ease her down onto the couch.

She welcomed his weight and the hardness of his arousal pressing against her thigh. His hand splayed across her rib cage. Her breast ached in anticipation, yet he made no move to touch the nipples that puckered against the lace of her bra. A whimper escaped her as she deepened the kiss, begging him to touch her.

His lips broke away, and she heard his ragged breath. "No. Wait. Stop."

She blinked up at him, too stunned to comprehend.

Had she misread his attraction? Or had he changed his mind at some point during the kiss? "I'm sorry. I—"

She grabbed at her blouse to cover herself, but his hand stopped her. When she looked into his eyes, she saw tormented desire rather than rejection.

"Do you have any idea how badly I want you right now?" he said.

Relief spread through her. "I rather hoped you did." She managed a shy smile. "Because I want you, too."

With a moan, he captured her lips, teasing and tasting. His hand moved down over her skirt, then up along her bare thigh. She quivered as his fingers slid beneath her panties to cup and squeeze her bottom. Only, when she pressed her hips against his, he pulled away.

"Wait," he rasped, tearing his mouth from hers. "We have to stop."

"Why?" She frowned up at him.

"Because . . ." A line formed between his brows as his gaze dropped to her half-exposed breasts. "I didn't invite you here for a one-night stand."

"And I didn't come here for one." She fought down equal measures of uncertainty and frustration. She longed to tell him she'd waited half her life for him, and she didn't see any reason to wait anymore. "Brent," she sighed, cupping his face so he would look at her. "We practically grew up together. Would it be so wrong if we sort of skipped the 'getting to know each other' stage?"

A laugh escaped him. "I never know what to expect from you." Leaning down, he kissed her lips, gently, sweetly. She lifted her arms to pull him closer.

"Naw-uh." He pulled back, grinning. "If we're going to do this, let's do it right."

Before her dazed senses could sort out the words, he

stood and pulled her up to stand beside him. Her blouse gaped open, and she reached to close it. Stopping her, he took her hand in his and brought it to his mouth. "Even on short notice, I think I can manage something a bit more romantic than the sofa."

Apparently, in rising, she'd left her boldness behind, for his words brought a blush of heat into her cheeks. She tried to duck her head, but he lifted her chin with a chiding smile. "Never be embarrassed by the things that give you pleasure."

With her hand still caught in his, he walked backward, leading the way to a door she hadn't yet been through. He pushed it open on its silent hinges, revealing the master bedroom. In the silver-blue shadows, she could barely make out a massive bed. Its black metal posts rose upward nearly to the ceiling. The dark masculinity beckoned her like a den of forbidden pleasure.

A moment ago she'd wanted to surrender everything to Brent without a thought. Somehow this seemed different. More calculated. The sin her father had named it.

She felt Brent's eyes as he studied her face, sensed his withdrawal in some intangible way. "Laura," he sighed, brushing the hair back from her forehead. "We don't have to—"

"No." Her eyes sprang to his as need and uncertainty warred within her. What if giving herself to him drove him away? What if he found her body lacking? Maybe she should wait. But what if tonight was all she had?

She took a breath for courage. "I want you." When the doubt didn't leave his eyes, she cupped his face with her free hand. "And I want this."

The tension eased from his face as he kissed her briefly, then led her to the center of the room. "Wait here,'' he said, and went to the dresser to fumble in a drawer. Watching him in the dark, she placed a hand over her stomach to still her jittery nerves. *Please, don't let this be a mistake.*

With the scrape of a match, a tiny flame leapt to life. He touched it to the wick of a candle, softening the room with a romantic glow. Above the flickering light, she saw her reflection in the dresser mirror. She looked more apparition than flesh, all golden and white, floating in the darkness.

He moved to stand behind her, a part of the shadows rather than the light. He was so much taller, broader, more solid than she, and so devastatingly male. She watched, transfixed, as he slipped the blouse from her shoulders. It floated downward and out of sight like a worry soon forgotten.

His hands shook as they came to rest on her shoulders. She watched in the mirror as he lowered his head. His firm-looking lips touched her neck the same instant she felt their softness. The reality of his touch contrasted sweetly with the illusion in the mirror, beguiling her senses. Her eyes drifted closed, and she relaxed against him, absorbing the feel of his hard body and tender hands. She felt the tug and release of her bra and imagined it following her blouse, drifting away like mist in moonlight.

His hands cupped her breasts. The thought of him watching her embarrassed and thrilled her as he fondled her nipples, bringing them to aching peaks.

''I've thought about this for so long, wanted to touch you like this.'' He breathed the words against her hair. The evidence of that wanting pressed firmly against her backside.

The nervous fear subsided in her stomach, replaced

by an empty yearning. This was right. This man, this night. The certainty of it settled over her as his hands traveled downward along her stomach, drawing a quiver from deep within.

As if lost in a dream, she felt him remove the rest of her clothing, until she stood naked with him pressed behind her once again. One of his hands returned to her breast, the other moved lower, holding her firmly against him. She could feel him straining against the confines of his slacks, knew he stood fully clothed, gazing at her nakedness in the mirror.

"My God, Laura," he breathed against her temple, "you are so beautiful."

Her eyes drifted open, and she saw herself: pale and thin, yet somehow, wrapped in his solid, dark strength, she was beautiful—ethereal yet earthly. Her breath caught at the expression in her own eyes, at the hunger that glowed beneath her heavy eyelids. When she realized he watched her face, that he too saw the naked hunger, she wanted to turn away. But the image before her held her entranced as his strong hands smoothed over her soft skin.

"Since that night, in the car," he said, "I've wished a hundred times I'd been watching your face when I touched you. That I'd seen your eyes when you came undone."

His hand moved down her stomach to toy with the patch of golden curls. A whimper escaped her as his hand slipped between her thighs, igniting her desire. Embarrassment won over boldness. She turned in his arms to bury her face against his chest.

"Love me, Brent—I mean—" She raised her gaze to his. "Make love to me."

A smile flitted across his features as he lowered his mouth to hers. The mind-numbing kiss calmed her down, kept her from thinking. She twined her arms around his neck as he lifted her and carried her to the bed. Even as he laid her on the mattress, she clung to him, kissing him with her whole heart.

"Laura," he whispered, moving from her mouth to her neck, "do you need me to wear anything?"

"What?" She frowned, thinking he was wearing too much already. Her hands tugged at his shirt, wanting to touch his naked flesh.

"Do I need to wear a condom?" he clarified, helping her with his shirt. "I'm okay without one, unless you . . ."

Embarrassment returned a hundredfold. "No, no, I'm on the Pill. I mean—" She bit her lip, knowing pregnancy was a minor concern compared with the more recent consequences of having sex. "I'm okay, if you are."

"Clean as a whistle." He gave her a cocky grin, then climbed off the bed and stripped with provocative slowness. His body emerged, firmly muscled, lean, and sleek. He was every fantasy she'd ever had, dark, alluring, with a hint of danger. But when he came to her, he did so with tenderness and restraint.

The restraint, for Brent, was the hardest won, for never had he had a woman give herself so openly. The trust in her eyes excited him as much as the feel of her skin. She was as soft and fine as cashmere, responding to his slightest touch. He watched her face as he caressed the damp folds between her thighs. Her response embarrassed her—he could tell by the way she bit her lip to suppress a moan—but the pleasure was too tempting for her to resist.

Slowly, methodically, he touched her more deeply,

thrilling to every whimper and gasp. She was so close to the peak, so close, he could feel it in his own body's response. At last, she arched and twisted, reaching for his shoulders. "Oh, Brent. Brent, I—" Her fingers dug into his arms, pulling him toward her.

"Shh, I know." He tried to gentle her with kisses as he shifted his weight on top of her. Her hands grew more impatient. When her legs came around him, he gritted his teeth in a bid for control. He buried one hand in her hair; the other he wrapped about the small of her back. Her moist heat nudged against him, beckoning him in. Groaning, he broke the kiss.

"Look at me, Laura," he rasped.

Her heavy eyelids lifted a fraction, just enough for him to witness her dazed wonder as he pressed himself slowly but fully inside her tight heat.

With a gasp, her head arched back. He felt her spasm and watched in awe as she remained arched, suspended in a world of ecstasy. That he could send her soaring so quickly made his chest swell with pure male pride. She sighed and floated back to earth, her body relaxing beneath him. A smile spread across her face as she drifted toward sleep.

"Oh, no you don't," he chuckled as he nuzzled her lips. With slow, thorough strokes, he moved inside her. She purred against his mouth, returning his kiss full measure.

God, she excited him. Her blend of boldness and shyness touched something deep inside his chest. A small part of himself that he'd always held apart from the world slipped past his rigid control.

Rising on his arms, he gave himself up to the demands of the flesh. He plunged into her and over the edge, into a free fall of pleasure. As he descended, he realized Laura was right there with him, gasping for breath, arching with pleasure. Her arms opened, and he collapsed into her embrace, letting her hold him through the aftershocks that quaked his body.

When his heartbeat steadied, he rolled onto his side, pulling her with him. She gave a blissful sigh as she curled against his chest. As the hum of pleasure faded, doubt crept in. He hadn't meant for their first real date to end in bed. He closed his eyes to block out the memory of how she'd looked at him moments ago. There in her eyes he'd seen the one thing he didn't want to see.

Laura Beth Morgan imagined herself in love with him.

He had no idea what to do about that, what to say. As he lay in the darkness, struggling with his conscience, he heard her breathing even out, felt her body relax into sleep. Turning his head, he marveled at the contentment on her face. Her total trust reached inside him and twisted everything into knots. He didn't deserve this—and she deserved better.

"Ah, Laura." He kissed her forehead. "What am I going to do with you?"

Laura woke slowly to a delicious soreness in her muscles. Opening her eyes, she saw that Brent had also drifted off to sleep. She slipped her hand beneath her cheek and watched him. He looked so peaceful, she hadn't the heart to wake him. But Melody was expecting her.

She raised her head enough to see the clock on his nightstand. One A.M.! How had it gotten so late? She glanced about, trying to decide what to do. A phone sat beside the alarm clock, but if she used it, she might wake Brent. If he awoke, would he insist on getting dressed and taking her to Melody's? For a moment, she was torn, not knowing if he wanted her to stay, but knowing that was what she wanted. Very much.

Only what if her father called Melody's in the morning, looking for her? While she might be a grown woman, entitled to make her own choices, she had no wish to cause more friction than necessary with her father. And Melody might be worried.

Easing from the bed, she blew out the nearly spent candle, then slipped into what she assumed was the master bathroom. Cringing at the glare of light, she saw that the room was small, as most bathrooms were in older homes, but newly remodeled with gray, navy, and burgundy tile. After splashing water on her face and combing her hair, she found a navy-blue robe hanging on the door. The homey feel of terrycloth delighted her skin as the scent of aftershave tickled her nose.

She turned out the light and, in bare feet, tiptoed across the bedroom into the den. A flash of lightning flickered beyond the patio windows. She stopped for a moment, distracted by the rapid-fire lightning and wildly dancing trees. She was tempted to linger, but . . . But she needed to make her phone call and hurry back to bed.

Rummaging through the dark, she found her purse, retrieved Melody's phone number, and headed for the phone in the kitchen.

Melody answered on the first ring. "Piper here," her friend said over the blaring sound of Celtic flutes and drums.

"Melody?" she whispered, glancing toward the bedroom. "It's me. Laura."

"Hold on." The music went down in volume. "Okay, go ahead."

"I'm sorry to call so late." Beyond the window over the sink, another shaft of lightning splintered through the sky.

"Is it late?" Melody asked.

"It's one in the morning."

"Oh. Well, time flies when you're working. So what's up?"

"I wanted you to know, I'm still at Brent's."

"Let me guess." Laura could hear the smile in the other woman's voice. "You aren't coming here tonight."

"Do you mind?"

"Shoot no! In fact, I really didn't expect you. I take it things are working out between you and the news hunk?"

"I guess. I hope." Thunder rolled softly over the house.

"You okay?" Melody asked. "You sound kind of down."

"No, I'm fine." Laura hesitated. "Although I need to ask you a favor."

"Sure. Name it."

"If my father calls in the morning, can you say I'm in the shower or something, then call me here?"

Melody gave a deep throaty chuckle. "God, to feel like a teenager again. Give me the number, kid."

Finishing the call, Laura hung up the phone and let out a breath. She was committed to staying now and devoutly hoped Brent wouldn't take it the wrong way.

Cocking an ear, she listened for him to stir. The quiet of the room settled about her. She had the oddest sense that the house slept, as if it were an extension of its master. And just as she enjoyed watching Brent sleep, she couldn't resist wandering through the downstairs, smiling at the molding he thought needed to be replaced, running her fingertips along the polished surface of the dining table.

In the den, she saw the movie had run to the end and rewound itself. She ejected the tape from the player and slipped it back into its sleeve. As she set the tape in its proper place, she smiled at the other movies lined up in alphabetical order.

Brent was a man who liked things well ordered, completely opposed to the chaos of his early life.

Turning, she noticed they'd left their wineglasses on the coffee table. She picked up the glasses to put them in the sink before returning to bed. Only when she reached the kitchen, she saw their dinner dishes still in the sink. Brent must have been distracted indeed to have left them unwashed. The thought brought a smile to her lips. Deciding to wash them for him, she reached for the lemon-scented dishwashing liquid and a sponge. Before setting to work, she cracked the window over the sink to enjoy the smell of the rain and the feel of the cool air against her cheeks. Humming softly to herself, she filled the sink with sudsy water.

How ironic that she would so enjoy doing one of the very things she'd wanted to leave behind—being the happy homemaker. But this was Brent's house. And the simple act of washing his dishes pleased her immensely.

CHAPTER
14

~⌒~

Thunder rumbled in the distance. Brent stirred as the sound seeped through his layers of sleep, like the echo of angry voices. He tried to shake himself awake, but darkness clung tenaciously to him, trapping him in that cramped spaced filled with old terrors.

Within the darkness, he could still hear his mother's pleading voice and his grandmother's angry objection.

"You can't leave that kid here. Lord, I just got you and your brothers raised. Now you want me to raise him, too?"

"I don't have any choice, Momma. Wayne and I got married today. He's my husband now. You know he and Brent don't get along, but they will. Wayne just needs time to get used to the idea. Brent's a good boy, mostly. You know that. He won't be any trouble at all."

"He better not be, or he'll feel the back of my hand."

Light exploded through the room, jolting Brent awake. He bolted upright, panting for breath as the flickering light faded. Thunder rattled the windows.

Jesus. He wiped a hand over his face, feeling the sweat. When was the last time he'd had that nightmare? He glanced sideways, hoping he hadn't disturbed Laura.

And found her gone.

Cold panic gripped his chest. She'd left him. Without waking him to say good-bye. Just as his mother had.

Realizing the source of his panic, he drew his thoughts up short. Laura wasn't the type to sneak off in the middle of the night never to return.

So why was his heart still pounding?

He forced the irrational terror back down where it belonged. Grown men did not waste time on little-boy fears. Climbing from the bed, he pulled on his pants and went in search of her. She'd probably just had trouble sleeping, or needed a glass of water. Absently, he rubbed his chest as he crossed the den. Lightning exploded beyond the windows. When it died, he saw the glow coming from the kitchen.

He crossed to the door and stopped at the sight that greeted him. Laura stood at the sink in his navy-blue robe washing dishes and humming a cheerful tune. He watched her for a moment, willing the sight of her to soothe him.

"Laura?" he called.

"Oh!" She whirled, then sagged against the sink. Her neatly combed hair framed her face as she smiled sweetly at him. How could a woman who'd been thoroughly ravished so recently look like a cross between June Cleaver and Pollyanna? "You scared me," she laughed.

He rubbed harder at the knot in his chest, irritated that the tension persisted. "Next time you can't sleep, I'd appreciate it if you'd wake me as well."

"I'm sorry. I—" Lightning flickered in the window behind her. Her brows drew together as she noticed his hand pressed to his chest. "Is something wrong?"

"No. Of course not." Dropping his hand, he forced himself to forget the nightmare. Laura wasn't his mother, and she certainly hadn't abandoned him. "Are you coming back to bed?"

"As soon as I dry these last few dishes."

"Fine." His jaw tensed around the word. A hurt look flickered across her face, and he cursed himself for his curtness. He started to raise his hand back to his chest but balled it into a fist instead. "Take your time."

He turned and left her standing there.

In the bedroom, he sat on the edge of the bed and told himself to get a grip. Her inability to sleep in his bed was not a personal insult. Most people had trouble sleeping in strange places.

At the sound of bare footsteps in the doorway, he glanced up and found her silhouetted in the light from the den. She hesitated, as if uncertain whether to enter the darkened room.

"Are you coming to bed?" he asked, his voice sharper than he intended.

"Perhaps I should go to Melody's instead."

A blow from his grandmother had never knocked the air from his lungs so quickly. "Is that what you want? To leave?"

"No. . . ." She folded her arms about her chest, hugging herself. "Brent, what's this all about? Does my being here upset you?"

"No, your being here doesn't upset me. I just don't appreciate waking up and finding you gone, all right?"

She came forward and knelt before him. With a reassuring smile, she took his hands in hers. "I just went into the kitchen to call Melody, to tell her not to expect me till tomorrow."

He forced his lungs to take shallow breaths as lightning danced about the room. "Why didn't you tell me?"

"Because . . ." Her eyes chided him as she placed her hand against his cheek. "You were sleeping."

Her gentle touch prickled his skin as thunder rumbled outside. Closing his eyes, he placed his hand over hers, willing himself to calm down. Still, every muscle in his body trembled. If he had any sense, he'd go upstairs and lift weights until the old fears subsided back into the darkness where they belonged. But Laura was touching him, gently stroking his cheek.

"I didn't mean to upset you," she whispered softly.

He gritted his teeth as her fingertips brushed through his hair, sending shock waves through his system. He needed to tell her to stop, before he jerked her hard against him and lost himself in an exertion more primal than pumping iron. She deserved better treatment than that. Any woman deserved better. If only she'd stop touching him.

"Forgive me?" She said the words teasingly, completely unaware of the battle that raged inside him. Another volley of lightning lit the room as she kissed his temple, his cheek. Her clean honeysuckle scent drifted down inside him and wrapped his gut in a fist of need. Her lips traced his clenched jaw as she cradled his face in her soft hands.

The instant her lips touched his, his control snapped. With a groan, he caught her head in his hand and slanted his mouth over hers. His tongue plunged into her honeyed warmth, ravaging her sweetness. She stiffened in surprise when he pulled her down on the bed. Pinning her there, he raised his head. "Don't do that again, okay? Don't get up and leave without waking me."

"Okay." Laura blinked up at him as her heart leaped into her throat. She'd never seen anything more savagely

exciting than Brent at that moment, looming over her in
the darkness. His chest heaved with his breaths as lightning danced behind him.

His gaze dropped, and she realized the robe had
fallen open, leaving her exposed. Her breasts rose and fell
with her own labored breathing. Cupping one mound, he
lowered his head to take the tip in his mouth. Pleasure
knifed through her, as thunder rolled over the house.

She gasped as he sucked the nipple into his mouth.
She wasn't sure what had upset Brent, but she sensed he
needed her with a desperation that startled and thrilled
her. She moved against him, offering him the comfort
of her body. Somehow he managed between devouring
kisses to shed his trousers, while she became hopelessly
tangled in his robe.

She reached out to touch him, but the sleeves pinned
her arms to her side. His mouth and hands moved over
her body, kissing and kneading her flesh, driving her into a
world of frantic pleasure. She couldn't think, could barely
breathe as he settled between her thighs.

Lightning exploded through the room as he drove
inside her. Unable to touch him with her hands, she
arched upward, opening herself up to his hunger, his
need. Her head tossed as desire built inside her, so sharp
and keen, she wept his name. She knew he felt it, too, the
unbearable edge of ecstasy riding him as hard and fast as
he rode her. When it burst around them, he stiffened over
her, his back arched, his head thrown back. In a daze, she
watched him, and a wave of tenderness overwhelmed the
pleasures of the flesh. Knowing she'd filled some elemen-
tal need in him, given him some kind of solace, made her
feel more womanly than the climax that had just crashed
through her.

As the air left his lungs, he sagged on top of her. She welcomed his weight as she kissed his damp forehead. Warm currents of satisfaction flowed over her, and she let herself drift, listening to the storm.

When he finally shifted his weight to lie beside her, he drew her against him, holding her close. "Thank you," he whispered, kissing her forehead.

She moved her head against his shoulder to see his face. "For what?"

He smiled, and even in the darkness, she could see the tension was gone. "For staying."

Snuggling against him, she tucked his smile into her heart and drifted to sleep.

When Brent turned into the parking lot of Laura's third interview, he stifled a groan. The dilapidated office building sat in the middle of a barrio. This on top of her other two disastrous interviews made his heart sink in sympathy.

He glanced sideways to gauge Laura's reaction. She stared up at the building with the same nervous yet determined expression she'd been wearing all morning. "You know," he said cautiously, "if you don't want to go in for this one, you don't have to."

She turned to him with wounded eyes. "Surely I'm not that hopeless."

"No, I didn't mean that." He reached over to squeeze her hand. "I only meant, you don't have to keep every appointment you made if you can tell from the outside that the job isn't right for you."

"Brent . . ." She gave him an amused smirk. "How can I tell that if I don't go inside?"

"Just look at this place." He stared at it in horror. "It's a dump."

"It's not that bad." Her nervous look returned. "Besides, the doctor that bought Dad's practice went to school with Dr. Velasquez and had all kinds of wonderful things to say about him. According to him, Dr. Velasquez could have opened a pediatric practice anywhere but chose to come back to his old neighborhood because this was where he felt most needed."

"How noble."

She scowled at him. "I thought you liked noble causes."

"I do. I just don't like the idea of you working in this neighborhood."

"Well, with the way things have gone so far, I doubt you have much to worry about."

"Laura," he gave her hand another squeeze, "you know finding a job takes time."

"I know." Her gaze dropped to their joined hands, shielding her eyes with her lashes. "But the first doctor took one look at my résumé and politely brushed me off."

"The man was obviously a moron."

"And the second doctor didn't even bother keeping the appointment. He just had one of his nurses take my application and tell me they'd get back to me if they were interested."

"Another moron."

"They can't all be morons," she said quietly.

"Would you stop taking this so personally."

"You're right. You're right." With a deep breath, she lifted her eyes to the two-story structure with its ugly metal stairs and battered doors opening to an outside landing. "And I'll never find a job sitting out here."

"Just one thing, though," he said as she gathered her purse and reached for the door handle. "You don't have to take the first job you're offered. Okay?"

She smiled. "Let's just hope I'm offered one."

"You will be." He grinned.

"Thanks." She kissed his cheek. "Now wish me luck." With that she climbed out of the car and headed across the parking lot.

He kept his smile in place until she climbed the stairs and disappeared through a door on the second level; then he let loose the groan he'd been holding back. If she got this job, he'd shoot himself. The woman had no business even interviewing in a neighborhood like this. He never should have encouraged her to move to Houston.

Now that she was here, though, the least he could do was see her properly settled. That way, when they broke up, he wouldn't have to worry about her quite so much. And even after last night, he knew they would break up. It was inevitable. His relationships with women never lasted.

As he waited for her to finish her interview, he wondered how long they'd have together—and how well he'd handle it when she dumped him. The few other breakups he'd weathered hadn't been too bad. There'd been some yelling, some angry accusations about his refusal to commit himself to a relationship, followed by the slamming of a door or two. After which he'd heaved a huge sigh of relief and turned his mind back to work.

Perhaps Laura would have more patience with his inability to get close to a woman. Maybe she'd understand, because she'd know the reason behind it: He feared abandonment because his mother had abandoned him as a child. A first-year psychology student could figure that out without even cracking a book.

Women needed emotional commitment. They deserved it. But he couldn't give it. When they figured this out, they left.

He probably ought to spell it all out for Laura. Only, if he did that, she might leave immediately rather than a few months down the road. Selfish as it might be, he wanted those few months. He planned to savor every moment of them. Was that so wrong?

He glanced again at the office building, wondering how long this interview would last. The first two had been over before he even settled into waiting. Several minutes ticked by while he watched the traffic and checked his watch five times. Maybe he should go in and make sure she was all right.

Just as he reached for the handle, she reappeared on the second-floor balcony. The moment she turned, her face lit with such a brilliant smile, he swore he felt it clear across the parking lot. His body, which should have been thoroughly sated after last night, leapt to attention.

He shook his head at his physical reaction to the mere sight of her as she skipped down the metal stairs and headed toward him.

~

Laura resisted the urge to holler *yes* as she hurried across the cracked pavement toward the patch of shade where Brent had parked. The interview had gone well. Really well. She could feel it in her bones. The minute she and Dr. Velasquez shook hands, something had clicked between them. The pediatrician was slight of stature with gentle hands and a quiet voice, and yet she'd sensed a strength to his character that demanded respect. A mother couldn't ask for a better doctor for her children, and Laura couldn't imagine a better boss.

Hopping into the car, she leaned over and gave Brent's cheek a kiss. "Guess what?"

His face went stiff. "You got the job."

"Maybe." She could feel the smile beaming from her face. "The interview went well. Really, really well."

"And?" His smile looked a bit frozen, but after the morning she'd had, he probably didn't want to get his hopes up.

"I won't know for a couple of days. Dr. Velasquez said he had a few other people to interview. But I think I got it. I hope so, anyway."

"Laura . . ." He stared at her as if she'd lost her mind. "You truly don't have to take the first job you're offered."

"I know. But I want this job. I like Dr. Velasquez a lot, and so will you when you meet him."

"If you say so," he muttered as he started the car.

She studied him in silence while he drove across the parking lot. "Are you feeling all right?"

"Sure. I'm fine." When he glanced her way, his eyes didn't quite meet hers.

"You sure?" she persisted.

"Of course," he said. "Why wouldn't I be?"

"I don't know. I just thought you'd be happier for me, that's all."

"I am happy for you," he insisted a bit too strongly. Then, as if catching himself, he sighed. "I just have a lot on my mind, that's all."

"Oh?" She cocked her head to see his eyes. "Anything you want to talk about?"

Ignoring her question, he pulled into traffic. "What street did you say I need to take?"

Sighing, she gave him directions to Melody's house, but she couldn't brush off the feeling that some barrier had risen between them.

CHAPTER
15

On the opposite side of Buffalo Bayou from where Brent lived, Melody's neighborhood had a completely different flavor. Rather than stately brick houses with walled-in backyards, here colorful Victorian "painted ladies" mingled with single-story clapboard houses. Most of the homes had been lovingly restored as private residences or converted into lawyers' offices, but a few looked ready to be condemned. An esplanade ran down the center of the main street with trails for joggers and cyclists. Occasional statues, gazebos, and gothic streetlamps with sea serpents holding the lamp globes provided a romantic touch.

"Nothing like a neighborhood in transition," Brent muttered, seeming to notice the run-down elements more than the whimsical ones.

"I think it's charming," Laura countered, her spirits still soaring from her interview. Spotting the street sign she'd been watching for, she pointed toward it. "This is your turn." As he steered the Porsche onto the side street, she checked her notes and gestured to a clapboard house in the middle of the block. "It's this one, here."

Over the privacy fence that enclosed the entire yard, front and back, she saw a sapphire-blue house with white

and ruby trim. She smiled in delight at the colorful jewel
nestled beneath a tangle of oak, pecan, and pine trees. "It
looks just like a place where an artist would live."

"I guess," Brent said. As soon as they climbed out of
the car, he engaged the alarm.

Ignoring his odd mood, she took in a greedy breath.
Beneath the smell of the traffic and smog, she caught
the heady fragrance of flowers from a profusion of beds
in a neighbor's yard. Mockingbirds and bluejays hopped
through the branches overhead, adding their noisy ruckus
to the distant sounds of humanity. In contrast to the se-
date pace of Beason's Ferry, here her senses were constantly filled to overflowing.

As they approached the house, she noticed two
square holes about chest high in the gate. Before she
could venture a question as to their purpose, she heard a
series of deep throated *woofs* followed by the frantic
scratching of paws against wood. Two massive black and
tan heads popped through the openings, startling a laugh
out of her. With tongues lagging, the dogs grinned at their
visitors.

"Oh, aren't they cute?" Laura reached out a hand to
pet one of the massive heads. "They look just like grinning gargoyles."

Brent stepped back, as if unsure what to make of the
dogs.

"Karma! Chakra!" Melody shouted from the other
side of the fence. "Get down!" A noisy battle ensued,
followed by silence. "Okay, I got 'em. Come on in."

Opening the gate, Laura peeked around. Melody
stood in a vivid purple caftan with the collar to a wiggling
Rottweiler in each hand. "Is it safe?"

"Only if you don't mind getting licked to death."

Laughing, she shook her head. "To think Roger gave me these big babies as guard dogs."

"Roger?" Laura asked as Brent came in behind her and closed the gate.

"My ex-husband." Melody let the dogs go. One ran instantly to Laura, the other to Brent, each sniffing and wiggling. "He didn't like the idea of my living alone."

"I didn't know you'd been married," Laura said as she scratched and cooed over one of the dogs.

"That was in a past life." Melody shrugged.

Out of the corner of her eye, Laura saw Brent tentatively offer the back of his hand for the other dog to smell. That was all the incentive the beast needed to slide to the ground and lie on his back at Brent's feet. Brent glanced at her with startled pleasure lighting his eyes.

"Some guard dogs, eh?" Melody laughed.

"Oh, Melody, this is Brent." Laura straightened to make the introductions. "Brent, Melody Piper, artist extraordinaire."

"Well, I don't know about that." Melody offered Brent a firm, friendly handshake. "It's good to meet you."

"Same here." Brent's smile was cool but cordial.

"So come on in," Melody said. With Karma and Chakra charging before her, she led the way up the steps to the front porch. "Let me show you around. Then you can tell me how your interviews went this morning."

"You bet," Laura answered, then glanced back at Brent. "You coming?"

He gave the house a wary frown but followed her inside.

A hodgepodge of Middle Eastern accents, Tiffany lamps, and old furniture covered with batik slipcovers filled the entry hall and living room.

"The bedrooms are on opposite sides of the house—mine in the front, yours in the back—with a connecting bathroom in between, though I doubt sharing it will be a problem. I'm a late-to-bed, never-to-rise-before-noon type. So you'll have the bathroom to yourself in the mornings." Her caftan floated about her as Melody led the way through the dining room. "My studio's in the garage out back, right outside your window, but hopefully I won't keep you up nights." They passed through a large kitchen with wooden cabinets that went all the way up to the high coffered ceiling. "You're on your own if you drink coffee, since I only stock herb tea." The back bedroom opened directly off the kitchen. "This will be your room. Like I warned you, I don't have any spare furniture. I did get down my old sleeping bag and an air mattress, though, for tonight."

Laura glanced around at the mattress on the floor and the big windows that looked out on the backyard. Sheets had been tacked up and swagged back to serve as draperies. "This is perfect. I've never had a room to decorate on my own."

"You're kidding!" Melody laughed. "Well, we'll have to hit the garage sales. I know where to find all the really good ones. Karma, Chakra, no!" she shouted as the dogs padded over to flop on the mattress. Shaking her head, Melody grabbed their collars. "Why don't I lock these two in my room while you bring in your stuff. Otherwise they'll slip out that gate in two seconds flat. The last thing I need is another citation from the dog catcher—or Mrs. Carsdale next door, screaming about her flower beds."

The room fell silent when Melody dragged the dogs through the connecting bathroom to the bedroom beyond. Laura turned to Brent. "Well? What do you think?"

He glanced over his shoulder to be sure Melody was out of earshot. "I don't know. . . ."

"What?" She frowned.

"It just seems a bit . . . rough." He glanced around. "And unfurnished."

"I know. But it's only for the summer. Then, depending how things work out and how much money I've saved, I may look for a place of my own. In the meantime," she said, desperately wanting him to share her enthusiasm, "I guess I should get my things."

Brent's brooding scowl grew darker as they went outside to unload the car. The minute she reached for the overnight case, though, he stopped her. "Wait a second."

She dropped her hand and turned to face him.

He took a deep breath, as if struggling for words. Several seconds slipped by. He plowed his fingers through his hair, took another breath, then looked her straight in the eye. "Move in with me."

"Do what?" A startled laugh escaped her.

"All you need is a place to stay until you get settled, right? Well, you can stay with me. And since you won't have to pay rent, you won't be pressured to take a job until you're sure it's what you want. You can take the whole summer to look around, get to know the city, decide what you want to do."

"And then what? Move out?"

He shifted uneasily. "Well, yeah, I suppose."

"Brent, I . . ." She placed a hand over her stomach to calm the emotions rioting through her. The idea of living with him was thrilling—and entirely too tempting. "I can't move in with you."

"Why not?" He scowled.

"Because it would completely negate my reason for coming to Houston."

"No, it wouldn't," he argued. "It would simply help me look after you while you're getting settled."

"Look after me?" She stared at him, struck by the irony that so many people depended on her for so many things, then turned right around and thought of her as incapable of taking care of herself. That Brent would be one of those people hurt. "I don't need anyone to look after me, Brent. What I need is a little freedom to take care of no one but myself for a change. And I can't very well do that by going straight from being my father's dutiful daughter to your live-in girlfriend."

He stared at her a moment, his face blank but his eyes filled with hurt. "Fine." He jerked her overnight case from the backseat and handed it to her.

She took it on reflex, then frowned at him in confusion. "That doesn't mean I don't want to see you."

"Whatever." Her garment bag came next. "It's your choice."

She took the bag, wishing she could take her words back as easily. When she realized what she was thinking, she stiffened. He was the one who should apologize, not her.

In spite of the anger, a sinking feeling settled in her gut. "Will I still see you tomorrow?"

He drew up short, clearly affronted. "I told you I'd drive you home, didn't I?"

She wrapped her arms about her bag, clutching it to her breast. "I can take the bus if you'd rather not."

"Christ." He started to turn away, then whirled back. "Why are you being like this?"

"Like what?" She stiffened. He was the one acting strangely!

"Just tell me what time to pick you up."

"Nine o'clock," she answered, not entirely sure she wanted him to drive her home if he was going to act this way.

"Fine, I'll see you at nine." He glanced at his watch. "Right now, though, I need to get to work. Let's get your stuff inside."

"I've got it." She blocked him with her shoulder.

"Okay, well, I'll see you in the morning then." He gave her forehead a quick, impersonal kiss, got in his car, and drove off.

She stared after him, not sure whether to be angry or hurt, and not sure which of those emotions Brent was feeling. But dammit, she refused to be treated as a helpless weakling.

"So you want to tell me what that scene outside was all about?" Melody asked as Laura lowered herself to sit cross-legged in front of the coffee table. They'd spent the afternoon rearranging Melody's studio, something Melody claimed she'd wanted to do for months but had needed an extra set of hands. Between Melody's vivacious chatter and the dogs getting underfoot at every turn, the tension in Laura's stomach had begun to ease. Something in Melody's tone put it right back, though.

"What?" she asked cautiously as she set a bowl of popcorn on the table and joined her friend on the floor. Karma, the female Rottweiler, sat before her with hopeful eyes glued on the popcorn as she licked her chops.

"That little discussion you and Brent had by his car," Melody said as she sprinkled sea salt over the bowl.

"Oh," Laura said softly. Growing up in a small town had taught her the dangers of confiding in the wrong person. But Melody didn't strike her as the judgmental, gossipy type. Sighing, she gathered a handful of popcorn. "Brent asked me to move in with him."

"Oh?" her friend prompted.

"I told him no."

"Boy, I'll bet that's a word he doesn't hear much!" Melody laughed as she tossed a kernel toward Chakra. The big male caught it in midair.

Laura started to nod in agreement, until a thought occurred to her.

"What?" Melody asked.

She glanced up, then shook her head. "Nothing."

"Ah, come on, Laura. We're roommates. And this," she waved a hand over the coffee table full of health food—"is a slumber party."

"Another first for me." A sad smile crept up on Laura. "I've never been to a slumber party."

"You're kidding." Melody shook her head, then took on a big-sister expression. "Well, the first rule is: All secrets, confessions, and fantasies about men will be shared. Rule number two: No tape recorders, taking notes, or little brothers allowed. And last but not least: No judgments tonight, or embarrassment tomorrow. So spill it."

Offering a kernel of popcorn to Karma, Laura tried to gather her thoughts. "I think you may be right, about Brent not hearing the word *no* very often. Not because he's irresistible, which, by the way, I happen to think he is, but because . . ." She frowned. "I don't think he leaves himself open to rejection very often."

"Then he must have really wanted you to move in with him."

"I don't know." As Karma settled beside her, Laura stroked the Rottweiler's coarse coat. "I think the offer surprised him as much as it did me."

"Are you sorry you said no?"

"Actually," she smiled. "I'm rather proud of myself. *No* is a word I've been trying to work into my vocabulary. I just . . ." The frown returned. "I just wish it didn't hurt to say it."

"Hurt others? Or hurt you?"

Laura looked at her. "It's the same thing, isn't it?"

"See?" Melody gestured toward her. "*This* is the problem with people who have too much blue light in their aura."

"What?" Laura laughed.

"People with blue auras. You're entirely too self-sacrificing and motivated by the needs of others. You have a very nice sky-blue aura, by the way, with pretty streaks of sunshine yellow."

"Thank you. I think." Laura frowned.

"I, on the other hand, am all orange and green. Not bad, but not very lofty." Melody spread her arms, showing off her caftan. "I keep wearing purple, hoping it will stimulate my spiritual chakra, but I fear I'm simply too entrenched in the physical plane. I like good food, hot sex, and a soft comfy bed. So sue me."

Laura hid a smile as she munched on the popcorn.

"You, however, don't have enough orange light." Melody tilted her head and squinted toward her. "Or at least you didn't. I'd say last night must have been pretty steamy."

"What makes you say that?" Laura froze with a kernel halfway to her mouth.

Melody raised her hands and danced her fingertips around Laura as if touching a field of light. "You have these little orange sparks floating around you, like fireflies."

"And?" Laura prompted, fascinated.

Melody tossed another piece of popcorn to Chakra. "Orange light comes from the sexual chakra. And yours has been sadly repressed since I met you. Good thing you and Greg finally parted ways, or he'd have snuffed the orange light right out of you."

Blushing, Laura glanced away, and noticed the time. Brent's newscast would be on soon. "Would you mind if I watch the news?"

"Lord, is it that late already?" Muttering about how time always seemed to get away from her, Melody fumbled through the seat cushions on the sofa for the remote control. Turning back to the TV, she began flipping channels. "Speaking of Greg, now *there's* a man who needs to get his chakras adjusted. His orange lights are completely out of whack."

Laura grinned. "I'll have to tell him that, the next time I see him."

"Now *that* I'd like to see." Melody gazed off into space. "I can just picture his baby-smooth cheeks turning all red, and those hazel eyes of his blinking behind those cute little glasses."

"You have a good memory."

"I'm a people watcher." Melody shrugged. "Speaking

of people and auras," she gestured toward the screen, "he certainly has an interesting one."

Laura turned, and her breath stilled at the sight of Brent speaking into the camera, so calm and collected. He seemed like a different man from the one she'd stood with on the sidewalk mere hours before, or the lover whose bed she'd shared last night.

"Can you really see people's auras?" she asked. She had been around enough holistic medicine to believe in the existence of auras. She wasn't sure she bought into the claims about prophecy and healing, but she wasn't ready to brush the entire idea off as hogwash, either.

"In person, yeah I can read 'em pretty well," Melody said. "Can't see a dang thing through a TV screen, though."

"Tell me about Brent's," Laura asked, mesmerized by the sight of him, even with the volume turned low.

Melody studied his image, as if to help her memory. "It's very colorful and full, like a rainbow. Except . . . he has this hole, a big black one surrounded by a ring of red, right over his heart chakra. I noticed it that day in Beason's Ferry, when he dragged you out of the club-house."

"He didn't drag me," Laura insisted.

Melody just smiled. "I noticed it again today, the minute he came through the gate. Then, when the two of you were talking out front, the red ring started glowing and pulsing like crazy."

"What does that mean?" Laura glanced at her friend.

"Well, the black hole is probably an old wound. Being near you seems to aggravate it, kind of like picking at a scab, which is what makes the red pulsate. But then, sometimes we have to pick at old wounds in order for them to heal. I just hope your blue lights don't get sucked down in his black hole in the process."

The phone rang before Laura could respond.

"I'll get it." With the dogs bounding after her, Melody headed for the kitchen. She returned a moment later. "It's for you. Dr. Velasquez."

"Oh!" Laura leapt up. "My last interview." With her heart racing, she sidestepped the dogs and snatched up the phone. She pressed a hand to her stomach to compose herself, took a deep breath, and answered.

"Yes!" she exclaimed minutes later and threw her arms around Melody in a spontaneous hug. "I got the job!"

"I thought you wouldn't know for a while."

"He decided not to wait. He wants me to start right away. Day after tomorrow, if possible. I'll need to go home to pack my things, get my car, and come right back."

"Why don't we take my van so I can help you move," Melody suggested.

"Really, you mean it?" Laura felt as if she were floating off the floor. Melody's van would allow her to get everything in one trip. Not that she had much to move, but her car was a fuel-efficient compact that would never hold all her plants, books, and boxes of clothes. "That would be great. As long as you don't mind— Oh! Wait, I need to call Brent to tell him I don't need him to come get me tomorrow. What time is it?" She glanced at her watch. "The news is still on. I'll leave him a message to call me."

Brent dropped into the chair at his desk. Now that the show was over, he had nothing to keep his mind off of Laura and the stupid way he'd acted that afternoon. What had possessed him to ask her to move in with him?

He was supposed to be taking things cautiously to ensure she stayed around longer than a couple of dates, so that the end, when it came, was relatively painless for both of them. Instead, he'd made a fool of himself, first by getting too protective, then by getting mad and storming off. If only she didn't tie him all in knots, he'd be able to think when he was around her.

"Good show, Michaels," Connie said as she took her seat at the desk facing his.

"Thanks." Nodding in acknowledgment, he picked up his phone. He had several messages in his voice mail. The last one was from Laura saying she had something to tell him and for him to call as soon as he could. From the excited tone of her voice, he assumed the news was good.

When he called, Melody answered the phone. "Wait a second, I'll get her."

"Brent!" Laura's voice came on the line, sounding as excited as she had in her message. "Guess what?"

You've changed your mind about moving in with me, he thought impulsively, then squashed that thought with a smirk. "I haven't a clue."

"I got the job! The one I wanted. With Dr. Velasquez, the pediatrician."

His stomach clenched. "Laura, I don't think it's safe for you to work in that part of town."

"Don't be silly. I'll do fine."

"You aren't even used to locking your doors, much less doing the hundreds of other things that will keep you from having your car stolen or getting mugged."

"Then I'll learn." Her voice turned surprisingly stern.

"You can't be serious." He battled back another surge of protective instincts. But dammit, this was Laura, and the thought of her getting hurt made his heart stop. "You had two other interviews today. Why don't you wait to hear from them before you make up your mind?"

"Because this is the job I want."

"Why do you do this?" He raked a hand through his hair. "You're always chasing after lost causes. When are you going to start looking after yourself for a change?"

"I *am* looking out for myself!"

Brent noticed people listening and dropped his forehead to his hand. "We'll talk about it when I pick you up tomorrow."

"Actually, that's why I called," she said in a stilted tone. "I don't need you to come get me after all. Melody's going to take me back to Beason's Ferry to get my things."

The coldness crept outward from his chest. "Laura, I said I'd take you home, and I will."

"No, really, it's not necessary. Melody has a van, so I'll be able to move all my stuff in one load."

He couldn't help but wonder if Melody's van was just an excuse not to see him again. Had he blown it that badly with Laura that afternoon?

"Are you there?" she asked.

"Yeah, I'm here."

Another silence fell. "Well, that's all I needed to tell you," she said at last.

"Fine. Look, I've got a lot of work to do here."

"I see." She hesitated. "I guess I'll let you go, then."

"Laura, wait." He pinched the bridge of his nose. "Call me when you get back in town . . . if you want to talk. All right?"

"Yes, of course." The silence grew thicker, more painful.

He tightened his grip on the phone, wishing he could reach out and grab hold of her, hold on so tight she'd never leave him. But he could feel her slipping through his fingers. "Drive safely, okay?"

"Okay." She paused. "I guess I'll see you when I get back then."

"Sure." He squeezed his eyes shut as he hung up the phone. *Stupid, stupid, stupid!*

"Hey, Michaels, you okay?" Connie asked.

"Yeah, I'm fine. Perfect." *If you count being a perfect ass as fine.* At least now he knew how he'd feel when Laura eventually dumped him—as if someone had opened up his chest and ripped his heart out.

CHAPTER
16

Laura stared out the front window of the old Chevy van, too numb to feel anything. A mere two days ago, this same view of sunshine and wildflowers had seemed so full of promise, in spite of her argument with her father about her moving.

At least she'd understood that argument and her father's reasons for trying to control her. Brent, however, made no sense. He was the one who'd encouraged her to stand up for herself—then, when she'd gone after what she wanted, he'd behaved as if she'd insulted him. And after she'd rearranged her whole life just to be near him . . . Although, that wasn't fair. She'd rearranged her life because it needed rearranging. If nothing else, she should thank him for adding the extra incentive to do what she should have done years ago.

"Hey, you okay over there?" Melody gave her a concerned look.

"Hmm?" She blinked to bring herself out of her fog and found Melody watching her. In spite of how late they'd stayed up the night before, the woman looked surprisingly fresh with the air conditioning blowing her long red curls. "I'm fine. Just a little tired."

"Sorry." Melody wrinkled her nose. "I guess we sort

of overdid it on movies and girl talk for your first slumber party."

"No, I enjoyed it. Really." Laura laid a hand on Melody's arm to convey her gratitude. After she'd spoken to Brent, she'd been too stunned even to cry. Melody had somehow understood she wasn't able to talk about it, so they'd stayed up most of the night watching *Lethal Weapon* movies and drooling over Mel Gibson.

Although as another mile marker passed by the window, she remembered that Brent wasn't the only concern she had to wrestle with. She still had her father to face. "Melody, I think I should warn you about something. My father isn't exactly thrilled about my moving to Houston, and he may be a bit . . . unpleasant today."

"Unpleasant?" Melody scowled. "In what way?"

"Not physically, or anything like that," she hastened to explain. "No, he's more the master of guilt. By the time we leave, you won't even have to open the door for me. I'll feel low enough to slide right under."

"Ah." Melody gave a knowing nod. "Sounds like my father."

"Oh?" Laura cocked her head to study her new roommate more closely. The woman wore her carefree style like a badge, but there were currents beneath the surface that hinted at deeper emotions.

"Yeah." Melody sighed. "My father could hurl guilt and belittling insults like fists, always knowing exactly where to jab to cause the most internal damage."

"Could?" Laura frowned at the past tense. "Is he no longer living?"

"Oh, he's still alive. We just live in two different worlds. Literally and figuratively." At Laura's puzzled look, Melody explained. "My father's in petroleum and has lived most of his life overseas. I grew up in the Middle East. That's how I met Roger."

"Roger? Your ex-husband, right?"

"Yeah. Colonel Roger Piper." Her voice caressed the name with fondness. "Of course, then he was a lowly second lieutenant. My family lived as civilians on base."

"That must have been fascinating, growing up in the Middle East," Laura said.

"It's not as exciting as it sounds." Melody's mouth twisted with distaste. "At least not if you're a girl. Every time you leave the base, you have to make sure your whole body is covered. Even then, there's not much they allow you to do other than shop. I was bored stiff."

Laura nodded, thinking it sounded a lot like growing up in a small town.

"Then I turned sixteen and discovered men." Melody flashed a wicked smile. "Ah, to learn that I, the stupid girl who couldn't do anything right, suddenly had tremendous power over male hormones simply by growing breasts."

"I know what you mean." Laura chuckled softly, then glanced from her moderate chest to the generous bosom that filled Melody's purple halter top. "Though not to the same degree, obviously."

"Hey." Melody stuck out her chest. "Like we always tell the men: It's the quality that matters, not the quantity."

"And you obviously got more than your share of both."

"We all have our crosses to bear." Melody sighed dramatically.

Laura laughed, enjoying the moment of closeness.

Melody shook her head, sighing. "You know, I'm not

sure why I picked poor Roger as my first serious target. He was quite a bit older than me, and not the best-looking guy on base. But the more he tried to treat me like some bothersome child, the more I turned on the heat.''

"I take it you got your man."

"Oh, yeah." Melody snorted. "Unfortunately, I also got pregnant."

After one quick sideways glance, Laura hid any show of surprise. A good portion of the girls in her graduating class had found themselves in the same predicament. As much as she loved children, she wouldn't have traded places with any of those girls. To go straight from childhood to raising children seemed even more stifling than the life she'd led.

"I expected Roger to be as horrified as I was," Melody said. "If he was, he never showed it. Instead, he went right to my father to ask for permission to marry me. I'll never forget him standing there taking all the blame, letting my father rant and rage at him. But the minute my father tried to turn on me, Roger nearly came unglued. I think that's when I fell in love with him."

"And the baby?"

Melody's gaze remained fixed on the road. "I lost it. I was never able to have another."

"Oh, Melody." Laura heart twisted. "I'm so sorry."

"Yeah, me, too." A sheen of moisture rose in Melody's eyes. Blinking it away, she pasted on a false smile. "You know, though, sometimes I think it was for the best. No, really. Not that I didn't want that baby like the very dickens once I got used to the idea, but the truth is I wasn't old enough, emotionally, to be a mother."

Laura swallowed the knot that had formed in her throat. "How long were you and Roger married?"

"Twenty years. We've been divorced nearly four." She let out a breath. "Which means I'm now pushing forty."

"Forty's not that old," Laura insisted.

Melody laughed, looking youthful even in the harsh Texas sun. "You're right. It's just that, here I am at an age when most people are trying to figure out how to pay their kids' college tuition, and I'm still lagging behind trying to figure out the basics, like what life is all about."

"I know how you feel," Laura sighed.

"I figured you did. Although you've got a whole lot more going for you upstairs then I ever did."

"Oh, I don't know about that." Laura smiled. Melody had a quirky sort of wisdom she found admirable. "So what happened with Roger?"

"Well, now we're back on the subject of guilt." Melody released a long breath. "I never could live with the fact that I'd trapped the poor man into marriage and stuck him with more of a daughter than a wife. I know he loved me, still does in some ways. And I tried to play the housewife bit." Melody shrugged. "But I hated every minute of it. Which taught me that no matter how badly you want to please someone, you can only put up a false front for so long. The whole military wife routine was smothering me. I didn't fit in with those people, and I hated myself for crying about it to Roger all the time."

"So what'd you do?" Laura asked.

"Became an artist," Melody said, as if such a feat were as simple as breathing. "Ironically, Roger was the one who encouraged me to start painting as a way to gain a sense of self-worth. Of course," Melody grinned, "he meant it to be a hobby, not a career. But the day I took my first real art class was the day I found myself. And the more I learned about who I was, the more I realized I didn't belong in the role I was trying to fill."

Laura frowned, thinking of her own role as Dr. Morgan's daughter and town do-gooder.

"The problem was," Melody said, "how could I possibly leave Roger? I mean, here was a man who'd nurtured me and encouraged me through my teens and twenties. He'd been more of a father to me than my old man ever was. And the minute I finally get my head on straight, I want a divorce? Now there's a guilt trip for you."

"What did you do?"

"I toughed it out for a few more years, until we were both so miserable, I realized I wasn't doing either of us any good."

"And?"

"And . . . I finally worked up the courage to tell him how I felt. There were lots of tears, and 'I'll always love yous,' and 'if you ever need anythings.' He helped me find a place to live, even painted it for me and gave me the dogs. Then one year later, nearly to the day, *pow*—he up and marries the widow of one of his air force buddies!"

Laura's eyes widened at Melody's vehemence. "Were you jealous?"

"I was stunned! The woman is boring with a capital B. She's one of those steady-as-she-goes types. Totally competent and self-sufficient. She drives poor Roger crazy—even crazier than I did. He can't stand not rescuing people. Although I have to say, it's nice seeing him get rescued for a change. I hate to admit it, but they're perfect for each other."

"But you're still jealous," Laura guessed.

"No, actually, I'm pissed."

"Why?"

"Think about it." Melody raised a hand. "After all the agony and guilt I put myself through, my leaving Roger turned out to be the best thing that ever happened to him. I was beating myself up for nothing."

Laura frowned over that revelation, wondering if the same would hold true in the case of her and her father. Could it be that sometimes you have to hurt people to do what's best for them? She wasn't sure she liked that notion, but it definitely gave her something to think about for the rest of the drive.

When they arrived at the house, Laura directed Melody to park around back, next to her own car. She noticed her father's car was gone and breathed a small sigh of relief.

"At least we'll be able to pack in peace," she told Melody as they climbed the steps to the back door. To her surprise, the knob didn't give when she turned it. "That's funny," she muttered. "We never lock this door during the day."

She dug into her purse for her seldom-used key. But the key didn't fit.

"What's wrong?" Melody asked.

"I don't know. Maybe the lock is rusted." Something cold settled in the pit of her stomach as she bent down to inspect the lock. It was as shiny as a new dime. Through the sheer curtain on the door's window, she saw a shadow move. "Clarice?" She knocked and waited as the woman shuffled toward her.

"Oh, Miss Laura Beth." Clarice's eyes filled with tears as she opened the door. "I'm so sorry."

Laura's heart lurched. "What? What's happened?" She stepped inside to soothe the woman. "Is it Dad? Is he sick?"

"No." The elderly maid sniffed, then thrust out a mutinous chin. "Though I wish he were. I'd like to put him in the hospital myself."

"What!" Laura straightened. "Clarice, what happened?"

"He's the one what had the locks changed. Made me promise to keep 'em locked till you got here." Her eyes filled again with tears. "And that's not all he made me do. All your things is packed." The woman's chin trembled. "I'm so sorry, miss, but if I hadn't done it, he'd have throwed everything out in the yard."

"My things?" Laura whispered. Turning toward the back hall, she hurried up the stairs with Melody right behind her. She halted in the doorway to her room. In the middle of the floor sat a pile of cardboard boxes. The four-poster bed had been stripped of the eyelet-and-lace bedding her mother had picked out for her. Even the ruffled canopy and matching draperies had been taken down. The vanity where she'd learned to put on makeup and the desk where she'd done her homework stood devoid of picture frames, perfume bottles, and knickknacks.

Through the open door of the closet, she saw only bare hangers. Numbly, she walked to the dresser, pulled open a drawer, and found it empty. Even knowing Clarice was the one who'd packed her things, the total invasion of privacy tore at something deep inside of her.

"I don't understand," she whispered, staring into that empty drawer. "How could he have done this?"

"He said—" Clarice hesitated. "He said to tell you that if you went through with this nonsense, you weren't to ever come back, and he didn't want no reminder of you left in the house."

All the guilt Laura had felt at leaving home vanished in a snap. She slammed the drawer closed and turned to face a startled Clarice. "Oh, he did, did he?"

She glanced around again and saw the ploy for what it was, a calculated move designed to have her running home, begging for forgiveness, and promising never to leave him alone again.

"Well, Clarice," she said with deadly calm, "you can tell my father that two can play at this game."

The maid blinked in confusion. "Excuse me, miss?"

"You heard me," Laura said, ignoring the quiver in her stomach. "Tell Dr. Morgan that when he decides he wants his daughter back, he knows where to find me. In the meantime, I have work to do." She turned to Melody. "Would you care to help me load these boxes?"

Melody gave her a questioning look, then nodded in understanding and support. "I'd be happy to."

"Clarice," Laura said as she lifted a box of her Madame Alexander dolls and set them aside to load last, "if you're not too busy, could you make some iced tea? I have a feeling we're going to build up quite a thirst loading all these boxes."

Clarice stared at her a moment, clearly startled that she wasn't caving in to her father's command. Then slowly a grin spread over her face, rearranging the wrinkles. "Yes, ma'am."

The maid turned and left with more spring in her step than Laura had seen in a long time.

Picking up one of the boxes filled with her clothes, Laura started down the stairs with Melody following suit. Trip after trip she hauled the bits and pieces of her life out of the house and stacked them beside the van. Melody took care of arranging the boxes in the cargo space that was usually used for hauling her booth and artwork across the country.

"How many more of these?" Melody asked as she hoisted a heavy box of books.

"One more trip ought to do it." Laura turned to head back into the house, but the sound of a car pulling into the drive stopped her. For a split second, her heart jumped with the hope—and fear—that her father had changed his mind, that he'd come home to confront her in person. Then she turned and saw Greg, in his familiar zipper-fronted pharmacist's shirt, stepping out of his conservative blue Chrysler.

She heaved a sigh, not sure if she was disappointed or relieved.

"Who is it?" Melody asked, poking her head out the back of the van. "Oh, him." She sounded unduly irritated. "This is all we need."

"Hello, Greg," Laura greeted him with poorly disguised impatience as he walked up the drive. They hadn't spoken since the day after the Homes Tour, when she'd told him she was moving to Houston.

"Laura Beth." He rushed toward her, concern lining his brow. "Clarice called to tell me you were here."

When he reached her, he enfolded her in his arms. She suffered the embrace in silence, telling herself not to take her anger at her father out on Greg. Still, dealing with Greg's stubborn refusal to accept their breakup as final was not what she needed at the moment.

"I'm so sorry, sweetheart," he whispered against her hair. "I can't believe your father is acting this way."

"I can."

He made a sound that was almost a laugh. "Yes, I guess I can, too. Stubborn old goat." He stepped back to study her face. "Do you want me to talk to him?"

"No, I don't want you to talk to him." She frowned at him incredulously. "I'm perfectly capable of dealing with my own father."

"Yes, but if he understood your move to Houston is just temporary, he'd quit taking it so hard."

"Greg . . ." She stared at him. "How many times do I have to tell you that this move is *not* temporary? The only part of this that's temporary is my rooming with Melody."

"And that's another thing." He straightened abruptly. "I can't believe you're going to live with that— that—"

"Hey there," Melody called cheerfully to Greg from inside the van. "Are you going to help, or just stand around and watch?"

Greg spun about, his cheeks turning bright red. "What are you doing here?"

"Helping Laura move." Melody leapt from the van and planted her hands on her hips. "What does it look like I'm doing?"

Greg's gaze swept over her purple halter top and skintight blue jeans. "Yes, but . . . you . . ." He drew himself up. "If you don't mind, this is a private conversation."

"Suit yourself." Melody shrugged, then turned around and bent forward to pick up another box. Greg's eyes widened as the worn denim of her jeans stretched over her shapely derriere. As Melody straightened, she cast him a knowing smile over her shoulder. "You two just pretend I'm not here."

"Laura Beth." Greg stepped toward her and lowered his voice. "Could we go inside to talk?"

She started to protest, then shrugged in defeat. "Sure. Why not. You can help me get the last two boxes."

Leading the way into the cool interior of the house, she told herself to stay civil and she'd get out of the house that much quicker. Eventually, Greg would have to realize she was serious about leaving Beason's Ferry.

"I can't believe you intend to live with that—that hippie," Greg muttered as they reached the top of the stairs.

That did it! Laura whirled on an unsuspecting Greg. "Melody Piper happens to be one of the nicest, most genuine people I've ever known. And I wish you and everyone else would give me a little credit for choosing my friends."

He took a step back, surprised at her outburst. *Well, fine!* She was tired of playing little-miss-walk-all-over-me.

"You don't have to take it personally," Greg said. "I only meant I can't picture the two of you rooming together, that's all. You're so . . . different."

"So what if we are?" she demanded. "There's a lot more to getting along with someone than being just like them. Heck, Greg, look at us. On the surface, you and I are just alike. We both come from small-town East Texas German families, but when it comes to the really important things in life, we've never seen eye-to-eye on anything."

"That's not true—"

"Yes, Greg, it is." Turning, she marched into her bedroom with him dogging her heels. He hesitated awkwardly at entering such a forbidden space. "For one thing," she picked up the box of dolls she'd left on the dresser and thrust it against his chest, "you happen to be a prude."

He staggered back, then straightened with indignation. "I am not."

She raised a brow. "Then why do you turn beet red every time you look at Melody Piper?"

His mouth moved soundlessly as color flooded his cheeks. "I—I do not turn beet red."

"Yeah, right." She turned to gather the last box off the floor, too emotionally drained to care what she said. "If you ask me, the subject of sex has always embarrassed you."

"I beg your pardon." The flush of color in his cheeks went a shade brighter. "If this is about the fact that I did not pressure you to consummate the physical part of our relationship right away, it's simply because I happen to have more respect for you than that."

"Respect!" She stared at him, remembering how long they'd dated before they'd gotten past the kissing stage. "Greg, have you ever heard the expression 'A lady in the parlor, a wanton in the bedroom'? Well, I hate to tell you this, but it goes both ways. Women don't always want a man to be a gentleman."

He stepped back, as if some blinding revelation had just struck him. "Are you saying this . . . phase you're going through is because I'm not hot enough between the sheets?" His eyes blinked behind his glasses. "Good Lord, Laura Beth, loving someone is about more than just sex."

"Maybe so." She shook her head. "But you act as if the two have nothing to do with each other."

He set the box back on the dresser, as if afraid he'd drop it. "That's it, isn't it? You really did run off to Houston to be with Brent Michaels—just like everyone's been saying."

So her father's prediction had come true; people were talking behind her back. "I left Beason's Ferry for a lot of reasons."

He turned to face her. "Do you deny Brent Michaels is one of them?"

She looked away, refusing to answer. What went on between her and Brent was nobody's business but theirs.

"All right," Greg said at long last. "I can accept that."

"Accept what?" She frowned, thinking he seemed a little too calm all of a sudden.

"Accept," he made a motion with his hand, "you needing to . . . you know."

"What?" she asked warily.

"Well, it's not as if this is that different than what most of us go through in college," he said defensively. "Only you never lived on campus, so you . . . well . . . never had a chance to get it out of your system."

" 'It'?" She arched her brow. "As in what? My wild oats?"

"All I'm saying—" he stepped toward her and set her box on the floor so he could take her hands in his—"is that I understand."

She stared at him, not believing her ears. "Understand what?"

"That you need to, well, see what's out there before you settle down." He gathered her hands close to his chest. "And I want you to know . . . I'm willing to wait until you do."

With a snort of laughter, she pulled away. "Let me see if I get this straight. You think I'm carrying on a wild

lascivious affair with Brent Michaels, and that's hunky-
dory with you, just as long as I come back to Beason's
Ferry to become your dutiful wife when I'm done?''

His brows furrowed. "This isn't the dark ages, you
know. We've advanced enough as a society to accept that
women have the same needs as men. And you have led a
rather sheltered life. I just think it's better for you to get
this out of your system *before* we're married.''

She stared at him, not sure whether to be angry or
amused. Even if they did have a chance to get back together, how could any man who truly loved a woman
accept what he was suggesting? It suddenly dawned on
her that no man could. She'd lived in a household filled
with infidelity long enough to know people didn't "accept" and "understand" that kind of betrayal without a
great deal of pain. Which meant Greg didn't love her. He
thought he did, but he couldn't possibly say such a thing
if he truly loved her.

All these months she'd agonized over how to let him
down gently, and he didn't even love her!

"I don't believe this!"

"What?" he asked with a frown.

Turning away, she made a wide gesture with her arm.
"All my life I've sacrificed my own dreams to smooth the
way for everyone else. No matter that smoothing those
rough spots left me bleeding inside. As long as everyone
else was happy, who cared about respectable, sensible
Laura *Beth*?''

She whirled back to face him. "Well, Greg, you know
what? I'm sick and tired of sitting here docilely while life
passes me by. I happen to have a whole field of wild oats
to sow, and I have every intention of sowing them. So you

go ahead and wait for me. You wait just as long as you like.

"But I'm telling you this." She poked her finger in his chest, pushing him backward until he plopped ignobly on her bed. "While you're sitting here turning gray, I'm going to be out there grabbing hold of life with both hands to follow it wherever it takes me."

With that, she scooped the box off the floor, gathered the one from the dresser, and marched from the room.

CHAPTER
17

While Laura was out of town, Brent decided that when she returned, he'd apologize for his strange fit of possessiveness and assure her such behavior was totally out of character for him, at least where women were concerned. He still didn't understand why he'd acted the way he had, but since he wasn't sure he wanted to understand this new quirk in his psyche, he chose not to examine the incident too closely.

That plan, however, went out the window when two days passed without a word. Bewilderment turned quickly to anger when two days turned into three. Had she decided to end their relationship because of one little fight? If that were the case, he'd be damned if he called her first. As juvenile as it sounded, even to his own mind, she'd agreed to call him when she got back to town, and he meant to stick to that agreement.

Besides, it wasn't like he didn't have other options for female companionship. One of the advertising sales reps at the station made eyes at him whenever they passed in the hall. Or he could call up the midday anchor at the rival station who he'd taken to a few awards functions. Except, the ad rep was too eager for his taste, and he'd never felt any real sparks for the anchorwoman.

Not like he'd felt with Laura.

By the weekend, he'd come up with several scenarios of what he'd say if Laura ever did get around to picking up the phone. First, he'd chew her out for worrying him; after all, she could be dead on the side of the road for all he knew. Not that he really believed that, but saying it would put her in the position of apologizing to him.

On Sunday evening, he worked up enough indignation to decide he wouldn't forgive her right away when she offered that apology. He'd also started wondering if maybe she really had been in an accident.

Monday and Tuesday he could barely concentrate on work as images played in his head of her broken body lying in some hospital bed with no one thinking to contact him.

Unfortunately, that little scene shared equal billing with one of her calling him up to say she'd changed her mind about moving to Houston and had decided to stay home and marry the blond wimp with the wire-rim glasses.

By Thursday night, his stomach was tied in so many knots, he didn't even care if she *had* decided to stay in Beason's Ferry and raise a dozen kids with another man—if only she'd call. He lay awake, staring into the darkness with sweat sticking the sheets to his body, wishing he knew how to pray. At that moment, he'd have offered God anything just to know Laura was safe.

As dawn crept through the window of his bedroom, he realized he couldn't go on like this. One way or another, he had to know she was all right—even if she chewed him out and called him an overprotective jerk and said she never wanted to see him again.

Besides, in addition to being worried sick, he missed

her. At some point during the lonely hours of the night, he realized a part of him had missed her for years. She was the only person he'd ever felt truly comfortable around. He was tired of having to watch every word he said for fear people would find out he was a fake. Laura already knew he was a fake, and for some reason she liked him anyway.

He needed that in his life. Seeing Laura again had made him realize that, for all his vast circle of acquaintances, he had no real friends. He was as alone in the world now as he'd been as a kid. And he was tired of being alone.

⟋⟍

Laura glanced up from her computer screen as Cathy, the physician's assistant, entered her office. "You all done for the day?" she asked.

"With the patients, at least," Cathy answered as she went to the locker behind Laura's desk to collect her street clothes. Since the doctor didn't see patients past noon on Friday, the staff frequently took a long lunch before returning to tackle any make-up work they had to do. "I promise you, though, things aren't always as crazy as they were this week. We just wanted to break you in right."

"You definitely did that." Laura chuckled, thinking of how hectic the week had been. For that, she was grateful, since she'd been too busy to think about Brent more than—well, a couple hundred times a day. Her brow puckered as she tried for the millionth time to understand what had happened between them. She couldn't believe things were over before they'd really even started. And all because of one argument. What else was she to think, though, when the days continued to slip by without one word from him?

"Oh, man, would you look at that," Cathy exclaimed from behind her. When Laura glanced over her shoulder, she found the nurse staring out the window that overlooked the parking lot. "Hey, Margarita!" Cathy called loud enough for the other nurse in the outer area to hear. "Come check this out!"

Margarita strolled into Laura's office, looking frazzled from a morning of sick children and fretting parents. "I'm done restocking the exam rooms," she told Laura. "Unless you have anything else for me to do, I'm headed for lunch."

"No, that's fine," Laura said.

"No, wait." Cathy waved a hand toward her coworker as she stared down at the parking lot. "You got to see this."

Dragging her feet, Margarita went to the window, then stiffened to full alert. "*Papacito!* Now that's what I call one gorgeous baby."

"Good enough to make me drool," Cathy said.

Laura cast the women a puzzled frown. While her coworkers frequently cooed over a particularly cute child, their voices had a decidedly avaricious edge to them.

"*Dios mio!*" Margarita stood on tiptoes to keep the "baby" in view as it moved beneath the window. "I think he's coming up here."

"No way!" Cathy jostled the other woman aside to get a better view. "What would *he* be doing coming into a place like this?"

"I don't know." Margarita craned her neck to see

over Cathy's shoulder. "But if he does come in, I get to take his temperature."

"Personally, I'd rather give him a temperature."

Laura stifled a grin as understanding dawned. During her first week and a half of work, the two women had provided her with an endless source of amusement. While they could bash men with the best of them, they quickly changed their tune whenever a particularly fine-looking male came into sight.

Apparently, the most recent cause of their combined high blood pressure moved out of the field of vision, for they gave twin sighs of disappointment and turned from the window.

"So, Laura," Cathy asked, "you going to Loose Willie's with us?"

Loose Willie's, she had learned, was a hole-in-the-wall bar where the staff went for their long Friday lunches and happy hour after work. "No, I still have to fill out this insurance appeal and make out the deposit. Maybe you could bring me something back, though."

"Not me. Dr. V gave me the afternoon off," Margarita said. "So come on, Laura, come with us."

Laura's first impulse was to say no. Aside from being busy, she had the distinct impression that Loose Willie's wasn't much more respectable than Snake's Pool Palace back in Beason's Ferry. But wasn't that what her declaration of independence was all about? To do what she wanted when she wanted with whom she wanted?

"You know," she said, smiling, "I believe I will join you."

Before Margarita could respond, the receptionist, Tina, poked her head around the door. "Psst!" Tina's eyes looked wide as saucers, and her voice came out as a frantic stage whisper. "Laura!"

"Yes, Tina?" Laura frowned. "What is it?"

"There's a *man* here to see you."

Laura's skin prickled as Cathy and Margarita went perfectly still behind her. "Did he give a name?"

"Didn't have to," Tina said. "I recognized him from the news. He's, you know, that Michael Somebody?"

Laura's heart skipped a beat, then galloped ahead. After a week and a half of willing the phone to ring, the last thing she expected was for Brent to show up in person. Had he come to make up or to break things off officially?

"Tell him I'll be right there," she managed in a hollow voice.

To give her body a minute to stop trembling, she restacked the patient charts on her desk. She could feel Cathy and Margarita watching her and feared they saw through her calm act. Nevertheless, she rose on shaky legs, smoothed her tailored linen skirt, and headed for the reception area.

The minute she turned the corner, she saw him, and her lungs swelled with air, making her feel light-headed. He stood in the middle of the cluttered room amid the jumble of toys and miniature plastic furniture. He had his hands in his pockets and a frown on his face. She'd never seen a man look so out of his element, yet so compellingly masculine. The only thing that kept her from bursting with joy at the sight of him was the scowl on his face as he took in the shabby decor. Apparently, his opinion of her chosen workplace hadn't changed.

"Hello, Brent," she said in her coolest voice, folding her hands before her.

His head snapped up. For one instant, relief washed over his features, followed by emotions too startling to name. But the look vanished quickly, hidden behind that slow, sexy smile he'd perfected over the years. His gaze traveled downward, making her aware of the new wardrobe she'd purchased. Though similar to her old style, the sage-green skirt, loose jacket, and white silk tank-top seemed brighter and younger than the colors she usually wore. She'd even splurged and bought high-heeled sandals to finish the outfit.

The journey of his gaze stalled halfway between the short hem of her skirt and her new shoes. "I, uhm—" he began, then blinked and raised his eyes to hers. "I was in the neighborhood."

The mischievous gleam in his eyes told her the words were a blatant lie. Brent Michael Zartlich was the most exasperating, confusing, unpredictable person she'd ever known. She should be furious with him for not calling. And yet, she realized with chagrin, she couldn't stay mad at the man any more than she'd ever stayed mad at the boy.

Not that she was going to let him off the hook that easily. She raised an eyebrow. "Were you now?"

"Actually," he tipped his head slightly, "it's a gorgeous day, and I was in the mood for a picnic. I understand you close at noon, and since I happen to know a great spot on Buffalo Bayou, I thought I'd try to persuade you to join me. A man can't have a proper picnic by himself." As he came slowly toward her, she saw something flicker beneath his playful expression, some glimpse of loneliness and need that tugged her heart. "So what would you say to joining me?"

He didn't stop approaching until he stood directly

before her. She caught the scent of his aftershave, the freshly laundered fragrance of his clothes, and a hint of musky maleness. The enticing scents awakened memories that made her knees tingle. She closed her eyes, but the lack of sight only made the images more vivid.

She remembered too clearly the feel of his hands caressing her skin, the touch of his lips, the sound of her own gasps of pleasure.

"Have lunch with me, Laura." The softly spoken words strummed her senses. This man disarmed her too quickly, too completely. Could her heart survive another effortless fall into his arms—only to be left alone again?

"I . . . can't. Really. Just because we stop seeing patients at noon doesn't mean I have the rest of the day off. Besides, I promised the nurses I'd go with them to lunch."

"Shoot, Laura," Cathy called from behind her, "Dr. V won't mind if you take a long lunch, and you can go with us anytime."

"There, you see," Brent said. "You're free after all."

"I don't know," she stalled, wanting to be with him but fearing it, too. He had the power to wound her too easily. And if he cared for her, if he really wanted to be with her, why hadn't he called?

"I see." He gave a resigned sigh. When she looked up, she saw his mask had fallen in place. Could he possibly be as hurt and confused as she? "Never mind, then. I just thought . . ."

He started to step away, stopped, then turned back. "Ah hell, Laura, have lunch with me. Just this once. I—" His gaze flickered toward the hallway behind her, and his voice lowered. "I have some things I really need to say, and I'd prefer to say them in private."

If he hadn't put the emphasis on the word *need*, she might have resisted.

"Very well." She sighed in exasperation, then gave him a mock scowl. "On one condition."

"Ah! Here it comes." He slapped a hand to his chest as if wounded. How quickly he bounced back to the playful charmer. "Okay. Go ahead. Shoot."

"You let me drive."

"You want me to leave my car in this neighborhood?" He looked so incredulous, she nearly laughed.

"No, silly. I meant you let me drive *your* car."

His eyes widened for several seconds, before he took a breath as if bracing himself. "All right. You're on."

Brent kept the conversation on nothing more important than Laura getting settled as Melody's roommate as she maneuvered the yellow convertible through the harrowing Houston traffic. Even if he'd wanted to discuss something more intimate, he was too busy gripping the armrest and trying to look calm. Although, he had to admit, Laura drove with a swift aggression that surprised him. She looked entirely at home, and sexy as hell, slumped low in the leather seat with one hand on the steering wheel and the other on the gearshift as the wind played with her hair.

When they reached the bayou, which ran like a river just north and west of downtown, he retrieved the bag of deli sandwiches and a blanket from the backseat.

"Oh, this is perfect," she said, climbing out of the car.

"Yes, I thought—" he glanced up in time to see her

remove her suit jacket; the silk tank-top beneath bared her shoulders and a good deal of her back— "you'd like it."

His thoughts remained scattered as he led them to a secluded spot in the shade. They spread a blanket on the grassy shore where joggers and bicyclists moved by in a constant stream. Yet there under the oak tree, watching the sunlight dance through the leaves to play upon her hair, he felt isolated, as if they existed in a world all their own.

As they ate, he racked his brain for how to ease into the speech he'd rehearsed. He glanced sideways and found her watching the ducks that scavenged for scraps along the bank. He wanted to stay that way forever, quietly sitting beside her with no hurt emotions to come between them. As the silence stretched on, though, he saw her picking at her sandwich more than eating it. They couldn't possibly be comfortable together until they cleared the air. He wanted that comfort—even more than he feared her answer to his opening question.

Pulling his eyes away from her nearly naked shoulders, he braced himself. "Laura, why didn't you call when you got back in town?"

A heartbeat passed before she turned toward him with a startled look. "What?"

He almost let it slide, almost said to hell with it, let's pretend the last week and a half never happened, that there was never an angry word spoken. Let's just go back to the morning we woke in each other's arms, and start again from there.

Instead, he forced himself to look at her. "When you got back from Beason's Ferry, why didn't you call me?"

"Brent . . ." A breathy laugh escaped her. "I was waiting for you to call *me*."

His brows snapped together in a scowl. "But we agreed on the phone that you'd call me when you got back."

"No, we didn't. All we said was we'd talk when I got back." She hesitated, then frowned. "Didn't we?"

"No." Something relaxed in his chest, like a fist that had been clenched too long suddenly letting go. "I specifically asked you to call me, *if* you wanted to talk about . . . things. So when you didn't call, I assumed . . ." He let the rest trail off in embarrassment. God, he felt like an idiot. Of course Laura would expect the man to do the calling.

"Oh." The whispered word echoed the regret in her eyes. "I . . . I'm sorry. I guess I was upset and wasn't really listening."

He shook his head, disgusted with himself. "Actually, I think that's my line—the one about being sorry. Laura, I—"

"No, don't apologize." She pulled away when he started to reach for her. Wrapping her arms about her knees, she let her head fall forward. "God, I can't believe this." Sad laughter rippled from her. "All this time, I thought you didn't want to see me again."

"I never meant for you to think that." He cringed inwardly as he realized she'd felt as awful all week as he had. All because of his stubborn pride. Not that she wasn't just as stubborn, but still—"I should have called. I'm sorry."

"It's okay." She sighed. "Maybe it was even for the best."

"Oh?" he prompted.

"Yeah." She tossed the rest of her bread to the ducks. "After what happened at home, I've had a lot to think about this last week. I needed some time alone."

"I take it your father has been up to his usual tricks?"

"You might say that." Her shoulders sagged. "Only this time, he's come up with a little different angle. Instead of clinging to me, he's washed his hands of me completely."

"What do you mean?" A frisson of alarm snaked up his spine.

When she finally spoke, she did so without turning to face him. "The day I left to bring you your car, he told me if I walked out the door, I'd never be welcomed back through it. Apparently he was serious. When I got home," her muscles shifted, as if she were withdrawing inside herself, "I found the locks on the doors changed and all my belongings packed in boxes."

"You can't be serious." His body tensed for battle. Though he'd never particularly liked her father's possessive attitude, he'd never thought the man was cruel. Looking at Laura's curved spine, though, he saw the signs of deep pain. "What the hell did he say to you?"

"Nothing." She turned her head to rest her cheek on her knees and regarded him with resigned eyes. "He wasn't even there. He didn't have to be. His message was clear enough—either I move back home, or I'm no daughter to him."

"That self-centered, manipulative son of a bitch." He clenched his fists, wishing he could hit something.

"I know he seems that way." She sighed. "But there are things about him you don't understand."

"There's no excuse for the way he treats you, Laura. There never has been."

She smiled at him—a sad smile that tore at his heart. "Not even love?"

"This isn't love. This is sheer domination."

"He's just trying to protect me."

"Protect you from what? Growing up?"

She looked away. "From the world that killed the one person he loved more than anything else."

He stared at her in confusion, realizing she wasn't so much resigned as emotionally exhausted. For that he could happily wring her father's neck. He couldn't believe that in addition to his not calling her all week, she'd had this to deal with. Alone.

"Do you remember my mother?" she asked after a moment.

"Not really," he answered distractedly. He found it difficult to carry on a casual conversation with his blood doing a slow boil. "I know there were some rumors about her, but I always discounted them. She was so beautiful and gracious. You know, the perfect wife for Beason's Ferry's most respectable citizen."

"Yes she was. But that doesn't mean the rumors weren't true. In fact, I doubt the folks in Beason's Ferry know the half of it. Even in a small town, some skeletons can remain safely hidden in the closet." Her manner grew hushed and still. "There were a lot of skeletons in the house where I grew up."

She seemed so fragile, he feared she would shatter at the slightest touch. Forcing his anger aside, he leaned forward and draped his arms over his knees. "Care to tell me about them?"

She remained silent so long, he knew the thoughts in her head were ones she'd never shared with anyone else.

"I think my mother was . . . abused . . . sexually as a child. By . . . her father."

He forced himself not to react, to remain perfectly still even as everything in him rebelled at the thought that something so ugly had touched Laura's life.

"I think," she continued slowly, "that's why she was so self-destructive. No matter how much my father loved her, and he truly did love her, she never thought she was worthy of him."

He watched silently as she stared into the distance.

"They met when Dad worked at a hospital here in Houston. She'd just been kicked out of college and sent home. Her parents, my grandparents, live on a ranch north of here. I don't really know them. Dad has always refused to let them anywhere near me."

"Good choice," Brent said with controlled calm.

"Anyway, my parents met when my mother was brought into the hospital. She'd been beaten up."

"By her father?"

"No, just some man," Laura said the words quietly, without meeting his eyes. "I doubt if she even knew his name. He was just someone she'd picked up in a bar. My father patched her up and sent her on her way. A week later she was back in the emergency ward from an overdose of barbiturates."

Laura sighed at some far-off memory. "I always thought of her as a beautiful bird with a broken wing. Dad never could resist healing the wounded. He tried everything he could to save her from her own self-loathing."

"I take it his efforts didn't work?" Brent asked softly.

"For a time, I think they did. When they first married and he brought her to Beason's Ferry, I think she was better. At first people saw her as my dad did. Kind-hearted, generous, gracious. But that's not how she saw herself. And by the time she died, she'd made sure other people saw her the same way she saw herself."

She looked right at him. "Isn't it strange that how we see ourselves and how others see us as is often so at odds?"

The truth behind the question made him frown, for he'd always seen Laura's life as the opposite of his own, only to learn now that she'd had her own demons to conquer. Yet maybe he had sensed this sadness and this strength inside her. Maybe this was the common ground that had let them be childhood friends.

"How did *you* see her?" he asked.

"She was a good mother. The best," she said with conviction. "I like to think she was happy when she was around me. She seemed happy."

"How could she not have been?" He smiled. "Any mother would be proud to have you as her daughter."

Laura looked away. "I wasn't enough, though. Nor was Dad. Not enough to make her feel whole."

"Do you blame yourself for her death?"

"No." She sighed. "But Dad blames himself. He knew she was clinically depressed, but he thought he could treat her himself. He thought he could be everything to her—doctor, counselor, husband. She tried to get well for him. I know she tried."

Laura shook her head. "That's why she never slipped up in Beason's Ferry. Whenever she went on one of her self-destructive binges, she'd go to Houston, or Galveston, or anywhere she could lose herself in alcohol and drugs and men."

She fell silent for a while, and he waited patiently, sensing she needed to tell him more.

"Do you know how she died?" she asked at last.

"In a boating accident, wasn't it?"

Laura nodded. "Except there was a lot more to the story than ever reached home. The yacht she was on belonged to some Galveston drug dealer. Apparently, he was throwing a wild weekend party that got out of control. His yacht collided with another boat at full speed, killing several people—even though he escaped without a scratch." She sighed to expel the bitterness that had crept into her voice. "I lost more than my mother that day. I lost a part of my dad. I saw it on his face the day he brought her body home for burial. Something inside him had died."

"Is that why he's so overprotective of you? He's afraid he'll lose you, too?"

She glanced toward him. "I'm all he has left, Brent."

"I still say it's no excuse."

"Actually, I agree." Straightening her legs, she rested her weight back on her hands. "However—I also know he isn't solely to blame. He wanted my life to be perfect, so I fell into the habit of pretending that it was." Dropping her head back, she stared at the sky. "But then, who would have guessed that living in a perfect bubble wouldn't be enough?"

He stared at her, distracted by the graceful arch of her neck. She turned her head sideways and smiled at him. "Truth is, I've discovered that I'd rather fall on my face a few times than never experience anything outside Beason's Ferry. And that's what he can't take: the thought of me suffering one moment of pain."

Brent's gaze lingered on the soft curve of her cheek

before meeting her eyes. "Can't he see that he's the one hurting you?"

"Probably." She lowered her weight to one elbow, turning slightly toward him. "And if I know Dad, he's home right now steeped in guilt, with no idea how to make everything right again. And sadly, I can't tell him not to worry, or assure him that I'm okay."

"Why not?" He fought the urge to lean back on his elbow as well so he could recline alongside her.

She shrugged. "He made the mistake of drawing this stupid line in the sand. For once in my life, I refuse to toe the mark. If he wants to resolve things, he's the one who has to make the first move."

"But are you really okay, Laura?" He studied her closely.

"Yes. No. I don't know." She gazed off toward the water. "I guess I'm more confused than anything. About a lot of things. Like why we go through life playing so many games. Why can't we just let down our guard and be ourselves?"

"What do you mean?" He sat up a bit straighter and wished she'd do the same, especially since her skirt had started to inch up her thigh.

"It just seems like we all pretend to be someone we're not, or that we see people as something other than who they are." She rolled to her back, so her weight rested on both elbows, and her silk tank-top stretched enticingly over her breasts. "And I'm the worst of all. While I was trying so hard to pretend my life was perfect, everyone started seeing me that way. Dr. Morgan's daughter, so respectable, responsible, so kind and good. *Blah!*"

"It's not an insult," he said, trying not to laugh at her expression. "Besides, you are those things."

"Maybe. Some. But it isn't enough." She looked up at him, and a devious smile lit her eyes. "Sometimes what I really want to be is exactly the opposite."

"Excuse me?"

"Just once, I'd like to walk into a room and have every man turn and look." She seemed to savor the image for a moment, while he struggled not to.

Against his will, a memory stirred through him of how she'd looked and felt lying beneath him, their bodies tangled in passion. He cleared his throat. "I have a feeling men notice you more than you think."

She tipped her head to give him a sidelong look. "Do you think wanting to be bad makes a person bad? I don't mean being really bad, just a little bit bad?"

He shifted his weight to accommodate his unexpected arousal. Didn't the woman have any idea how sexy she was? Or that talking about it was turning him on? "I assure you being a little bit bad can be a lot of fun at times."

"Really?" She sat up. "Like when?"

He laughed. "Oh, no, you aren't going to sucker me into that conversation."

"Oh?" She blinked in a way that made him want to lay her down and show her just how bad he could be. "You think if you share some wild tale about you and some other woman that I'll get jealous?"

"As we say in the news business: I have no comment."

"Fuddy-duddy." She wrinkled her nose.

"To answer your *earlier* question—no, I don't think

being a little bad now and then makes a person bad. It's probably healthy, in fact."

"That's what I've been thinking."

"I'm not exactly sure I like the sound of that." He scowled at her, thinking her father had had the right idea after all about keeping her sheltered.

"Well," she grinned, "you don't exactly have much say in the matter, now do you?" The words rolled off her tongue as a jest but fell into silence between them.

"True." His scowl deepened. "Which is why I wanted to talk to you."

"About what?" She turned wary.

He took a breath for courage. "Us."

"Oh?" Her smile faded, and he nearly changed his mind. But no, he'd made a decision last night, and he meant to stick to it.

"Laura," he said, "I don't want you to take this the wrong way, but I don't think we were meant to date."

She regarded him for a moment, then wrapped her arms around her legs. "I see."

"It's not what you're thinking," he hastened to say. "This has nothing to do with your desirability, or how much I enjoy your company. In fact, I'd like to go on seeing you, but I think it would be best for both of us if we see each other as friends."

"You want to be friends?"

"Absolutely. Trust me on this that platonic relationships last longer than lovers, and I'd like for what we have to last."

She studied him with narrowed eyes that probed too deeply for his comfort. He prayed she couldn't see what he really wanted, which had very little to do with being friends and everything to do with stripping that skimpy tank-top off her luscious little body.

Finally, she nodded. "All right."

"You agree, then?" He frowned, wondering why her words didn't make him happy. There just didn't seem to be any pleasing him lately. "No problem? No anger? No tears? No telling me to go to hell?"

"Nope." She gathered up the deli wrappers and crumpled them in her hand before tossing them into the bag. "Not even a pout."

"Okay," he said, thinking he should feel a lot more relieved than he did. "So how about tonight?"

"What about it?"

"Well, it is Friday." He shrugged. "Some of the news crew is planning to get together at Chuy's after work." Or at least they would be after he invited everyone.

"After work?" She stopped cleaning up their picnic long enough to look at him. "But you don't get off until midnight."

"So?"

"Don't you think that's kind of late to start your evening?"

He flashed her a teasing grin. "Now, how are you going to be bad if you aren't even willing to stay up past your normal bedtime?"

"You know, you're right." A light dawned slowly over her face, turning her lips up in a mischievous smile. "In fact, tonight would be perfect."

Now why did that sound as if she were planning something he wouldn't like? "You'll meet me, then? At midnight?"

"Absolutely." The mischievous look turned calculated. "I wouldn't miss it."

CHAPTER
18

So Brent wanted to go back to being just friends, did he? Laura snorted at the absurdity of that notion as she pulled into the parking lot of Chuy's, a trendy Mexican restaurant, fifteen minutes after midnight. She and Brent had stepped too far over the line for her to go back to thinking of him as "just a friend" even if she wanted to. Which she most certainly did not. She wanted more from Brent than that. Much more.

When she spotted his car, she released her breath in a rush. He was already there, just as she'd hoped. Now, if she could work up the courage to go through with her plan, she and Brent would be back on very "un-friendly" terms before the night was over.

Pulling into a parking space, she cut the engine of her economical compact. She gripped the steering wheel and assured herself she looked sexy, not vampish. The dress was a simple cotton-knit sundress: a hot red, form-fitting sundress she'd seen a week ago when she'd gone on the first shopping spree for her new life. She'd been tempted to buy it at the time but hadn't been able to justify the extravagance while shopping for a new work wardrobe.

Today, however, Brent's well-intentioned words had made her so angry—not angry at him, but at the image she'd lived under for too long—she'd driven to the Galleria after work, marched into the shop, and plunked down her credit card without even trying on the dress. Not until she got home and slipped into the clingy red knit did she realize just how sexy it was. Or maybe she just wasn't used to wearing something that so blatantly stated "Look at me boys, look at me and drool."

Glancing in the rearview mirror to check her makeup, she tried to visualize herself walking into the crowded restaurant. No, not walking, prowling. That's the word Melody had used in the last-minute pep talk Laura had received when she'd almost lost her nerve. "When you get to the restaurant," Melody had said, "stroll through the door like the queen of cats deigning to prowl among the kittens."

A nervous flutter rose up from her stomach, like a thousand butterflies trying to escape through her throat. *I can do this*, she told herself. Besides, what were her choices? She could go into the restaurant and possibly make a fool of herself while trying to wake Brent up to a few basic facts of life. Or she could chicken out, go home, and spend the rest of her life as a respectable spinster.

She'd already decided that if she couldn't have the man she deeply, passionately wanted, she didn't want anyone. Brent was that man. And if it took playing a few games to get him, she'd put everything on the line, bend the rules, and even cheat if she had to. Whatever it took to win.

Clinging to her resolve, she opened her car door and swung her high-heeled, red leather–sandaled feet to the pavement. As she stood and locked her car, the short skirt swished against her naked thighs. She still couldn't believe she'd let Melody talk her into going out in public with nothing on beneath her dress. "Trust me, Laura. Going without panties will make you feel so wicked, you'll positively exude pheromones."

She didn't know about her pheromones, but both sets of her cheeks were definitely blushing as she strolled across the parking lot.

Nervously, she smoothed the bodice of the dress that hugged her from breasts to hips. A cuff at the top formed off-the-shoulder sleeves. Hopefully, in a place like Chuy's, which was known for its garish decor, no one but Brent would notice her bright red dress. That brief hope died when three college-age boys sitting on the patio turned to stare. One of them let out a long low whistle. She wasn't sure if she should feel encouraged or offended.

Walk slow, she reminded herself as she strode through the bright purple door with the lemon-yellow molding, into a montage of noise, velvet Elvis paintings, and brightly painted wooden fish hanging from the ceiling. A mirrored ball spun in the middle of the bar area, reflecting light on the trunk of a 1950s pink Cadillac that served as a food buffet.

"How many?" the frazzled hostess asked over the clamor of noise bouncing off the orange concrete floors.

"Actually, I'm meeting a group of people," Laura shouted back. So much for keeping her voice low and sultry. "From KSET?"

"Oh, yeah, they're in the back-corner booth."

Following the direction the hostess pointed, she spotted a half-dozen people crowded into a large semicircular booth that looked like it had come from a Las Vegas lounge. Brent sat in middle of the horseshoe bend, the obvious center of attention.

She stopped for a moment, caught by the sight of him

as he enthralled his audience with some tale. Even in the tacky restaurant, she was struck by an image of King Arthur holding court at his fabled round table. He was so at ease, so obviously admired, her heart swelled with pride. This was what he'd been born for, to be a leader among his peers.

His gaze flickered past her toward the door, then shot back. An arrested look came over his face as he stared at her, his eyes drinking in every inch, first in disbelief, then with a flare of hunger that reached across the crowded restaurant to burn her skin. Never in her life had she felt so attractive, confident, and nervous all at the same time.

A fist of desire struck Brent right in the gut when Laura began walking toward him. Though the dress covered her discreetly, it hugged every curve, from her gently rounded breasts and the inward dip of her waist to the subtle flare of her hips. Below the midthigh hem, a pair of spike-heeled red leather sandals showcased her long shapely legs.

The room seemed to blur as she moved in the slow, purposeful strides of a woman who knew she could have any man she wanted. Only, her eyes stayed focused on him, as if she'd singled him out among all the other males who were no doubt drooling in her wake. He'd never seen that devious I-want-you look smolder so strongly in Laura's eyes. What game was she up to tonight?

And what had she done to her hair? It floated about her face like a fluffy golden-white cloud that somehow made her lips look fuller and her eyes bluer. He wanted to drag her into the nearest bathroom and wash that kiss-me-red lipstick off her mouth. Either that or lick it off with his tongue.

Beside him, someone asked a question, but the words

efused to register in his brain. As Laura came to stand
directly before the table, a slight hush fell over the booth.
Some of the boldness slipped from her expression, revealing the uncertainty beneath. In spite of the seductive
dress, an innocence still surrounded her, a sweetness that
always reached inside his chest and grabbed hold of his
heart.

"Hey, Michaels." Connie snapped her fingers before
his face. "You in there?"

"Huh? What?" He blinked to find several pairs of
amused eyes glancing between him and Laura.

"Are you going to introduce us?" Connie asked. "Or
are you planning to gawk at the woman all night?"

"Oh. Yes." He shook his head to clear his senses, then
struggled to get out of the booth, which forced half the
occupants to stand and move out of his way. Thankfully,
he managed to keep his napkin discreetly held before him
as he made the introductions. "Everyone, this is Laura
Morgan. Laura, this is Keshia Jackson, my coanchor, and
her fiancé, Franklin."

Keshia flashed one of her winning smiles that always
made her teeth appear startling white against her smooth
mocha skin. Her stockbroker boyfriend gave Laura a
friendly nod, then shot Brent an amused look, as if he
knew exactly how Brent felt, which he probably did. Being engaged to a knockout like Keshia couldn't be easy.

Brent scowled at the remaining males in the party as
he finished the introductions. "This is Jorge, one of our
cameramen, and his buddy Kevin, who works in one of
the control rooms."

"Hi." Jorge waved at her. "We met, remember? Behind the clubhouse?"

Laura's cheeks flushed at the reminder of when Jorge caught them kissing.

"And this," Brent said hastily to smooth over the moment, "is my producer, Connie Rosenstein."

"Sooo," Connie grinned, "you're Laura Beth, Brent's high school sweetheart from Beason's Ferry. Brent has told us absolutely nothing about you."

"Actually, there's nothing to tell." Laura leaned forward to shake Connie's hand, a move that displayed a mouthwatering length of bare thigh. At least she wasn't wearing stockings. He definitely would have had to drag her off then, to the nearest phone booth or dark corner. In a voice that carried a hint of mischief, Laura went on to explain, "Brent and I were just friends growing up. Still are. Isn't that right, Brent?"

He snapped his gaze away from her legs to find her smiling at him over her shoulder. He narrowed his eyes in warning. "Yeah. Friends."

"Come have a seat," Connie ordered, waving at Laura with her cigarette. Jorge tried to slip in behind her, but Brent stepped in his path with a pointed look that even a hormone-crazed kid couldn't miss. Sliding into the booth beside her, he found himself wedged into the back with Laura on one side, and Jorge and Kevin on the other.

"So, Michaels," Franklin said from across the table, "you going to finish that story?"

He suddenly remembered the story he'd just started when Laura had come in. "Uh, no, I think I'll save that one for another time."

"Ah, come on!" Kevin, a pimple-faced college kid, whined. "You were just getting to the good part."

He glanced about at the circle of expectant faces and tried to think of a less racy story to substitute.

"Yeah," Connie gestured with her chin, "you were just about to tell these kids why Sandra Wilcox was traded to a sucky market in Idaho from a prime-time slot in Denver."

"Sandra Wilcox?" Laura asked Connie.

"She used to be a hotshot newscaster at the last station where Brent worked," Connie explained.

"Oh, what happened?" Laura asked in total innocence.

"Yeah, Michaels, what happened?" Connie asked in that teasing tone that alternately amused and aggravated Brent.

"You know perfectly well what happened, Connie," Brent said with a smile as taunting as hers.

"Of course, I do. But these youngsters haven't heard the story yet, which is why you were about to fill their impressionable little ears with a great piece of newsroom gossip."

"Hey, we ain't that impressionable!" Kevin complained. " 'Sides, it ain't like everyone and their dog don't already know how she got that anchor job."

"Well, it sure wasn't for her talent," Keshia put in with disgust.

"Oh, I don't know." Jorge snickered. "From what I hear, she has a very talented mouth."

"Not for reading the news, though," Keshia said.

"Well, if y'all are going to gossip, you might as well get the story straight," Brent said.

" 'Y'all,' " Connie mimicked as she leaned toward Laura. "I just love it when he talks like a Texan."

Laura's eyes shone with laughter as she turned toward him. Beneath the table, their bodies pressed together from hip to knee. He could feel her heat seeping through the thin bit of cloth separating them. Determined to ignore the effect that heat was having on his groin, he concentrated on his story. "As most of you obviously know, Sandra got the anchor job by, uhm—"

"Screwing," Kevin supplied with a grin.

"*Sleeping with* the news director," Brent corrected.

"The news director? As in Ed Kramer?" Keshia's lip curled. "Lord, she must have *really* wanted the anchor job. That man is gross."

"Maybe," Connie said. "But we *are* talking evening anchor in a major market."

"True," Keshia allowed. "But still gross."

"Well, apparently," Brent said, "Sandra thought so too, because at the same time she was getting Kramer's jollies off, she was having her own fun with one of the cameramen."

"You camera guys have all the fun." Keshia blew Jorge a kiss that made him blush.

"So what happened?" Kevin asked eagerly. "They get caught with their pants down?"

"Actually . . ." Brent felt the heat of embarrassment creep up his neck. Why had he thought an evening out with Laura and his coworkers was a good idea? She'd probably want nothing to do with him after meeting these bozos. He should have kept the group down to just Keshia, Franklin, Laura and himself. But that would have been too much like a double date. And this was not a date. It was *definitely* not a date.

Brent forced his mind back to a story he wished he'd never started. "They didn't exactly get caught in 'person.' You see, Sandra and the cameraman were into some pretty kinky stuff, including him filming her playing with an interesting selection of, uhm, toys."

"Filming?" Jorge sat up straight. "As in, up close and personal?"

Brent shook his head, laughing in spite of his embarrassment. "We are talking major up close and personal."

"Cool!" Kevin nodded.

"And how would you know?" Keshia demanded of Brent. "A little backroom bragging among the boys?"

"No." Brent drew the word out to build suspense. "I know because the idiot cameraman used station equipment and forgot to take the tape out after one of their sexathon weekends."

"No way!" Keshia screamed.

"Score two points for the cameraman!" Jorge shouted.

Brent glanced at Laura and found her hand clamped over her mouth, her eyes dancing with laughter. She really was an intriguing contrast in her sexy red dress with that becoming shade of pink on her cheeks.

"Tell them the rest," Connie said over the excited chatter.

"There's more?" Kevin leaned forward.

"Yeah," Brent chuckled. "The guys in the control room found the tape and made copies, which they sent to friends in stations all over the country."

"No way, dude!" Kevin nodded his head to some tune only he could hear. "Too cool!"

"Jeez," Keshia snorted. "No wonder they got fired."

"Actually, I think the cameraman still works there."

"What!" Keshia's tone turned militant. "They trade Sandra to some Podunkville station in Outer Mongolia but keep on the cameraman? That's the most blatantly sexist thing I ever heard."

"True, but then, we live in a sexist world, Keshia," Brent pointed out. "Get used to it."

"Brent Michaels, if I thought for one moment you actually felt that way, I'd kick you under the table."

"Sorry, sweetheart." Brent grinned. "I'm not into kinky stuff."

"Yeah, right, and I bet you didn't stand around the control room with the rest of the men drooling over Sandra's homemade porno flick either."

"Hey—" he held up his hands— "I'm innocent!"

"Like hell you are. Bunch of sexist pigs," she mumbled, than turned on her fiancé. "And just what are you grinning at?"

"Nothing, baby," Franklin held his hands out much in the manner Brent had. "I'm not saying a word."

"You better not be saying anything, if you know what's good for you."

Franklin leaned over to nuzzle Keshia's neck. "I guess this means we won't be borrowing Jorge's camera tonight."

"Not on your life," Keshia snapped. "And don't you be sneaking that hand toward me under the table, Franklin Prescott. Frank-*lin*!"

Keshia screeched and squirmed as Franklin tickled her without mercy.

Chuckling, Brent glanced at Laura. She too was laughing at the couple's antics, but when her eyes met his, her laughter stilled. Too clearly he could feel her thigh pressing against his as his gaze ran over her slender neck, the curve of her bare shoulders. At the base of her throat, her pulse throbbed. He longed to lean forward and kiss her there, to feel her heart beat against his lips. As if reading his mind, her skin flushed. He watched her throat move as she swallowed.

Dragging his eyes upward, he saw the hunger burning in her gaze. He didn't want her to look at him with such naked desire, as if remembering all the ways they'd touched each other's bodies. As if she wanted them to touch that way again.

No, he didn't want her to look at him that way, but nothing in his life had ever aroused him more. Only, if he gave in to the hunger that burned between them, would she still look at him like that a month from now? A year? Or would she turn away in anger when she realized he could satisfy her body but not her heart?

Women like Laura deserved the best a man could give. His best would never be good enough, no matter how much he wanted it to be. He knew his limitations, accepted his flaws.

Unfortunately, that didn't stop his body from craving hers.

CHAPTER
19

After one long, heated look, Brent turned back to his friends and proceeded to ignore Laura for the rest of the evening. She sat beside him, sipping her margarita, wondering what to do next. Her plan had been to flirt with him, not outrageously, but enough for him to admit that the sparks that flew between them went beyond mere friendship. But how could she flirt with a man who spent the entire evening swapping news stories with his co-workers?

She glanced at Franklin, the only other nonnews person in the group. Unfortunately, Franklin was seated at the far side of the booth with a satisfied expression on his face. From the subtle way Keshia kept shifting in her seat, Laura imagined the interchange going on beneath the table was as lively as the conversation above.

If only she had the courage to "talk" to Brent that way, to tell him she wanted him with the caress of her hand along his thigh; to ask him if he wanted her too by nudging his knee with her own. Would he answer yes by increasing the pressure of his leg against hers? Or would he shift his body to break contact?

With a sigh, she took another sip of the frothy lime and tequila drink. She'd had such high hopes for this evening, but nothing was going as she'd planned. Staring into her nearly empty glass, she could see her whole life stretching out before her, with her sitting quietly in the midst of a party while everybody around her had fun. Oh, but let those same people need a hard worker to organize a charity bazaar, and Little Laura Beth was the first one they'd turn to.

It wasn't until her second margarita came that she started to ask herself *why* she put up with being so blithely dismissed. And why on earth was she sitting there letting her well-laid plans crumble to pieces? She'd had Brent's attention when she first walked through the door. Was she willing to call it quits at the first obstacle he presented? She'd never caved in at the first sign of rejection when she'd done fund-raising. She'd learned, when going for donations, never to accept the first no because sometimes yes was just a word away. If she could forge ahead through uncomfortable situations for other people's benefit, why couldn't she do the same for herself?

She glanced at Brent's profile as he and Keshia debated the wisdom of some reporter who'd broken a story without confirming his facts with a second source. She loved this man. And if she didn't do something, she'd spend the rest of her life wondering if there could have been something more between them than one brief, wondrous night of passion if she'd only pushed him a little more.

Now was her chance. Maybe her only chance. *Just do it*, she told herself.

Even though she took a deep breath to strengthen her resolve, moving her hand from her own lap to his was the hardest thing she'd ever done. She hesitated midair, her fingers trembling. She felt as if her whole life hinged on this one action, or rather his response to it. If he shifted away from her, she'd never have the courage to try again. She'd likely never have the courage even to face him again, but if she didn't try, she'd never know.

Before she could change her mind, she lowered her hand to his thigh. His muscles tensed beneath her palm as his lower body went perfectly still. Though his conversation with Keshia barely faltered, she felt his attention shift toward her. An eternity passed as she waited for him to glance her way. She'd have her answer then, whether it be an encouraging smile or an angry frown.

Only he didn't turn. He didn't even glance at her.

Mortified, she started to snatch her hand away, but his leg shifted and nudged against hers. She held her breath, wondering if she'd mistaken the move. When she remained frozen, his leg moved again, in a slow, hard rub against hers. She wanted to sag in relief and shout for joy. Instead, she sat very still, pretending to listen demurely as she had for the past half hour, while under the table she curled her fingers to squeeze his thigh.

Brent jumped at the feel of her fingertips pressing into him, and an arrow of heat shot straight into his loins. Did the woman realize how sensitive a man's inner thigh was?

"What!" Keshia demanded of him. "Don't tell me you disagree."

"Hum?" Brent struggled to remember what they were talking about. *Oh, yeah, confirming sources.* "Of course I don't disagree."

"Than why are you frowning like that?" Keshia asked.

"I'm not frowning." *Was he frowning?* "I was thinking." Thinking he'd like to take hold of Laura's hand and move it half an inch up and just a fraction to the left. Either that, or drag her outside and demand to know what was going on. She wasn't at all herself this evening. Maybe the strain of moving and her argument with her father were getting to her. He should ease away from her before things got out of hand. Instead, he found himself shifting his knees apart to give her easier access to his thigh. As if he'd drawn her a road map, her fingers zeroed in on an erogenous zone halfway between his groin and his knee.

His body jerked so violently, he half-expected everyone to turn and look at him as if they knew what was going on beneath the table. He reached for his drink in hopes of covering up his sudden movement. That, and squelching the bonfire that was spreading through his system. Damn, the room was getting hot. Setting his glass down, he gave Laura a look that demanded to know what she thought she was doing. To his surprise, she smiled back at him as if nothing at all were going on.

All right, he told her with his eyes, *two can play at this game. We'll just see who cries uncle first.*

Turning back to Keshia, he picked up the debate where it had left off as he slipped his hand under the table. He ran his palm across the top of Laura's thigh. She squirmed when he made contact with her bare knee. The satin softness of her skin tantalized his fingertips as he drew the hem of her dress upward to make small circles on her flesh. From the corner of his eye, he watched her breathing go shallow. He wanted to smile when she reached for her drink to take a hurried sip. His smile faltered, though, when her other hand traveled downward toward his own knee and back up. She repeated the journey again and again, each time going a tiny bit higher.

Sweat formed on the back of his neck, even though

he knew she would never, surely never, go all the way up his thigh to the bulge that strained against his trousers. He shifted his legs to accommodate the growing pressure and prayed she didn't take his movement as an invitation. If she touched him there, he was not going to be responsible for the result.

To his relief, she redirected her assault to the top of his thigh, and he relaxed slightly; not much, but enough to lean back in the booth and enjoy the game. She might be in a strangely brazen mood, but she was still an amateur, and he'd have her begging him for mercy any second.

Unfortunately, he wasn't exactly an old pro at these games either, since he'd focused most of his life on work rather than women. In fact, touching her thigh, feeling the supple muscles play beneath his hand, seemed to be having more of an effect on him than her. He was glad when Franklin took up the debate with Keshia, since his brain was having a hard time putting two words together in a coherent manner.

Laura, on the other hand, had turned to Connie and was chatting away about Beason's Ferry and her family history. All the while, she made torturous circles with her fingertip, drawing random patterns that made him hold his breath every time she started toward the junction of his thighs. At some point he quit fearing she'd touch him there and started hoping to feel her hand cup him. Before long, he wanted her touch so badly, his teeth ached.

What had started as a flirtatious game turned into a battle of the sexes. Male ego demanded he make her quit first. He just hoped she surrendered soon, because if her fingertips brushed across that spot inside his thigh one more time, he was going to whimper.

His hand flexed about her thigh at the thought. God, she had incredible legs. He wanted to slide beneath the table and spend an hour kissing every inch of them, from the slender ankles on up to the hot nest he knew waited at their apex.

In a last-ditch effort to turn the tables on her, he leaned toward her, catching the scent of some spicy new perfume. "You know, Laura," he whispered, "if we keep this up much longer, you could wind up very embarrassed."

"Oh?" She turned to him, blinking innocently, but her eyes were dilated with desire. Victory was almost his. She was in over her head, and soon he'd hear her admit it.

"That's right," he breathed near her ear. "Or have you forgotten that night in my car? The way I made you scream? Is that what you want me to do? Make you scream with pleasure in front of all these people?"

For a moment she just stared at him as if too tantalized or horrified to speak. Then, to his relief, she snatched her hand away from him. Even though he'd wanted her to stop, he nearly groaned at the loss of her touch. Reaching for his drink, he offered her a whispered consolation. "I will say this: It's a good thing you weren't wearing stockings under that dress, or this little game really could have gotten out of hand."

To his surprise, a laugh escaped her lips.

"Brent," she whispered back as he took a deep gulp of his margarita, "I'm not wearing *anything* under this dress."

He choked, gasping for breath, until Jorge slapped him hard between the shoulder blades and asked if he was all right.

"Fine. I'm fine," he managed to gasp. "I just remembered something I have to do, though."

"What?" Several voices asked.

"I, uhm . . . I need to get home, that's all. *Now.*" He grabbed Laura's hand. "Sorry to bust up the party, but I really have to go."

Ignoring the stunned faces of his coworkers, he shoved Jorge and Kevin out of the booth, dragging Laura behind him.

"What in the world could you possibly have to do at home in the middle of the night?" Keshia asked. Beside her, Franklin dissolved with laughter.

"A project." Brent's brain refused to function, and he rattled off the first words that came to mind. "I'm replacing some molding, and Laura promised to help me pick out the paint."

"In the middle of the night?" Keshia gaped at him.

Brent gave her an exasperated look as he fumbled for enough money to cover his part of the bill. "What's the use of living in a big city if you don't take advantage of the all-night hardware stores?"

"Hardware?" Franklin clamped his arm about his stomach to control his laughter. "Oh, God, that's rich, Michaels. Maybe I'll have to get me some of that *hard*ware."

Tossing down his money, Brent grabbed Laura's hand and headed for the door.

"Brent, slow down," Laura said as she stumbled after him into the parking lot. Before she could utter another word, he'd opened the passenger door of his car, put her inside, and dashed around to the driver's side. The minute he closed the door behind him, he leaned toward her, all but trapping her in her bucket seat. "Prove it."

"Excuse me?" She stared at him, still panting for breath. She wasn't quite sure how she'd gone from sitting in the restaurant to sitting in his car, but there she was with him leaning over her in the darkness. Beyond the car, she heard music underscored by laughter from the patio bar. Moving headlights sliced through the back window of the Porsche, illuminating his eyes. He looked determined and deadly serious.

"Prove you're not wearing anything under that dress," he said.

"How do you expect me to do that?" Her heart raced as his eyes traveled downward to her lap, then back up.

"It's very simple, Laura. Just lift your skirt and let me see."

"I can't do that!" She gaped at him, horrified at the suggestion, and incredibly excited. Even more shocking than his suggestion was her reason for refusing. She knew she'd die of embarrassment if she lifted her skirt and he saw the moisture glistening between her thighs. Then he'd know just how excited he'd gotten her in the restaurant.

"Not so brazen now, are you?" His mouth turned up into a slow smile so filled with male smugness, she wanted to wipe it right off his lips.

She smiled up at him, in the slowest, most seductive way she knew how. "You want to see what I'm wearing? Look for yourself."

"You think I won't?" Her heart went still as his hand dropped to the hem of her dress while his eyes remained fixed on hers. Slowly he lifted the dress to her waist, and the night air brushed the curls between her thighs.

His gaze dropped to her lap, and he went utterly still. "Oh, God." He breathed the words in reverence, and his gaze shot back to hers. For a moment, they just stared at each other, then his mouth was on hers in a demanding, searing kiss that stole her breath. She couldn't think as his hand dropped beside the seat, and the back reclined slowly, lowering her seductively beneath him. His hands moved to caress her legs and squeeze her bottom.

He broke the kiss and dropped his forehead to hers. "Oh, Christ." He panted the words like a plea for strength. His head lifted, and he stared straight into her eyes. "Don't move."

With her head still whirling, she remained exactly as she was, slumped down in the seat, her dress bunched at her waist, her knees slightly parted. With a flick of his wrist, Brent brought the car to life with a roar of the engine and drove out of the parking lot. Some part of her brain screamed at her to sit up straight, lower her dress, and try to regain some semblance of modesty. But the moment she tried to do that, his hand shot from the gearshift to her knee, holding it exactly where it was. She looked up at him and saw him watching her out of the corner of his eye.

"Oh, no you don't," he said teasingly. "You started this game, and you'll finish it. Unless you're willing to concede defeat now."

Game? she wondered. *What game?* She vaguely remembered the challenging look he'd given her in the restaurant. Apparently this was all a game to him, a thrilling, tantalizing game she was more than willing to play. She just wished she knew the rules. "What happens if I surrender?"

"Why don't you say uncle and find out?" His hand crept up her thigh to lightly tease her blond curls. Heat shot through her, melting her legs until they fell farther apart. Maybe it was crazy, and she couldn't believe she was actually doing this, but she'd never felt more alive than she did at that moment.

In the darkness of the car, she opened herself to his every touch. Thankfully, his house was mere blocks from the restaurant. Still, she could feel the pressure building as she writhed against his hand, aching for release.

"Not yet, sweetheart," he said, casting her a sideways look. "I'm not letting you off that easily."

She moaned as his hand left her to return to the gearshift. Tires squealed as the car turned a corner. Then he slammed on the brake, pitching her to a sitting position. She stared in surprise at the dark silhouette of his house. Then the car door opened beside her, and Brent was half-helping, half-hauling her out. He kissed her again, pressing her against the car with his body. She felt his arousal thrusting against her belly as he rocked his hips.

Before she could wrap her arms around his neck, he broke the kiss and dragged her behind him along the path to the porch. She laughed as they stumbled up the stairs to his front door. He fumbled to put the key in the lock, cursing when he couldn't make it fit. Feeling outrageous, she wrapped herself against his back, splaying her hands against his chest. "What happens if you surrender to me?"

"I won't," he laughed, then groaned as she ran her hands downward, over his taut stomach. "God help me."

As if in answer to his prayer, the door opened, and they fell through it together. He spun around, closing the door and trapping her against it. His mouth covered hers as his hands ran over her hips. She felt him gather her dress about her waist, felt him press his hardened length against her heated flesh. All that separated them was his trousers, but even that was too much. She moaned and rubbed against him, desperately needing release.

"Oh, jeez." He lifted his head, panting for air. "Laura, wait, give me a second."

"Are you saying I win?" Disappointment vied with triumph as she wondered if winning meant they would stop.

He narrowed his eyes. "Not a chance."

With staggering skill he kissed a path over her chin, down her neck. "You want me, Laura. You know you do. All you have to do is admit it, and I'll give you everything your body's begging for."

Is that what she got for admitting defeat? Him satisfying the ravenous need inside her? Suddenly losing seemed like a very pleasant proposition. She felt him lower the cuff that formed the top of her dress, trapping her arms against her sides. In a daze, she watched him cup her naked breast, then take one nipple into his hot, wet mouth.

Her head fell back as her eyes closed. The sucking motion of his mouth tugged all the way to the aching emptiness between her thighs. The words "I surrender" came to her lips, but when she opened her mouth to speak, the words changed to: "What happens if I win?"

He kissed and nipped his way upward until his face hovered over her. A wicked grin lit his eyes. "Then you get to do anything you want to my body."

The image of him lying naked on a bed completely at her mercy nearly sent her over the edge. He must have seen the reaction in her eyes, for he gave a low, sexy laugh that tantalized her senses. "Only that's not going to happen," he said as he nibbled her neck. His teeth grazed her earlobe. "Because, my sweet little Laura, in about two seconds, you'll be begging me to take you."

"Wanna bet?" She rallied her senses enough to grin as she worked her hands between them. She found his rigid length through his trousers. His breath hissed in as his body jerked taut. "Maybe you'll be begging me," she said.

"You may be right," he breathed as he moved against her hand. The intent expression on his face, the feel of him so big and hard against her palm, thrilled her. She didn't care who won, only that she felt him inside her.

Abruptly, he pulled her hand away. "Laura," he panted against her lips as he took her mouth in another hard kiss. "Wrap your legs around me."

Too lost in desire to argue, she let him hoist her up, and she wrapped her legs about his hips as she freed her arms to drape them over his shoulders. Their tongues entwined as he turned and started walking. Every step he took rubbed his hardness against her sensitized flesh. She was mindless with need by the time they fell together onto his bed.

She tried to pull at his clothes, but he eluded her hands. Her red-knit dress came up and over her head, leaving her with nothing on but her high-heeled sandals. When she tried again to reach for him, he clasped her wrists in one hand and pinned them to the mattress above her head. Stretching out beside her, he thrilled her with long, drugging kisses as his free hand played over her body. She whimpered in despair when he left her abruptly.

Dazed, she opened her eyes to see him standing beside the bed, pulling off his clothes. With his eyes devouring her, she became aware of her nudity and the fact that she lay sprawled on his bed, her hands above her head, her knees raised and wide apart as the spiked heels of her sandals dug into his mattress. Self-conscious, she started to close her legs.

"No, don't." His hand dropped to her knee, holding it in place. "Just, please, don't move."

Grinning, she wondered if he realized he'd just said "please"—the magic word of surrender. Then her gaze lowered to his straining arousal, and her thoughts fled as he sprawled beside her.

Clasping her wrists once more in his hand, he took a pebble-hard nipple in his mouth and suckled until she moaned and thrashed beneath him. Then he moved lower, kissing a trail over her quivering belly. He released her hands to spread her thighs.

One of his fingers slid slowly inside of her. When she whimpered with pleasure, he glanced up at her and grinned.

"You are so incredibly beautiful," he breathed in wonder before he lowered his mouth to her. Just as the world started to spin beneath her, he pulled back, watching her intently as she floated back down. Then he did it again and again, driving her toward the brink of release, only to pull back at the last moment. She wanted to scream in frustration when she heard him chuckle. "Say the words, Laura."

"Yes, yes, I want you."

"And you'll have me. Just say you surrender."

"I surrender. You win. Anything, just please, Brent, please make love to me."

He slid up her body and sealed his mouth over hers. Weeping his name, she reached for him. "Shh." He smoothed the hair from her face as he kissed her temple and cheek. "I'm here. I'm right here."

"I want you. Now, Brent. Please. Take me. Love me. Now, please, now."

He drove inside her, and the world shattered. She shuddered and convulsed, feeling as if she were dying, only to be reborn with fire and fury.

She couldn't get enough of him. She needed him harder and deeper, all of him touching her, taking her. In answer to the pleas that tumbled from her lips, he hooked his arms behind her legs and pressed her knees to her shoulders.

Pinned beneath him, she planted her hands against the headboard to increase the impact of every hard driving thrust. She should have felt helpless, but instead she soared with power and desire as she watched the expression on his face, the straining muscles in his shoulders and arms. She wanted to give him more than her body; she wanted to give him her very soul. Arching her head back, she opened her heart to him and felt herself soar with the excruciating pleasure of being in love.

In that instant, he stiffened against her and spent himself in one glorious burst that shot them both to heaven.

CHAPTER
20

~

Slowly the world drifted back into focus. Laura could feel the weight and warmth of Brent's body pressing her into the mattress. He'd released her legs, and they lay weakly alongside his. She lowered her arms to cradle his head, which rested on her shoulder.

"I guess it's true what the French say." She sighed as a smile tugged at her lips. "It really is like a little death."

She expected him to laugh. Instead, his body went very still. With a moan, he lifted his head. What she saw in his eyes startled her. He looked almost frantic. "Did I hurt you?"

"No," she laughed, but sobered quickly at his expression. "I'm fine Brent. In fact," she grinned, "I'm more than fine."

He rolled onto his back to lie beside her with his hands over his face. A surge of concern dispelled the last of her euphoria. "Brent? Are you okay?"

"I'm not sure." He lowered his hands and looked at her. "Laura, I . . . I didn't mean for this to happen again. I'm sorry."

Her body, so hot and happy a moment before, went cold as the events of the evening played back through her head. She'd thrown herself at him, intentionally seduced him. He'd given in, and now he felt guilty. He felt guilty because she was his friend, and he'd used her for sex. But the guilt and embarrassment rightfully belonged to her.

"I see," she said, marveling at how calm she sounded. Sitting up, she swung her feet to the floor. She wanted to stand and reach for her clothes but feared she'd topple off her ridiculous high heels if she did. "If you'll give me a minute, I'll be out of your way."

"Laura, no. I didn't mean it like that!" She felt the bed sag as he came to her. He turned her toward him, cradling her face in the crook of his neck. "I didn't mean I didn't want this to happen. Or that I didn't want you. Believe me, I want you very much, even now. Jeez, even after what we just did, I still want you."

"Then why are you sorry?"

He heaved a frustrated sigh. "Because I don't want to hurt you."

"But you didn't hurt me." She pulled back to see his face.

"Maybe not physically." He gave her a lopsided smile. "But I still took advantage of you."

"Brent, that's ridiculous. I threw myself at you."

"Because you believed there was something to gain from it. Something besides good sex. No, make that spectacular sex. But I know you, Laura." He touched her cheek. "No matter how attracted you are to a man, you would never have done this if you didn't think it might lead somewhere."

A coldness settled about her heart as she realized he was rejecting her—gently but completely. She turned her head away. "I see."

"No, you don't." He took her chin and turned her back to face him. "And that's why we need to talk." She

watched him struggle for the right words. "I meant to sa
this earlier today, when I took you to lunch. Only I jus
couldn't seem to get the words out."

"Actually, you stated very clearly that you wanted u
to be friends and nothing else."

"Yes, but I didn't say why I wanted that." He sighed
"Laura, I've never told you this, but I admire you. I ad
mire your ability to cherish the very things so many peo
ple take for granted. The things you want out of life are s
basic and honest, they should be very simple. Unfortu
nately, they are the very things I am completely incapabl
of giving you."

She frowned at him. "And what things are those?"

"A home, a husband, and children."

Something fluttered inside her, and she realized that
in spite of all her avowals to want more than a small-town
life, the dream of a home and a family still drew her
That, however, was not what Brent wanted to give her
"There's more to life than marriage," she said, as if his
rejection didn't hurt.

"Laura . . ." He reprimanded her with a look. "You
aren't listening to me."

"Of course I am," she insisted. "You have no interest
in marrying me now or anytime in the future."

"I said I'm not capable of marrying you, which is a big
difference." He ran a hand through his rumpled hair
"Look, I'm sure you'll agree it takes more than a house to
make a home, right?"

She nodded.

"Well, it also takes more than a marriage certificate
and some glibly spoken vows to make a husband. And it
damned sure takes a lot more than what we just did to
make a father."

"Don't you think I know that?"

"Yes, I think you do. After the things you told me today, I think you understand it better than I'd like. But what you lived through does not come close to what happened to me as a child." He shook his head. "The last thing in the world I want to do is sound like one of those whiny people who blames all his problems on his childhood, but the fact remains that how I was raised damaged me inside. I don't feel the same emotions other people do. And nothing you or I can do will ever, *ever* change that."

"Are you saying that because you weren't loved as a child, you're incapable of feeling love as an adult?"

He looked her straight in the eye. "That's exactly what I'm saying."

"I don't believe you."

With a curse, he leaned against the headboard. After a moment of brooding silence, he nailed her with a direct look. "Did you take Mr. Wilburn's psychology class in high school?"

"Yes." She frowned warily.

"Do you remember learning about the wolf-boy who was found by that British doctor around the turn of the century?"

"I remember."

"Well, I remember it, too," he said. "I remember it very clearly. Because until then, I had the same dreams a lot of kids have, about growing up and having kids of my own so I could give them all the things I never had. But that day, sitting in Mr. Wilburn's class, I started to realize that would never happen. At least not for me."

She stared at him, incredulously. "Because you learned about some boy who'd been raised by wolves?"

"If you remember, that boy was perfectly healthy and

of normal intelligence when they found him, and y
he was never able to adapt to life among humans. H
couldn't talk, Laura." His gaze bored into hers, as if wil
ing her to understand. "Not because there was anythir
wrong with his vocal cords, but because he hadn't bee
exposed to human sounds as an infant."

"Which proves what?"

"It proves that, if a child doesn't develop certain abi
ities by age three, they can't develop them later. It's phy
ically impossible."

"That has nothing to do with the ability to feel emo
tions," she insisted staunchly.

"All right, let's say, for the sake of argument, I wa
able to fall in love, get married, and have a couple of kid
What kind of a father do you think I'd make?"

Warmth tingled through her at the thought. "I thin
you'd make a wonderful father."

He looked at her as if she'd lost her mind. "Have yo
ever seen the statistics on child abuse? A huge percentag
of abusive parents were the victims of abuse themselve
They don't know how to communicate with their chi
dren any other way, because getting slapped upside th
head and screamed at was all they knew growing up."

The warmth vanished. "Are you saying you wer
abused? I mean physically?"

His body went rigid. "I am not going to get into tha
A blow-by-blow description of my childhood would onl
upset you and put me in a really rotten mood. I've worke
through all that, accepted it, and gotten on with my life a
best I can."

"Have you, Brent? Have you really worked throug
it?"

"I've worked through it enough to know I'd make a horrible husband and a worse father."

"I don't think you give yourself enough credit." She offered stubbornly. "I think you would make a terrific husband."

"See, I knew it." He gestured toward her. "I knew you'd say something like that. Which is exactly why I didn't want to get involved with you like this. I knew, no matter how honest I was up front, you'd go into a relationship with all these starry-eyed notions and false expectations."

"Now you're not giving me enough credit." Her back straightened. "Just because I said you'd make a good husband, doesn't mean I want you to be *my* husband."

He gave a skeptical snort, obviously seeing the lie for what it was, a blatant attempt to salvage her pride.

Angry and hurt, she plunged ahead. "I did not come to Houston with some naïve assumption that you and I would fall hopelessly in love and live happily ever after. And I sure didn't come here on a husband hunt. If all I wanted was a husband, I'd have stayed in Beason's Ferry, where a perfectly wonderful, caring man has been after me to marry him for the past six months."

"Well, that's just what every man wants to hear when he's sitting naked in bed with a woman—how wonderful and caring some other guy is."

"The point I'm trying to make is that I'm not trying to trap you into some lifetime commitment here. My whole life is topsy-turvy right now, and all I'm capable of handling is each day as it comes. I don't expect any more from you than that." *Because I can't face the thought of choosing between you and my dream of marriage and family. Not yet.*

"Can't two people just take things a day at a time and be together because they enjoy each other's company without worrying if it's going to last forever?" she asked. "I'm having enough trouble handling the here and now to even think about forever."

"I know. I'm sorry." Brent caressed her arm. "I'm just scared to death I'll break your heart."

"Oh, Brent," she laid a hand against his cheek, "you can't do that unless I let you."

Time ticked by as he studied her. "Just promise me one thing. Promise you won't do anything stupid, like start thinking you're in love with me, okay?"

Emotions prickled her eyes, but she hid the tears with a smile. "How about if I promise not to blame you for anything stupid I might do?"

He studied her a long time. "Okay," he said slowly.

"Okay as in 'we'll see each other as more than friends'?"

He surprised her with a wolfish grin. "Okay as in 'I won't kick you out of my bed.' For now anyway."

"Why, you—" She pushed against his chest, then laughed when he caught her wrists and pulled her to him. His mouth covered hers, stealing the sound of her mirth. She melted in his arms, twining her own about his neck.

"Hmm." He lifted his head to smile down at her. "No, I definitely won't kick you out of my bed."

"That's good to hear." She grinned. "Since you owe me something."

"What?" His expression turned leery as he loosened his embrace.

"Welll." She straightened primly. "You know earlier when we were . . ."

"Yes?" He smiled at her blush.

"Technically, you did surrender first."

"I did not!" he said with obvious offense.

"You said please before I did," she pointed out.

"When?"

"When . . . when you were undressing . . . and I was . . . lying down with . . . Well, you did!"

He thought for a moment, then laughed. "You're right. I did."

"So," she battled down shyness, "does that mean I get to do whatever I want to your body?"

He fell back on the bed with his arms flung wide. "I'm all yours."

CHAPTER
21

Laura's advice to take things one day at a time worked like magic for Brent. He wondered why he hadn't adopted the philosophy in his personal life before, since he frequently used it at work in order to get through a crisis. Yet, this was the first time he'd allowed himself to truly relax on a personal level and let time proceed at its own pace without constantly questioning its direction.

For the most part, Laura maintained her separate residence with her roommate, a fact that mildly irritated him but he decided not to dwell on it. Besides, he had her to himself on the weekends. He'd even adapted to her bringing the Rottweilers over, since part of her rental agreement stipulated she baby-sit the big mutts whenever Melody went out of town.

True, the dogs had dug up his yard, chewed a corner off his Navajo rug, and scratched up his wood floors. He'd discovered a secret, however, about dealing with dogs. Even big, pampered babies could learn words like "sit," "down," and "drop that shoe or die," if the commands were spoken with authority. Surprisingly, he also discovered he rather like being greeted with enthusiasm and utter devotion when he slipped through the front door on Friday nights. Especially since the presence of the dogs meant he'd find Laura curled up on the sofa, where she fell asleep every Friday while waiting for him to come home.

He didn't think he'd ever get used to the feeling that welled inside him when he stood in the dark and watched her sleep. Then she'd stir and stretch and give him that incredible welcome-home smile as he bent down to kiss her. She always felt so right in his arms as he'd lift her from the sofa and carry her to his bed. The easy, honest way she gave herself up to their shared passion never ceased to thrill him. In the darkness afterward, when she'd snuggle against him and drift back to sleep, he'd lie awake and wonder what he'd ever done right in his life to deserve Laura—for however long she stayed.

For however long she stayed.

That annoying thought popped into his head less and less frequently as the summer progressed. By mid-August, as he drove to the office where she worked to take her to lunch, he found he could push the worry out of his mind with hardly any effort. Everything in his life was damned near perfect. As long as he didn't do anything stupid to screw it up, he didn't see any reason why things couldn't continue exactly as they were indefinitely.

Entering the doctor's office, he waved to Tina, the receptionist.

"Hey, Brent." The receptionist's expression brightened at the sight of him.

"Hi, Tina." He smiled in return. The more he got to know Laura's coworkers, the less he worried about where she worked. The women had apparently taught her a few city survival basics like carrying Mace and parking under streetlights and never walking to her car alone after dark.

"Laura will be out in a minute." Tina leaned forward,

giving him a flirtatious grin. "She's in with the doctor trying to untangle some insurance snafu. From the sound of it, she could be a while. But you're welcome to talk to me till she's done."

"And run the risk of getting you in trouble with the boss?" Brent pretended to be horrified at the thought. "No, I better just have a seat and mind my manners."

Hiding a grin at Tina's pout, he headed across the waiting room. This close to lunch, the place was deserted, but he could tell from the toys and books scattered across the floor that the morning had been a busy one.

Picking his way through the clutter, he took a seat in one of the adult-sized chairs. There didn't appear to be any *Sports Illustrated* to read, and he couldn't work up much enthusiasm for thumbing through *American Baby*. On the battered coffee table, he spotted a copy of Dr. Seuss's *Green Eggs and Ham*, and thought, what the heck. He'd never actually read a Dr. Seuss book and figured now was as good a time as any to broaden his literary horizons.

Settling back in the chair, he started skimming the lines of quirky verse. A few pages into the book, he heard footsteps and glanced up, hoping to see Laura. Instead, he saw a young woman headed for the counter to settle her bill.

No sooner had he turned back to his reading than the book flew forward to slap against his chest. Startled, he stared at the grinning face of a young boy who'd barreled into him.

"I kn-know you," the boy said, leaning against Brent's legs.

"Oh, you do, do you?" Brent stifled the urge to laugh at the boy's complete lack of inhibition.

"Yeah. You're thhhe g—" The boy struggled for a
moment as if his tongue had stuck to the roof of his
mouth. "*Guy*—that makes the nnnews."

"Actually, I just report the news. Other people make
." Brent grinned, but apparently the joke went right
over the top of the kid's head. "Do you like to watch the
news?"

The boy laughed and shook his head with enough
force to send it flopping from side to side. "I like caaar-
oons."

"Oh." Brent had preferred cartoons to the news at
hat age, too. "Cartoons are cool."

The boy giggled, and Brent found the sound oddly
infectious. He'd always considered kids something to
avoid, but this one wasn't too bad. He was kind of cute
even, in a squirrelly sort of way with his squinty brown
eyes and big front teeth. Short black hair stuck straight
out from the kid's head, adding to the goofy look.

"So, uhm, were you here to see the doctor?" Brent
asked.

The boy nodded with a floppy, jerky motion.
Yyyep," he said in the nasal voice of someone with a
stuffed-up nose.

"You have a cold or something?"

"No!" The kid erupted with laughter as if the ques-
ion were hilarious. "Seb-ber pollly."

Sebber polly? Brent frowned. Then his eyes swept over
he boy, taking in the squinted eyes, the wobbly stance,
and the constant motion of the head. "You mean cerebral
palsy?"

The boy nodded, still grinning.

Brent felt as if someone had kicked him in the chest
as he stared at the face before him. It was the face of any

normal, healthy elementary-school-age kid, and yet i wasn't. This child would never be completely normal and healthy like his classmates. He'd always be different, held apart through no fault of his own.

"So yyyou here to see the doc?" the boy asked.

"No. No, I'm to see Laura Morgan."

"Yeah?" The boy's eyes lit up. "Pretty hot nnnum ber."

"What?" Brent blinked, not sure he'd heard right.

"Miss Mmmorgan. Pretty hhhot."

Brent didn't know what he expected from a chile with cerebral palsy, but humor wasn't it. He couldn' help but smile back. "Yes, I guess I'd have to agree with you on that one."

"She your gggirlfen?"

"Something like that."

"Rrrats." The boy made a face.

"Hey!" Brent gave a mock scowl. "You been hitting on my girl?"

"She thinnnks I'm c-cute."

"Oh, she does, does she? Well, I just might have to talk to her about that."

The boy giggled and wobbled while Brent fought the urge to steady him.

"Robby," the young woman called. When Brent glanced up, he saw she was little more than a kid herself with a dark braid that hung to the waist of her peach polyester maid's uniform. *"Vente, mi hijo."*

"Sí, mammma." As the boy struggled to stand straight, Brent realized he wore braces on both legs. With a sway-and-step motion, he made his way across the room to take his mother's hand. At the door, he turned around a gave Brent a wave. "See yyya."

"Yeah, see ya." Brent waved back as the boy and his mother left. He had the oddest feeling in his chest, as if everything were turning to warm mush. Even after the door closed, he sat there staring after Robby. How could anybody with a healthy body complain about his lot in life?

Guilt pricked his conscience for every time he'd indulged in self-pity. Perhaps life had dealt him a rotten hand in some respects, but it had also given him one very powerful trump card: a healthy body and a face that had opened a lot of doors.

"Sorry to keep you waiting," Laura said as she breezed into the waiting room, "though I see you've kept yourself entertained," she added, eyeing the Dr. Seuss book. An odd look came over her face, more tenderness than amusement.

"Yeah, uh, riveting stuff." He set the book aside and rose to give her the quick kiss they always exchanged when he picked her up for lunch.

"What would you think about going to the Ol' Bayou for some Cajun food?" she asked. "Unless you'd rather have green eggs and ham."

"Whatever," he answered absently, his mind still on the boy.

"Hey." She tilted her head to catch his eyes. "You okay?"

"Hmm? Oh, sure, the Ol' Bayou sounds fine."

The smile that swept over her face finally captured his full attention. "I missed you last night," she whispered.

"I missed you, too," he whispered back. That warm mushy feeling shifted and spread outward as he stood staring at her. Sometimes he wondered if being happy affected a person's brain. He seemed to spend a lot of time simply staring at Laura without a single thought in his head. But since she seemed to suffer from a similar malady, he decided not to worry about it too much. He'd just enjoy it—while it lasted.

~~~

Laura savored a bite of rich étouffée as she watched Brent. He seemed oblivious to the quaint atmosphere of the Cajun restaurant, with its odd assortment of copper pots, antique beer signs, and fishing nets that covered the rough-paneled walls.

"So," she asked, more curious than piqued, "are you going to pick at that jambalaya or eat it?"

"What? Oh, sorry." He gave an embarrassed laugh. "What were we talking about?"

"The idea of you throwing a party for the people you work with." She'd been gently prodding him for weeks to have some people over. He had a beautiful house that deserved to be shown off, just as he deserved the praise and acceptance of friends. Only he'd never have close friends if he continued to hold everyone but her at arm's length. "If the idea of entertaining bothers you that much, I'll quit pushing."

"No, no, it's not that." He shook his head. "And I didn't mean to ignore you. I just have other things on my mind, that's all."

"Like what?" she asked, wondering what excuse he'd come up with this time to postpone the party.

"Just things." He shrugged.

"What things?"

"*Things*," he insisted. At her exasperated look, he

sighed. "I was just wondering if anyone had ever come up with a cure for cerebral palsy, that's all."

"Cerebral palsy?" She stared at him a moment before understanding dawned. "Ah. You've met Robby."

"He came into the reception area while I was waiting for you."

"He's a real heart-stealer, isn't he?"

"He's friendly, I'll give him that," Brent agreed.

"That he is." She smiled, as she often did when she thought of Roberto Gonzales. As always, though, the grin faded quickly, crowded out by the reality of his situation. "Unfortunately, the answer to your question is no, there is no cure for cerebral palsy. It's a type of brain damage, not a disease. Robby's one of the lucky ones, though, if there is such a thing in these cases."

"What do you mean?" He finally gave her his undivided attention.

"He has no mental retardation, and his balance and motor skills are remarkably good. He could even learn to walk with a fairly normal gait if—" she took a breath as the frustration built inside her. "If we could just get him the physical therapy he needs."

"What's the holdup?" Brent asked as he reached for a piece of cornbread. "Even if he doesn't have private insurance, shouldn't Medicaid cover it?"

"Oh, they do." She snorted. "Only Medicaid has gone to the new HMO system. Do you have any idea the kind of hoops I have to jump through to get referral approval for a patient?"

He shook his head.

"Okay, example." She set her fork aside. "Dr. Velasquez wants Robby to have physical therapy once a month for a year to see if that helps. So I call the insurance company to request approval for twelve sessions. No problem. They approve all twelve sessions, except—get this—he has to have them all in a row."

"You mean one a day for twelve days?"

"Exactly." She threw up her hands. "Have you ever heard of anything so ridiculous?"

Brent's fork went down. "Have you explained this to the insurance company?"

"About a million times," she said. "Unfortunately, the people who dole out the referral numbers are little more than college kids with a computer full of guidelines. If the computer says the treatments have to be on consecutive days, then far be it from some medical doctor with years of experience to tell them differently. And if I try to explain the error in their guidelines, they act as if I'm trying to pull a fast one."

"Have you talked to someone higher up?"

"I'm trying, Brent. Don't you think I'm trying?" Taking up her fork, she stabbed a shrimp in frustration. "I just get so angry. I've been filing appeals for weeks and getting absolutely nowhere. It's like nobody cares. To them, Robby's just one boy. What does it matter if one child falls through the cracks, as long as the majority are served?"

With a calmness that surprised her, Brent reached for a paper napkin and pulled a pen from his pocket. "What's the name of his insurance company?"

"Why?" She sat up straight. "You're not going to call them or anything are you?"

"I'm going to do a lot more than call them. I'm going to put them on the six o'clock news."

"Are you crazy?" She grabbed his hand. "Do you want to get me fired and Dr. Velasquez sued?" When he frowned at her, she went on to explain. "Everything I just told you is protected by patient confidentiality."

"You're right." She could almost see the wheels turning inside his head. A smile spread over his face. "Which is why you're going to call Robby's mother as soon as you get back to work and talk her into calling me. Maybe you can't give me permission to report this story, but she sure as hell can. We'll see how fast the insurance company changes their tune."

"You mean it?" A giddy thrill rose inside her. She wasn't sure whether to laugh or cry or throw her arms around Brent and cover him with kisses. "Thank you, Brent. This could make a huge difference."

"My pleasure." He smiled back, and she knew he cared for Robby's plight as much as she did. How could any man with such a capacity for compassion doubt he'd make a fabulous father?

A hollow ache opened beneath her heart, an ache that was growing more difficult to ignore. Six weeks ago, she claimed she wanted more out of life than marriage and children. And every day since then she'd spent more and more time picturing herself with Brent's baby in her arms. At odd moments in the day, bits of fantasy would flash through her mind: images of Brent teaching their son how to hold a baseball bat, or Brent smiling proudly as their daughter performed in a school play. When she'd walked into the waiting room and seen him holding a Dr. Seuss book, she'd pictured him with a child snuggled in his lap as he read aloud.

Only those children would never exist. Brent had stated firmly he didn't want them. And she'd assured him she respected his feelings on the subject. So why did she find it so hard to live with that decision? Had she secretly hoped he'd change his mind? Or that she'd be able to change it for him?

She frowned at the thought, for if she'd entered the relationship with such expectations, she was setting herself up for heartbreak. Unless . . .

For one tantalizing moment, she let herself wonder what the future would hold if Brent did change his mind.

~

By the following day, Brent had approval from Robby's mother and his news director to do the special report. In fact, the station liked the idea so much, they decided to pull out all the stops and use the special for the upcoming ratings week. Connie had even agreed to produce it, though she normally didn't work in the field.

With Laura helping on the research end, Brent soon realized they'd stumbled onto a much bigger story than one boy's fight for physical therapy. Though he wanted the focus of the report to remain on Robby, he expanded the script to explain that this was not an isolated case but a widespread problem in the medical community. Legislators at both the state and national level had been addressing the issue for the past few years, but until a solution was found, patients across the country were going without vitally needed medical treatment.

The taping of the segment was done over a period of days, all of it during Brent's off hours. Laura set up a taped interview with Dr. Velasquez and arranged for Brent to take a camera crew into one of Robby's hardwon physical therapy sessions. Not that he couldn't have arranged the tapings himself, but he enjoyed working with Laura. She was efficient, professional, and enthusiastic about the project. He often thought it a shame she hadn't gone into journalism. She'd have made one hell of a reporter.

When he mentioned that to her, she just laughed and said it took more than gathering facts to make a good reporter. It took talent, of which he had plenty for the both of them. The compliment made the warm glow he'd been carrying around all summer grow a bit brighter, and the silly grin he wore a bit more noticeable.

Connie, of course, teased him unmercifully about his "sappy look." But he laughed it off, which surprised him. Normally, any hint that he was "falling in love" would have set alarm bells ringing in his head.

The final day of taping took place on a Saturday on the banks of Buffalo Bayou, near the spot where he and Laura had had their picnic nearly two months before. Being August, the crew arrived early in the morning, when the temperature would be a tolerable eighty-six degrees and the park would be relatively empty. Two cameramen, the key grips, and the field director set up the equipment near the duck feeding area. They would use a mounted camera to film Brent's intro into the report, then use a hand-held camera to get shots of Brent and Robby feeding the ducks and walking through the park. These latter snippets would be interspersed with interviews and other scenes, with Brent doing the final voice-over in the studio once everything was spliced together.

While they waited for the taping to begin, Brent stood with Connie, Robby, and Robby's mother in the shade of a tree. Connie fanned herself with her notes. "How you ever talked me into doing an outdoor shot in August is beyond me," she groused.

"You owed me a favor, remember?" Brent said.

"Yeah, but I never expected the payback to involve standing outside in weather like this. It's so hot, I swear my brain is melting. How do you locals take it?"

Brent chuckled as he dabbed his face with powder to absorb the shine. By noon the heat and humidity would make even breathing difficult. "I hate to say this, but it's not any easier for us. In fact, every year about this time, I think seriously about buying a cabin in Colorado and escaping until October."

"Good idea," Connie sighed and reached for a cigarette. "When do we leave?"

"D-do I have to wwwear that gggunk?" Robby asked, watching Brent finish with his makeup. Brent hid a grin, since he had little liking for the stuff himself. Fortunately, with his dark complexion he rarely had to wear any outside of the studio, and then he wore as little as possible.

"It's not so bad," Brent assured him. "Once you get used to it."

"It's fffor girls!" Robby crinkled his nose.

"And movie stars," Brent added, thinking quickly. In the last few days, he'd learned Robby could be as temperamental as any seven-year-old. Strangely, he found he liked the kid all the more for being so natural. With Robby, no one ever had to wonder what he was thinking—because every thought was instantly voiced. Brent glanced at Robby's mother, Maria. "What's Robby's favorite show?"

"*Walker, Texas Ranger*," she answered in her accented English.

Brent squatted down to Robby's level. "I bet Chuck Norris puts on makeup."

"Who?" Robby frowned.

Brent rolled his eyes and tickled Robby's stomach. "The guy that plays Walker."

"Wwwalker doesn't wear mmmakeup," the boy protested between giggles.

"Sure he does. Every guy that gets in front of a camera wears some kind of makeup." Brent dabbed the sponge into translucent stage powder. "And that's what you're going to do today, play out a scene in front of a camera, just like *Walker, Texas Ranger*. Pretty cool, eh?"

Robby scowled dubiously at the round sponge in Brent's hand. "I g-guess."

Not giving him a chance to change his mind, Brent started swiping the boy's face. "After all your friends see the show, you'll be a regular star."

"Yyyou think s-so?"

"You bet." Brent smiled at the boy's excitement. He'd already learned that being camera shy was not a problem with this kid.

Just then Laura drove up and parked along the curb behind the TV van and other cars. Getting out of the car, she headed toward them with a bakery bag in one hand and an ice chest in the other.

"Sorry I'm late," she said as she drew near. "But I thought y'all might need a few thousand calories to keep the energy up."

Spying the bag, the crew abandoned their work and headed for the shade tree.

"What did you bring?" Connie asked.

"Doughnuts, danishes, and croissants so buttery, they'll make you drool," Laura announced with glee.

"Oh, bless you, my child." Connie went straight for the bag as Laura spread a blanket in the shade. "I don't suppose you brought any coffee?"

"In this heat?" Laura shuddered, then opened the ice chest. "I brought orange juice and soft drinks."

Connie made a face but reached for a small plastic bottle of juice.

"I'm g-going to be a mmmovie star," Robby told Laura.

"You are," she answered with the proper amount of awe. "Well, that calls for a celebration. Pick your poison, orange juice or soft drink."

"Yyyou have orange s-soda?"

"You bet!"

"No orange soda!" Brent, Connie, and the field director shouted at once. The last thing they needed was for Robby to have an orange mustache when the cameras rolled.

"Okay, okay," Laura cringed playfully.

Brent took one look at Robby's mutinous face and quickly intervened. "How about a Coke now and an orange soda later?"

"Okkkay." Still pouting a bit, Robby swayed and stepped his way over to the blanket.

"You have children?" Maria asked softly beside him.

Brent startled at the words. "No. None. Why do you ask?"

"You're very good with them." Maria smiled.

"I—thank you." A strange tightness crept into his chest as Maria turned to watch her child. The pride and love she felt for the boy shone clearly in her eyes. Yet he knew raising Robby couldn't be easy, and not just because of the cerebral palsy, but because Maria was young and single.

Just as his own mother had been.

In the last week, he'd wondered many times why two

women in the same situation would react so differently. Robby's father had apparently abandoned Maria before the child had even been born. Maria had dropped out of high school to take care of her baby and now worked as a hotel maid to support them both. He admired her for refusing to give up her child, even though keeping him made her life more difficult.

Brent's mother, on the other hand, had put up little more than a token resistance when she'd found a man who wanted to marry her and take her to California, but only if she left Brent behind. Though she'd promised to send for Brent later, none of the Zartlichs ever heard from her again.

For as long as Brent could remember, he'd blamed himself for her leaving, but now he wasn't so sure. What if the weakness was with her character, not his?

He thought of all the years he'd spent trying to be perfect out of fear that everyone would abandon him if he weren't. Even as an adult, he worried about letting any-one get too close, for fear that they'd see his flaws and want nothing to do with him. Yet Laura knew all about his shortcomings, that he could be stubborn and selfish at times and embarrassingly insecure at others.

She knew all that and she still brushed his flaws off as simply being human.

"Okay," Connie called as she finished her danish. "Let's get this show on the road."

As the crew grabbed for the last few pastries, Brent gratefully turned his attention to work. Here at least was safe ground, a place where he didn't have to be anything but the man on the surface for the camera to film.

CHAPTER
22

⁓

Two weeks later, Laura rushed through the front door of Melody's house. "Melody, are you home? It's me!"

The dogs charged toward her from the back of the house, yelping in doggy ecstasy. Since Melody hadn't had an art show that weekend, Laura had left the dogs home rather than take them to Brent's.

"Yes, Chakra, yes Karma, I'm happy to see you, too," she said, as she waded through their happy gyrations on her way to the kitchen.

"Hey there, stranger," Melody said as she came into the kitchen through the back door. The dogs bounded toward her, eager to be petted. Melody bent forward to comply as she spoke to Laura. "What are you doing here on a Saturday?"

"Looking for some serving bowls," Laura explained as she rummaged through a lower cabinet. "No, Karma, I don't need your help." Pushing the eager female out of the way, she dove back into the shelves of cookware. "Can you believe, after weeks of me nagging Brent to have some people over, he up and tells me this morning—*this morning*, mind you—that he's invited the entire station over for fajitas at his house this evening. This evening!"

Moving on to another cabinet, she muttered to herself, "One would think a man with such a well-stocked kitchen would have a few bowls for serving chips. Or that he'd give me more than a few hours to prepare for a party."

"So what's the occasion?" Melody asked.

Backing out of the cabinet, Laura gave her friend a startled look. "Didn't you watch the news last night? I left a note telling you all about it."

"Oh, that." Waving a hand, Melody headed for the refrigerator and poured a glass of ginseng tea.

"What do you mean, 'oh, that'? Didn't you watch it? Didn't you see Brent?"

"Laura." Melody looked at her as if she had a screw loose. "Brent's on the news every night."

"Not the national news. The network picked up his special report about Robby. It was on the *national* news!"

"I take it this is a big deal."

"It's a *huge* deal. Brent was so excited when he got home last night, you should have seen him." Heat rose in her cheeks as she remembered exactly how "excited" he had been. He'd come through the door and swept her into his arms, laughing and twirling her about. They hadn't even made it to the bedroom before they'd tumbled to the floor and he'd kissed her into mindless oblivion. Considering how preoccupied they'd both been with each other's bodies the rest of the night, she supposed she could forgive him for not mentioning the party until the next morning.

"Ah-ha!" she exclaimed, finding some bowls she could use for chips and salsa. "Now, all I need to do is change clothes and get back to Brent's before his guests start arriving—or before Brent has a nervous breakdown at the thought of hosting his first party." With the dogs hurrying along beside her, she headed for her bedroom. "Honestly," she called over her shoulder, "that man is worse than the entire Bluebonnet Homes Tour fund-raising committee when it comes to worrying over every little detail."

Still, she could hardly complain, since she knew what a big step this was for Brent to open up enough to let people into his home.

"Speaking of Beason's Ferry," Melody said as she followed Laura to the bedroom, "I have a couple of phone messages for you."

Laura's heart lurched as she backed out of her closet. "Phone messages?" she asked hopefully. "From my father?"

"Sorry." Melody gave her a sympathetic look. "They're both from Greg."

"Argh!" Laura growled and went back to rifling through her clothes. Selecting a brightly colored shorts outfit, she carried it to the bed. "What did he want this time?"

"Oh, nothing much, just to tell you he's coming to Houston to see you—tonight."

"He's coming to Houston?" Laura gaped.

"Tonight." Melody had the audacity to grin. "See, I told you this would happen if you didn't return his phone calls."

Laura groaned. "I was hoping if I ignored him long enough, he'd take the hint and go away." Stripping off her T-shirt and jeans, she pulled on the multicolored outfit. "Honestly, I don't understand that man. I really don't. He was never the possessive type while we dated. So why is he acting that way now?"

"Apparently, he thinks there's a chance you'll get back together."

"Well, there isn't," Laura said.

"Are you sure?" The teasing note left Melody's voice, and she sounded almost hopeful. "I mean, are you really truly sure you'll never get back with him?"

Laura glanced up, confused by the change in her friend's mood. "Of course, I'm sure."

"But what if you and Brent broke up? Would you go back to Greg then?"

"Absolutely not." She nearly laughed at the notion. "You know perfectly well I didn't turn down Greg's proposal because of Brent. I turned him down because I realized we'd both be miserable if I married him. Don't get me wrong, I think Greg's a great guy, and he'll make some nice girl a wonderful husband someday. I just hope he finds that girl soon, so he'll leave me alone."

Melody gave a rude snort. "If a nice girl was what he needed, he'd have done well to marry you."

Laura studied her friend as she sat on the bed to change her shoes. "You okay, Mel? You seem a little down tonight."

"Yeah, I'm fine, I guess." Melody sat beside Laura on the bed. Sensing his mistress's mood, Chakra laid his head in her lap. Melody rubbed his floppy black ear as he gazed up at her with big sorrowful eyes. "I guess I've just been feeling a bit old lately."

"You're not old." Laura laughed softly.

"Maybe not, but lately I seem to spend more time talking to your ex-boyfriend than people my own age."

"Oh, Melody, Greg's only eight years younger than you, so it's not like he's a kid and you're ancient."

"I feel ancient."

"Well, you don't look it." She hugged her friend's shoulders. "You look great!"

"Thanks." Melody managed a weak smile. "You know, it's weird—emotionally, I feel like I'm barely ready to start adult life, and here mine is half over."

Laura frowned, knowing she needed to get back to Brent's but not willing to leave her friend in such a mood. "Hey, why don't you put up the paints for one night and come to the party with me?"

"No." Melody shook her head. "When I get on one of these downers, I've learned it passes more quickly if I just give in and wallow for a while. And the sooner you get out of here, the sooner I can start wallowing."

"You sure?" Laura asked. "I could stay for a few minutes if you want to talk."

Melody looked ready to say no, then sighed. "I just keep having all these crazy thoughts lately."

"Like what?"

"Like, 'Do I really want to spend the rest of my life alone?'" Chakra whined, and Melody resumed rubbing his ear. "When I left Roger, I thought I wanted freedom, independence, to escape the constraints of married life. Only lately I've started wondering if maybe the opposite was true. Maybe I left him because I was finally ready to *be* a wife."

"I'm not sure I follow you."

Melody shrugged. "Roger was more a substitute father than anything else, and I'd outgrown my need for that. I wanted, or *want* rather, a real husband: a partner, a spouse, a man who is both lover and friend." She turned and looked at Laura. "You know what I mean?"

"Yeah." Laura sighed, thinking of Brent. "I know exactly what you mean."

"Well, at least you seem to have found a man who fits the bill."

"I'm not so sure." Restless, Laura went to the dresser to brush her hair.

"Oh?" Melody prompted, watching Laura's reflection in the mirror. "I thought things were going great for you two. Every time I see you together, he's practically eating you up with his eyes."

Laura toyed with the hairbrush, picturing the look that so often came into Brent's eyes when he looked at her. Sometimes she felt as if the words "I love you" were on the tip of his tongue. Yet he never said them. How long could she wait to hear those words? Would he bolt if she said them first?

"Laura?" Melody asked. "Things are okay with you and Brent, aren't they?"

"Hmm? Oh, yes, of course." When her friend raised a brow, Laura sighed. "Well, maybe not perfect, but whose relationship is?"

"What's the problem?"

A complicated question, Laura thought, *with no clear answer*. "Mostly, I guess, it's that Brent isn't interested in marriage. Now or ever."

"Hmm." Melody frowned. "How do you feel about that?"

"I don't know!" Setting down the brush, Laura turned to slump against the dresser. "I thought I could accept it, but lately . . . lately, I think about marriage all the time. And children. When I was little, I used to dream about having babies of my own. Then time passed, and thirty got closer, and I convinced myself I could live without ever being a mother, without ever knowing how it felt to hold my own child in my arms. But these last weeks with Brent I just . . ."

"What?"

A rise of tears blurred her vision. "I just love him so much."

In a quick, fluid motion, Melody left the bed and enfolded Laura in her arms. "I know, it hurts to love sometimes. It shouldn't, but it does."

"Especially when you can't even tell the one you love how you feel. I'm so afraid he'll run if I do."

"Honesty is always frightening," Melody said, "and usually carries a high price."

"So what should I do?" She pulled back to search her friend's face.

"Oh, Laura." Melody sighed. "If I were twenty years younger, I'd say something like 'Anything worth having is worth taking risks for,' or 'Sometimes we have to go through a little pain to get to the happiness on the other side.' " She shook her head. "Unfortunately—even though I believe both those things—I've learned that going after what you want always comes with a bigger price tag than you expect and no guarantee that you'll be satisfied with what you get in the end."

"Have the risks you've taken paid off?" Laura asked.

"Some. Not all. But then, none of us gets to win all the time." She tucked Laura's hair behind her ear in a motherly gesture. "The game of life just doesn't work that way."

"That's what I'm afraid of."

"Join the club." Melody laughed.

Before Laura could comment further, a knock came at the front door. Karma and Chakra took off in a noisy imitation of the guard dogs they were supposed to be as Laura stared at Melody. "You don't think that's—"

"Greg!" Melody's eyes went round as she laughed in a complete lack of sympathy for Laura's predicament.

"What am I going to do?" Laura whispered.

"You could start by answering the door."

"I can't do that!" She glanced toward the window, wondering if she could crawl out, sneak around front, and make it to her car without him catching her.

"Don't even think it," Melody warned as the dogs bounded back into the room. "Just answer the door, tell him you don't have time to talk, and leave."

"How about if you answer it and tell him I'm not here."

"Only one problem with that: Your car's out front." Melody reached for the dogs. "I'll put these two away while *you* answer the door."

"Thanks a lot," Laura groused as she watched Melody try to sweet-talk the dogs into the other bedroom. Dragging her feet, she went to the front door, assuring herself she wasn't a coward—she was just giving Melody time to lock up the dogs.

With a sigh of resignation, she glanced through the peephole and saw Greg standing on the front porch frowning at his feet. Habit forced a smile to her face as she opened the door. "Hello, Greg."

"Laura Beth." His face lit up when he saw her. For a moment, he stood drinking in the sight of her. Even though he no longer interested her in a romantic sense, she had to admit he looked handsome in the lengthening shadows of early evening. In deference to the warmth of September, he'd worn a golf shirt and slacks, much the

same attire Brent preferred. Somehow, though, Greg
didn't fill the clothes out quite the same way.

"I was, uhm . . ." His expression turned sheepish.
"I was afraid you wouldn't be here, I mean, since you
didn't return my calls. You did get my message that I was
coming, didn't you?"

"Yes, well, I just got it a second ago." She felt a
twinge of guilt for all the calls over the summer that she
hadn't returned. "The truth is, I was just on my way out.
Brent and I are giving a party this evening, and I really
need to go."

"Oh."

His face fell in disappointment, and she felt as if she'd
just kicked someone's dog. "I do have a minute, though, if
you'd like to come in?"

"Yes." The light leapt back into his eyes. "Yes, I
would, if that would be all right."

Trying not to sigh out loud, she motioned him to
follow her into the living room. "Can I get you anything?"

"No, I'm fine." He glanced around in overt curiosity
to see where she lived. From his furrowed brow, she assumed he didn't care for Melody's decor.

"I, uhm, just need to get something from the
kitchen." She started in that direction, and he followed as
she went to retrieve the bowls she'd left on the counter.
"So . . ." She glanced nervously about, wondering
where Melody was. Considering that her friend and Greg
struck sparks off each other like two pieces of flint, she
almost hoped Melody didn't join them. "How's everyone
back home?"

"Fine, I guess. Though they all miss you. Hardly a day
goes by that someone doesn't ask me if I've heard from

you. Except for your father. Whenever your name comes up in conversation, he changes the subject."

She frowned, saying nothing, though a twinge of pain struck her heart.

"I take it you two still aren't speaking?" Greg asked.

"No."

"I'm sorry," he said softly. "Look, Laura Beth, I know you're in a hurry, so I'll get right to the reason I came. I've done a lot of thinking these last months about the things you said. You were wrong, you know, when you said I had no faith in you. I have the utmost faith in you, on every level."

"I appreciate that, really, but—"

"No, no, let me finish." He took a deep breath. "I realize Beason's Ferry isn't the most exciting town in the world, but I also know you weren't always so anxious to leave it. When I first met you, and you still managed your father's office, you seemed happy. So I started thinking, maybe all you really needed was some renewed sense of purpose in your life, a real job, instead of just charity work, that would make you feel less restless."

"Greg," she sighed, feeling the tension build behind her eyes. "I came to Houston to find more than a job."

"I know, just hear me out." He shifted his weight. "When we were dating, we uhm, talked a lot about the pharmacy, and well, you always had a lot of good ideas about how I could improve business. Like the espresso bar. I never would have thought of putting that in, but it's paid off really big. And so I've been thinking, even though things haven't worked out for us personally," his eyes finally lifted to hers, "how would you like to be my business partner?"

"What?" She gaped at him, startled and flattered

and, for one unexpected moment, tempted. Only moving back home would mean giving up Brent and her new job and friends. Her shoulders slumped. "Greg, I—"

"You don't have to answer right now," he said quickly. "Think about it, and maybe tomorrow or sometime next week we could get together and talk."

"Talk about what?" Melody asked from the doorway, and Greg whirled to face her.

"Greg just asked me to be his business partner," Laura said.

"Oh, that's rich." Melody laughed. "And clever. Very clever, Gregory."

"What exactly is that supposed to mean?" He went poker stiff.

"If you can't win her with a wedding ring, dangle your business before her, is that it?" Melody smirked.

"That was not my intention at all," Greg said with an excess of indignation.

"Yeah, right!" Melody snorted.

"Laura Beth happens to be an excellent office manager who has inventive ideas on how to improve business."

"Why, you slime." Melody eyed him up and down as if discovering a mutant form of insect. "That's the whole reason you wanted to marry her, isn't it?"

"Not the whole reason, no, and I resent you suggesting such a callous motivation." Greg's face turned so flushed, Laura wondered if Melody was right. The thought cut deep, that he'd wanted her as a business partner more than he desired her as a woman. But it certainly explained their less-than-heated love life.

"For your information," Greg persisted, "I have the deepest admiration for Laura Beth as a person."

"Admiration!" Melody scoffed. "For your information, it takes more than that to make a happy marriage."

"So you're the one who's been filling her head with all these ideas about relationships between men and women, as if all that matters is physical attraction, and—and lust!" His gaze swept to the oversize shirt Melody wore open down the front. Beneath, a sports bra and bicycle shorts boldly displayed her body.

"You got something against a little honest lust?" Stepping toward him, Melody pulled the shirt further open to plant a hand on one hip. "As a pharmacist, you of all people should know the benefits of a healthy sex life."

"Guys," Laura tried to interrupt as Greg stumbled through some convoluted retort. "Uhm, guys?" She tried again as Melody fired back with a scathing rebuttal. "If y'all will excuse me, I have a party to get to."

Neither of them spared her a glance as they went toe to toe and nose to nose. Deciding she'd heard more than enough, Laura scooped up her bowls and headed for the front door. Behind her, she could still hear them arguing and didn't know whether to laugh or do some hollering herself. Had Greg's marriage proposal really been so self-serving? Even if it had, surely his ulterior motive hadn't been intentional. Greg was not the type of man to consciously use anyone. Still, this furtive proof that he had never really loved her bothered her. It bothered her as much as what he'd said about a relationship needing more than lust to survive.

Not that her relationship with Brent was based solely on lust. Was it? No, of course it wasn't, she assured herself.

So why did Greg's words make her feel all queasy inside?

Because, she realized as she drove, if Brent felt something more for her than physical desire and friendship, he'd want to marry her—no matter how much the idea of commitment frightened him.

But what if he didn't love her?

The question echoed in her mind as she pulled into his driveway. She could see him through the kitchen window, and for a moment she sat simply watching him. How much was she willing to sacrifice in order to be with this man? How long could she go on seeing him without saying the words "I love you" and hearing them in return?

She waited for some answer to come, some magical solution that would show her the way to win his heart. If only she could walk through that door, put her arms around his waist, and tell him everything she felt, everything he meant to her.

Only she'd lose him if she did, because he wasn't ready.

So for tonight, as with all the other nights they'd shared, she'd be there with him and for him as his lover and his friend. If her patience strained, she'd deal with it as she'd been dealing with it, by biding her time—for however long it took.

CHAPTER
23

Brent heard a car in the drive and peeked out the kitchen window. "Look, Hal," he said into the phone, "I need to go. Laura's back."

"Oh, sure," his agent replied, wrapping up a long-winded monologue. The two had spoken more in the last twenty-four hours than they had in the last two years. But then, they hadn't had anything to discuss until yesterday afternoon. "I'll call you Monday," Hal said, "the minute I have the contract in hand."

"Just do me a favor," Brent said. "Keep it discreet until everything is signed."

There was a heartbeat of silence. "You're not having second thoughts about this, are you?" The agent's tone rang with alarm.

"No, of course not." Brent turned away from the window. "Are you kidding? This is the deal of a lifetime. I'd just rather the station hear it directly from me than through the rumor mill. I owe them that."

"Just be sure you don't wait too long," Hal said. "And Brent—congratulations. You've worked hard for this one."

"Thanks." Hanging up the phone, Brent stared blindly into space. The people at the station weren't the only ones he needed to tell about the deal he'd been offered. He hadn't said a word to Laura. He'd meant to last night, but his excitement over the biggest job offer of his life had spilled into passion, and they'd spent half the night making love. Then this morning there'd been the party to prepare for.

Sooner or later, though, he had to tell her and deal with her response, good or bad. If only he could know if she'd greet the news with a burst of joy and an agreement to move halfway across the country or a cool "congratulations" and "good luck with your life."

The back door opened, jarring him back to his senses. He grabbed a cutting board and knife in an effort to look busy. "Did you find some bowls?" he asked over his shoulder. Seeing her hands full, he dropped the knife. "Here, let me help you with that."

"Sorry I took so long." She brushed her hair off her forehead as he took one armload. "I got hung up over at Melody's."

"No problem." He leaned down to give her a quick kiss, started to pull away, then changed his mind and went back for another. The instant punch of desire stole the breath from his lungs, as it always did. She rose up to meet him, to twine her arm about his neck and hold on as he devoured her sweet, giving mouth. He'd never be able to give this up. He'd wither and die without Laura in his life.

But what if she forced him to choose between her and his career? Could he give up everything he'd worked for to stay with her? He'd seen other anchors do it: pass up a chance for advancement in order to stay in the town where their spouses worked and their children went to school.

But he and Laura weren't married. The only thing that held them together was friendship, respect, and this flare of passion that ignited every time they touched. Would it be enough? It had to be, because he couldn't imagine letting her go. His mouth slanted over hers as he deepened the kiss, needing to taste all of her.

She moaned when he finally lifted his head. "Mmm." Her eyes fluttered open. "If I'd known that was waiting for me, I'd have hurried a bit more."

"Well, I was planning to rip your clothes off and have my way with you before the guests arrived, but I guess it's too late for that now."

"We could always make them wait out on the front porch," she teased.

"Don't tempt me." Laughing, he stepped back to a safer distance and prayed his body would cool before the guests arrived. "Did you find some decent salsa?" he asked, taking the bowls to the counter.

"Knowing how picky you are, I bought three kinds." She set the grocery bag beside the bowls and proceeded to pull out one jar at a time. "Wimpy. Gourmet. And hot-enough-to-burn-the-roof-off-your-mouth. Which do you want to sample first?"

"Give me the hot stuff." He wiggled his brows.

"All right, tough guy. Just remember, you asked for it." Opening a bag of tortilla chips, she dipped one in the jar and brought a bite of salsa to his mouth with one hand held below to catch any drips.

"Not bad," he said, and then the afterburn kicked in. "*Hhaa! Hhaa!* Get me a beer." Breathing fire, he headed for the ice chest and twisted the cap off a cold lager from a local microbrewery.

"What? Too hot?"

"No, it's good." He took another pull off the beer. "Just be sure you keep that stuff away from Connie. It'll kill a Yankee like her."

"Oh, I don't know. Connie's pretty tough."

Yeah, he thought, Connie was a tough old bird on the outside—and pure marshmallow underneath. He was going to miss her and all the others. He'd formed more friendships at this station than anywhere else he'd worked, mostly due to Laura and her easy way of socializing.

"So what can I do to help?" Laura asked, surveying the chaos of the kitchen.

He took in all the work still to be done. What had ever possessed him to invite the entire station over? "Call everyone and tell them not to come?" he suggested hopefully.

"Brent." She looked at him in exasperation. "We're not going to go through this again, are we?"

Apparently his expression conveyed the state of his nerves, for she walked forward and framed his face with her hands.

"Listen to me very carefully," she said. "Everything does not have to be perfect. Even if the food stinks, which it won't, and the house is a wreck, which it isn't, people will have a good time because they aren't coming merely to eat and drink. They're coming because they enjoy your company. People like you, Brent. They admire you and respect you. That's not going to change if you play the wrong music or serve the wrong beer. So take a deep breath and relax."

"I have a better idea," he said as he wrapped one arm about the small of her back. "Take your panties off."

"What?" she stared at him as if he'd spoken Greek.

"I can't think about how nervous I am if you're in the same room without any panties on under your shorts."

"Brent!" She laughed, ruining the effect of her scandalized expression. "I will not take off my underwear."

"Come on, Laura." Setting his beer on the chopping block, he kissed her neck just beneath the ear, right in the spot that always made her quiver. "Be wild. Be daring. Give me your panties."

"No," she laughed as he walked her backward, kissing her neck as they went. "I . . . can't." Her head tipped sideways, giving him free access to her neck. He drew her earlobe into his mouth and nibbled it with his teeth. "Really," she said in a breathy voice. "I'd be too embarrassed."

"Come on," he coaxed as he pulled her shirt free of her shorts and slipped his hands inside to caress her warm, bare skin. "It'll be fun."

"Brent, stop," she laughed in false protest and wiggled against him, thrilling his body with the feel of her soft curves against his hard planes. He moved his mouth to her lips and covered them in a greedy kiss. She opened her lips eagerly, accepting and returning every sweep of his tongue. His nimble hands unfastened her shorts.

When her shorts fell to the floor, his fingertips caressed her skin along the edge of her panties, then slipped between her thighs to find the fabric wet. He lifted his head to gaze into her eyes as he stroked her through the thin silk. "God, I want you."

Her eyes turned heavy and dilated. "We don't have time." He glanced at the clock. "We've got five minutes, at least. Plenty of time."

She hesitated for a heartbeat, then attacked the buttons of her blouse. "Be fast."

He sucked in a breath as the blouse opened to reveal her lacy white underwear. The demi cups of her bra barely covered the rose-colored nipples he knew waited beneath. With one hand still between her thighs, he dipped his head to kiss the swell of her breast just above the lace. "You drive me wild, you know that, don't you?"

She moaned deep in her throat as she leaned back against the counter and widened her stance. He stroked her until neither of them could stand the torture a moment longer, then he peeled the lace and silk panties down her long legs.

"Oh, yes," she breathed as he lifted her to sit on the edge of the counter. She wrapped her legs about his hips and reached for the button on his slacks. "I want you inside me," she told him in a husky voice. "Hurry, Brent. Please hurry."

Together they fumbled with the fastenings of his slacks. The moment he sprang free, he thrust deep into her welcoming heat. Her head fell back as she gasped in pleasure. With her half-reclining on the countertop, her blouse gaping, he ran his hands over the curve of her hips and the dip of her waist as he moved inside her. He lowered the cups of her bra to suckle her breasts until the nipples rose to hard peaks in his mouth.

No matter how many times their bodies joined, he never got enough of her. He could go on touching her forever and knew he'd sooner die than stop.

Her legs tightened about his hips, begging him to move harder, faster. He trailed a hand down her stomach and found her sensitive bud with his thumb. She arched against him as her climax rocked through her. He followed a beat behind, pouring himself into her—all of his emotions and the things he couldn't say rushing out of him and into her in that moment of perfect pleasure.

Spent, he slumped forward and gathered her into his arms. They remained entwined, their breathing heavy, as he cradled her to his heart. Then slowly, he straightened to stand between her legs. She blushed a bit as he tugged the lacy bra back into place. "Was that fast enough for you?" he asked, teasing her.

"Yes," she answered, smiling.

Tenderly, he smoothed her hair back into place and felt a calmness settle over him. She'd brought that into his life, a sense of stability to balance the turmoil. He couldn't imagine her not being there for him. Losing her simply was not possible.

He cupped her cheek, telling her with his eyes how much she meant to him. The fear of sharing his news had vanished during their lovemaking, slipping back into the darkness where it belonged. "Laura," he began, "there's something I need tell you."

"Yes?" Her eyes searched his. Any barriers that remained between them crumbled in that instant as he looked in her eyes and saw her heart. She loved him. Why, he couldn't begin to fathom, but she loved him with a completeness that both lifted him up and laid him low.

He took a deep breath, ready to tell her about the job offer. "Laura, I—"

The doorbell rang. They both jumped as the bubble surrounding them burst—and they realized they were half-naked, disheveled, and about to be descended upon by an entire TV station.

"Ohmygod!" Laura gasped as she scrambled off the counter.

"It's okay. Don't panic." Brent tucked in his shirt and fastened his trousers.

"Maybe you should answer the door and stall them," she suggested as she reached for her panties and shorts on the floor.

He snatched up the panties first. "No way, those are mine."

"Brent!" She grabbed for them, but he thrust them into his pants pocket.

"You can have them back—*later*." She started to protest, but he handed her her shorts. "Better hurry."

Muttering to herself, Laura grabbed the shorts while Brent went to the sink to wash his hands. In spite of her indignation, another part of her mind soared with everything that had just happened. Had Brent been about to say what she thought? The way he'd looked into her eyes, she'd seen what she had longed to see for so long. He loved her. Really, truly loved her. More than that, he'd seemed ready to say it. If the doorbell hadn't rung, would she finally have heard the three most precious words known in any language? She held the possibility close to her heart as she righted her clothes and smoothed her hair.

Once they were presentable, they answered the door to find Keshia and Franklin. Laura's euphoric smile shifted to one of welcome. "I'm so glad you could make it," she said with genuine enthusiasm. They'd become casual friends over the summer, seeing each other at the station's after-hours get-togethers.

"What a great house," Keshia exclaimed, taking in the foyer.

"No kidding," Franklin added. "From the way you

described it, Brent, I expected a construction site with torn-up floors and half-painted walls.''

"Well, it does still need some finishing touches," Brent insisted.

"Never mind him." Laura laughed. "Come on in, and we'll show you around."

After a tour of the downstairs, Laura and Keshia headed for the kitchen to chop onions and grate cheese for the fajitas.

"There they go," Franklin chuckled. "Off to talk about us behind our backs."

"Oh, hush." Keshia waved a hand at him. "You two go do something manly, like start the grill."

The minute the kitchen door closed, Keshia turned to Laura. "So?" she asked, her face alive with intrigue. "Is Brent going to make any big announcements tonight?"

Laura blinked, completely confused.

"Oh, I know," Keshia said, moving toward the cutting board on the island. "I'm not supposed to talk about it 'to *anyone*,' right? But I'd hardly call you anyone. I mean, he's bound to have told *you*, even if he is being tight-lipped with everyone else."

The ground shifted under Laura's feet. Keshia had said the word announcement. As far as Laura knew, there were three basic announcements people made during their lifetimes: birth, death, and marriage. Was that what Brent had been about to say before the doorbell rang? Not merely "Laura, I love you," but also "Will you marry me?"

"H-how—" She swallowed hard. "How did you know?"

Keshia shrugged as she selected an onion and tossed it

into the air like a tennis ball. "I caught him talking on the phone yesterday when he thought no one was around."

Laura's mind raced as she grated the cheese. Who could Brent have been talking to that would tip off Keshia? A jeweler, perhaps? Was Brent planning on the whole traditional proposal scene, complete with a diamond engagement ring?

"Hey, Laura?" Franklin poked his head through the door. "I think we're ready for the meat out here."

"Oh. Sure." In a daze she moved to the refrigerator and pulled out a plastic container.

Franklin lifted the lid and gave her a strange look. "Not that I don't love leftover lasagna, but I thought we were having fajitas tonight."

Laura laughed as she saw what she'd handed him. "Oh, sorry." Shaking her head, she exchanged the lasagna for the marinated meat that would be grilled, cut into strips, and served wrapped in flour tortillas. With the meat balanced on the ice chest of cold drinks, Franklin headed back to the patio. The doorbell rang, and Keshia called out that she'd get it.

Laura found herself alone in the kitchen. Beyond the door, she could hear a crowd of guests arriving. Brent called out from the patio, telling everyone to come join him. He sounded confident and jovial, the perfect host.

She closed her eyes to savor the moment, every sound, every scent, every tingle that danced along her skin. The dream she'd almost accepted as beyond her reach was about to come true. She and Brent would marry, have a family, grow old and gray in each other's arms.

The rest of the evening went by in a blur. She laughed and visited with all the friends she'd made from the station. But nothing really touched her—not the music or the festive mood. She felt as if she floated above the picture-perfect scene.

Landscape lights lent a fairy-tale quality to the brightly blooming flower beds. The montage of people who made up the KSET staff laughed and mingled as they devoured the Tex-Mex feast. Brent moved among them looking self-assured, as if he'd hosted a thousand parties. She watched as he accepted the congratulations over his special report with grace and humor.

From across the yard, his gaze connected with hers. *I love you, Brent Michael Zartlich*, she told him with her eyes. *With all my heart*. As if hearing the words, his face softened, and she felt his answer as if he'd spoken aloud. She gathered the feeling close and held it long after they each turned away to see to their guests.

Not until midnight did the last of the guests finally leave. Laura went with Brent to the front door as he bade them good-bye. Calling a final "thank you for coming and drive safe," he closed the door. Silence filled the house. Leaning against the door, he stared at her as a huge grin spread across his features. "Thank God," he said. "I thought they'd never leave."

"And here I thought you were enjoying yourself," she teased, even though she'd been ready for the stragglers to take off an hour ago. "You realize your first party was a smash hit, don't you?"

"Thanks to you." Coming forward, he scooped her up and twirled her around. "And thanks for talking me into it. I had fun."

Laughing, she clung to his neck as his mouth settled over hers for a long kiss. She sighed as he lifted his head.

"Does that mean you'll throw another one? Say, for Christmas?"

"Maybe." He set her down and gave her a look so filled with boyish exuberance, she felt giddy. "Enough about parties, though. I have the greatest news!"

Her heart jumped right into her throat. "What?"

"No, not here." His eyes twinkled as he stepped back. "Wait for me in the den. I'll be right there."

Battling an attack of the jitters, she went to wait on the sofa. She wished she'd worn something besides a casual shorts set. A woman should look special the night her husband proposed. When the kitchen door swung open, she jumped, then folded her hands in her lap to keep them from shaking. A smile washed over her when she saw he carried a bottle of champagne in one hand and two fluted glasses in the other.

"Champagne?" She held a hand over her heart. "This really must be a special occasion."

Taking a seat beside her, he popped the cork, filled both glasses, and handed one to her. His eyes danced as he held up his glass. *Oh God, this is it,* she thought.

"How would you feel," he said slowly, "about toasting the network's newest political reporter in Washington, D.C.?"

She blinked as she tried to make sense of his words. "Excuse me?"

His smile broadened. "I got a call from my agent yesterday. I've been offered a job as political reporter for the network, Laura. The network!"

"I don't understand." *What did this have to do with them getting married?* "I thought reporting was a step down from being an anchor."

"On the local level, yeah. But we're talking the big

time here. This is exactly what I've dreamed about. Being back in the field, doing investigative reports. Oh, God!" He shook his head, laughing. "I can't believe this is happening! Even though I've been working for it, I still can't believe it's finally happening."

A chill brushed her skin. "Then . . . you mean to take the job?"

"As soon as my agent hammers out a contract." He touched his glass to hers and drank deeply.

"I see." Her fingers went numb. Afraid she'd drop the glass, she put it on the coffee table without taking a sip. This was the announcement Keshia had meant. It had nothing to do with marriage and family, or a life filled with love and the laughter of children. Every fantasy she'd played out in her mind during the past few hours returned to mock her.

"What is it?" he asked, apparently sensing the shift in her mood.

"Nothing. I'm happy for you. Really." She tried to smile, but her lips trembled. "If this is what you want, I'm glad." Afraid she'd cry, she turned away.

"Hey." He caught her chin and turned her back to face him. She swallowed hard as tears stung her eyes. If she'd been wrong about the proposal, had she also been wrong about him loving her?

"Laura?" He sat his glass aside and took her hands in his. "You're cold as ice. What's wrong? Is it the thought of moving to Washington? I promise you'll love it. It's a great town. And I'm sure you'll be able to find a job. Look how well you've done here."

She searched his eyes for some sign that she was wrong, that he did love her and meant to marry her. "Brent, what exactly are you asking me?"

"Damn." He slumped. "I guess I did this out of order." Taking a deep breath, he fixed his gaze on their joined hands. Her heart fluttered with renewed hope.

"Laura, these last weeks, I've been thinking about . . . about a lot of things. I never really pictured myself in a long-term relationship, but things have been going so well between us. I mean, we get along great and you seem happy. So I guess I just assumed . . ." He finally looked at her. "I'd like for you to come to Washington with me."

Come to Washington with me. Not "Laura, I love you, please marry me," just "Come to Washington with me." She rose and crossed to the windows. The fairy-tale scene of yard lights and flowers looked abandoned and forlorn.

"Laura?" He came up behind her. In the glass, she saw his reflection as he started to reach for her, then hesitated. "What is it?"

"You said come with you to Washington." Her voice sounded so calm. "What exactly did you want me to come as?"

"I'm not sure I understand."

"Did you mean for me to come with you as your lover?"

His reflection went rigid, as if she'd insulted him. "If that's what you want to call it."

"That *is* what you call it, Brent." Numbly, she turned to face him. "When two people sleep together outside of marriage, they're called lovers."

"Laura . . ." With a sigh, he reached up to brush the hair off her forehead. "What does it matter what people call it? I need you. And well, I want to be with you."

"For how long?"

He blinked. "What do you mean, for how long?"

"I mean, how long will you 'want' to be with me?"

"I don't know." He pulled away. "How can anyone know such a thing?"

"Okay, so you want me to drop everything, move to Washington, and find a new job and a new place to live, so that we can go on being lovers. Is that about it?"

"Actually," his gaze lowered, "I was hoping you'd reconsider living with me. You have to admit, it would be more practical. Especially given the price of housing in D.C."

"Oh," she said, crossing her arms. "So you want me to be more than your lover. You want me to be your mistress."

"Why are you making such a big deal out of this?" Stepping away from her, he made a dismissive gesture with his hand. "People live together all the time. Nobody thinks anything of it."

"Call me picky, but I like to nail down these little details before I make a decision."

"Fine." He thrust his hands into his pockets and faced her from across the room. "What exactly do you need nailed down?"

"When we're out socially, how will you introduce me? 'Hey, everyone, I'd like you to meet my lovely shack-up, Laura Morgan'?"

"Why are you doing this?" He stared at her as if she were intentionally trying to be difficult. She didn't care. She was dying inside, and all she could think was *why*? Why did she always fall short of the mark? What was so wrong with her that she didn't deserve to be loved?

"And what about children, Brent?" she asked, battling tears. "Do you introduce our children as Joey and Suzy, your cute little bastards?"

"Stop it, Laura. Stop it right there!" He raked both

hands through his hair. "Christ," he muttered. "I've already told you I have no intention of having children."

"Accidents happen." She tightened her arms about her waist. "What are you going to do if we accidentally make a baby? Dump me so you don't have to vicariously relive the pain of growing up illegitimate?"

"It's not like it's that big of a stigma, for Christ's sake," he insisted. "People have kids outside of marriage all the time."

"So being born a bastard doesn't bother you?" He didn't respond, and her patience evaporated. "You look me in the eye, Brent Zartlich, and you tell me it didn't bother you to grow up as a bastard."

"I will not have this conversation." He turned away as if to leave the room.

"And I will not let my children grow up without a proper home and loving parents."

He whirled back, his eyes blazing with fury. "A marriage certificate is the last thing that guarantees that."

Laura simply stared at him, watching as he reined in his temper, locking the demons away inside himself where he could pretend they didn't exist.

"For Christ's sake," he sighed. "I said I needed you, didn't I? So it's not like I'm looking for an easy out the first time we have an argument. But you must understand I *can't* marry you."

"Why?" Her voice wavered with confusion and hurt.

"I just can't!" His jaw clenched as his control slipped a notch. "It's not something I can explain. I just can't do it."

"Brent, I—I know the idea of being a husband and a father frightens you, but—"

"You're not listening to me!" he shouted, then took a deep breath when she stepped back.

She watched him run a hand over his face and knew she had nothing to fear from him physically. No matter what he thought of himself, he was not a man who would allow his temper to run loose. She feared instead what he would say.

"All right," he said. "Since you're determined to have this out, I'll tell you again how I feel. *Exactly* how I feel. Every time I even *think* about getting married, my whole chest constricts and I can't breathe. I tried to explain that to you before. I thought you understood."

With perfect clarity, she remembered how she felt every time she thought about marrying Greg: as if she were suffocating. Only her aversion was to Greg, not to marriage. Brent's chest constricted at the thought of marrying *her*. Tears rose up to clog in her throat as she realized he truly didn't love her.

"I see," she managed to say, breaking eye contact. "I guess I thought—Never mind." She needed to get away, quickly, before she crumbled. Blindly she moved past him, heading for the kitchen to retrieve her purse.

"Wait a second." He followed her but stopped in the kitchen doorway. "What are you doing?"

"I—I need to go." She clutched her purse to her breast. What a fool she'd been. What an utter fool!

"Laura, wait!" He stepped toward her but stopped when she backed away. His eyes turned panicked and pleading. "What's this about? You can't just walk out like this."

"I can't stay. Not like this. Not feeling the way I do."

"Like what? Tell me." He moved toward her. "Talk to me."

Swallowing hard, she gazed at him through her tears. "I love you, Brent. I love you."

Utter silence fell as she watched his face. She'd waited so long to say it, had imagined a dozen different reactions. But none of them came close to the confusion and pain she saw playing in his eyes.

"You can't say it, can you?" she said.

"It isn't that I don't care about you," he managed. "I . . . I *care*, all right?"

She shook her head as despair pressed down upon her. "It's not the same, and it's not enough. If you loved me, you'd want to marry me, no matter how much the idea frightens you. You'd find the courage . . . if you loved me."

"So that's it, is it?" He demanded, the anger snapping back into his voice. "Marry you, or it's over?"

She looked away, knowing she'd lost him.

"I can't believe this!" He raked his hands through his hair. "Three months ago, you sat in there on my bed and said you could handle this kind of a relationship. Was that all a lie?"

"Three months ago you weren't asking me to give up my job and my friends while you offer nothing in return," she shot back. "Is it too much to ask for something so simple as love?"

"There is nothing simple about love," he said. "And just because I can't say a few glib words or a make some meaningless vows does not change how I feel about you."

"The words aren't meaningless to me. And if you can't understand that, we have no future together." *I love you, Brent. I will always love you, but I won't stay with you if you can't return that love.* "I won't settle for less than I deserve."

At her words, the hot emotion drained from his eyes, replaced by a coldness that chilled her. He turned away.

"Get out." He said it so softly, she wasn't sure she'd heard right. But when he turned back and impaled her with a look from his wounded eyes, she knew he meant it. "Now, Laura. I want you out of my house. Now!"

She stumbled out the door and stood for a moment on the drive, her legs trembling. From behind her, she heard a crash, as if he'd swept the countertop with his arm, sending bowls and platters crashing to the floor to break into a million jagged pieces.

Just like that, in the blink of an eye, their life together had been shattered.

CHAPTER
24

Laura drove home in a state of shock, along the banks of Buffalo Bayou, past the restaurant where they'd talked about Robby. The esplanade that ran through the middle of Melody's neighborhood looked lonely and surreal in the moonlight.

Had she been wrong to tell Brent how she felt about marriage?

No, she decided. By bringing up the subject, she'd learned the bitter truth. He cared for her, probably even loved her in a way, but not the way she longed to be loved. She was to him what Greg had been to her. A comfort. A convenience. She deserved to be more than that, and to give more in return.

Learning the truth now, before she gave any more of herself, was for the best. She just wished she didn't feel so empty. And so totally numb.

Turning the corner onto Melody's street, she saw Greg's car still parked in front of Melody's house, and the numbness vanished in a heartbeat. For one desperate moment, she thought about not stopping. The last thing she wanted was to face anyone right then, especially Greg. Where would she go, though, if she didn't stop?

Resigned, she pulled over and got out of the car. She

stood, listening to the night sounds of the wind rustling through the trees and katydids chirping their continuous song. How could everything seem so ordinary when her world was falling apart?

Passing through the front gate, she tried to imagine why Greg was still here. He seemed to have accepted that things were over for them romantically. Surely this idea of them becoming business partners didn't warrant him waiting hours for her to return. Especially since, if she and Brent hadn't broken up, she wouldn't have come home tonight at all.

From inside, she heard something that sounded like sitar music. She assumed Melody had pulled out all the stops in trying to run Greg off. She was surprised it hadn't worked.

Opening the door, she found the lights dim. She started to call out a greeting, but the sheer quiet of the place stopped her. Cautiously, she stepped past the entry-way into the living room—and stopped in her tracks, stunned by the scene that lay before her.

Greg and Melody sat on the floor facing each other in the lotus position of meditation. Their eyes were closed, their hands rested palm up on their knees. Incense smoke spiraled upward from a burner that rested on the floor between them.

And they were both stark naked.

From Melody's bedroom, one of the dogs barked, breaking the silence. Greg's eyes cracked open, then flew wide. "Laura Beth!" He grabbed for his discarded clothes.

Melody startled out of her trance, blinking in confusion. "Laura Beth? Oh, Laura! What are you doing home?"

"I can explain!" Greg struggled to cover himself with his shirt and slacks.

A small giggle of hysteria escaped Laura. *Just when I thought I couldn't possibly feel worse . . .* Though why finding them together should hurt, she had no idea.

"Oh, Greg, for heaven's sake," Melody said. "Would you stop blushing?" As if she weren't blushing as well, albeit to a lesser degree, Melody shrugged into the over-size shirt she'd been wearing earlier. "It's not as if Laura's never seen you naked before."

"Laura, I swear—" Ignoring Melody, Greg gave her a pleading look. "This isn't what it looks like."

"It's exactly what it looks like," Melody insisted, appearing more disgruntled at Greg than embarrassed about Laura finding them together. Then she caught the expression on Laura's face, and her frown turned to one of concern. "Hey, you're not upset about this, are you?"

"No, I'm not upset," she said, with a total lack of inflection. In truth, she wasn't sure what she felt, other than stunned. "If y'all will excuse me, I think I'll go to my room."

Thankfully, neither of them tried to stop her as she crossed the room and disappeared through the kitchen into her bedroom. Closing the door, she leaned against it. Laughter came first, followed by tears—silent wrenching tears that wracked her whole body.

Long moments passed before the quiet knock came, and she realized she'd been waiting for it. Straightening, she wiped her cheeks and opened the door. Greg stood there, once again dressed, his head slightly bowed.

"Can I come in?"

"Of course." She stepped back.

He took a long time closing the door, then stood for a

while, staring at the doorknob. "Laura, I—I don't know what to say."

"You don't have to say anything."

"Even though you've made it clear that things are over between us, my behavior tonight was inexcusable."

"Why?" she asked. "Because you think we could still get back together?" When he didn't answer, she knew she was right. "So that's why you offered me a partnership in the pharmacy. As a way of getting me back."

"No!" He finally looked at her. "Of course not. Well, at least not completely. No." As if realizing he'd protested too strongly, he sighed in defeat. "Well, all right, perhaps that was part of the reason. Although I really did think we'd make good business partners."

"Did?" She raised a brow.

She could see the thoughts flicker across his face as he searched for a graceful way out of an awkward situation. "Yes, well, uhm, Melody pointed out that you and I might not be the best business partners, seeing as how we both lean toward the analytical. She, uhm, suggested that I might, well, want someone of a more creative nature who understands marketing and new trends in wellness products, and possibly a gift section . . . and, uhm, such." His words dwindled with a hopeless look of apology.

In spite of everything, Laura had to bite her lip to keep from smiling. "I don't suppose she had anyone in particular in mind for the job?"

He gave her a sheepish look, reminding her so much of the shy man she'd nearly fallen in love with five years ago. "Actually," he cleared his throat, "Melody is quite knowledgeable on the subject of holistic health. In fact," he added, as if surprised by his own thoughts, "she really is the most remarkable woman, once you get beneath the strange clothes she wears—I mean—'' His face went crimson.

"That's okay." Laura held up her hand.

"I meant, intellectually," he rushed to explain.

"I know what you meant, and I quite agree. Melody is a very intelligent, wonderfully genuine person."

"Yeah, she is, isn't she?" His embarrassment shifted to pride.

Laura blinked, wondering if he'd ever felt that silly sort of enchantment for her. "You really like her, don't you?''

He shrugged, hedging. "She's just so different from anyone I've ever known. She's frustrating, irritating, and completely exasperating, but I can't seem to stop thinking about her. And she knows it, too. From the first moment I met her, that day of the Homes Tour, she's had this way of looking at me, all smug and amused, like she can read my mind and knows how attracted I've been, even though I didn't want to be. You've got to believe me, I never meant to think about her like that."

"Greg, it's okay. It's not like you cheated on me or anything."

His gaze dropped to his shoes. "I just want you to know I didn't mean for—for tonight to happen. I'm not even sure how it did. One minute, we were yelling at each other—even though I never yell; you know I never yell. The next thing I know, we're tearing each other's clothes off like a couple of sex-crazed teenagers."

"Greg, please, you don't have to explain." Her hand went back up. "In fact, I really wish you wouldn't."

"Sorry." He studied her a moment, then tilted his head in surprise. "You're not angry."

"No, I'm not. Surprised. Shocked, maybe, but not angry. I just never pictured you and Melody, well, you know."

"I did." He grinned. "Picture it, I mean. A little too often. I guess somehow I knew how it would be. She drives me nuts, but at the same time, tonight I felt more alive than I ever have. Ever. With anyone." Realizing what he'd just said, he rushed to add, "Not that it wasn't great with you—"

Laura shook her head. "It's okay. I'm happy for you, Greg. I mean that. And I think that whatever this is between you and Melody, you ought to give it a chance."

"You really think so? You don't think it's weird us being together, I mean with me being younger and all?"

"Does being younger bother you?" she asked.

He thought about it a moment, then grinned. "Actually, no. Not in the least."

"Then no, I don't think it's weird."

"Thanks." He sighed. "You know, you've been a good friend. I hope we can keep that, at least."

"Me, too."

They stood for a moment, staring at each other. Then, with a laugh, they stepped forward and embraced. The hug was friendly and filled with the warmth of many fond memories.

"You take care of yourself," she whispered.

"Hey, you don't have to say it like we'll never see each other again. I have a feeling you may be seeing a lot of me if things work out with Melody."

"I hope so. But either way, take care," she said. "You're a very special person."

"You, too."

With a final nod, he turned and left. As soon as the

door closed behind him, she sank to the bed, dropped her face into her hands, and wept. The sorrow didn't come from his accepting that their relationship was over, or that he'd found something special with Melody. The sorrow came from knowing that door to her life was finally, irrevocably closed. Even though she wanted that, it was still an ending, and every ending—even a welcome one—left a small hole with its passing.

A few moments passed before Melody rapped lightly on the door, then poked her head inside. "Hey there."

"Hey." She managed a weak smile.

Melody frowned. "You okay?"

She started to say yes, but when she opened her mouth, a tiny sob escaped. "No."

"Oh, honey." Rushing forward, Melody enveloped her in her arms. The tears came hot and fast as Melody rocked her. "I'm sorry. I swear I didn't know you still cared for him. Please believe me, I never would have let this happen, no matter how attracted I was to him. I swear I didn't think you'd care."

"I don't."

"You don't?" Melody leaned back to study her face. "Then why are you sitting here crying your heart out?"

She shrugged. "I guess it's not every night a girl gets dumped by two men."

"*Two* men?"

"Brent and I . . ." She took a breath and forced herself to say it, to accept it. "Brent and I split up."

"No!" Melody's face registered disbelief, then sorrow. "Oh, honey, what happened?"

Laura explained the whole evening. As she spoke, a nagging suspicion wormed its way into the back of her mind, that maybe, if she hadn't jumped to the assumption that Brent was going to propose marriage earlier in the evening, she might have reacted differently to the proposal he *had* offered. From the expression on Melody's face, her friend had come to the same conclusion. "What?" she asked, hoping she was wrong. "What is it?"

"Nothing," Melody insisted quickly.

Laura stood in a rush, needing to move. Would the evening have worked out differently if not for her sudden attack of old-fashioned values? But dammit, those values weren't wrong. She glanced back at Melody and caught her friend's pitying expression. "You think I acted unreasonably, don't you?"

"I didn't say that."

"But you thought it."

"No, I—" Melody slumped. "I'm not saying you're wrong to feel the way you do, but—"

"You think I overreacted."

"I'm just saying issuing an ultimatum usually isn't the best way to deal with people, especially men."

"I didn't give him an ultimatum."

Melody arched a brow.

"I never said 'propose marriage or I'm out of here.' " But neither had she denied it when Brent had said it. Self-conscious under her friend's steady gaze, she straightened the items on the top of the dresser. "I simply stated the facts as I saw them. He doesn't love me, not truly, so what would be the point of my moving to D.C. with him?" Yet the idea of staying behind felt like a knife twisting in her heart. "If I went with him, it would only get worse, Melody. Can't you see that? Emotionally, I'd starve to death by slow degrees waiting for a few crumbs of commitment from him. I can't live like that, so it's best I get out now."

She glanced over her shoulder, pleading for her friend to understand. "Don't you think?"

Melody studied her for a long moment. "What are the facts as Brent sees them?"

Her shoulders slumped. "That I lied to him, deceived him, tried to trap him."

"I doubt he phrased it quite so harshly," Melody said. "And even if he did, he was probably just lashing out because you'd hurt him."

That stiffened Laura's spine. "Well, he hurt me, too. Don't my feelings count?"

"Of course they do." Melody came off the bed to take Laura's hand in her own. With her other hand, she brushed the hair off Laura's forehead. "You have every right to be upset. In fact, do what I do, and wallow in it a while. Then, tomorrow morning, when you've both calmed down, you can call him and work this out like two rational adults who care deeply for each other."

"I will *not*." Laura stepped away from Melody's comforting touch. The mere thought of calling Brent sent waves of panic through her. She'd made a big enough fool of herself already. The last thing she would do was open herself up to more pain by chasing after him.

But am I willing to give up what I have just because I can't have it all? she wondered. The temptation to give in to such naked longing, to sacrifice her dream of a family in order to stay with Brent, hurt as much as the thought of losing him. But to call him and apologize?

"No," she said, striving for conviction. "I won't call. If he wants to work things out, he can call me. I'm through making all the sacrifices. If Brent wants to be with me, it's time he made a few of his own."

Melody sighed, but Laura refused to look at her.

She'd made her stand, and if she backed down now, she'd lose the only thing she had left: her self-respect.

"Laura," her friend said at last, "I know you're hurting. But if there's one thing I learned from being married to a military man, it's that you have to offer the enemy a way to surrender and still save face."

Laura turned around, horrified at hearing Brent called an enemy. "I'm not asking him to surrender. I'd just like someone besides me to do the bending for a change."

"You know, Laura, there's something I've noticed about you," Melody said. "You aren't nearly as flexible as people think. Oh, ninety percent of the time you are, but then there's that ten percent when you dig in your heels and refuse to budge. Take this standoff with your father, for instance. Don't you think that man knows he's in the wrong for the way he acted?"

Laura frowned but didn't answer.

"You've said it yourself, he's likely eaten up with guilt," Melody continued. "Given that, don't you think he'd rush to meet you more than halfway if you just made the first step? Sometimes you have to take the first step, even if you're in the right, so the one who's wrong can salvage a little pride."

"What about *my* pride?"

"Is your pride more important to you than a relationship with Brent?"

Laura frowned. What if she did take that first step toward Brent, only to find out he'd changed his mind about wanting her to move with him to Washington? Or what if she moved to D.C., secretly hoping that someday he'd come to love her enough to offer marriage? Would that be fair to him—or to her? "I won't call him." She said the words more quietly this time, but with no less conviction. Wrapping her arms about herself, she refused to meet Melody's sorrowful gaze. "If Brent wants to make up, he can call me. And that's final."

"Oh, Laura." With a sigh, Melody shook her head. "I wish you hadn't said that."

"Why, because you think I'm wrong?"

"No. When it comes to love, there is no right and wrong. Just be careful you don't back yourself into a corner you can't gracefully get out of, or you really will have to sacrifice your pride."

The truth of those words made her turn away. "Don't you understand, Melody?" she said softly. "It's not just a matter of pride."

"Then what is it?"

"It's a matter of facing reality." Laura closed her eyes, feeling suddenly drained. "Brent has always been my impossible dream. For a while, I forgot that dreams don't last. Eventually, the time comes when you have to wake up." She bit her lip to keep it from trembling. "And that's what I have to do, wake up and get on with my life."

CHAPTER
25

"This is Brent Michaels, reporting from the nation's capital." The words rolled off Brent's tongue by rote, as so many words seemed to do lately. Standing on the steps of the capitol building, he felt oddly detached—as if he were standing outside himself watching a successful news reporter wrap up another live feed. Even the chill of the November wind slicing through his overcoat barely registered on his senses.

"Good job, Brent." His producer's voice filled his ear through the IFB. The woman was young, competent, and aggressive, but there were times when her peppy enthusiasm irritated the hell out of him.

He missed Connie's deprecating humor and Keshia's quick comebacks, which had often made keeping a straight face on the air a challenge. As the cameraman took his mic and loaded up the van, he realized how much he missed Jorge's odd blend of street smarts and naïveté. He missed going out for Mexican food with the crew at midnight. He even missed the damned Rottweilers slobbering all over him when he came through the front door.

And he missed Laura.

God, he missed her so much, he felt as if someone

had carved a hole in his chest. How could anyone hu
this much without actually bleeding?

He'd thought the wretched pain would ease wit
time. Yet after two and a half months, he still couldn
take a full breath without feeling as if something migh
break loose inside. Out of sheer self-preservation, h
knew he had to keep a lid on his emotions. Because onc
the pain broke loose, it would devour him whole.

"Mr. Michaels," the cameraman called, "I'm a
loaded up, if you're ready to go."

He stared at the boy's energetic face, bright with th
chill of autumn. If he had to get in that van and listen t
the kid's cheerful banter all the way back to the statior
his control would snap. "No, you go on. I'll catch th
Metro."

The cameraman shrugged as if Brent were crazy bu
climbed into the van. A moment later, Brent was alone
Blessedly alone. Turning up the collar of his overcoat t
ward off the wind, he shoved his hands into his pocket
and walked down the middle of D.C.'s famous mall, no
really caring where he went. With the summer touris
season over, the grassy park that stretched from the capi
tol building to the Washington Monument appeared vir
tually deserted. A few transients slept on the benche
before the numerous buildings of the Smithsonian and a
occasional jogger passed by.

Decorations on the lampposts reminded him that to
morrow would be Thanksgiving. He'd always hated th
holidays, and this year he dreaded them even more thai
usual. Holidays reminded him too keenly that he was a
outsider. Only with Laura had he felt a part of the worl
around him. A part of something vital.

With a few shallow breaths, he pushed the though

aside and concentrated on the present, on the crunch of the brittle grass beneath his feet, the sting of the wind in his face.

He'd wanted this job so badly. Perhaps too badly. When his agent had called with the offer from the network, his first response had been disbelief. Was that why he hadn't told Laura right away? Had he simply needed time to let it sink in?

No, he admitted in a moment of brutal honesty. He hadn't told her because he'd known what her answer would be; and he'd needed a whole day to convince himself he was wrong—that she would blithely follow him anywhere he went.

Weary beyond belief, he settled onto an empty bench in front of the building known as "The Castle." Even deserted as it was today, the merry-go-round that stood before it struck him as a snapshot of the American dream, something young couples with cozy homes in the suburbs brought their children to ride; then returned to those homes to share an evening meal as a unit, a whole. Did such happiness really exist, or was it all a myth?

As if to taunt him, an image rose in his mind of Laura lifting a little girl with a ponytail and glasses onto one of the brightly painted horses. He could almost hear the laughter as the little version of Laura turned to him and cried, "Look at me, Daddy."

He shook his head to dispel the vision as pain speared through him. As a realist, he knew better than to indulge in such flights of fancy. A home and children were Laura's dream, not his. Besides, what was so great about marriage anyway?

He waited for the righteous tirade to come, like a tape that had played repeatedly in his head for the past

two months—on how Laura had claimed she accepted
him as he was, then turned on him in the end. Unfortu
nately, the angry words died more quickly with each pass
ing day. In their place, silence stretched all around him, a
silence he wasn't sure he could face much longer. Still it
remained, growing more vast until he thought he would
sell his soul just to have the quiet broken with the sound
of Laura's voice.

Other times, he could almost hear her whisper in the
back of his mind, *If you loved me, you'd want to marry me
no matter how much the idea frightens you.*

Of all the things she'd said, that one had struck the
deepest chord of truth. He was afraid—deathly afraid to
open himself up a second time after what had happened.
He'd told her he needed her, that he cared. And she'd
acted as if that meant nothing.

He stood abruptly and resumed walking away from
the capitol. Leaving the mall, he crested the hill of the
Washington Monument and started down the grassy slope
on the other side. No matter how far he walked, though,
her words still hounded him.

*If you loved me, you'd want to marry me, no matter how
much the idea frightens you.*

He picked up his pace until he reached the reflecting
pool before the Lincoln Memorial and could go no
further. He stopped and stared down at his own reflection, at the desperation that ravaged his face—and he accepted the truth. He loved Laura Beth Morgan. How that
was possible, he wasn't quite sure, but she was so much a
part of him, he knew the feeling was real and it would
never go away.

Closing his eyes, he tried to picture telling her.
Would she leap into his arms, filling his life with joy? Or

would she turn him away, ending all chance of winning her back? But even if she did turn away, could he possibly hurt any more than he did right now? He opened his eyes and stared at the leaden sky. One way or another, this had to end. He simply couldn't go on any longer without hearing her voice.

His hands shook as he fumbled in the pocket of his overcoat for his cell phone, then he hesitated. What if she refused to even talk to him? Perhaps he should wait until evening to call her at home. But he couldn't wait. He had to talk to her now. Pulling her work number from memory, he punched it in.

"Doctor's office, may I help you?" a cheerful voice answered.

"Tina?" His heart raced, to be this close to Laura by the magic of a telephone. "This is Brent. Is Laura in?"

"I'm sorry, this isn't Tina. She quit," the new receptionist announced cheerfully. "I'm Angie."

"Oh, well, hi, Angie." He smiled at how youthful the girl sounded. "This is Brent Michaels. I need to speak with Laura Morgan, please."

"I'm sorry, she's not in today. Would you like to leave a message? Or maybe someone else can help you."

"No, I don't think anyone else can help with this," he admitted with a smile. "It's personal."

"Oh, are you calling about the wedding? If you are, you might try Laura at the house. Although she's probably still at the alterations lady, picking up her dress."

The air left his lungs in a painful rush. *Wedding!* He nearly shouted the word out loud before his years of experience as an investigative reporter took over. "Uh, yes. Yes, of course. The wedding." He pinched the bridge of his nose as his mind took a dizzy whirl inside his head.

"I'm, eh, a friend of the family, and I seem to have mis
placed my invitation. I don't suppose you have the time
and place for the ceremony, do you?"

"Oh, sure. It's on Laura's calendar. Hang on, and I'll
go grab it."

As he waited, he forced himself not to panic. Maybe
it wasn't her wedding. How could it be? He'd only been
gone two and a half months. She couldn't possibly have
fallen in love with someone else so quickly. Unless she'd
decided to marry Greg Smith. No, she'd sworn that was
over, that she didn't love Greg, and he couldn't see her
marrying for anything less than love.

Except she wanted a home, a family. Children.
Would she marry Greg simply to have all that?

"Here it is," Angie announced. "Let's see, the cere-
mony will be at the First Methodist Church in Beason's
Ferry on Saturday at four o'clock with a reception at the
VFW Hall to follow. Do you need the addresses?"

"No. I know where they are." His clenched teeth
made the words come out as a snarl. "Does her calender
mention the name of the groom?"

"Well, no, but everybody knows it's Greg Smith."

"Son of a *bitch*!" He jammed his thumb against the
off button and nearly hurled the phone into the reflecting
pool. She was really going to do it. She was going to marry
that whey-faced, mealy-mouthed pharmacist!

"Like hell she is!" he growled. Turning, he stalked
toward the nearest Metro station, his mind racing with
every step. The ceremony wasn't until Saturday, which
gave him plenty of time to get to Laura and inform her
she wasn't going to marry anyone but him!

As he walked, he punched in her home number, but
all he got was Melody's answering machine. Just as well,

he decided. For something like this, he needed to talk to her face to face, not over the telephone. He stopped to make another call before he descended into the underground Metro station. His producer's voice came on the line.

"Margie, look, I need to leave town unexpectedly. Family emergency. Can someone cover my beat for a few days?"

"Well, sure, I guess, if it's an emergency." Concern filled the woman's voice. "There hasn't been a death, has there?"

"No," he said. "But there might be," he added under his breath. He'd break every bone in Greg's body before he let some other man marry Laura. "I need a plane ticket to Houston right away. What travel agency do we use?"

She looked up the information on her Rolodex and gave it to him. When he got through to the travel agent moments later, he lost what little control he had left. "What do you mean, you can't get me a flight out of here until Monday!"

"I'm sorry, Mr. Michaels, but it *is* the Thanksgiving weekend."

"Thanksgiving! Who cares about *Thanksgiving*?" He tried and failed to rein in his temper. "You don't understand. I *have* to get to Houston." After a few more minutes of fruitless arguing, he hung up on the woman and stalked into the Metro station to catch a subway to the hotel where he rented a room by the week. Even after two months, he hadn't been able to bear looking at houses without Laura. Every time he saw a place that needed renovating, he remembered the weekends they'd spent together fixing up his house in Houston.

Damn! There had to be some way to get to Houston,

other than hanging around the airport hoping for a standby ticket. If the flights were as booked as the travel agent claimed, he couldn't take a chance. He needed to get to Laura. Now.

By the time he reached his hotel room, a plan had formed in his mind. He had three days to get from D.C. to Texas. His Porsche was the next best thing to flying. Grabbing a suitcase, he packed in record time.

Thirty minutes later, he hit the interstate doing a hundred and five. He checked the radar detector and settled back for the drive. Barring any major complications, he'd make it to Laura in plenty of time to stop the wedding.

CHAPTER
26

Laura hesitated at the front door, not sure if she should ring the bell or just open the door. It felt odd, being faced with such a decision while standing on the front step of the house where she'd grown up. Would the door even open if she tried to turn the knob? Too well she remembered the last time she'd come home and found the house locked against her.

Squaring her shoulders, she decided to try the knob. If it gave, she'd walk on in. If it didn't . . . If it didn't, she'd ring the bell and keep right on ringing it until her father answered. Melody was right. This nonsense had gone on long enough. Thanksgiving Day was meant to be shared by family. And she would share it with the only family she had, whether he'd invited her or not.

To her relief, the knob gave. Easing the door open, she stepped hesitantly over the threshold. The moment she closed the door against the cool autumn air, the stillness of the house enveloped her like an old friend welcoming her in a warm embrace. The familiar sights and smells filled her senses. She took a deep breath and smiled at the scent of lemon oil and floor wax—and something else. Was that the smell of fresh-baked turkey and home-made rolls?

She should have known better than to imagine her father sitting in the dark, starving from his own stubbornness on Thanksgiving Day. In Beason's Ferry, neighbors looked after one another, even if the one who needed looking after was the town's most obstinate widower.

The sound of football on TV drew her to the den. She made the trek slowly, noting the cleanliness of the front parlor. Filtered sunlight glowed on the cherry wood coffee table with its porcelain figurines all in their proper places. At least her father had had Clarice these past months. Even if the two rarely exchanged a word, the mere presence of another human in the house could be a comfort. She knew that all too well, since loneliness had descended upon her the minute Greg had come to Houston to whisk Melody off to his parents' house in a neighboring town for the holiday.

Not that she begrudged Melody and Greg their happiness; but she was somewhat amazed at how warmly Melody had been welcomed by Greg's small-town, ultraconservative family. The Smiths apparently looked on their future daughter-in-law with a sense of awe for her artistic talent. Likewise, the people of Beason's Ferry had taken to the pharmacist's bride, especially the fundraising committee, who'd already roped Melody into organizing the arts and crafts show for the next Homes Tour.

Still, Laura had felt a bit abandoned when her friend left. That, combined with a nagging image of her father being equally alone, had finally prodded her to take the long-overdue first step toward reconciliation.

A burst of cheers and an announcer yelling "touchdown" pulled her the last few steps to the den where she and her father had spent so many evenings. He relaxed in his recliner, facing the TV. A quiet warmth filled her as she leaned against the doorjamb, savoring the sight of him. He'd never been much of a man for watching sports, preferring a good John Wayne movie on a quiet afternoon. Still, not watching the Longhorns and the Aggies on Thanksgiving was next to sacrilege in Texas. And Dr. Walter Morgan was as proud of being a UT alumnus as he was of being a Son of the Republic.

He was a man who liked tradition, her father: a man who clung to the tenets of strength, honor, and integrity. Above all, he believed a man's role in the world was to protect and provide. Providing had never been a problem for him. Her heart ached, knowing he saw himself as a failure in the other regard. He hadn't been able to save his wife from her own self-destruction, or to spare his daughter the pain of growing up.

Tears unexpectedly prickled her eyes. She sniffed to hold them back. At the sound, her father glanced around, then bolted from the chair. Emotions flickered across his face, from surprise to joy to something that looked like guilt before the mask dropped firmly into place.

"Hello, Daddy," she said with a sad smile. She'd known this wouldn't be easy, but she hadn't expected the discomfort to strike quite this close to the bone. He made no move to answer, and she fought the urge to fidget. "I know I should have called first, but . . ."

But I was afraid you'd tell me not to come. She wanted to shout "I'm your daughter! And I'm hurting, too!" Instead, she sighed in resignation, pleading with him to understand. "Dad, it's Thanksgiving. Whether you want to claim me or not, we're still a family. And I don't see any reason why either one of us should spend this day alone."

"I'm, uhm—" He eyes darted toward the kitchen,

and to her surprise a hint of color rose up his neck. "I'm not exactly alone."

"Walter, dear?" a feminine voice rang out from the kitchen. "Do you want whipped topping on your pecan pie?"

Laura's eyes widened. She knew that voice. She knew she knew it, she just couldn't believe it. She stared at her father for confirmation, but he stood ramrod straight, his chin raised as his face turned red.

"Walter?" The woman's voice grew louder as she appeared in the doorway opposite Laura, an apron tied about her waist, a pie plate in one hand. She halted abruptly when she spotted Laura.

"Miss *Miller*?"

"Close your mouth, dear," Miss Miller said. "It's unbecoming to gape."

"Yes, ma'am," Laura said. The woman looked neat as always in a shirtwaist dress.

"Well, Walter?" The schoolteacher gave Laura's father a pointed look.

"Well what, Ellie?" He grumbled.

Miss Miller propped one hand on her narrow hip. "Are you going to stand there all day, or are you going to ask your daughter to join us for a bite of pie?"

Her father's lips thinned, like a child refusing to speak.

"Thank you anyway," Laura hastened to say. "But I'm not hungry . . . just yet. Maybe later?" She added the last hopefully, glancing back to her father. His eyes softened, even if his posture remained rigid.

"Oh, for heaven's sake!" Miss Miller marched into the room like General Patton in two-inch pumps. "Walter, sit." She pointed at his recliner. To Laura's surprise, her father sank obediently into his chair. "Now, eat your pie and visit with your daughter while I go finish the dishes."

"I'm not hungry," he said.

"Fine!" Miss Miller slammed the plate onto the table beside her father's chair, picked up the remote control, and hit the mute button. "Then you won't have your mouth full when you tell her how glad you are to see her. Laura Beth." The woman turned with eyes narrowed. "Have a seat and catch your father up on how you've been these last months. He's plumb eaten up with worry, even if he won't admit it."

Laura sat on the sofa.

Miss Miller turned to go but hesitated at the door. As she looked at Laura's father, her face softened in a way that almost made her pretty. "Walter Morgan, you are the finest man I have ever known, but so help me, if you keep punishing that child for her mother's sins, I swear I'll keep walking right out that back door."

Her father's back snapped straight. "I have never punished Laura Beth for anything her mother did."

Miss Miller shook her head, her eyes pleading. "Let it go, Walter. You are never going to be free of that woman and the pain she put you through until you let it go."

The moment Miss Miller left, silence settled over the room. Laura waited. Now that she'd made the first step in coming, she was determined that her father make the next. From the corner of her eyes, she saw him fidget slightly and frowned. She'd seen her father angry, stoic, and proud; she'd even seen him emotionally shattered. But she couldn't remember ever seeing him nervous.

"I . . ." he cleared his throat. "I hear you're working for a pediatrician."

"Yes. Dr. Velasquez." Laura folded her arms, then unfolded them and smoothed the pleats of her pants.

"I've heard he's very good." Her father drummed his fingers on the arm of his chair. "You enjoy working for him?"

"Very much. Although I'm thinking of applying for a position as director of ways and means for KIND, Kids In Need of Doctors. It's a national organization that raises money to help children receive medical treatment."

"Oh?" He prompted.

Laura clasped her hands, wishing she hadn't brought the subject up. She'd learned of the job opening through a friend she'd made while helping Brent with his special report. The foundation was based in Washington, D.C., and she'd all but been told the job was hers if she'd just apply. That, however, was a decision she wasn't ready to face. Not today.

"Yes, well, I haven't made up my mind yet, but I think I'd enjoy the work."

She wasn't sure, but she thought she saw a smile of pride tug at his lips. "Yes. You always did enjoy helping others."

"I guess I get that from you," she offered. "You're one of the most caring people I've ever known. I always admired that about you."

He turned his head, and she saw his throat move, as if trying to swallow a painful knot.

Taking a deep breath, she searched for a different subject. "I assume you heard Greg Smith is getting married."

"Yes. Yes I did." His voice sounded too tight for his casual manner. "Quite a shock that, him up and marrying his former girlfriend's roommate. Had all the old hens around here clucking for days. Some of the young ones, too."

"I imagine it did." She glanced away, knowing that if he'd heard about where she worked and about Greg and Melody, he'd heard about her breakup with Brent. Small-town grapevines had far-reaching roots. She prayed he wouldn't bring it up. Not yet. Maybe later, after they got through this first awkward meeting. *If* they got through it.

"You all right with that?" he asked. "Greg marrying your roommate?"

"I couldn't be more pleased." Her smile was genuine if fleeting. "In fact, I'm going to be Melody's maid of honor. The ceremony is this Saturday, at the First Methodist Church."

"So I heard."

"Would you, uhm . . ." she straightened the crease of her slacks—"care to come?"

A short silence fell. "I might." His fingers drummed on the chair arm. "If you think the bride and groom wouldn't mind."

"They'd be delighted."

"Do you think they'd mind if I brought a . . . date?"

Her eyes widened in surprise. "I—I think it would be fine if you brought a date. In fact, I think it would be wonderful."

"You do?" His gaze finally met hers.

She blinked back tears. "Yes, Daddy, I really do."

"Then you don't mind about me and Ellie."

"No! Of course I don't mind! Did you think I would?"

"I don't know." He looked frustrated and confused.

"Children are funny sometimes, about this sort of thing. And I just—" He broke off abruptly as his face crumbled.

In a flash, she crossed the room and knelt before him. His arms pulled her into a crushing embrace. She felt him kiss the top of her head as he stroked her hair.

"Oh, God, Laura Beth, I've missed you. I've missed you so much, but after all the things I said, I knew I'd hurt you, and I didn't know how to make it right. I couldn't face you, even though I've been so worried. I know I wasn't a very good father. And I'm sorry. I'm so sorry."

"Who says you weren't a good father?" She pulled back to look into his eyes. "You were the best father a girl could have, in spite of everything you were going through. Raising a daughter alone would be hard for any man. Yet you were always there for me, and I never doubted how much you loved me."

"You were the one who took care of me." He cupped her face and gave her a sad smile. "I never quite knew what to do with you. Even as a child, you were such a quiet, solemn thing, like a miniature adult. At least when your mother was alive, she knew how to make you laugh and play like other children. Then, suddenly—" A tear rolled down his cheek.

She reached for his hand and squeezed it.

"Suddenly, she was gone," he said. "And I was so caught up in my own grief, I—I forgot to take care of you. I just sat here, sunk in my self-pity, letting you look after me. Then the next thing I know, you're all grown up and wanting to leave home, and I couldn't quite figure out how it happened. All those years I threw away— And I wanted them back, Laura Beth. I still want them back."

"Oh, Daddy, I'm sorry." She hugged him again,

breathing in the scent of fabric starch and Old Spice. "Can you ever forgive me?"

"Sweetheart, there's nothing to forgive you for. I'm the one—"

"No." She leaned back and covered his mouth with her fingertips. "Hear me out. You're not the only one who floundered out of not knowing what to do. All those years I took care of you, I was keeping busy so I wouldn't have to grieve. Only I forgot to give you the one thing you needed most: to feel needed. I should have let you take care of me some, too. In fact, I should have stomped my foot and made you. Instead, I left you alone, because it was easier for me. I can't give you back the years we lost, but if you're willing to try, we can go forward from here."

He shook his head. "If I could only take back the things I said that day—"

"No. No regrets." She narrowed her eyes at him. "Let's just take it from right here, right now, and see where that leads us. Agreed?"

When his face softened, she saw more clearly the man who lived behind the proud mask. He looked lonely and humbled and more vulnerable than even she had suspected. "Agreed," he said at last.

She resisted the urge to throw her arms around him again, knowing he needed time to compose himself. "So," she said with forced brightness, "what do you say I take this here pie into the kitchen and have Miss Miller put the proper topping on it? After all, if she's going to hang out around here, she needs to learn my daddy likes ice cream on his pecan pie, not whipped cream."

He gave her a mock scowl. "Are you trying to take care of me, young lady?"

"Sorry." Laura bit her lip, but let laughter dance in

her eyes. "Maybe we could take it into the kitchen together?"

"On one condition. That you call my gal Ellie." His voice dropped to a whisper. "She says being called Miss Miller makes her feel like an old maid."

"Oh." Laura refrained from pointing out that Miss Miller was an old maid. Although seeing the twinkle in her father's eyes, she wondered how long that status would last. "Ellie it is," she agreed, and rose with her hand held out.

The moment his hand slipped into hers, a sense of rightness settled over her. No matter how many years they'd lost, he'd always be her daddy, and some part of her would always be his little girl.

~⌒⌐

Brent cursed when he recognized the sound of a second cylinder misfiring, followed by a third and then a fourth. The first one had started popping shortly after his last fill-up, outside of Memphis, where he'd apparently bought some corrupted gas. Any hope that the fuel injectors would magically unplug themselves died when the car lagged as if hitting a wall of water. He took his foot off the gas pedal and let the Porsche roll onto the shoulder of the highway.

Getting out, he slammed the door and went around back to check the engine compartment. Nothing appeared to be wrong; all the fluid levels looked fine. He stared at the engine, knowing it had to be the injectors. Which meant the whole fuel system would need to be cleaned by a competent mechanic.

Slamming the hood, he glanced up and down the

deserted highway. According to the sign he'd passed a few miles back, he was still hours away from Little Rock. Telephone lines stretched along the road, disappearing into the distance with little else to break the horizon but some hills and trees. Overhead, a vulture circled in the cloudless sky.

Returning to the car, he snatched up the cell phone and road map. The closest town was little more than a dot on State Highway 70, which ran parallel to the interstate he was on. A moment later, directory assistance patched him through to Earl's Auto Shop.

"Yello," a man answered on the other end of the line. In the background, Brent heard children screaming. A woman hollered, "Carter, you hit your sister with that Mutant Ninja Turtle sword one more time, I'm gonna Nin-ja you, you got that?"

"Excuse me." Brent frowned. "Is this Earl's Auto Shop?"

"No, but this here's Earl. What can I do ya for, mister?"

"I'm broken down out on I-40 and need a tow."

"Well thankye Jesus, there is a God!" the man announced with feeling.

"Honey?" the woman in the background called. "That ain't a call coming through, is it?"

When Earl answered, his voice sounded distant, as if he'd dropped the phone to his chest. "Yeah, baby, I'm real sorry about this, but we're gonna have to leave your momma's right away."

"But Eeeaaarl," the woman whined over the screaming of children and the barking of a dog. "You promised this year we could stay and visit all Thanksgiving Day."

"I'm sorry, baby," Earl said unconvincingly. "But I

got me a motorist out on the interstate that needs a tow. You tell them kids to say good-bye to all their cousins now and get 'em loaded in the truck. I'll be right there.''

"See, Marlene," another woman said, "I told you not to marry yourself no tow-truck driver. Every time you come to visit, he's rushing ya right back out the door.''

"Sorry 'bout that," Earl said to Brent. "Can you tell me where you're at?''

Brent glanced around. "Try the middle of nowhere.''

"Yeah, there's plenty of that hereabouts. What was the last exit you saw?''

After a few minutes, Earl assured Brent he knew right where he was. "You just sit tight. I'll be there before you know it.''

Hanging up, Brent slumped against the car, weary beyond belief. He'd driven straight through the night, stopping occasionally on the side of the road to rest his eyes. Only, every time he drifted toward sleep, images of Laura danced through his mind: the way she looked laughing, smiling, and flushed with passion—or how she'd looked with tears in her eyes as she'd told him good-bye. But the image that always jarred him awake was the one of her standing at the front of a church dressed in white as she gazed up at Greg Smith with adoring eyes as the preacher pronounced them husband and wife. He'd see himself charging into the church—too late. Always too late. Shaking his head, he wiped a hand over his face to scrub away the vision. The scratch of his whiskers reminded him he hadn't bathed or shaved since yesterday morning. He was even still wearing his suit, minus the overcoat, which he'd shed after leaving the Tennessee mountains.

He looked up and down the deserted highway, then

glanced at his watch. Four twenty-eight. He had forty-seven hours and thirty-two minutes to break up Laura's wedding and convince her to marry him instead. Plenty of time. Tipping his head back, he grinned at the vulture that still flew in lazy circles overhead. "Buzz off, pal. I ain't dead yet."

CHAPTER
27

By noon on Friday, Brent had decided the world is at its darkest just before it goes completely black. Standing in the doorway to Earl's garage, he stared at the mechanic in disbelief. "What do you mean, you can't fix my car until Tuesday?"

"Fuel filter needs replacing," Earl said, wiping his hands with a red rag. "I'll have to order one from Little Rock. Soonest they can get it here is Tuesday."

"Look, you don't understand," Brent said. "You have to fix the car today, because I have to get to Beason's Ferry by four o'clock tomorrow."

"Oh, I understand," Earl answered. "But, you ain't gonna make it anywhere in this car until Tuesday."

"Fine." Rubbing a hand over his face, Brent glanced about the yard of the auto shop for some alternative form of transportation. The place looked even more depressing than when he'd first arrived, but then yesterday he'd been too exhausted to take note of his surroundings.

Now that he'd caught up on his sleep, he couldn't quite believe he'd spent the night in a broken-down RV behind an auto shop. Not that he'd had much choice. The town that had been a dot on the map was even smaller in reality. At least he'd had a chance to shower, shave, and change into something more casual than a suit.

Not that any of that mattered. All that mattered was getting to Laura. To do that, he needed a car. He cast one apologetic look at his Porsche, hating the thought of leaving such a prize in Earl's hands. Desperate times, however, called for desperate measures. And he had never felt more desperate in his life.

"All right." He reached for his wallet. "If my car can't make it, what kind of transportation do you have around?"

"You mean to buy?" Earl laughed as he tucked the oily rag into the back pocket of his overalls. "What does this look like, a car lot?"

"Not exactly," Brent answered as diplomatically as possible. The place looked like a junkyard, but surely even junkyards had vehicles for sale. "I'll buy anything with wheels that runs."

"Tell you what, mister," Earl said. "I ain't got anything to sell ya, but I do have I car I'll loan ya till yours is fixed."

"You do?" Brent stared in disbelief. "All right, although I'll be happy to pay you—"

"Nawh, you save your money. 'Sides, I owe you for rescuing me from the Thanksgiving-Day-from-hell." Earl led the way to the office to get the keys. "Not that this car's much to look at, mind you, but she'll get ya where you're going."

At five minutes to four on Saturday, Laura slipped the string of pearls she'd inherited from her mother around

Melody's neck. "Here you are—something borrowed."
Glancing up, she caught her friend's reflection in the mirror. "Oh, Melody, you look just like a 1950s movie star."

"That was the general idea." Melody twirled around,
then struck a Jane Russell pose in the tea-length ivory
gown. "After all, if one has to play to a conservative
crowd, one ought to do it with a statement."

Laura laughed, for Melody definitely made a statement in that dress. They'd found it in a vintage clothing
store that catered to the theater set in Houston. While
Laura had had some doubts upon entering the store, she
had to admit the final result was stunning.

The soft peach maid-of-honor dress she'd found com-
plemented Melody's off-the-shoulder tea-length style.
That morning they'd ventured to Betty's Beauty Shop to
have their hair sculpted into finger waves that fit the time
period of the clothes.

Gazing at herself in the mirror, Laura imagined she
looked a bit like Grace Kelly, very classy and elegant. She
wondered what Brent would think if he saw her dressed
like this. The thought brought the usual pang to her
chest. The pain of losing him hadn't lessened over the
past months. If anything, it had grown worse.

"Well, I guess I don't have to ask what my 'something
blue' will be," Melody said.

"What?" Laura looked over her shoulder and saw her
friend's exasperated look. "Oh. Sorry." She tried to paste
on a bright smile, but Melody only shook her head.

"When are you going to quit this nonsense and call
the man?"

Laura busied herself with the bouquets that waited
on the minister's desk. The office they'd used for chang-

ing suddenly seemed far too small. "We've been through this before, Melody."

"And you're still being stubborn!" Melody growled in frustration. "Didn't making up with your dad teach you anything?"

"Certainly." Laura frowned as she straightened a rosebud. "It taught me that sometimes you have to let people stand on their own two feet rather than doing everything for them."

"And what about taking the first step to reconcile your differences with people who are too mule-headed to admit they're wrong?"

The tears that never seemed far away made Laura's throat ache. "I can't, Melody," she whispered.

"Why not?"

"Because there's one major difference between my father and Brent." She took a slow breath. "You see . . . my father loves me."

"And you think Brent doesn't?" Melody demanded incredulously.

"If he did, he'd have tried to contact me at least once these last two months." She looked at Melody, silently pleading. "Don't you think?"

Melody shook her head. "What I think is that the man is probably hurting every bit as much as you are."

Laura turned away as guilt joined the sorrow in her heart. Could Melody be right? Could Brent be hurting, too? But if he was, why wouldn't he call? "I'm sorry, Mel. This is the last thing we should be discussing on your wedding day."

"Oh, Laura." Melody's shoulders slumped. "The best wedding present you could give me is a promise to call Brent, just to see if getting back together is possible."

"I can't, Melody. I just can't."

"You're that convinced he'll say no?"

Laura nodded.

"You know what?" Melody propped her hands on her hips. "All these months, I've listened to you say what a wonderful man Brent is, if only he'd believe in himself. Well, maybe that's what you need too, Laura, to believe in yourself. You're an incredibly kind, intelligent, fun person who deserves very much to be loved. Who *is* loved. By a lot of people. Including Brent."

Laura wanted desperately to believe her. Before she could say as much, a knock came at the door.

"Is the bride ready?" the minister called.

Melody jumped as if she'd been pricked by a pin. "Oh, my gosh, is it time already? Do I look all right?"

"You look great," Laura assured her, and set her own sorrow aside to concentrate on her friend's happiness. "In fact, you look stunning. So what do you say we get you married?"

⁓

Brent tightened his grip on the steering wheel. He should have called. The thought repeated in his mind for at least the hundredth time as he headed down I-10, pushing the seventy-six Ford Pinto for everything it was worth— which was about two cents. The driver's side window wouldn't close, and baling wire kept the door attached. Still, if he hadn't had that flat, he'd have made it with time to spare. Glancing at his watch, he realized the wedding would start any second, and he was a good ten minutes from the First Methodist Church.

If only he'd called. What he had to say, though, was

best said in person—not over the phone with him stranded on the side of the road trying to change a flat tire. Looking up, he saw the city limits sign, and relief washed over him. Perhaps he'd still make it before the service was over; before the minister pronounced Laura another man's wife.

"Come on, baby," he chanted to the car as he coaxed it to go a little faster. Just then, a flicker in the rearview mirror caught his attention. He looked up and saw flashing red and blue lights. "Shit!"

He'd never be able to outrun a sheriff's deputy in a broken-down Pinto. Although, he realized, he didn't have to outrun the patrol car—he just had to keep going until he reached the church. Then whoever was behind him could write him every ticket in the book, or throw him in jail, for all he cared. As long as he stopped the wedding first.

Bracing his hands on the steering wheel, he hit the off ramp into town without letting up on the gas. The sirens came on as the sheriff's car closed the gap between them. Brent looked in the mirror long enough to recognize Sheriff Baines behind the wheel. Great, he thought. He probably *would* get arrested. With grim determination, he took the turn onto First Street with tires squealing. One way or another, he would make it to the church.

"Dearly beloved, we are gathered today in the eyes of the Lord to join together this man and this woman in the bonds of holy matrimony. . . ."

Laura's eyes prickled as she watched Melody and Greg standing together, facing the altar. For all Melody's appearance of calm over the past weeks, she now shook so hard, her dress trembled.

"Marriage is not a state to be entered into lightly," the minister continued in reverent tones that rang to the polished oak rafters. Chancing a sideways peek, Laura found that Greg, who'd been a wreck for days, stood straight and solid, without a hint of nervousness. When he looked at his bride, his eyes filled with such certainty and pride, Laura knew she'd never make it through the service dry-eyed.

No, marriage was not something to be entered into lightly, or to push someone into before they were ready. But when the time was right, nothing was more wonderful to behold.

Loneliness settled about her like a well-worn cloak as she wondered if she would ever know this joy firsthand. She thought back to what Melody had said. Could she really get back together with Brent? Did she only need to take the first step and have faith in herself?

The faith, she realized, was the hardest part. She'd never seen herself as a woman to inspire great passion. But marriage was more a matter of devotion than desire. It was the depth of love that made it endure, not the height and flash of its fire.

That, however, was something to think about later. Right now, she needed to keep her attention on the service and enjoy the glow of the candles, the scent of the flowers. If only that siren wasn't shrilling in the background. Apparently others in the congregation heard it as well, for a buzz of speculation started at the back of the church. One would think the sheriff would have more sense than to drive by the church during a wedding with sirens blaring.

To the distress of all present, the patrol car skidded to a screeching halt right outside of the church. The minister valiantly raised his voice to be heard over the slamming of car doors and the shouts of men.

Then a dark figure burst through the doors at the back of the church.

"Laura! Stop!"

Laura whirled about, her eyes wide. She saw only a silhouette framed in the daylight that poured through the door, but her pulse leapt as she recognized the voice. *Brent?*

Tears of startled joy sprang to her eyes. She covered her mouth to keep from crying out. Brent was here. He'd come for her. Why or how, she didn't know. Didn't care. He had come for *her*!

Brent's mind reeled with confusion as he stood frozen in the aisle. The scene before him was just like his nightmare—the bride and groom held hands about to say "I do"—only the bride had red hair. The groom was definitely Greg, but Melody, not Laura, stood beside him.

Where the hell was Laura?

Then he saw her, standing beside Melody. Relief nearly sent him to his knees. She stood with one hand clasping a bouquet to her chest, the other covering her mouth. When his eyes met hers, he saw her tears shimmer in the candlelight.

Then slowly, his vision took in the rows upon rows of gawking faces. Karl Adderson, along with his plump wife and three kids, sat to his right. A row behind him, Miss Miller sat with a stunned, yet oddly approving look on her face. Beside her, Dr. Morgan regarded Brent with an unreadable expression.

Someone slapped Brent on the back, and he realized

the sheriff had followed him into the church. "Well heck, son, why didn't you just tell me you were speeding to stop a wedding?" Sheriff Baines drawled. "Although aren't you supposed to bust through the door calling out the name of the bride?"

Humiliation struck Brent square in the chest as he glanced about.

"I—" He took a step back, unable to meet anyone's eyes. "I'm sorry. I'll wait outside." *Outside. As he'd always been in this town.* Only this time he feared Laura wouldn't join him, even though she'd always been there in spite of what others thought. He couldn't even look at her as he turned toward the door.

"No, wait!" A woman shouted so loud, the entire congregation jumped. He looked back to see Melody reaching toward him, a panicked expression on her face. She glanced from him to Laura and back again. "Brent Michaels, don't you dare walk out that door."

"Melody," Greg said, looking as mortified as Brent felt.

"Greg, please." Melody sent her groom a look filled with silent meaning, then turned back to Brent. "As long as you've interrupted my wedding, the least you can do is tell us why."

"I, eh . . ." Brent looked about the church, at the sea of familiar faces. He couldn't quite bring himself to look at Laura. "I heard Greg Smith was getting married," he began, in a hollow impersonation of his well-trained voice. "And I thought . . ." He closed his eyes, reliving that gut-wrenching moment when he'd thought Laura was marrying another man. He'd driven halfway across the country to stop her, to tell her he loved her, to beg her to marry him. Now that he was here, was he just going to slink off to nurse his embarrassment? Or was he going to do what he'd come here to do: win Laura back—at any cost?

He raised his head and looked straight at her. All he could see was her eyes above the hand she held over her mouth. "I thought you were marrying another man," he said in a resonant voice that carried through the church. "I couldn't let you do that."

She blinked rapidly but made no move to encourage him. Taking his courage in hand, he walked slowly, steadily down the aisle. "I couldn't let you do that, Laura, because I happen to be in love with you."

She made a tiny sound he prayed was joy as the tears tumbled down her cheeks. Reaching her, he held out one hand, needing to see all of her face as much as he needed to touch her. She slipped her hand into his, and he saw, to his relief, that she was smiling. A bright, dazzling smile.

The sight filled him with a dizzy relief. He'd had three days to agonize over what to say when he saw her, but now that he stood before her, fear of her rejection nearly closed his throat.

"Laura . . ." His voice cracked, and he swallowed hard. "Laura, these last weeks without you have been the worst of my life. I need you too much to go on alone. I can't promise what kind of husband I'll make, but I can promise this: If you'll marry me, if you'll be my wife, I promise to honor you and cherish you, to hold you in my heart every day of our lives."

For a moment, she simply stared up at him as more tears tumbled down her cheeks. Sheer determination pushed the last few words from him. "I love you, Laura Beth Morgan. . . . Will you marry me?"

"Yes!" She laughed through her tears as she leapt into

his arms, clinging to his neck as he spun her about. "I'll marry you, and love you, and cherish you, and all the rest forever and ever! I love you, Brent Michael Zartlich. I love you with all my heart."

He held her against him, absorbing the feel of her in his arms. Slowly, though, he remembered where they were and looked up. Melody had a smug grin on her face, though her groom and the minister looked anything but pleased. Glancing at the rest of their audience, he saw a blend of amusement, approval, and delighted titillation.

For once he didn't care if he was the subject of town gossip. Then his gaze fell on Laura's father, who had his arm wrapped about the shoulders of Miss Miller. Dr. Morgan gave him a subtle nod of approval. No accolade or gesture of acceptance had ever meant so much.

"Excuse me," the minister said, clearing his throat, "But if it's all the same to you, we were in the middle of a wedding here."

"Oh, yes," Brent said, surprised he no longer felt the least bit embarrassed. "By all means, continue."

"Well, thank you." The minister bowed his head mockingly. Brent didn't care. Laura was leaning against him with her arm about his waist as if she'd never let go. As the ceremony continued, he almost felt like they were the ones being pronounced husband and wife.

So perhaps it was only natural that, as they left the church in the wake of the newly married couple, he scooped Laura into his arms and kissed her right there on the steps.

When the kiss ended, the wedding guests cheered. He spared them a smile before turning back to his future wife. "So, Squirt, is this what you had in mind when you invited me home to be a bachelor in your dating game?"

"Maybe," she laughed. Sunlight danced in her eyes and hair as she placed one hand against his cheek. "I've always thought that any game worth playing was worth playing for keeps."

For keeps. Brent decided he rather liked the sound of that as he lowered his lips back to hers, for he definitely planned to keep Laura. Forever.

ABOUT THE AUTHOR

As a fifth generation Texan, Julie Ortolon draws inspiration from her native state for both her writing and her artwork. Her pastel paintings can be found in collections across the United States and she is currently working on her next Texas-based novel.

She and her husband live on the shores of Lake Travis in the Texas Hill Country. You can learn more about Julie Ortolon at *www.ortolon.com* or write to her at JulieOrtolon@aol.com.